A COOL PROPOSITION

"I would request, my lord, that you mention this visit to no one," she said, her voice amazingly cool, even imperious. He had to admire her nerve. "This interview has been pleasant for neither of us. I am persuaded you will agree it is best forgotten."

She turned to go, and without thinking, he strode across the room and grabbed her by the wrist. Her sleeve had ridden up a bit and his fingers touched her bare flesh. The feel of her skin startled him, almost burned; he tightened his grasp and pulled her closer.

"Our interview is concluded, my lord," she stammered, trying unsuccessfully, he thought, to resume her imperious tone. "You are not interested in my terms. There is nothing more I can offer you."

"Oh, I wouldn't say that," he murmured insolently, his eyes sweeping pointedly over her.

Her eyes widened and she colored, but instead of delivering the slap on the face he expected, she merely looked curiously at him.

"I hadn't thought of that, my lord," she said quietly. "Indeed, I—I hadn't thought of that at all."

A NOBLE MISTRESS

GOTHICS A LA MOOR—FROM ZEBRA

ISLAND OF LOST RUBIES
by Patricia Werner   (2603, $3.95)
Heartbroken by her father's death and the loss of her great love, Eileen returns to her island home to claim her inheritance. But eerie things begin happening the minute she steps off the boat, and it isn't long before Eileen realizes that there's no escape from *THE ISLAND OF LOST RUBIES*.

DARK CRIES OF GRAY OAKS
by Lee Karr   (2736, $3.95)
When orphaned Brianna Anderson was offered a job as companion to the mentally ill seventeen-year-old girl, Cassie, she was grateful for the non-troublesome employment. Soon she began to wonder why the girl's family insisted that Cassie be given hydro-electrical therapy and increased doses of laudanum. What was the shocking secret that Cassie held in her dark tormented mind? And was she herself in danger?

CRYSTAL SHADOWS
by Michele Y. Thomas   (2819, $3.95)
When Teresa Hawthorne accepted a post as tutor to the wealthy Curtis family, she didn't believe the scandal surrounding them would be any concern of hers. However, it soon began to seem as if someone was trying to ruin the Curtises and Theresa was becoming the unwitting target of a deadly conspiracy . . .

CASTLE OF CRUSHED SHAMROCKS
by Lee Karr   (2843, $3.95)
Penniless and alone, eighteen-year-old Aileen O'Conner traveled to the coast of Ireland to be recognized as daughter and heir to Lord Edwin Lynhurst. Upon her arrival, she was horrified to find her long lost father had been murdered. And slowly, the extent of the danger dawned upon her: her father's killer was still at large. And her name was next on the list.

BRIDE OF HATFIELD CASTLE
by Beverly G. Warren   (2517, $3.95)
Left a widow on her wedding night and the sole inheritor of Hatfield's fortune, Eden Lane was convinced that someone wanted her out of the castle, preferably dead. Her failing health, the whispering voices of death, and the phantoms who roamed the keep were driving her mad. And although she came to the castle as a bride, she needed to discover who was trying to kill her, or leave as a corpse!

Available wherever paperbacks are sold, or order direct from the Publisher. Send cover price plus 50¢ per copy for mailing and handling to Zebra Books, Dept. 2169, 475 Park Avenue South, New York, N.Y. 10016. Residents of New York, New Jersey and Pennsylvania must include sales tax. DO NOT SEND CASH.

A NOBLE MISTRESS

BY JANIS LADEN

ZEBRA·BOOKS
KENSINGTON PUBLISHING CORP.

ZEBRA BOOKS

are published by

Kensington Publishing Corp.
475 Park Avenue South
New York, NY 10016

Second printing: April, 1990

Printed in the United States of America

Also by Janis Laden: *Sapphire Temptation*

For my parents, Claire and Samuel,
from the first one that came along.

"My father's wit and my mother's tongue,
assist me!"

— "Love's Labour Lost"
William Shakespeare

Acknowledgments

Once again, my deepest gratitude to my agent, Florence Feiler, and to my editor, Wendy McCurdy.

To Marjorie Miller, Diane Bouchard, and all the Westwood writers, for all their support, and to Mabel Mossman, my typist.

To my children, Tamar, Naomi, Abigail, and even little Gideon, for understanding, and always, to my husband, Michael, from his Scheherazade.

Come to me, my mistress fair,
In the sultry heat of summer's air.
Come to me, my sweet delight,
In the fragrant dew of summer's night.

But come in joy, deny me not,
For grief and shame all ill begot.
Oh, love's a high and noble quest —
How few of us are e'er so blest!

—Sir Isaac Mariner

Chapter 1

Justin Traugott, Viscount Roane, sipped his claret with deliberate calm and regarded his opponent dispassionately. Beads of sweat glistened on Landon's upper lip and brow as he stared at his cards. Presently Landon ran a hand through his hair, the once jet black locks now sprinkled with gray. He signalled to a passing footman for more brandy, and the viscount shook his head almost imperceptibly. Thomas Landon was a fool, for all he was playing right into the viscount's hands. It would be obvious to all that Landon was digging his own grave, deliberately playing too deeply and injudiciously becoming muddled with drink in the bargain. Landon had insisted on this game, wanting to redeem some of his markers, and Roane had offered no objection. For he had been steadily winning pieces of the Landon fortune for years. He had, in fact, quietly orchestrated the downfall that was now imminent.

Indeed, it had not been difficult to orchestrate such a fall. Landon, compulsive gambler that he was, had been most obliging. It would have been very easy to sit back and watch him gamble away the last of his assets in one random gaming hell or another. But Viscount Roane, with his personal score to settle, did not wish for that. Rather, he had to be sure that when the end came, *he* held all the markers, innocent though it would all look.

No, society would not hold Roane to account, nor did he fear retribution from any of the Landon family. There was no direct male heir, of that he was certain. There were two daughters, both still in the schoolroom, he believed. Needless to say, they would be powerless to do anything about the loss of their family's estate to their nearest neighbor.

If Roane now felt a pang of conscience at the thought of taking the estate whose lands had marched with his own Roanbrooke for generations, he quelled it as he always stilled such pangs. He had only to remember his family, destroyed at the hands of a Landon. His father, his mother, and his beloved little sister, Nell—Nell with her golden ringlets, her little life snuffed out cruelly at the age of four. So long ago, yet her face was so vivid to him still.

Shaking away those disturbing images, Roane lowered his goblet and gazed casually at the plush but understated furnishings of this particular saloon at White's. The panelling was a rich, dark oak. It had the strong, fresh smell of beeswax, which not even the cigar smoke could quite overcome. The high-backed green leather chairs and deep carpets seemed to beckon gentlemen to come in and take their ease. But, at the same time, the very stateliness of the room, not to mention the deference of the servants, seemed to demand a certain decorum, a certain softness of tone and reticence of manner.

Perhaps it was for this reason that there were no more than four men gathered around the corner table at which Roane had been sitting with the baron these many hours past. Their audience said nothing, betraying no emotion save several rather sharp intakes of breath each time another rubber went to the viscount. We English are capable of an amazing degree of restraint, Roane mused to himself. Every man in this room—for each table in the saloon was yet occupied, despite the lateness of the hour—was well aware that the baron was at his last prayers. Landon's unfortunate, improvident ruin would be grist for the gossip mills of the ton for days. There was nothing havey cavey afoot, after all. It was a straightforward game of piquet. Landon was a fool at best, pathetic at worst. It was all most unfortunate, but inevitable.

Such would be the thinking of every gentleman present tonight, Roane told himself. His own part in it all, when the story was repeated, would be almost incidental. But Wykham Abbey, however deeply mortgaged, would be his. As would every painting and furnishing it contained, every bit of Landon cattle, every conveyance, indeed, every tree on the ancestral estate of the Barons Landon.

The clock chimed the second hour of the morning and Landon glanced around uneasily. No footman was about at the moment, and he requested a short break. "In need of a bit of refreshment, eh what?" he said with a travesty of a smile. Roane agreed, not at all minding the opportunity to stretch his long legs for a bit. He ignored the hushed murmurs that followed them both as they rose and left the table.

It was in the corridor that he encountered the Earl of Westmacott. As usual his uncle was genuinely glad to see him, and as usual he immediately launched into a discussion of the political state of the country.

"Now, Uncle George, you know full well I've no intention of embroiling myself in politics. You, sir, are a brilliant statesman, which I can never be. I daresay the Empire will survive without me," Roane remarked dryly.

"On the contrary, Justin, we need new blood, young blood. I don't know any other young man who commands the attention you do whenever you choose to express an opinion. And you do speak on political issues, even if your arena is Gentleman Jim's, or one of your clubs, and not the Lords," replied the earl, reclining his trim, medium high frame against the richly panelled wall, swirling his drink in his right hand.

"Nevertheless, Uncle, I am not interested," Roane said. He felt a great deal of affection toward his uncle, but he was beginning to wish the man at Jericho. Another round of piquet awaited him, and he was eager to get on with it.

"You *ought* to be interested, Justin," countered the earl. "You know full well the kind of disorder and violence that's plagued the country since the War. All those damned agitators! The government needs as many sane, rational men as we can recruit," Westmacott continued earnestly. He had to look up at his tall nephew, but Roane recognized, as always, the unmistakable authority in his voice.

"You flatter me, Uncle George," replied the viscount after a moment's pause. "But with all due respect, I am not your man. Perhaps Drew might —"

"My scapegrace son will make a fine country gentleman, and he's already an acknowledged pink of the ton. He's an engaging fellow, and solid, but rather a nodcock for all that," said the earl genially, the laugh lines around his eyes becoming more pronounced. Roane noted what a handsome man he was still, despite the graying hair and lines creeping out from the eyes and etched into the pale pink cheeks. "You, on the other hand, Justin, are no more a hardened gambler than you are a town dandy. You've merely been playacting these several years past, for

14

what purpose I am afraid to guess," the earl added pointedly.

"Then pray do not, Uncle. Now if you will excuse me—" Roane tried to move toward the open door just beyond them but his uncle stood erect and blocked his way.

"I half raised you, my boy. I know you better than you know yourself. You have tremendous drive, untapped abilities. You need a mission in life, just as I do, just as your father did."

Roane's eyes narrowed at the mention of his father and drifted to the door of the card room. The baron was already seated, waiting for him. The earl followed his gaze. "Perhaps I already have one," Roane said quietly.

"Give over, boy," said the earl softly. "The past is gone, best off buried and forgotten. Do not pursue this course further."

The viscount arched his brows in all innocence. "I cannot think what you mean, Uncle. Landon, as everyone knows, is a wastrel, bent on his own ruin. I am merely a gentleman in search of an interesting card game."

"You may gammon the entire ton with that pose, Justin, including my dear son and heir, but not me. Give it up, I tell you. Vengeance most hurts those who reap it, Justin. Remember that." The older man gave his nephew a firm pat on the shoulder and, with one last glance into the card room, padded slowly away.

Roane slipped into the card room and took his seat across from Landon. The room was nearly silent, the same four men flanking the table, as Roane bent to his cards. This was not the time to consider politics or Uncle George or untapped abilities, he reflected, and gave himself over to the game.

As the hour ticked away Roane allowed his long, tapered fingers to stroke his square jaw in a slow motion that belied his determination. He had been very patient, planning his strategy carefully over several years, ever since he'd sold out of his regiment and made his appearance in Town. But his mind had always been racing inexorably toward his goal. Now in his twenty-eighth year, he was firmly established as a man of fashion in the ton. He was much sought after by hostesses, for his countenance was considered handsome and his conversation witty and engaging. And despite the steady stream of mistresses known to have graced his bed over the years, he was considered a prime catch on the Marriage Mart. A title and a rather enormous fortune went a long way toward obscuring any peccadilloes a man might commit, he had oft reflected wryly. He had little use for the fawning attention he received from ambitious mamas and was merely amused by the admiration of his fellow Corinthians. For though he enjoyed the excitement of London now and again, in truth he missed the quiet of his beloved Roanbrooke, his family's seat. But a man driven as he was did not have the luxury of rusticating whenever the mood struck him. No more could he eschew the card tables when he would have preferred to immerse himself in his books or estate business or even, he had to admit, politics.

The viscount was known, he was well aware, as a man who played fairly, when at the gaming tables or in the bedchamber. He pursued such activities only with those who knew what they were about. He was not one to lead green young bucks astray in the gaming hells of London, no more than he would dally with innocent young girls. His own instincts and the gentlemanly code of honor that was his birthright would have insured such behavior, but Roane had a further reason for wanting to cultivate such a reputation. He must be above reproach; it was all part of the plan. It was a matter of minutes now before Landon capitulated, admitting his final defeat. And no one, no one at all, would know that the Viscount Roane had quietly brought about the ruin of the House of Landon. He frowned at the thought that his uncle might very well guess, but the earl, he knew, would keep such conjecture to himself.

The Viscount Roane stared at his opponent, whose entire face was now flushed and covered with beads of sweat. Roane stilled a momentary pang of sympathy — he could not feel sorry for Landon. Nor could he think of himself as bent on revenge. Uncle George was wrong in that. Rather, Roane believed he owed a debt to his family, a debt that must be paid.

Chapter 2

"He is not 'out of sorts,' Finch, as you know full well!" exclaimed Moriah, her red lips pursed in vexation. "He is foxed! He is—oh, Finch, pray do not look so very shocked. You know I have my few cant terms from Papa himself. He is drunk, as he has been these two days past. Oh, you may gammon Mrs. Trotter if you like, for I own she fairly dotes on Papa. And the rest of the household may choose to be bamboozled, but I cannot afford such luxury." Moriah stood, arms akimbo, at the door to her father's sitting room. She had been unable to advance further than the doorway these two days, what with her father's valet guarding the sitting room and the bedchamber beyond with such fervour. But she had waited long enough, and Finch's loyalty was, she felt, quite misplaced.

"Miss Moriah, please. The baron is not—er—quite well, you see. Now, you wouldn't want to be raisin' your voice in just that way, would you? I reckon the noise'd be quite—er—distressin' to the baron, beggin' your pardon, miss," said Finch. The ruddy face of the short, wiry valet turned a shade redder, and his normally superior expression looked almost pleading. But Moriah held her ground.

"I'll warrant the noise would indeed be distressing,

18

Finch. But not half so distressing as what may happen if I am not able to speak with him very soon. Not another drop of brandy is he to have, Finch. You must brew him that dreadful concoction for which you are so famous and see that he drinks it down. Pray inform my father, when he is sufficiently recovered, that I shall wait upon him in his study one hour before tea time." She spoke in the tone of command she had learned over the years to assume when necessary. It was not her nature to be high in the instep. But Moriah had run her father's household for too long to become missish now, when it mattered so much. For she was certain that something was dreadfully wrong.

Finch continued to look doubtful, and Moriah's tone suddenly softened. She needed Finch's full cooperation and, knowing that he was in her father's complete confidence, felt comfortable in what she had to say next. "Finch, I fear that any delay may result in rather . . . unpleasant consequences for Papa and perhaps for the entire household. Oh, I know he has come up from London in such a state before, but never has his . . . indisposition lasted so long. His creditors may follow rapidly upon his heels, as you must know, and I can hardly deal appropriately with them without knowing the full extent of his—his losses. Somehow I fear that this time is worse than the others. You must see that to indulge him now would be foolhardy, Finch." Moriah's rather deep, clear voice had dropped to almost a whisper, and her large eyes had narrowed in concern.

She thought the valet's face paled somewhat. He looked anxiously at her and then at the half-closed door to the sitting room, as if waging an inner battle with himself.

"Very well, miss," he said at length. "I—I shall

attend the master straight away, as you say. And I — I do hope he ain't of a mind to bring down the rafters when he discovers what next I'll put in his goblet," he added with a wry smile.

"Thank you, Finch," was all she said, and watched the valet disappear into the sacred masculine chambers.

Moriah allowed herself the indulgence of a deep sigh before gathering up her skirts and making her way down the corridor. She was relieved that she'd been able to elicit Finch's cooperation with no further explanation. For she had no desire to overset him nor alarm anyone else in the household with what she really feared above everything. It was not merely Papa's two-day indisposition that made her think this time was worse than the others. No, it was what she had seen early this morning, when she had wandered into his study. Papa might be in his cups, but part of him had been lucid enough to be thinking terrible thoughts, self-destructive thoughts. For the pistol cabinet had been left slightly ajar, and she could see that Papa had been cleaning his perfectly crafted pearl-handled pistol. He rarely did so, and now the thought of that beautiful, deadly weapon made her shiver.

Thank God no pistols had been missing from the study, else Moriah would have bolted to her father's rooms straight away. Finch would have been horrified to see a lady enter a gentleman's chambers — that the gentleman in question was her father being quite irrelevant — but she would have paid no heed. After all, one could carry proprieties just so far. But for now, she knew it would never do to rush to his chambers. Her father, despite his befuddled state, would raise his eyebrows and mutter that it was not at all the thing and wait until Finch ushered her out.

And so, as on most days after breakfast, Moriah walked briskly to the beautifully appointed morning room of the Abbey. It was furnished in the delicate chairs and tables of Thomas Chippendale, and made warm and inviting by the chintz curtains and upholstery done in shades of plum and primrose pink. Her mother had decorated this room when she was a bride. And though the baroness was gone these many years now, Moriah had effected only one change in the morning room since she'd taken it over as her own.

Her charming, light hearted mother had enjoyed the use of a spindle-legged, gilt-edged ladies' escritoire that sat in the bright light of the front bay window of the room. But Moriah was not her mother. It was she who now virtually ran the Abbey, and so she had substituted for her mother's escritoire a large, serviceable mahogany desk with numerous drawers and cubbies. It was to her desk that she now came, but she was too restless to sit down. She found herself instead slowly encircling the desk, her fingers playing now with the inkstand, then with the carved ivory letter opener, and now again with the dictionary she always kept there.

If her steps were slow, her mind was churning. Sometimes she wondered, looking down at her plum-colored morning dress, whether all she and her mother had had in common was a decided preference for the same colors. The late baroness, when not flitting about London, had spent her days lounging on her couch, receiving visitors, and writing short missives at her escritoire. But Moriah was of a much more practical turn of mind. And she was too energetic to sit back, as her beautiful mother had done, and allow her loving though inefficient father to make a muddle of household and even estate affairs.

Lady Clarissa Landon had died when Moriah was twelve years old. Somehow it seemed as if that event had catapulted her, if not into adulthood, then well on her way. Her beloved little sister, though only three years her junior, had seemed to need her so much, and Moriah became like a mother to her. Gradually Mrs. Trotter had begun bringing domestic problems to the young Miss Moriah, rather than troubling the master, and soon Reeves, staid butler that he was, had followed suit. Thus it was that by the time she was fifteen years of age, she was the acknowledged mistress of Wykham Abbey. Her father, now spending more and more of his time in London, had not seemed to mind a bit.

Moriah had always been very observant, and it did not take her long to realize that all was not as it should be with regard to finances at the Abbey. She'd heard whispers, even while her mother was alive, about her father's gambling tendencies, but she had, of course, never understood the ramifications. But as Moriah took on increasing responsibility of the household and even the estate itself, she began to notice things. Her father would frequently be absent for weeks at a time in London. That had never overly disturbed her—she'd assumed that was de rigueur for a gentleman and, of course, he'd done it even when her mother was alive. But when he'd come home, Moriah would often notice Mrs. Trotter in quite a pelter. Sometimes a painting would disappear from its age-old place on the wall, or several antique porcelain statuettes, which Moriah knew to be of great value, might likewise vanish. Reeves and Mrs. Trotter had maintained a conspiracy of silence whenever she'd questioned them. And when she'd broached the subject to Mr. Thornton, the estate agent, he was scandalized that a young lady might

22

wish to sully her ears with such talk of money. The fact that she was called upon daily to think of money in her household management did not sway him in the least.

It was left to kindly old Mr. Fairley, the family lawyer, whose father had been the family lawyer before him, to enlighten her. Her father, with his compulsive gambling, had been steadily depleting the family resources for years. Her mother had known but had long before her death given up trying to change him. Probably no one could; certainly not the languid baroness, who had quite adored her dashing, good-natured husband and was always willing to make excuses for him. Mr. Fairley had looked hopefully at Moriah, as if she might be able to wean her father from his disastrous propensity for squandering the family fortune.

But despite her youth, for she was but seventeen at the time, Moriah had immediately grasped several things. One was that her father would never change. Try as she might, it would be hopeless. And her practical nature condemned him. It angered her that he could be so irresponsible as to jeopardize her future and that of her sister, not to mention the servants and the many estate dependents. But in her heart Moriah could only feel pity for a man who was so obsessed that he must act in a way that would of a certain lead to disaster. Pity and a great deal of love. He was her father, and they had always enjoyed a warm, affectionate relationship.

There was one thing more that Moriah had understood the day Mr. Fairley had taken her into his confidence. One day Papa would ruin them. He would not mean for it to happen, but it would come about nonetheless. He would return home from London one day, and no sale of paintings nor horses nor jewels would be to any avail.

Moriah still missed her mother, but sometimes, in the ensuing two years, it had crossed her mind that perhaps the influenza that had carried her off had been for the best. The baroness could never have endured what Moriah knew the Landons would someday come to. Her mama needed to be surrounded by a bevy of servants and every luxury, and would have died at the thought of losing the Abbey, which had been in the Landon family for generations.

But Moriah would not die, and she was prepared to hold the family together, no matter what it took. Tess, though sixteen, was very much still a child. She was a bit too much like their mother, but Moriah still had hopes of instilling some degree of frugality into her nature. It was Papa that had Moriah most frightfully concerned just now. She sat at her desk, staring at the papers and quills neatly arranged in their cubbies, and pondered the problem.

Instinct told her that the worst was upon them. But she must make her Papa see that there were better alternatives than the pistol. To lose Wykham Abbey and everything it represented would be bad enough; to lose Papa as well would be intolerable. Yet if he had lost everything, including their marriage portions, he would feel desperate indeed. Moriah must make him see that somehow, as a family, they would survive.

Chapter 3

"Oh, Papa, how good to see you up and about!" exclaimed Moriah with a forced cheerfulness as she approached her father's desk. She noted that the glass and oak pistol cabinet was closed now, all of its contents seemingly in place.

The baron took her hands and made an attempt at a smile. "You are looking well, my dear. It is always so good to come—to come home to you," he said a bit hoarsely, and then he bade her sit down.

She took the soft leather chair he indicated across the massive burr walnut desk from his own. As he resumed his seat, she gazed intently at him. His normally pink complexion held a ghastly white pallor, and his eyes were bloodshot. Really it was useless to dissemble.

"How bad, Papa?" she asked quietly. She thought he winced slightly before he covered his eyes for a moment with his hands. Then he looked back at her and his face softened into a smile that did not quite reach his gray eyes.

"Now, my dear, things are never so bad as they seem, are they? And what mischief have you and my little Tess got up whilst I've been gone?" The forced cheerfulness was his now, but still he could not hide the bleakness of his expression. Gone was the twinkle that so often enlivened those friendly eyes.

Ignoring his question, she said, "Papa, I am not a child, as I think you know. I must deal with the tradesmen who come dunning at the door. Surely you must see that I cannot be of very much use if I do not know the whole of it," she said softly, and briefly leaned over to cover his right hand, which lay stretched limply across the green leather desk blotter.

The baron took a deep breath. "Let us talk of other things my love. What say you to a brisk ride over the fields before dusk? It's a beautiful summer's day. And you, my dear daughter, are much too pretty to concern yourself with such mundane matters as money and creditors."

"Oh, Papa," sighed Moriah, standing up and becoming exasperated but determined not to lose her patience. She took a step back, one hand on her hip, thinking what to say next. Her eyes briefly scanned the room, barely taking in the rich, dark panelling and the familiar etchings of famous battle scenes.

"You know very well that I am not pretty, Papa," she said after a moment. "And besides, if *I* do not concern myself with such matters, who — that is — I've been doing it for years, as you are well aware. Someone must — there is Tess to consider, after all, and the servants and the tenants. Now come, Papa, whatever it is, I promise you we will contrive."

The Baron Landon gazed miserably up at his eldest daughter. When had she grown from child to woman? Indeed, had she ever been a child? She certainly didn't look like one, he thought, his eyes briefly travelling the length of the deep pink muslin gown that admirably became her woman's figure. But he supposed she was right — she wasn't pretty. She was too dark, when all the reigning beauties were fair-skinned. She was small, though well-proportioned. Her mouth was too generous, but then again, she had a heart-shaped face and very large, unusual amethyst eyes. Moriah was not what he would call a beauty, but though it was difficult for him to be objective about his own offspring, yet something told him she was deuced attractive. He was not certain exactly how that was, but surely some man—oh, but what was the use? There was no dowry now. What had he done to his daughters? Even Tess, who had inherited the blond, ethereal beauty of her mother, even she would have a hard time now.

Oh, God, he wondered, shifting his gaze from Moriah and staring into space. How had he allowed this to happen? He had been on a winning streak. He had been sure he was about to reverse his fortunes. And then . . .

"Papa?" inquired Moriah softly. But the baron was not fooled for a moment by her tone of voice. She would be relentless in her interrogation, and he supposed he owed her at least some answers.

If truth be told, Thomas Landon was a bit overwhelmed by his eldest daughter. She was only nineteen years old, but she was so capable, so—so strong-willed. And it seemed as if she'd always been so. Where had she got that determination, that strength of character? Not from his beautiful, frivolous wife and not, he admitted unhappily, from him. Probably from his own father, he thought irrelevantly. The sixth baron had been a formidable man, one who always got what he wanted.

"Papa," Moriah said again, breaking into his reverie. This time her voice was less gentle. But even she, with all her strength, would be unable to do anything now.

"How much, Papa?" came the voice that he had always thought a bit too husky for a woman.

27

"A great deal, Moriah," he answered, his head in his hands.

"How much, Papa?"

"Everything," he mumbled. Oh, why hadn't she left him to the comfort of his brandy? He thought fleetingly that there was no money now even to restock his supply.

"What do you mean—'everything'? Our remaining funds, our cattle, our—"

"No, my love. I mean everything," he interrupted, raising his head, his voice growing stronger as he realized the inevitability of her knowing, of everyone knowing. "The cattle, the few remaining paintings, the—the Abbey, Moriah. It has been—er—heavily mortgaged, I'm afraid." He paused here, as if expecting a reply, an outburst, some acknowledgment of surprise or chagrin at this last disclosure. But none was forthcoming. Had she known about the mortgages, then? Moriah's expression was non-committal; she waited patiently for him to continue.

"But now—well, I can no longer mortgage it. The Abbey is gone. Everything. We—we shall have to leave." The baron rubbed a hand across the back of his neck. "Dear God, I am so grateful your mother is not alive to see this. I—I am so sorry, my dear. I was so sure this time that I would recoup, and I vowed that when I did, I'd never again—but, what is the use? It does not help any, I know, but please believe that if I could undo—" Thomas Landon looked into his daughter's troubled eyes and sighed deeply. Why was she not angry? He actually thought he read sympathy in those huge amethyst pools, and he could not bear that. "I—I have ruined your chances and Tess's. It is unforgivable of me. Unforgivable." He spoke harshly, as if to repel her pity.

Moriah came around the desk and put her arm

across his shoulders. "Dear Papa, we forgive you because we love you. But this is no time for maudlin sentimentality. We must be practical and see what is to be done."

She left his side and resumed her seat, folding her hands on the desk as if she were about to begin a business meeting. How could she be so damned pragmatic all the time? Why hadn't she fainted? Why was she not succumbing to a fit of hysteria, as Clarissa would have done, as surely Tess would do when she heard? What manner of female was she? Suddenly, he realized that Moriah had not even been shocked. It was as if she'd known, all along, that it would come to this. Somehow that thought made him feel worse than anything.

He rose from his chair and walked behind it, none too steadily, to the large window that afforded a view of the rear gardens. He tried not to look at the hills beyond, the gentle hills of Herefordshire, which cradled Wykham Abbey and had been home to the Barons Landon since the time of the Stuarts. His title was older still, and with no male heir, it would go to some distant cousin in America. But the Abbey was not entailed. It should have gone to Moriah, to be passed on to her son. As it was . . .

"There is nothing to be done, Moriah. I have ruined your life and Tess's. And as for me — well, my life is over," he rasped, his back to her.

Moriah did not pretend to misunderstand him. She was at his side in a moment, and her tone was firm as she spoke. "Papa, I do not want to hear you talk that way. You are still young; your life is not over. And as for Tess and me — well, our lives will be different, perhaps, but we shall contrive."

Several ideas whirled about in her head, and wishing to distract him from his morbid thoughts, she

29

asked in a matter-of-fact voice, "if we were to redeem the markers, Papa, how much money would we need?"

Her father continued to stare out at the gardens, and she was glad that he could not see her blanch at the exorbitant sum he named. Actually she was rather surprised that anyone should take the Abbey, mortgaged as it was, for such a sum. But there it was, and she knew there was no chance this side of heaven ever to raise that amount. She and Tess between them possessed only a few jewels, and there were no relations to whom they might apply. There was, of course, her mother's older sister in Yorkshire, but she had washed her hands of the Landons long ago. At all events, such a sum was undoubtedly out of her league. There were moneylenders in London, Moriah knew, but they were reputed to be ruthless and, besides, with no hope of repaying them, such a course would be worse than useless. No, it was clear that some other solution must be found.

"Well, then," she said bracingly, "we needs must think of something else. We—"

"No, my dear. There *is* nothing else. You are being very brave, but it is over. All over."

Again Moriah did not pretend to misunderstand. She took her father's hand and turn him to face her. "No, Papa," she said firmly. "You must listen to me. I have a plan, but I will need your help. We will find lodgings and you shall stay with Tess whilst I seek work. I—"

"Work! Moriah, whatever can you be thinking?"

"Why, that I shall make a fine governess, Papa. Oh, I own I am young, but at least I am no beauty. Tess, of course, could never be a governess. But as for me, I think 'twill serve. My command of mathematics, French, and the classics is quite good. I can give a credible performance on the pianoforte. I—"

"Hold, hold, Moriah! I'll not hear of it! For a Landon of Wykham Abbey to hire herself out as a governess—why, it is unthinkable!"

"Papa, we shall no longer be the Landons of Wykham Abbey," she said unthinkingly, and then immediately regretted her words. The momentary life that had crept into her father's face left it again. Crestfallen, he sank back into his chair.

"I am too old, Moriah. I cannot face this."

"Papa, I'll have no more of this talk," she said almost sternly, striding back to the front of the desk. "You shall have to face it. What's done is done. But now—we need you, Tess and I. I certainly cannot go out to work and leave her alone. You must not desert us. And perhaps so drastic a step will not be necessary. But I must have time to think. Papa, promise me you won't—that is—oh, Papa, I—I couldn't bear it if we lost you. Give me time to think. I will find a way out of our difficulties. Pray do not do anything drastic."

But the baron's head was in his hands again and she could not be sure he'd even heard her. He was slumped down, and Moriah had the distinct impression that he'd retreated into a world of his own. Almost without realizing it, she began to pace the floor in front of his desk. She must think of something—and quickly. She did not wish to press him further; surely they'd talked long enough. But she did not know when next he'd be sober, and so she plunged on.

"Papa, who holds the markers?" she asked, the kernel of an idea beginning to take shape. But she had to act quickly. A debt of honour could not be forsworn, nor even postponed, unless . . .

"What does that signify, Moriah? And all of Lon-

31

don must know by now. I am a laughingstock. There is naught to be done."

"The markers, Papa? Who holds them?" repeated Moriah, trying not to let her growing exasperation with his self-pity become evident.

"What? Oh, Roane, don't you know. Roane of Roanbrooke Court."

"Roane? You mean the viscount?" asked Moriah, incredulous as she thought of the long-absent neighbor whom she'd never met. Heir to the Traugott fortune, he was much gossiped about by the local gentry, probably as much because of his constant absence as for his reputation as something of a rakehell in London.

"Yes, dear, the viscount. And I—I cannot really fault him. He came along only at the end, actually. I suppose if it hadn't been Roane, it'd have been someone else. I—I could not seem to stop, you see. I kept thinking . . . " His voice trailed off, and Moriah remained deep in thought.

"Papa," she said at some length, "is it not rather a coincidence that you have lost the Abbey to the Viscount Roane? I mean, when one considers his reputation and the fact that part of Roanbrooke marches with Abbey lands, well—"

"No, my dear. I am not a green boy to be led astray, nor is Roane a Captain Sharp. He may be something of a ladies' man, and he is a much admired Corinthian, but I am certain his behavior is always that of a gentleman. Besides, he seems to have little interest in Roanbrooke Court. He is a very wealthy man, with several rather large estates; it would be pure fantasy to conjecture that he deliberately set out to take the Abbey from us. Our lands only meet in one far corner at all events, and I cannot even think what he will do with the Abbey.

Ignore it and leave it empty, I suppose, much as he seems to have done with Roanbrooke," he finished bitterly.

Moriah did not like the far-off look of despair that seemed now to settle on the baron's face, and she forsook to point out her father's own near-neglect of the Abbey over the years. Instead, she walked behind the desk and stared out at the gardens. Surely there must be some way . . .

"How much time do we have, Papa?" she asked after a moment, not turning around.

"Close on a fortnight, Moriah. He was very good about it, really. I do believe he means to stop at Roanbrooke for a short time, I suppose until he has taken full possession of — of —"

The baron's voice shook and he could not continue. Moriah turned and came once again to the front of the desk. Her father rose, his eyes full of moisture. "Oh, God," he whispered. "Oh my God, what have I done?" He rushed past her and staggered toward the door, a kind of desperation in his movement.

Moriah darted to him, knowing she could hold him but a moment more. "Papa, let us say nothing to Tess or the staff. I may yet be able to find some remedy, so it will not serve for the story to be got about just yet." The baron shook his head sadly, looking suddenly much older than his forty-five years. "And, Papa, nothing drastic. Promise me. Give me a few days." The only answer she received was a hand lightly, tenderly grazing her cheek, and the baron turned and was gone.

Moriah took a deep breath to squelch her tears and resolved to speak with Finch straight away. She did not wish to involve any of the servants in this business, but Finch, of course, was in her father's confidence. And now he must be in hers. For she must convince the valet to filch the key to her father's pistol cabinet and to watch him carefully. She was acutely aware that he had made no promises to her, and his present state of mind was most unstable. Her father would be furious, of course, but such an emotion was much safer than despair, after all.

Chapter 4

Moriah disliked dissembling of any kind. And so she found taking tea with Tess and pretending that nothing untoward was afoot very trying. Moriah had attempted, over the last year, to acquaint her sister in some measure with her father's gaming tendencies and the true state of estate finances. Tess had always listened carefully, her clear blue eyes trained intently on Moriah and her lips pursed as though she were deep in thought. But when their little talk was over, Tess would always give a flirtatious toss to her blond curls — an accustomed gesture uncannily reminiscent of their mother — and declare herself glad to speak of less dismal topics. Moriah could only hope that her sister had heeded some of what she said and, truly, she did not despair of her.

Like their mother, Tess was one of those light-hearted, lovely females made to be surrounded by things as pretty as she was. Moriah had long known this, having also known that a kind of helplessness would inevitably characterize Tess, as it had their mother. As a result, Moriah had always felt fiercely protective of her little sister, who was not nearly so self-centered as their mother had been.

True, Tess might sing through her days as though life would never change, as though reductions in staff or one less painting on the wall really had nothing to do with her. She might read too far too many romantical novels and dream of a grand London come-out and elegant balls. But she would, Moriah knew, be horrified if even one retainer were turned off to help pay for it all.

Moriah's eyes wandered now about the Blue Saloon, where the family always took tea, and came to rest on the figure of her sister. The younger girl chomped away at a buttered biscuit as delicately as her healthy young appetite would allow. To Tess's credit—and perhaps just a little bit to Moriah's—the younger sister really had little idea of what an enchanting picture she made, sitting there, the midnight blue chintz sofa a perfect backdrop for her classic blond beauty.

No, Moriah did not despair of her. And she thought she had done right in dispensing with the services of a governess these two years past. It had become necessary to economize, and Moriah knew herself perfectly capable of instructing her young sister, though they both missed Miss Billingsley dearly.

Moriah's eyes darted again about the room, its pale blue walls interrupted here and there by muted landscape paintings and elegant brass sconces. The thick pile carpet was of a hue to match the walls. She would miss this room, Moriah thought suddenly, as she would desperately miss the whole of the Abbey. She felt her eyes become misty and forced herself to concentrate on what Tess was saying.

Moriah had previously steered the conversation away from their father, and now she realized that Tess was chattering about her morning's visits to several of the tenants. Such visits were Moriah's province, of course, but she was pleased that Tess had taken it upon herself to help.

"And truly, Moriah, I do wish there was something more we might do for poor Mrs. Grimes. Tommy's gone out to work, now that his father's ill, but he cannot possibly bring home enough to feed all the little ones. And when winter is upon us — why, I do not know if the children will even have shoes. Is there nothing we can do?" Tess said, her voice, taking on a pleading tone.

"I'm certain there is, love," Moriah replied, setting her teacup down on the rosewood table before her. "We must contrive to bring them what food we can, without offending their pride, and I shall see if some of the village women will send their mending to Mrs. Grimes. She has a neat hand with a needle, if I recall correctly."

Their discourse thereafter drifted to several other tenants, but Moriah found her own agitated thoughts wandering until something Tess said once again penetrated her reverie.

". . . and Briggs was all abuzz with the news, Moriah. They say he may arrive at Roanbrooke this very se'ennight. Is that not famous? Perhaps now someone will give a ball! Oh, I do so long —" Tess's eyes took on a certain dreamy look that Moriah knew well. She watched as her sister replaced her teacup on its saucer and clasped her knees with her hands.

But Moriah heard nary a word of Tess's monologue beyond the word "Roanbrooke." She had not wanted to think of the Viscount Roane but, of course, she must. Her father had said he'd be in residence, and Moriah suppressed a shudder at the thought that he might also be in residence at the Abbey very shortly. No! That must not happen! Who did he think he was at all events, to come swooping upon them to destroy their lives? But that was not fair and she knew it. Moriah frowned, trying to attend to what Tess was saying about who would be most likely to give a ball in the viscount's honour. A ball, Moriah thought with disdain. Why? Because he finally deigned to bestow the honour of his presence on his country neighbors?

In the next moment she was appalled that she might feel such bitterness toward a complete stranger. She mentally shook herself and was relieved when the tea cart was trundled away and Tess took her leave in order to practice several pieces on the pianoforte. Without quite realizing what she was doing, Moriah began wandering aimlessly through the corridors of the Abbey. It was rare that she did so but, then, rarely was she beset by such a dire problem as the imminent loss of her home. She meandered past the morning room and the closed door of her father's study, then rounded the corner toward the drawing room. She could hear the melodious strains of the pianoforte but continued on her way. Her fingers lovingly traced lines along the richly panelled walls of the wide corridors, but no solutions to her difficulties came to mind. Instead, she found herself thinking of the Abbey and all it stood for.

Founded in the thirteenth century, Wykham was nestled in this quiet corner of Herefordshire between the River Wye and the Welsh border. Once a great medieval monastery, it had fallen into ruin after the Dissolution until it became the property of the Landons. Now it was an elegant classical manor house, but Moriah had always been grateful that some portions of the monastery remained — the cloisters, the bell tower, the gatehouse.

She knew some of the Abbey's history from her father, and the rest she'd garnered from old family journals. The Abbey had been a great source of pride for the Landons for generations. It was even mentioned in some of the guidebooks, and occasionally Wykham had been honoured by a distinguished visitor who wished to view the ruins.

And now—now it would pass out of the family, naught but a marker in a game of piquet. The thought brought tears to Moriah's eyes but she dashed them away. She must think of something, she told herself firmly. She must not allow Wykham Abbey to fall into strange hands, even if he *was* a neighbor—and a titled one at that. At the least, she would not give up her home without a fight.

She had come now the sunswept picture gallery, the long, somewhat narrow room that had once been the southern portion of the cloisters. Moriah loved this room, with its long pointed lancet windows and its Gothic arches. The outer wall, with the beautifully symmetrical windows, remained just as she supposed it had always been. It gave off now onto a lovely, tranquil garden almost surrounded by yew hedges. Moriah wondered fleetingly whether the monks of long ago had had such a garden to view as they sat deep in their meditations. The wall opposite had undoubtedly once also consisted of rows of windows. But it had been panelled over when this remnant of the cloisters had been incorporated into the house. It now held the impressive array of family portraits, the late afternoon sun presently swooping down to illumine them.

This was a remarkably well-preserved room, Moriah thought, especially considering how much of the Abbey had been completely destroyed. She sank down onto a comfortable mahogany armchair and glanced upward at the ceiling. But pondering the unique architecture of the Abbey would not help her to save it from the hands of strangers, she admonished herself, and channeled her thoughts accordingly.

She rose abruptly and gazed out at the private garden, a frown puckering her brow. The Viscount Roane was indeed a stranger to her. He had hardly ever come up from London in recent years and so, of course, they had never met. She imagined few of the local gentry had set eyes on him in nearly a decade, with the exception of her father, who spent so much time in Town. That did not prevent the viscount from being a favorite topic of local gossip, however. There had been whispers of some long-ago scandal that kept him from Herefordshire. Never having heard any particulars, Moriah had discounted that, but she could not help giving credence to the stories of his rakehell activities in London.

That and the fact that he'd seen fit to abandon his principal seat for so long could not commend him to Moriah. And yet, as all the desperate thoughts of the day came back to her, she realized that he was her only hope of salvation. There was no one else to turn to. It was as simple as that. And though wastrel he might be, he was human, was he not? He must be possessed of a degree of simple human compassion, she told herself. And he was coming to Roanbrooke! Why, she need only go to him, explain her fears for her father, ask the viscount to—to . . .

To do what? she suddenly asked herself. To renounce his claim to the Abbey? But that was impossible. It was a debt of honour, and neither her father's pride nor the viscount's would allow it to be forsworn. And certainly her own pride would not allow her to beg. No, she must simply make some reasonable request of him, one that he would be hard put to deny.

Moriah sighed as she continued to stare out at the

garden, her mind methodically considering exactly what she might say to the viscount. But, despite her concentration, she could not help noticing that the roses were in bloom now. How she would miss this neatly laid out garden, now blossoming in a riot of color. Never mind the flowers, she admonished herself, and continued to mentally rehearse her exchange with the viscount. She knew know what she would ask of him. If he refused one request, she must have a second one at the ready, one that would seem even more reasonable. Her mind churned with possibilities, the flowers now a mere blur in front of her.

It was not long after that Moriah threw her shoulders back and lifted her chin, feeling better for having reached some decision. She must speak to the viscount as soon as possible, and she knew exactly what she would say to him. She turned and began to walk briskly the length of the gallery. But she slowed, realizing that she now faced two logistical problems. She did not know when the viscount was coming to Herefordshire. She must endeavor to find out without arousing suspicion about her curiosity, for until the matter of the debt was resolved, no one must know that there was any connection between Roane and the Landons.

The second problem might prove a bit more troublesome. She must go to speak with the viscount without anyone knowing. For a young lady simply did not venture out unattended to call on a bachelor neighbor. It was against every notion of propriety, and to call on a man whom she had never met — well, it was unthinkable! Yet it must be done, and so she would choose a time when few people were abroad. Perhaps early morning, or dusk.

She was confident that she would contrive it somehow. For now, she made her way from the gallery and headed toward the housekeeper's rooms. She and Mrs. Trotter must take inventory of the growing number of torn linens. It was not possible to replace any now, but those that could be mended ought to be sent to Mrs. Grimes. As long as there was still a roof over Moriah's head, she would see that their tenants did not starve.

Chapter 5

Moriah needn't have spared a moment's worry as to the date of the viscount's arrival. She was never so grateful for the servants' grapevine as on the very next day. For, by mid-morning, the news was all over the village and its environs that the long-absent lord would arrive at Roanbrooke Court that very evening. Moriah knew she must lose no time before going to see him, for she had less than a fortnight left. Besides that, her father had been "indisposed" again since their interview, and there was no telling what he might try to do.

And so it was that early the following morning Moriah appeared at the Abbey stables and ordered her sleek black mare saddled. Not for the first time she thanked Heaven that with all of the recent changes at Wykham, they still had several good horses, her light-footed Ruby among them. She knew it was much too early for a visit, even one so unconventional as this. But she often rode out just after daybreak, enjoying a brisk ride over the fields before breakfast. And so her departure from the Abbey, at least, would not be remarked.

She would, however, have to ride about for some time before venturing to Roanbrooke Court. And perhaps the exercise would help pluck up her nerve, for she was not all that confident of the outcome of this day's work. And she knew that the hour of her visit would not commend her to the viscount. She might interrupt him at his toilette or at breakfast. Worse, he might still be keeping Town hours and be yet asleep. But she had no choice. She must accomplish her mission well before the gentry began their round of morning calls.

The air was clear and mild as Moriah galloped over the green fields. She could not help thinking, with a kind of wistfulness, how very beautiful the Abbey and its surrounding lands were. Wykham Abbey could be approached from the south by riding for hours over rolling hills and gentle grasslands. As she rode now over those very grasslands, she espied several of the black and white timber-framed houses so typical of the region. Some called them magpie cottages, and she thought they somehow matched the white faces and brown coats of the cattle that seemed to abound hereabouts.

The Abbey might also be approached from the north, passing through the village of Much Henley. And though she had never been to Roanbrooke Court, she knew its aspect was similar, and that the proper way to approach the mansion would be from the front, thereby passing through Much Henley. For obvious reasons she could not do this, nor could she travel any well-trod paths. Moriah knew that the two estates met somewhere in the northeast corner of Wykham land. She resolved to make her way to Roanbrooke from that direction, so keeping away from any prying eyes.

It was sometime later that she found herself crossing onto Roanbrooke land, and though the manor house was not yet visible, she relied on her sense of direction to take her there. She passed several timbered cottages and one rather square-shaped gray-stone edifice before Roanbrooke Court came into view. She took a deep breath, heartened by the fact that she had encountered not a living soul thus far, and steeled herself for the coming interview.

Moriah slowed her mare to a trot as they neared the great country house. She brought Ruby to a halt before the spectacular horseshoe staircase, the outside focal point of the formal, classical brick mansion that was the viscount's home. One moment there had been no one in sight and in the next, as if from nowhere, there appeared a groom and then a footman in green and gold livery. The footman, his face impassive, helped her to dismount, and the groom, after throwing her a brief, somewhat saucy look, led her horse away. The footman escorted her up the great stone staircase and inside the front portico, where she was met by the butler.

He was tall, with neatly combed silver hair and an overlarge moustache that curled at the ends. From his great height he looked down at her, simultaneously raising his large nose high into the air, and inquired as to what he might do for her. Her reply that she wished to see his master was met with a disdainful narrowing of the eyes. She actually thought he sniffed before asking whether she had an appointment. An appointment! she thought, her temper rising.

"No," she snapped, thrusting her chin up, willing herself to remain calm. "I am a neighbor. If your master is not ready to receive, I shall be happy to wait." Her tone brooked no argument, and she knew it. Certainly not even this top-lofty servant would insist that a neighbor needed an appointment to come calling.

Still, his eyebrow shot up, and she knew her

unaccompanied state had probably shocked him. He offered no further impediment, though, and ushered her, however grudgingly, into the front entryway. This enormous hall, with its gleaming marble floor, was dominated by a massive crystal chandelier that hung suspended from the second-story ceiling. She had but a moment to remark it, however, before the butler led her up the wide circular staircase.

He settled her in a small sitting room that she surmised must be reserved for those whose welcome was in question.

"Whom shall I say is calling, ma'am?" he asked imperiously.

Moriah was not the least intimidated, but she *was* nonplussed for a moment. She had not anticipated having to give her name. What if the viscount should refuse to see her?

She drew herself up to her full height and decided to match arrogance for arrogance. "You may tell your master that a neighbor has come to call," she replied in clipped tones.

The butler's eyes widened for a moment, but otherwise he evinced no reaction and departed without another word. Moriah found herself pacing the carpeted floor, her mind churning over and over what she might say to the man who employed such a supercilious butler.

The Viscount Roane poured himself a second cup of coffee and continued to peruse the pages of the *London Gazette*. But he found that his mind would not remain long on the printed word. He was thinking instead about his triumph at White's the other night. He had finally driven Landon to the wall, and Wykham Abbey would be his in less than a fortnight.

Funny thing was that he did not feel at all triumphant. Perhaps that would come later, when word filtered from London through to the country. Landon's ruin had been quite a sensation in Town, but Roane had kept a low profile, wishing to keep his role in it all seemingly minimal. He had stayed in London just long enough to wind up his affairs, and then left for Herefordshire. And the gossip had not yet spread to this peaceful corner of the world, he knew, for the servants had not uttered a word. Roane, of course, had no intention of telling anyone; he would not want to appear to gloat.

And in truth he was not gloating, though he should have been. Instead he felt rather empty and restless. His fierce need to settle his score with the Landons had driven him for so long. Now that the deed was done, he felt cast adrift, much as a soldier when the war is over. He folded the newspaper, setting it down on the white damask tablecloth, and sipped his coffee without tasting it.

Well, he supposed he would find some new occupation for his mind before long. He certainly had no intention of returning to the gaming hells of London; he'd had quite enough of that. He would spend some time setting Roanbrooke to rights; really he had been absent much too long. And then there would be the Abbey to see to. Roane smiled to himself. Yes, he ought to enjoy that. Perhaps he would look to restoring some of the ruins, which were reputed to be of great architectural interest. Yes, perhaps he might do that . . . although, strangely enough, the actual possession of the Abbey did not excite him. He had no need for it; his own estates were extensive enough, of a certain. No, it was the winning of the Abbey that had so driven him, and now that it was done . . .

He slammed his coffee cup down rather too hard

onto the saucer. Damn! Now that it was done, he ought to feel at least a sense of satisfaction. He had paid his debt to his long-dead family. He had, in some small way, avenged them. Then why the hell . . .

His ruminations were interrupted by the entrance of Finley. The butler stood just inside the oak doorway, his face impassive, his body unmoving, waiting to be recognized.

"Yes, well, what is it?" Roane asked irritably, and then wondered when he had become so testy.

"Begging your pardon, my lord, but there is a—er—young person here to see you," replied Finley.

Roane regarded his servant quizzically. His use of the term "young person" and the decided sniff that accompanied it intimated that the visitor was a female of questionable birth and probably reputation. Roane could not fathom who she might be. Certainly no one had followed him from London—he had been more than generous with his last mistress when he'd given her her congé. And he'd not been in Herefordshire for more than the briefest of visits for years. Then whoever—

"A 'young person,' Finley? Did she, by any chance, leave a name?" he asked, amused by the assumed superiority of his retainer.

Finley unbent his body just a bit and the hint of smugness appeared on his lined face as he replied, "She declined, my lord, but said I was to tell you a 'neighbor' had come to call."

"A neighbor? Whoever—ah—where did you put her, Finley?" Roane asked, wondering why his butler had assigned a neighbor to his ignominious category of "young person," and why this "neighbor" had declined to give her name.

"She is in the small sitting room, my lord."

Roane suppressed a grin. The small sitting room, indeed. What an incorrigible snob was this butler of his.

"Does she have the manner of a lady, Finley?" the viscount asked, taking up his coffee cup again for a moment.

"As to that, I couldn't say, my lord." Finley had withdrawn behind the impassive mask considered de rigueur for those in his profession. His body was once more rigid, his long, thin arms crossed behind his back.

"Oh, do come down off your high ropes, my good man. Does she have the speech and dress of a lady?"

"I — er — suppose one might say so, your lordship." The butler sounded almost disappointed, and he lowered his nose a notch from its usual high perch.

"Then might one be permitted to ask why you put her in the small sitting room?" Roane leaned back comfortably in his chair. He endeavored to keep his lip from curling in amusement but could not keep the hint of sarcasm from his tone.

"The young person arrived quite . . . unaccompanied, my lord." The tips of Finley's moustache twitched and he permitted himself a slight smile of self-satisfaction.

"No maid?"

"No, my lord. She — er — came on a horse, you see," replied Finley, rather enjoying himself by now.

A horse? thought Roane. Strange way to pay a morning call. And as to that, it was a bit early in the morning, even for the country. Roane found his curiosity most definitely piqued.

He rose gracefully from the table. "Well, we mustn't insult a neighbor, now must we?" he asked genially. "Do escort the young lady to the Green Saloon and inform her that I shall join her presently."

For a moment Finley was betrayed into an unseemly expression of surprise, but he quickly pulled the impassive mask down over his features. "Very good, my lord," he said and bowed himself out.

Roane shook his head with a bemused grin after the servant departed. Wherever had his father found such a high stickler? he wondered. If he weren't so diverted by the fellow's toplofty antics, he might consider pensioning him off. Seating himself once again, he reflected that he ought to have a talk with Finley, at all events, to remind him that they were no longer in London. In Town a gentleman's consequence seemed to rise in direct proportion to the arrogance of his servants. Not so in the country; here he imagined the gentry would take exception to a butler so high in the instep. Roane had no wish to offend his neighbors, even if he might not go out of his way to cultivate them. Certainly this was no time to stir up controversy—not when he was about to take possession of the Abbey.

The viscount drained his coffee and poured another cup. He sighed inwardly as he remembered just how closed and judgmental country society could be. And gossip was often the breath of life in these isolated villages, where there was so little other diversion. That was one reason he'd stayed away so long— to let the last hints of scandal surrounding his family and the Landons die a natural death. It was not Justin Traugott who was to seem the villain in the downfall of the Landons, but Landon himself, as profligate with his cards as his father had been with his women.

Of course, Roane had also stayed in London all these years watching Landon slowly dissipate his fortune. Roane had struck when the time was ripe,

50

and now he was rather glad to be home.

He was not sure that Finley was, though. London had rather agreed with the man, giving him ample opportunity to administer his selective set downs. But now he had got to be brought down a notch. Finley's insufferable arrogance had quite come in handy several times in Town when one of Roane's high flyers had had the temerity to present herself at his London townhouse. But such would not occur at Roanbrooke. Should he decide to indulge, Roane would take his pleasures most discreetly. Finley must give his dubious talent for ferreting out "unsuitable" callers a bit of a rest.

The viscount's thoughts wandered now to his mysterious visitor. Whoever she was, she was most definitely not possessed of a great deal of discretion. Well, he mused, the encounter should prove interesting. He took one last sip of his coffee, and, deciding that he'd kept the "young person" waiting an appropriate amount of time, rose and sauntered from the room.

Chapter 6

She was staring out of the large picture window, her body still and her back completely erect. He could not see her face, but he knew, by the dignity of her carriage, by the quality of her midnight-blue riding habit, that his mysterious visitor was indeed a lady. Finley should have known, too, he thought, peeved. Really, the man was slipping.

He closed the door softly behind him and advanced into the room, waiting for her to realize that she was no longer alone. She seemed so lost in thought. Curious though he was, something compelled him simply to watch her for a moment. He stood some ten feet from her, his arm resting casually on the back of the tapestried wing chair. But suddenly she turned to face him, and he had the distinct feeling she'd known all along that he was there. A word of greeting rose to his lips, but somehow he could not utter it. His breath caught in his throat as he beheld the young woman, her features clearly visible in the bright early morning light.

My God, but she's beautiful, he thought. And then he frowned and gazed at her more intently. No, he amended, she was not exactly beautiful. But she was certainly stunning. There was a quality about her that he could not put into words. Her most striking features were two large amethyst eyes. He had never seen eyes that color, and if they were a bit too far apart for classic beauty, well, it did not seem to matter. Her nose was chiseled but strong, and her lips were full, a luscious red. Her skin was darker than most Englishwomen, but that somehow added to the indefinable quality that so attracted him. A saucy dark blue hat was perched on the side of her head, and he could see that her hair was jet-black, smooth, probably straight and thick. It was parted down the middle and caught in a full, soft bun at the nape of the neck, with tendrils escaping onto her shoulders.

"Thank you for seeing me, my lord," she said after a moment. The voice was deep, husky, but quite clear. Somehow, it fit her. She did not extend her hand nor come any closer. She simply stood, framed by the window, completely composed. Her hands were clasped loosely in front of her and her gaze was steady.

He found himself somewhat disconcerted by the direct gaze of those amethyst eyes and by her composure. A woman who had arrived in such an unconventional manner ought to be feeling somewhat defensive, which she obviously was not.

He strolled toward her. "It is my pleasure, ma'am," he drawled, inclining his head slightly, permitting not even the glimmer of a smile to curl his lips. "But I fear you have the advantage of me. Had we met before, I assure you, I should not have forgotten," he added smoothly.

"You are quite correct, my lord. We have not previously met. I am Moriah Landon."

Roane's eyes widened and he stopped short, barely three feet in front of her. Perhaps he hadn't heard her aright. "You are *who?*" he demanded, trying to keep his voice cool.

"Moriah Landon, my lord. Daughter of Thomas Landon." Moriah kept her voice steady but had the sinking feeling that he was going to make this interview very difficult. Her eyes flitted for a moment over his face, taking in the deep-set blue eyes, the high-bridged nose, the square, determined line of his jaw, the hard set of his mouth as he glared at her. She suppressed a sigh. No, this was not going to be easy.

"But that is impossible! Landon's daughters are— well, I was given to understand that Landon's daughters were still in the schoolroom," he exclaimed arrogantly.

Her eyes took in his tall, lean figure, clad in dark brown coat, buff-colored breeches, and brown top boots. She had the impression that beneath the beautifully tailored clothes there was a hard, muscular body. And that beneath that body was a hard, implacable man. But she would not allow him to faze her. "Obviously you were misinformed, my lord," she replied dryly.

"Obviously," he echoed, trying to wipe the shock off his face. As the reality of who she was sunk in, his eyes narrowed and a deep frown creased his brow. He did not exactly like the idea that Landon had a full grown daughter, and what the hell was she doing here? It passed all bounds of propriety, to be sure. Even so, he could not help his eyes slowly wandering the length of her.

She was small, but her figure was superbly proportioned. She was, in a word, voluptuous. His eyes went from her softly rounded hips to her small waist, then on to her full, high breasts. They seemed to be straining against the bodice of her riding habit, which, though of excellent quality, was well-worn and had obviously been made before her figure had fully ripened into womanhood. And that was exactly

54

what she was right now—ripe, like a juicy plum, waiting to be plucked.

He ran his tongue over his suddenly dry lips and sternly resisted the urge to run his hands down the sides of that curvaceous body. He did not deem it necessary to be overly nice in his manners toward a Landon, but that would be going a bit far, after all. A glance was one thing . . .

"Your gaze, my lord, is impertinent," she declared. Her tone was determined, but the huskiness of her voice only added to her unusual appeal. And just what sort of gaze did she expect, coming to a man's bachelor residence like this? He thought she wanted being set down a notch for such behaviour.

He chuckled softly, impudently. "And your unprecedented appearance, my dear, is brazen. Now, what do you want? Your father did not send you, surely?" he asked, thinking it shocking that Landon would have confided the sordid details of his downfall to his daughter, much less sent her to plead for him.

Roane watched her face carefully. She paled somewhat and her eyes widened for a moment, but her chin went up. "My father has no notion that I am here. He would be furious did he know and deeply chagrined."

So, Landon was not sunk quite that low. But she was certainly brazen. Roane folded his arms across his chest nonchalantly. "Well then, Miss Landon, I ask again. What do you want?"

She swallowed hard but spoke calmly enough. "I have come to speak with you."

He was suddenly struck by how young she was; she could not yet be twenty years of age. Such composure in the face of her youth quite unnerved him. But he reminded himself who she was and said sarcastically, "My limited faculties have enabled me to figure that out. However, I cannot think what we two might have to speak about. Pray do enlighten me."

He saw her flush and watched her ample breasts rise and fall, pressing against the fabric of her dress so that it looked as if the seams would burst. Nevertheless, her voice, when she spoke, was matter of fact. Or was there just a twinge of sarcasm in her tone.

"My lord, I do not wish to be rude. But I have ridden for several hours, and I would appreciate being permitted to sit down."

It was the viscount's turn to flush, but he did not apologize for a rudeness that was obviously his. He bowed slightly and with a sweeping motion of his hand indicated that she might be seated on the dark green camelback sofa. He watched the sway of her hips as she moved briskly to the sofa. There was a grace—no, more than that, a fluidity to her movement that made his blood race. As she passed by him he caught the rich scent of roses. Not for her, it seemed, the insipid lavender water that so many ladies seemed to prefer.

She sat down elegantly, despite the skimpy proportions of her habit. He checked the impulse to sit next to her and instead took a seat across from her in the tapestried wing chair. She drew her gloves off and placed them on the sofa table. He could not help staring at her and found himself imagining what her hair would look like tumbled down her back. He caught the flutter of her pulse at her throat and wondered if he was finally piercing that unnerving composure. Suddenly their eyes met, and held; he felt an intensity between them that jarred him. Quickly he blinked, but still a wave of desire coursed through him. This was ridiculous, he told himself, annoyed. She was just another woman, and a Landon at that. Hardly worth his notice. Best get this interview over with and then be rid of her.

He schooled his features to a mask of indifference, but his senses were reeling, assailed by the very presence of her. His eyes avoided hers but rested instead on her lips. They were slightly parted and looked soft, yielding, kissable. It was then that he realized what that indefinable quality about her was. She was alluring, to be sure, but it was more than that. Perhaps her dark skin gave her something of an exotic air, but even that did not quite define it. She had a certain look about her, as if . . . as if she were born to grace a man's bed. Sensuous, that was the word. She was completely and utterly sensuous.

Good God, he thought, no wonder Finley had reacted the way he had, however unwittingly. Roane's hand slid up to loosen his cravat; he felt decidedly warm. His mind had no difficulty conjuring up an image of Moriah Landon in a diaphanous negligee, stretched across his bed.

"My lord," the husky voice interrupted his reverie. Her tone was not questioning, nor unsure, nor apologetic. It was firm, the two words a simple reminder of her presence.

He certainly needed no reminder. He shifted uncomfortably in his chair and risked a look at her eyes. Again the direct, steady gaze. He wondered if she realized how enticing she was. Very possibly not, he thought, noting the candor in those eyes. And he supposed she was innocent, but only because she'd been buried in the country all her life. No woman who looked like that could remain innocent in London for long, baron's daughter or no, he thought cynically. And then he was angry, very angry at himself for allowing a Landon to so affect him. His face hardened into a sneer.

"Now, then, Miss Landon, you *did* wish to speak with me, did you not?" he drawled, as if it had been she, not he, who had been staring so rudely.

Her lips compressed for a moment but the large amethyst eyes never left his face. She folded her hands in her lap, seeming to compose herself to speak.

"I understand that you hold my father's markers, Lord Roane. You must know that we are unable to raise the sum owed to you. We are ruined, my lord, and Wykham Abbey is yours." She spoke slowly, deliberately. Where was the anger, the bitterness? he wondered. And damn it, why was she involved in this at all? It was between him and her father. Roane had no wish to deal with a female. In fact, her very existence was a rather unwelcome revelation. It was one thing to ruin a profligate gambler with a couple of theoretical daughters barely out of swaddling clothes. It was quite another to be presented with a young woman, an innocent victim of her father's and his own machinations. But no, he told himself, this was no time for foolish sentiment. He had wanted to ruin the Landons, all of them, male or female. Had not his mother been ruined and his family destroyed?

"Yes, I thought that might be the case," he said finally. "Your father is a most . . . improvident gambler," he added, summoning up a haughty indifference.

"I am aware of what my father is, my lord," Moriah said coldly. She strove mightily to maintain her composure. He must never know what it cost her to admit that Wykham was lost to them, nor to hear her father maligned, whatever his faults. She held her hands tightly clasped in her lap, the nails of her right hand digging into the palm of her left. She took a deep breath to calm herself and noted with mounting fury that his eyes flitted momentarily over her breasts. She was all too conscious of her tight, ill-fitting habit and had to still the urge to cover her chest with her arms. She would not give him the satisfaction of knowing that his glance discomfitted her. To her dismay, she felt the color rise in her, not for the first time, she knew.

Really, the man was insufferable, his blue eyes raking her outrageously, so—so unabashedly. But they *were* the most amazing eyes she'd ever seen, she had to admit. Already she'd watched them change from a cold, clear sky blue to a warm, intense deep blue. They were very deep blue now, and she stirred uncomfortably beneath their gaze. She felt a strange sensation in the pit of her stomach.

He raised his eyes and she forced herself to meet them. She read mockery there, as if he sensed her reaction to him. He crossed his legs and leaned back in his chair.

"Pray, go on, Miss Landon. You were saying that you know—er—what your father is."

Why did she have the disconcerting feeling that he was mentally undressing her? Once or twice she'd seen men size up the serving girls in a country inn in just that way. How dare he do the same to her! The man was unspeakably rude and arrogant! She reflected that he and that supercilious butler of his most assuredly deserved each other.

She drew herself up. "Yes, I do know what he is, my lord," she said finally. "But you do not. You see him as a wastrel. But he is also a very caring man, a loving father."

The viscount's mouth hardened. He'd had a loving father once, but his memories of him were those of an eight-year-old child. "And he shows his love by throwing away the very roof over your head in a game of cards?" he demanded caustically.

Moriah blanched at the bitterness and blatant incivility of his words, but she did not lower her eyes. She would not be cowed by him, nor would she allow him to make her angry. It would not serve her purpose and, besides, it was rare that she let her temper get the better of her. She certainly did not intend to give him the satisfaction of seeing her lose it. She dug her fingernails into her palms again, and her voice was strong as she said, "I did not come to discuss my father nor past events. What's done is done. I must look to the future now."

In spite of himself Roane had to concede a grudging admiration for her calm approach to what surely must be the greatest catastrophe of her life. Where were the hysterics so common to the females of his acquaintance? But he forced himself to remember the score he had to settle and said curtly, "I do not see how that concerns me."

Moriah ignored his last statement and went on. Best get this over with. "If it were just I who was concerned I should not be here. I should then accept what has happened and go on from there. But there is my sister to consider, and there is my father."

"Your father—who has brought this down upon you," he said disdainfully.

Damn him! Did he think she needed a reminder? "My father can no more help what he is than—than a wounded man can help crying out from pain," she retorted with more intensity than she'd intended. His eyes widened for a moment but he said nothing, and she went on, choosing her words carefully. "I shall obtain a position, of course. I see no problem with that. But Tess, my sister, is but sixteen years old, you must know. She needs my father to look after her if I am to be away. And my father — well, he — I have reason to believe he means to — to take his own life." She finished with her voice but a whisper and looked down at her hands for a moment. She would not abase herself by telling him that she could not bear to lose her father, let alone the Abbey. She took a deep breath and looked up again, bracing herself for a caustic reply.

Roane winced inwardly. He had not expected this. But perhaps she exaggerated, as females were wont to do. He forced himself to resume his tone of haughty indifference.

"Oh?" the viscount asked with a sneer. His tone told Moriah that he considered her problem no concern of his. Did the man have no feeling at all? she wondered. But she bit back a caustic comment of her own and forced herself to say what she had come to say.

"Yes, and I cannot believe, when you won at cards, that you meant for my father to lose his life. And so I have come to ask if you — if you would consider not laying claim to the Abbey. We would sell everything of value that we have in order to pay you. And the rest I — I would pay out gradually from my wages."

The viscount was quite taken aback and hadn't the faintest idea how to reply. Of course he did not wish her father dead, not but what he supposed there would be some justice in it — an eye for an eye and all that sort of thing. But now what was he supposed to do? Did she not know that a debt of honour needs must be paid straight away? It was a matter of honour for both parties involved, regardless of the consequences. And why was he discussing this with a female? It just wasn't done! He rose abruptly and strode to the fireplace, empty, this warm August morning, of a fire. He ran his fingers through his generous head of hair and then, resting his elbow on the gilt-edged mantel, regarded his visitor pensively.

Moriah's eyes followed the viscount as he moved. He turned to face her, and she noted again the deep-set eyes, a cool blue now as he studied her. His mouth was set in a hard line, almost a sneer. He would have been quite handsome, she thought, if not for that ever-present sneer and the lines of dissipation around his lips and eyes. He looked older than the twenty-seven or twenty-eight years she knew that he was. Her eyes went to his firm, square jaw and the dark brown, wavy hair, brushed forward in the Brutus cut. Ah, yes, he might very well have been handsome. . . .

He flexed his long, tapered fingers and put his hands to his hips. She could not prevent her eyes from sweeping up and down his person, taking in again the fine clothes and the fine lean body beneath them. She shuddered involuntarily. There was about him a sense of power, of drive, evident in the way he moved and spoke. He seemed to be a mass of coiled energy, ready to spring. He was completely unlike any men she'd ever met. There was a strength about him, a magnetism whose pull she could feel even though they met as adversaries. He was, she thought, a man to depend on, and a man to fear.

She saw him open his mouth to speak and steeled herself against his reply to her entreaty. "So you wish to pay me out of your wages. And just how long, my dear Miss Landon, do you suppose it would take you to pay me the whole?" he asked smoothly, arrogantly.

Fear was gradually being replaced by anger. She was not his "dear Miss Landon"! She looked down at her hands to hide the flash in her eyes. "A—a very long time, my lord," she replied, trying to sound humble.

"Yes, I had rather thought it might," Roane said dryly. He admonished himself to remember his family and not to soften simply because a beautiful young woman had made herself her father's emissary. Undoubtedly she was bluffing about Landon's imminent suicide, at all events. "I am afraid that would not answer, you know. I am not a patient man."

Moriah looked up at him, his face set implacably. "Well, in that case," she blurted, rather too quickly, "perhaps you would consider simply allowing us a bit more time. Just enough so that I might establish myself in a position and settle Papa and Tess some place suitable. That way Papa might be made to see that—that life can go on." She tried to still the hands twisting in her lap.

"Retrenching, are you, Miss Landon?" he inquired mockingly.

Moriah was furious, for that was exactly what she was doing. But she took a deep breath and forced herself to continue with the only logical argument she had. "Furthermore, my lord, I am persuaded that you will not commend yourself to our neighbors by preemptorily turning us out," she said, keeping her voice steady only with supreme effort.

"You needn't trouble yourself so very much over my reputation, my dear, although I do appreciate your concern," he retorted with thinly veiled sarcasm.

Oh! The man was impossible! she thought, her hold on her temper rapidly slipping. She tried to think of a suitable setdown, but the viscount must have sensed her reaction, for his smile became more pronounced. She would have liked to wipe it from his face, but he continued speaking.

"And just what sort of position did you have in mind, Miss Landon? You seem so very sure of obtaining one," he asked, reclining again against the mantel.

"Why, I shall find a place as a governess, of course," she replied confidently.

Suddenly his mouth widened into a grin and he erupted into a full, rich laughter that came from deep in his throat.

"You—a governess? Surely, you jest," he gasped. He looked years younger when he laughed, she thought, irrelevantly. She stood up, pulling herself to her full height, and marched across the green and gold Belgian carpet. She came to stand at the hearth, not three feet from the viscount.

She faced him and met his gaze defiantly. "Indeed, I am quite serious, my lord. I assure you I shall make a fine governess. Why, I have instructed my sister these two years past, and my qualifications are more than suitable. I can give a credible performance on the pianoforte, my embroidery is more than passable, my French is nearly fluent, and should there be any need, I am well versed in mathematics and the Greek classics as well."

She had spoken rather heatedly, but his voice in reply was a soft murmur as his eyes flicked over her. "I have no doubt you would acquit yourself well in the schoolroom, my dear Miss Landon, but you see, you would never get past the front door." The vestiges of laughter had gone from his face and she felt herself flush. Damn! She must not allow herself to become discomposed before this man. She looked down quickly at her dress, and then back up at him.

"Oh, you are referring no doubt to my dress. I daresay I had ought to wear something more sober-hued. And perhaps a governess oughtn't to have a riding habit at all," she said in a rush of words. "And I might dress my hair differently, but otherwise, I think it will answer. I know I am young, but it is not

64

as though I were a beauty, you must know."

Suddenly he straightened and took a step closer to her. The movement was graceful, yet she was made keenly aware again of the power, the strength that he exuded, like no other man she knew. She felt a sense of fear and of something else, which she could not define. He was very close to her now, and his eyes swept over her again, lingeringly. Once more there was that strange sensation in the pit of her stomach.

"Who told you that you are not beautiful?" he asked, his voice soft.

She cocked her head in curiosity. It seemed like a strange question. "Why, I have known it ever since I was a child."

He peered down at her, and she saw that his eyes were once more a deep, warm blue. Again the strange fluttering in her stomach. "I did not know you then," he murmured, "so I can venture no opinion. But surely you know that people change. And"—here he paused, his gaze, if possible, becoming even more intense—"there is more than one kind of beauty. Oh, no, my dear, you will never do as a governess."

Moriah swallowed hard, her eyes unable to leave his face. She was chagrined to feel that flush creeping through her again, chagrined that the softness of his tone and that warm gaze had transfixed her, even for a moment. She thought she preferred his insolence to this strange intensity; it seemed somehow safer. She mentally shook herself but could not raise her voice above a whisper.

"But surely I must try," she said.

His expression hardened again. How could a man put his daughter in such a position? He spoke harshly now, partly out of anger toward Landon, partly to frighten his daughter into running home where she belonged. She ought to leave men's business to men. Besides, she was much too attractive to be alone with any man. "And I ask you again, ma'am, have you any idea of how long it would take you to amass the amount of money you would need to dispatch your father's debt to me?"

"I said that we would sell everything of value in addition, my lord. There are still a number of paintings, a few jewels. . . . If that will not answer, then I merely ask that you give me time to establish myself. I would not ask for myself; it is only that I fear for my father's life." Her voice was strong again and she raised her chin, willing herself not to move away from him.

"But, my dear, I do not believe you would ever secure such a position," he said. "Certainly you will never remain long in one. Just let the family have an older son or a cousin or even a neighbor who cannot keep his eyes or his hands away from you." He did not know whether he was trying to frighten her or perhaps warn her of the pitfalls of her absurd plan.

But it seemed that Moriah Landon did not frighten easily. Her eyes widened and he caught a flash of anger. She turned and stormed to the sofa table, where she had placed her gloves.

So those magnificent amethysts have fire in them, do they? Roane mused. He contemplated the swivel of her hips as she sashayed across the room. He felt his blood surge and ran his tongue over his lips. Could she really be so completely ignorant of the effect she had on men?

She stood next the sofa table, her side to him, and bent to retrieve her gloves. Then she turned to him. "You are insolent, my lord," she snapped, her tone haughty as she drew on the left glove. "I came here because I fear for my father and because I have my sister to care for. I did not imagine that you had much need of the Abbey, nor did I think my proposals unreasonable. Neither would deny you your rightful winnings — 'twas only time that I asked for. As that is not to be, I shall take my leave." She drew on the second glove and folded her hands neatly in front of her.

She seemed amazingly composed, but her rather heavy breathing told him otherwise. Her mention of her family angered him, made him think of his own, and he was glad that he had in some way discomfitted her. But he suddenly realized that he did not wish her to leave. When she walked out his door it was quite likely that he would never see her again. And why the hell should he care? he berated himself.

"I would request, my lord, that you mention this visit to no one," she continued, her voice amazingly cool, even imperious. He had to admire her nerve. "It was improper of me to come here, and this interview has been pleasant for neither of us. I am persuaded you will agree it is best forgotten."

Somehow he did not think he could forget this interview. He did not know whether it was that or her mention of her father and sister, an unwelcome reminder of his own, which prompted his next action. She turned to go, and without thinking, he strode across the room and grabbed her by the wrist. Her sleeve had ridden up a bit and his fingers touched her bare flesh. The feel of her skin startled him, almost burned; he tightened his grasp and pulled her closer. He did not know what he intended to say or do. He could hear his own heartbeat, could see the movement of her breasts as she breathed rapidly. He felt heady from the scent of her. She looked down at her wrist, and then her eyes met his and there was that shocking intensity between them again. He could not put his whirling senses into words.

"Our . . . interview is concluded, my lord," she stammered, trying unsuccessfully, he thought, to resume her imperious tone. Her face was close to his; if he but bent his head, his lips would reach hers. He restrained himself with difficulty. "You are not interested in my terms," she continued softly. "There is nothing more I can offer you."

"Oh, I wouldn't say that," he murmured insolently, his eyes sweeping pointedly over her. Suddenly she stiffened, and he was recalled to his senses. My God, he hadn't said that aloud, had he? He released her immediately, assuring himself that she wouldn't understand the implications of such a statement anyway.

But apparently he had, and she did. Her eyes widened and she colored, but instead of delivering the slap on the face he expected, she merely looked curiously at him. "I hadn't thought of that, my lord," she said quietly. "Indeed, I — I hadn't thought of that at all."

Chapter 7

The viscount watched as Moriah Landon backed away from him and groped to place a hand on the sofa. Lord, she couldn't really be taking this seriously! And what in Heaven's name was he supposed to do if she did? He couldn't very well retract his improper offer. A man had his pride, after all, and *he* certainly could not apologize to a Landon. And, dammit, he hadn't made any offer in the first place! Whatever had possessed him to utter the words he had, he did not know. Never had he spoken so to a gentlewoman. It was unthinkable, no matter that she was a Landon, no matter what she looked like.

He saw her draw a deep breath and reflected that it really made no difference how she took his imprudent words. For, of course, she would refuse him and, if the momentary flash of temper he'd seen before was any indication, none too politely at that. But first would come the requisite hysterical burst of outrage, or an attack of the vapors at the least. He crossed his arms lazily over his chest and awaited her reaction, thinking that it would be amusing to see how Miss Moriah Landon refused his highly dishonorable offer that was not really an offer at all.

But the tears did not come, nor the outrage. Instead she raised her chin and spoke so matter-of-factly that he was taken aback. "I do not understand why you should want *me* instead of the Abbey, my lord. I am persuaded that there are many women more comely than I with whom you might — er — do this sort of thing."

What in the world? The viscount blinked in amazement. What was he supposed to say to that? "That is much beside the point, Miss Landon," he began, but seeing her face fall ever so slightly, decided he was being ungallant. "And I have already told you that you are no judge of that, you know," he heard himself saying softly.

"That's all very well, my lord, but what of the Abbey? Surely you must want — "

"I have land enough, Miss Landon, and houses enough." Why was he playing devil's advocate when he wanted her to refuse in the first place? Then he realized that it would be best to provoke her into a sharp refusal and have the whole absurd business done with.

"And mistresses enough, I warrant," she retorted with some asperity.

"Ah, yes. Well, I plan to make a rather extended stay in the country, you must know. And the nights can be long and lonely, do you not agree?" he said smoothly, thinking that surely he had incensed her sufficiently now.

"I do not imagine we should agree on very much, my lord, you and I," she snapped, and then clutched momentarily at her stomach.

A retort died on his lips and he found himself asking whether she was quite all right.

"Yes, yes, I — well, the fact of the matter is, my lord, that I have not yet broken my fast."

"You've not — are you saying you are . . . hungry, Miss Landon?" he asked, taking a step toward her.

"Yes, my lord."

Really, she was an original. As far as she knew, he had just made a highly improper and dishonorable proposition of the sort that would have sent any other female into a dead faint. But Moriah Landon, ever practical, was hungry. Roane suppressed a guffaw and went to the bellpull to summon Finley.

Finley was not quite able to mask his considerable surprise when the viscount ordered a substantial breakfast for his guest. But Roane ignored him, blithely escorting the "young person" into the breakfast room right under the nose of his disapproving butler. It occurred to Roane, as he seated Miss Landon at the table, that perhaps she was merely playing for time. Perhaps what she really wanted was not breakfast but time to formulate her reply to his offer. No lady could possibly eat at a time like this.

Moriah Landon could, however, and did. And though he was beginning to think her perfectly capable of discussing the topic at hand between forkfuls of scrambled eggs, he forestalled her. He insisted that they table their rather interesting conversation until her appetite had been sated. And so he sipped another cup of coffee as she consumed her eggs, nibbled dry toast, and drank a cup of coffee herself.

Finally, he leaned back in his seat. "And now, Miss Landon, I await your answer," he said smoothly, wondering how she was going to deliver a setdown to a man of whose hospitality she had just partaken.

She rose gracefully and strolled to the wall next the sideboard. She peered up at one of the pastoral paintings that adorned the room, running her fingers over the gold-leafed frame. Presently she turned to face him, her hands clasped in front of her as before. She was, as usual, the picture of composure.

"I was neither born nor bred to such as you

71

suggest, my lord," she said with great dignity. It was not the fiery rebuke he'd expected, but her next words surprised him even more. "But—but I suppose that, circumstanced as I am, pride, morality, and girlish dreams are luxuries I cannot afford."

He blinked and sat up in his chair. Was she actually going to consider becoming his mistress? Hellfire! This whole conversation was preposterous! How could she really think he would . . . would . . .

"Really, Miss Landon," he began, thinking that, somehow, he had got to get himself out of this with his pride intact. "I don't—"

"Oh, but my lord, surely you must give me time to think on 't," she interrupted earnestly. "I must make certain there are no—no other options—no other way before—before I would commit myself to such a course," she added quietly, her gaze never wavering from his face. As before, her nearly unflappable demeanor unnerved him. Any other female would have ranted at him through a veil of tears. But then, she was unlike any woman he'd ever met.

He cocked his head and gazed quizzically at her. She could not truly mean that she would consider coming to his bed, although the thought brought a warm flush to certain parts of his anatomy. But no, this seeming to weigh the options must simply be a ploy to gain time beyond the fortnight he'd promised her father. That *must* be it for, of course, she had no intention—or did she? My God, he thought, what would he do if she said yes? And, now that he thought on it, what would he do if she said *no?* He couldn't very well let her father kill himself, nor could he let her slave away as a governess, living in some cold garret of a room, to pay him money he had no need of. But he could not simply forego a debt of honour either.

Damn! What a coil it all was. He frowned and rose abruptly from his chair. And why was it *his* problem? It was Moriah Landon's problem, and that of her wastrel father. What the hell did he care what happened to the Landons? He hadn't maneuvered all this time to help Landon ruin himself, only to save his worthless neck in the end! But his daughter—what of his daughter?

He strode to where Miss Landon stood, stopping several feet before her. He could see clearly the movement of her full breasts as she breathed rapidly, and his eyes devoured her. She raised her chin with haughty dignity, as if in reaction to his scrutiny. For all her composure, he mused, she was no ice maiden. Oh, no, he was certain that beneath that luscious exterior there lurked a very passionate woman, although she had no idea of it as yet. And she wanted to be a governess, he laughed inwardly, and reflected that he would very much enjoy being her tutor, albeit not in Greek and Roman classics.

But, of course, that could never be. Landon or no, she was a lady of birth. And yet, if she agreed to come to him, would he really be able to turn her away? He swallowed hard and looked down into the amethyst eyes, assuring himself that the question was mute. Her decision was made; she was merely playing for time. Well, he would play along with her; he really was in no great hurry.

"You do understand that I cannot give you my— my answer just now, do you not, my lord?" she inquired calmly, but he sensed a bit of hesitation and thought her voice somewhat breathless. He wondered what it would be like to shatter that amazing composure utterly, irrevocably.

"I quite understand, Miss Landon," he found himself saying as he took a step closer to her. His blood was racing, but somehow he kept his voice as calm as hers. They might have been discussing the purchase of a thoroughbred mare. "I shall give you two days in which to decide. But it would, I think, be best for you if you did not come here again. I have a hunting box in the northwest corner of my land, near where it marches with yours. It is easily recognizable—the only greystone structure in the area." How had he managed to think so pragmatically at a time like this? It was just the sort of thing she would do, he realized.

"Yes, I—I passed it today." The voice was husky, unmistakably breathless now.

"Good. I shall await you there at this hour two days hence. You will, of course, come in person to deliver your answer." Now, why had he said that?

"My lord, you must understand that were I to—to consider this proposal of yours, I must have your word to maintain absolute secrecy." Her voice lowered at this last and she unclasped her hands, but her gaze met his steadily. "I would not have my family hurt by the dreadful scandal that would ensue if—if it became known."

Always her family. Did she never think of herself? But it was all quite academic, he told himself, and decided to enjoy this little repartee.

"My reputation would be rather blackened as well, Miss Landon. I assure you I should be most discreet," he replied with suitable gravity, one hand moving to rest casually against the wall.

"Yes, and we would have to devise some means of convincing my father that the debt was paid or of allowing him to win his markers back. We—"

"I *quite* understand, Miss Landon," he interrupted, caught between mirth and exasperation. Must she be so damned practical? One would think they were discussing estate business, not a highly indecent proposition. "I do assure you that if you— er—agree to come to me, I shall take care of . . . everything." He had meant to sound bemused for, indeed, the entire conversation, if taken in its proper context, was rather humourous. But as he stood looking down into those eyes, wide and luminous with a mixture of fear and pride and something else that he could not define, he found that his voice had grown soft. He knew that his eyes blazed with a hunger that he would rather she not see.

She flushed, and for some reason he was pleased that he had that effect on her. Impulsively, he took her hand and turned it palm upward. He planted a lingering kiss on the inside of her wrist and felt the rapid flutter of her pulse. He lifted his eyes to hers. "Until Friday, my dear," he whispered.

She swallowed hard. "Good day, my lord," she rasped, and then she turned and sashayed elegantly from the room.

Chapter 8

Moriah was never sure how it was that she managed to exit the viscount's house with some degree of
dignity, ride all the way home, and then appear in the
breakfast room as if she had done nothing more than
take an accustomed morning ride. But somehow she
must have, for she next found herself discussing
trivialities with Tess over the breakfast table. And
somehow she had the presence of mind to partially
fill her plate and make some pretense of consuming
her food, so as not to cause comment on her unusual
lack of appetite. But she could not, even one hour
later, have repeated a word of her conversation with
Tess, for her head was spinning with the words of
another conversation, one so extraordinary that she
could hardly credit its having taken place. She could
not later recall the excuse she made to Tess, but she
withdrew from the breakfast room as soon as she
dared and closeted herself in the morning room. It
was only then that she allowed herself to think, really
think, about what had transpired at Roanbrooke
Court.

She sat down at her mahogany desk, only to jump
up in the next moment and begin pacing the carpeted
floor. How dare he make such a suggestion to her!
How dare he! The man was a blackguard, completely

unprincipled and unfeeling. But then, had she really expected anything different? She had gone to him for lack of any alternative, but hadn't she known, deep down, that there was precious little chance of sympathy or help from the Viscount Roane? Perhaps, but she certainly had not expected his insolent manner, the insulting stare he trained on her, and the outrageous, ignominious offer he made her. And even that she might have anticipated, had she truly thought on 't, given the viscount's reputation as a ladies' man.

In truth, it was her own reaction that surprised and mystified her more than anything. What was it about him that had transfixed her, had made her heart beat so rapidly, had made her blush like a silly schoolgirl? But no, it was no schoolgirl blush she'd felt. Rather it had been a warm flush that had coursed through her body, a feeling not altogether unpleasant but most disconcerting, especially when engendered by a man so unscrupulous, so blackhearted as the viscount.

And yet, he *had* offered her a way out, a way to save her home and her father if she had courage enough to grasp the chance. She knew his offer was reprehensible, something that a well-bred young maiden should not or would not contemplate for a moment, no matter what the consequences of refusal. And yet, could she live with herself if, while she clung proudly to her honour, her father put a period to his existence?

She looked down at her desk top, at the pile of work awaiting her. How everything paled in significance compared to the problem now besetting her! She slid into her comfortable desk chair with its inlaid mother-of-pearl back. She propped her elbow on the desk and leaned her head on her open palm, her brow furrowed in thought. She had but two days in which to make a decision, but she knew that her options were pitifully few, perhaps non-existent. Still, she must leave no stone unturned. She resolved to pay a visit to Mr. Fairley in Much Henley this very afternoon, for he was intimately acquainted with Landon affairs. If there were some way that Moriah had overlooked, in which disaster might be averted, surely he would know of it.

She had little faith in eleventh hour miracles, however, and for the first time began to consider the consequences of accepting the viscount's offer. She rose slowly from her desk chair and ambled to the large bay window. She clasped her hands behind her back and stared out at the beautiful rolling lawns that marked the front of Wykham Abbey. To her right she could see one of the crumbling walls of the old gatehouse, its ancient stone a sparkling silver gray in the bright morning light. She closed her eyes for a moment and pressed her brow to the window-pane. All this, she thought, all this and my father's life, for the price of my honour, for the right to call myself a lady.

She blinked back unwitting moisture from her eyes and opened them, this time gazing unseeing out the window. The Viscount Roane was asking her to become his mistress. She gulped in dismay as she realized that she would be just another in a long string of mistresses. Her pride balked at that, but she knew it could not be helped, and she forced herself to consider what would happen if she accepted his offer.

She imagined that outwardly her life would change very little, except that she would have to sneak out of the house in the middle of the night and, much as she would dislike it, might be forced into lying now and again should she be excessively tired during the day. And that ought to be the worst of it unless—unless somehow it were to become known that Moriah Landon had become Lord Roane's mistress. She swallowed hard as she thought of the dire consequences of *that*. She would be cut by many, if not all, of their neighbors, and the family would not be received. And Tess—it would ruin her chances for contracting any kind of suitable marriage. Almost as an afterthought Moriah realized that she herself would never be able to marry, regardless of whether her liaison with the viscount became known. But that hardly signified; with neither dowry nor beauty, she had long ago accepted that she would not marry.

Moriah wondered fleetingly if any of their acquaintances would dare receive them if such a scandal should ensue. Probably not, she thought. Her friend Sarah would want to, she was certain, but her pompous husband would not allow it, nor would Sarah dare defy him. Olivia Crowley, though closer in age to Moriah than any of the neighbors, had never been a friend, and Moriah imagined that the haughty Miss Crowley would crow with delight at Moriah's fall from grace. Her mind went now to Mrs. Shoup, that kindly, refined lady of indeterminate middle years who lived just north of Much Henley. It had been rumoured for years that she had fled a cruel husband and perhaps even been granted a Bill of Divorcement before taking up residence in Herefordshire. But even such juicy tidbits were not quite enough for the country gossip mills, for rumour further had it that Mrs. Shoup was the mistress of a high-ranking nobleman who was a very important personage in the government.

Mrs. Shoup had lived in Much Henley for as long as Moriah could remember, and Moriah, never having heard any truth to the rumours and not really caring one way or the other, had befriended her.

Moriah found Mrs. Shoup to be good-natured and intelligent, unlike many of her neighbors, and thought it foolish, not to mention callous, to shun her company. Mrs. Shoup had always welcomed Moriah graciously but had warned her against coming too often, lest she damage her reputation. Well, Moriah thought, at least, if the worst comes to pass, I shall have *one* friend. Still, the thought was not very comforting, and Moriah resolved that her relationship to the viscount simply must remain secret. It oughtn't be that difficult, she reasoned. After all, Mrs. Shoup, if any of the rumours were true, had contrived to maintain secrecy. No one had ever seen the elusive nobleman nor could anyone guess at his name.

That was it then, Moriah thought, strolling now to the primrose pink sofa and sinking down into the plush cushions. She must be exceedingly discreet and her life, at least outwardly, should change little. But inwardly—that was another matter entirely. She felt a sudden shiver of fear and she did not know why. Would she look different? No, she did not imagine so. And she hoped she had enough sense not to act differently, no matter how she was feeling. And just what would she feel? And what was she afraid of? Not the act of coupling itself, she knew. She did not see how any young woman who'd spent her entire life in the country, surrounded by animals, could be afraid of what she knew to be a perfectly natural act. No, she did not fear the act itself nor, she realized with some degree of shame, did she fear the viscount's touch. She remembered the feel of his lips on her wrist, remembered the sense of strength emanating from him. She felt that warm flush again and quickly repressed it; she was sure such feelings were inappropriate, though she could not say why.

For although Moriah understood the mechanics of what went on between men and women, she had no notion of the feelings that accompanied the act. In truth, she could not fathom what all the fuss was about. Animals did not seen nearly so preoccupied with coupling as people were. Why did servants seem to gossip so much about it? And why did men seem to enjoy it so much that they would make a career of keeping mistresses? Did their women enjoy it as well? It was a question she had never had occasion to consider and, of course, there was no one she might ask. Young ladies simply did not concern themselves with such things, after all.

Moriah rose abruptly from the sofa, thinking that she had allowed her mind to meander quite long enough. It was time she did some work. She marched briskly to her desk, seated herself, and pulled the stack of bills toward her. But she could not focus on the task at hand. A pair of cool blue eyes rose in her mind, and in a flash, she understood what it was that she feared. If she went to the viscount, if she accepted his offer, she would change irrevocably. She did not know how, but it would be so. She would look the same on the outside, but inside she would never be the same again.

The Viscount Roane had stared at the closed door for several long minutes after Moriah Landon had departed. The room had felt exceedingly warm just moments ago when she'd been here, and there had been an intensity between them that he did not at all understand. What utter nonsense! he admonished himself, certain that he was being fanciful.

He strode from the room and down the hall to his study, wondering all the while what Miss Landon would say to him on Friday morning. Undoubtedly she would administer a clever, well-rehearsed little set-down by way of refusal of his so-called offer, and then depart from his presence with a great show of dignity. As he pushed open the double oak carved doors to the study, he assured himself that she would self-righteously take her virtue home with her and that her father would survive after all. He was not the first man to lose his fortune, and not all men blew their brains out because of it. The family would decline into genteel poverty, like so many before them. It was no more than the Landons deserved, he told himself as he slammed the doors shut behind him.

He marched across the Oriental carpet to the large picture window that overlooked the formal gardens and drew the curtains apart with a fierce jerk. He stood before the window, a scowl on his face, arms akimbo and feet apart. It was exactly what they deserved, he reiterated, and exactly what he had wanted. And as for the unprecedented Miss Moriah Landon — no doubt she would attract some hapless fellow who knew from the moment he saw her that he had to have her. And if marriage was the only way, then so it would be, dowry or no.

Damn! he thought, whirling about and glaring at the large walnut desk that stood in front of a wall of floor-to-ceiling bookshelves. He had a good deal of work to do, and suddenly he was in the foulest of moods. Would the Landons never leave him in peace? He stalked to the desk and, without sitting down, picked up one of the ledgers that he'd requested of his agent.

"Ahem. Your pardon, my lord."

Roane looked up from the still-unopened book and frowned. He hadn't even heard the butler come in. "Yes, what is it, Finley?" he snapped.

"This just came for your lordship," replied Finley at his most formal. The butler came forward with a silver salver in his extended hand, bowing correctly as Roane lifted the missive from the gleaming surface of the tray. The viscount waited until Finley departed before seating himself and breaking the seal. His frown gave way to eyes widened in incredulity as he read the formal invitation. It seemed that the honour of his presence was requested by Sir Hugo and Lady Crowley for a ball in honour of His Noble Lordship, the Viscount Roane!

"Oh, blast!" he muttered. Why, he hadn't been here for twenty-four hours! How did they manage to work so fast? And would it have been too much to ask to be informed of this singular honour *before* the distribution of invitations? He signed and then realized that there was a note scrawled at the bottom of the page.

"My Lord Roane," it read. "Please forgive the presumption, but we knew you would agree that this was a most fitting welcome for you after so long an absence. We look forward to seeing you Tuesday next. Please do us the honour of dining with us before the ball." The note was signed "Agatha Crowley," and Roane thought it sounded more like a summons than an invitation. He was quite sure the entire business had been Lady Crowley's idea, not her husband's. The baronet was a pleasant enough fellow, not without influence in the Commons. His wife, if Roane recalled correctly, was something of a viper.

Roane tossed aside the missive with a grimace, knowing he had little choice but to attend what was probably only the first of such entertainments in his "honour." He turned his attention back to his ledgers, but a pair of amethyst eyes swam before him. He found himself wondering whether Moriah Landon would attend the Crowley ball and what she would look like in an evening gown. Her shoulders and throat would be bare, and—

Enough of this! he commanded himself, and resolutely opened the first ledger.

Chapter 9

Lord Edward Chilton emerged from Albert Fairley's office with his usual expression of studied ennui. His boredom lifted, however, as did one eyebrow, when he saw the young woman ascending the steps just below. Wellborn, he thought, noting her manner of dress and the maid on the street below. She stopped just before him, murmured "Excuse me, sir" in a rather husky voice, and made as if to pass him. He stood still, however, blocking her path for a moment, and gazed rather intently at her.

Ah yes, wellborn, but definitely no lady, he reflected, as his practiced eye took in her voluptuous figure and sultry face. Most assuredly not a lady, he mused; he could always tells. He favoured her with a knowing smirk and caught the flash of anger in her violet eyes before she demurely lowered them. Then, with a slight bow, he allowed her to pass, thinking it might be amusing to discover her identity and pursue her. And then he wondered if she'd be at the Crowley Ball. That would certainly add a bit of spice to another of Agatha Crowley's rather prosaic entertainments.

Moriah's visit to Mr. Fairley yielded little more

than a sympathetic pat on the shoulder and a friendly admonition to keep her chin up. Of course, there had also been that rather distasteful interlude with the man outside the door. Though well dressed, he had not seemed at all a gentleman, for he had leered at her in a most disgraceful manner. Moriah reflected that the viscount had stared at her quite insolently as well, but somehow that was different. Lord Roane's gaze had infuriated her, but it had not been . . . unpleasant.

She had left Mr. Fairley's office knowing that she had a good deal of thinking to do, and Friday morning had come round all too soon for her comfort. Nevertheless, with typical resolution, Moriah found herself riding out once again in the clear light of daybreak. Once again she galloped over the open fields before venturing to Roanbrooke land. And though she knew precisely what she would say to the Viscount Roane, she welcomed the solitude and the opportunity to calm the flutters in her stomach.

And so here she was now, approaching his lordship's hunting box at the appointed time, the vigorous ride having greatly helped to perk up her courage. She drew rein in front of the hunting box and paused for a moment. It was a two-story rather boxy-looking graystone structure that somehow looked much more severe than when she had passed it two days previously. A thick layer of ivy clung to the walls and encroached on the oblong windows. Quickly Moriah dismounted and, wishing to keep her horse hidden from any prying eyes, walked Ruby round to the back. There was a small stable attached to the hunting box. Its door was ajar, allowing the morning light to stream through, and Moriah noticed a magnificent chestnut stallion in one of the three stalls. So, he was here, she thought with a somewhat sinking feeling. He *would* ride a chestnut stallion; it suited him perfectly.

She led Ruby into one of the stalls and settled her comfortably. Then she thrust her shoulders back and her chin up and slowly but determinedly walked round to the front door. The heavy wooden door creaked open at the second clank of the tarnished brass knocker. Moriah peered inside, but it was so dark that for a moment she could not see anyone.

"Good morning, Miss Landon," he said in deep, crisp tones, and then she realized that he stood just inside the doorway, his face bathed in shadows.

She was rather surprised that the viscount had answered his own door, but in the next moment she felt tremendous relief and even gratitude. His not having brought a servant with him would further insure that their meeting remained secret. She responded with a brief "Good morning" of her own, hoping that she might successfully mask her jumble of emotions.

The viscount opened the door wider and took a step back, indicating with a flourish of his hand that she might enter. She stepped over the threshold into the dark vestibule and the door closed immediately behind her.

"Welcome to my little retreat. Please come in," he said smoothly, too smoothly, and then turned that she might follow him.

Despite the shadows she could see that the floor of the hunting box was of stone and the ceilings were beamed. The ground level did not appear all that large. He led her into what must have been the sitting room. She noted immediately that the room was only a little less dark than the corridors, and her eyes went to the two rectangular windows. The curtains had been drawn back, but the ivy winding across the glass on the outside effectively screened much of the sunlight. Moriah loved the sunlight, but she could not deny the charm of this room. It was cozy, somewhat small, done in warm earth tones. The carpet was a deep green, and in front of the large brick hearth were two plump love seats upholstered in rust and gold and green. Numerous pillows were haphazardly strewn upon them and two had fallen onto the floor. A few rays of the morning sun crept through the ivy and rested on an oak sofa table, and she could see a thin layer of dust. The room, and probably the entire hunting box, did not seem to suffer the hand of servants, and somehow she found that comforting. It was the viscount's private retreat, where he tolerated few intruders. It was a very masculine room, and though the viscount had seemed to her a very cold man, she thought the warmth of it suited him well. She had the distinct impression that this was not a place to which he brought women. The thought pleased her very much, and she felt her courage rise.

She watched as Lord Roane walked briskly to the hearth and turned to face her. He wore no jacket and she thought she could perceive the muscles of his tall frame beneath the thin fabric of his buff-colored shirt. It was a soft shirt with wide, full sleeves, and it tapered into the close-fitting brown riding britches he wore. His hair was combed forward as before, but today it appeared attractively windblown. A loosely tied silk cravat rested at his neck, and altogether she thought he looked very much like a pirate. And though his pose and manner of dress were relaxed, she knew instinctively that *he* was not. He was a very dangerous man, this Viscount Roane, but for some reason she was not in the least afraid.

From his stance at the hearth Roane turned to face Moriah Landon as she stood just inside the doorway.

Again he felt that heat, that intensity enter the room when she did. It quite unnerved him, but he had no intention of letting her know it. He rested an elbow on the mantle as casually as he could.

"So, you came after all," he said silkily. "I had rather thought you might not."

She advanced several steps into the room and clasped her hands composedly in front of her as usual. "I gave you my word, my lord. I *always* keep my word," she said pointedly. He did not doubt that for a moment, and Roane had the fleeting suspicion that he was in trouble, though he did not know why.

"Won't you sit down?" he asked, for lack of a suitable reply.

"Thank you. I prefer to stand," she said calmly. His eyebrows rose almost imperceptibly. Amazing that she could appear so feminine, so—so womanly, and yet possess none of the feminine wiles, or at least use none of them knowingly. Any other woman would have made a great show of seating herself on the sofa with just the right amount of elegance, just the right flourish of skirts. But Moriah Landon simply sashayed across the carpet until she came face to face with him at the hearth. So, it was direct confrontation that she wanted, he mused, visibly relaxing and anticipating with some relish the set-down she had probably rehearsed the entire way here.

"As you wish," he countered, trying to match her calm tone and trying to keep his lips from twitching. She stood not two feet from him, and he let his eyes sweep the length of her. She was wearing the same midnight-blue riding habit as on their previous meeting, and her figure looked no less luscious. The same saucy hat perched on her jet-black hair, but this time more tendrils seemed to have escaped the confines of her bun. He found this pleasing and had to resist the urge to reach out and pull her hair completely free. And then their eyes met, and once again he found himself mesmerized, for just a moment, by those deep amethyst pools. He blinked and swallowed hard.

"My lord, I — I have thought much on your . . . proposal," she began, her voice even huskier than usual. "I have consulted with our lawyer, Mr. Fairley — "

"You did what?" Roane interrupted, pulling his hand from the mantle and standing erect. What manner of female discussed an indecent proposition with the family lawyer?

"I spoke with our lawyer," she repeated, seemingly unruffled, "and he has assured me that — that there is nothing to be done." Her voice became softer and she lowered her eyes, but raised them in a moment. "I cannot allow my family to be destroyed, my lord. And so — " she continued, inhaling deeply, "and so I have come to tell you that — that I . . . accept your offer."

"You what?" he exploded, his eyes wide and blazing, a mixture of fury and incredulity welling up inside him

"I — I accept your offer, my lord. I shall become your m — m — "

"But — but you can't!" he blurted, running his fingers through his hair in a jerking motion. "You cannot do such a thing! Nor can I!" He stalked several feet away from her and then whirled around to face her. He could not fail to note the rapid rise and fall of her breasts as she breathed deeply, but otherwise she stood still. "You are a lady of birth and I am a gentleman. It simply — it simply isn't done!" Roane was almost shouting, torn between anger and exasperation. He wanted to shake her

90

furiously for tempting him in such a way, and at the same time he wanted to kiss those full, luscious red lips, to kiss her until that unnerving composure crumbled completely.

"I see, my lord," she said quietly, her steady gaze never wavering. "You wish to retract your offer. Well"—here she paused and lowered her eyes to her clasped hands—"I—I quite understand. I *had* wondered why you should prefer *me* to Wykham Abbey. After all—"

"No, Miss Landon!" he barked, striding to her once again. "You do not understand at all. It has nothing to do with what I prefer. I don't even *want* your blasted Abbey!" He towered over her, clenching his fists at his sides to avoid touching her, anywhere. "And as for you—well, I—you are very desirable, Miss Landon, but—but I simply cannot—cannot take you dishonorably." His voice lowered at this last, and his eyes searched hers. How could such a woman imagine a man would not want her?

"You—you offered me a way to save my family from tragedy, my lord. You must know that I would not agree to such a thing for the sake of the Abbey alone. For much as I love it and much as it is a part of me, it is not worth the price you ask. But for my family—well, I have no choice but to accept. Am I to assume you no longer wish me to have that option?"

Hellfire! he thought. How had he ever gotten into this coil? He had never given her the option, never made the offer in the first place. And every time he tried to *un*make the offer, she either assumed he thought her an antidote or wanted to see her father die. "No, I—that is—yes, I mean you—you" He stopped abruptly, completely at a loss for words for perhaps the first time in his life. His wayward eyes moved from her face to caress the length of her. By

God, how he wanted her! A voice somewhere in his head told him to take her. It was poetic justice of sorts; he wanted her just as her grandfather had wanted . . . No! He silenced the voice firmly. Landon she might be, but he was still a gentleman and must act accordingly. Somehow he had got to navigate himself, indeed both of them, out of this imbroglio with some degree of grace.

He stepped away from her and moved to the window nearest the hearth, certain he could not think clearly if he stood so close to her. "Miss Landon," he began again, trying to be calm and rational and trying to keep his gaze on her face and not on her full breasts or rounded hips. But her eyes fascinated him and her red lips tempted him. He ran his hands through his hair again. Somehow they needed to be busy. "Miss Landon," he repeated, "you—you have no idea what you'd be getting into."

"Oh, yes I do," she countered quite matter-of-factly, and began to saunter toward him. "Enough, at all events. I have been around animals all my life. I have seen—"

"That—that is *not* what I meant, Miss Landon," Roane interjected quickly, a hand going to his brow in exasperation. She now stood close to him again, and he felt his blood race. About all he needed was for her to describe what she'd learned from the damned animals. "You—you would be ostracized from society. No one—"

"But you said no one need know, my lord," she interrupted gently.

"Yes, well, so I would hope. But—well, despite one's best efforts at discretion, these things sometimes have a way—well, it only takes but one pair of prying eyes, you know, my dear," he replied, and then realized that his tone had softened as well. Perhaps it was in response to those large amethyst eyes, gazing at him with a rare honestly and just a hint of distress in them. "And," he continued, determined to talk her out of the whole absurd business, "you could never marry, whether it became known or no."

"I realize that, my lord but, you see, I have never planned to marry. Despite what you say, I am not attractive to men. I know what beauty is. Tess is beautiful. I shall see her safely wed and shall end my days as a maiden aunt. Well, not precisely maiden, but—er—aunt nonetheless," she declared with a hint of a smile.

Roane was amazed that she could evince any humor whatever at a time like this, but he found himself laughing inwardly. Somehow he could never see her in the role of spinster aunt, maiden or no. And then he became aware of great anger rising inside of him. Anger at her for constantly deprecating herself, anger at her father, himself, all of society for placing a young woman in such a situation as she now faced.

He knew of a certain that he must divert her from the ignoble course she was determined to pursue. And as to her father—well, perhaps Roane could help. Help! Whatever was wrong with him? He remembered his parents and his sister and was ashamed of such softheartedness. It was not for him to help the Landons! But still, he must behave as a gentleman, and if reasoning with Moriah Landon would not do, he would try another tactic. Surely *this* time he could frighten her into fleeing his presence.

He took a step closer to her so that their bodies were almost touching. "You don't look the least bit like anyone's spinster aunt you know, my dear," he murmured, his voice deliberately intimate. She gazed up at him mutely and he continued. "But, if you are determined on this course—" He paused and brought his right hand up to lightly graze her cheek. It felt soft and very warm, almost hot. He had to remind himself that he was trying to scare her away; it was not likely that he would ever touch any part of her again. "Are you certain, Miss Landon, that this is what you want?" he asked, his voice almost a whisper as he looked deeply into her eyes.

He thought he felt her quiver beside him, but her gaze never wavered. "Yes, my lord," she replied softly, "I am certain."

Blast! he thought. Was she unflappable? How much closer did he have to get to bring home to her the enormity of what she intended? And just how close *could* he get before he lost all control? Roane could see that she was breathing rapidly now, and he resolutely kept his eyes from straying below her throat.

"Well, then, Miss Landon, perhaps we ought to become better acquainted." He took her gently by the elbows and pulled her to him. He waited a moment, expecting her to back away, but she did not. His eyes searched her face and then he could wait no longer. He brought his lips gently down onto hers, trying to convince himself that he was merely doing this to convince *her* to leave and never come back. He thought she would flinch or stiffen or put up a hand in protest. But she did not move. Her lips met his calmly; they were soft and lush and yielding, just as he'd known they would be. He'd intended no more than a tentative kiss, but somehow he found his lips pressing harder and his arms encircling her. He told himself he was fully in control as his hand slid to the nape of her neck and pulled her closer to him. He barely noticed her hat fall slightly askew as he wedged his fingers through her tightly secured hair. And then suddenly her body seemed to mold to his and her lips opened to receive his tongue. He could feel her full breasts pressed against him and he could not keep his hands from sliding up and down her body even as he held her close. Suddenly his right hand closed over her breast, and he could feel her shiver through the fabric of her dress.

It was that tremor that brought him back to reality. Was it a shiver of fear? Was that not what he'd wanted? Slowly he drew his lips from hers and gently, reluctantly, he pushed her from him. It jarred him to realize how hard it was to let her go. He waited for a slap in the face or an angry diatribe before she turned and fled back to her precious Abbey. His eyes scanned her face and he realized that he was holding his breath awaiting her reaction. But it was neither fear nor anger that he read in those amethyst eyes, but rather . . . bewilderment. Bewildered about what — his behaviour or her own? Ah, but what did it matter? She would be gone in a moment.

"My lord," she whispered, quite breathless, "d-do you — do you still . . . want me?"

Did he still — my God! What was she saying? That she intended to stay? And did she think he'd been testing her?

"I will always want you, Miss Landon," he rasped. Now why had he said that? "But that is much beside the point. Do you not realize — ?" He stopped abruptly, remembering that he was supposed to frighten her. Problem was she didn't seem to frighten easily. He ran his fingertips down her cheek again and let his eyes sweep her body suggestively. "Are you still of a mind to come to me, my dear?"

She nodded and met his gaze. "Yes, my lord," she said softly.

Damn! What would it take to unnerve this unnerving female? He decided to play his trump card.

"Good," he countered, and gave her a knowing smirk. "Then I suggest we begin this night. You've no objection, I trust, have you, Miss Landon?" he continued smoothly, certain that finally would come the tears or at least the narrowing of eyes in horror. But those beautiful amethyst pools never left his, and she stood perfectly still. Only the slight tremor in her voice betrayed her. "I—I—no, my lord T-tonight will . . . be fine."

Hellfire! What was he to do now? It was his own eyes that narrowed as he tried to read beneath the depths of hers. He had one more card to play, and he did not like it one bit. It was simply not the sort of thing one spoke of to a lady, and she was, despite everything, very much a lady. But this was hardly drawing room conversation at all events, and so he plunged on.

"Since you fully comprehend—er—what we are about to embark upon, my dear, then you will agree with me that some precaution must be taken," he said, affecting a confidence he was far from feeling just now. If this ploy did not work, then what? . . .

"Yes, I quite understand, my lord. We must insure that we—we will not be found out," she replied, only a slight hesitation in her voice. "I will naturally not venture out until everyone at the Abbey is abed. What—what time shall I arrive? I presume we are to—to meet here?"

Damn that practical nature of hers! Did she want a scheduled list of the evening's activities as well?

He put his large hands on her shoulders and kept his voice low, almost a caress. "Er—yes—well, of course we must be discreet, but that was not the sort of precaution I had in mind. I meant—well, you are

96

aware, are you not, that there are ways—er—precautions as it were to—er—prevent the—er—advent of a child."

He watched her face pale and felt her stiffen beneath his fingers. He breathed an inward sigh of relief. Thank God that at last . . .

Good Lord, Moriah thought, she had completely forgotten the possibility of a child! She had thought of scandal, of her family, the neighbors, but never—but never a *child*. She swallowed hard, willing herself to remain composed. Now that she thought on 't, she knew from servants' gossip that there were ways for a man or a woman to prevent such an occurence, but she had no idea at all of the particulars. And so she was enormously grateful to the viscount for his willingness to take care of it. She managed a tremulous smile, but all in all she felt quite dizzy, as much from the effect of Lord Roane's touch as his words. She hoped he could not tell how fast her heart was beating ever since he'd kissed her. She had not at all understood what had happened to her body or her mind those few short minutes ago. And even now, with his warm hands on her shoulders, she felt a strange tingling throughout her body, the viscount's disturbing words notwithstanding.

"My lord, I—I thank you for—making mention of—of such a delicate matter. Of course, I realize such a thing must be taken care of," she replied finally and then, feeling decidedly uncomfortable with the whole subject, repeated here previous question. "What time did you want me to—to come her tonight?"

What the devil? Roane's eyes widened and for a moment he could do naught but stare at her. He dropped his hands from her shoulders and took a step back. He was dumbfounded, nonplussed, completely at a loss. He'd thought he'd pushed Landon to the wall, and now his daughter, this little slip of a girl—well, a woman—had done the same to him. He was vanquished. Totally. He did not have another card to play. He was too much the gentleman to take her to his bed, and he knew she was too much the proud lady to accept any charity from him. But she *was* a lady, he told himself. She would never go through with this.

"My lord, I—I really must return now, lest my absence be remarked," she said, interrupting his thoughts. He watched her straighten her hat and tidy her thick black hair. Moriah Landon, ever practical. No matter what the topic at hand, she would remember her stomach or hair or whatever. "Shall I come at midnight, my lord?"

Should she come at midnight? How the hell was he to know? She shouldn't come here at all, but then, of course she wouldn't, he reminded himself. Even the indomitable Moriah Landon would break down at the last minute. Yes, that was it. He would humour her now. It was the only thing he could do. He certainly had no intention of starting another discussion about whether or not he desired her.

"As you say, I shall await you here at midnight," he said impassively. "Until then, Miss Landon."

"Yes. I—ah—until then. But—ah—my lord, I . . . must know . . . how often you will require—that is—for how long will I be your—your mis—"

"Miss Landon," he interrupted, somehow not wanting her to say the word and finding himself more than a little exasperated with her penchant for pragmatism. He decided to make one last attempt to frighten her. He stepped closer to her again and traced the line of her lips with his thumbs. He let his fingers slide down her throat and then fall away before he spoke, his voice low and silky. "My dear, surely you know that it is customary for a woman to remain under a gentleman's protection until — until he tires of her."

Moriah took a deep breath to steel herself. How could he kiss her so warmly and then speak so callously? She knew she had got to leave soon before her courage gave way.

"Y — yes, of course, I — I see, my lord. I — good morning," she said, and turned as if to leave.

"Ah, Miss Landon," he said quickly, and she turned back to him. Somehow he felt the need to detain her, as if he regretted his harsh words. "I fear I have been remiss in my duties as host. There is not much here, but may I offer you some refreshment?"

"No. No thank you, my lord. I — I am not very hungry just now. If — if you'll excuse me . . ." She let her words trail off and hurried from the room.

The viscount contemplated the unforgettable swivel of her hips as she did so. He found a soft smile slowly creeping onto his face. So, Moriah Landon wasn't hungry, was she? Had he begun to pierce the armour of her composure at last? Well, well. He heard the outer door of the hunting box slam, but he remained where he was, savouring the memory of her. He had been completely unable to talk her out of meeting him tonight. Never in his long experience — why, *she* was practically seducing *him!* Opening her lips so invitingly, asking if he still wanted her. Innocence can be very dangerous, he mused, and then remembered something else. At least she would take proper precautions; he would not want to get her with child. And how the hell did she know about such things, anyway? Surely not from her farm animals!

The viscount caught himself up short, the smile

changing to a scowl. What was he thinking? What difference did it make what she knew of precautions? It would never come to that! He had no intention of—or had he?

On impulse he stalked to the front door of the box and yanked it open. The woods were silent, empty, and he stood in the doorway without moving, wondering if she would ever cross his threshold again. What would he do if she did, and how would he feel if she didn't?

Chapter 10

"Well, it was a vigorous ride you had, Miss Moriah, an' I make no mistake," chuckled Mrs. Trotter good-naturedly as Moriah hurried up the stairs to her chamber. "Why, your hair is all askew. Lost track of time, did you, love?" the housekeeper asked with the intimacy of one who had known her charge even in the womb.

Moriah nodded lamely. The first lie, she thought. How many more would there be? "Tell Tess I'll join her in a moment, Mrs. T., as soon as I've changed my clothes," she said.

But once she reached the security of her room, Moriah found that she could not hurry. She sat down on the canopied bed and stared down at the satin coverlet with its brilliant floral pattern. The violet and pink flowers on the coverlet and matching canopy always cheered her, but today she hardly noticed them. She sighed and let her eyes drift upward to sweep the pale pink walls and the Georgian highboy with its Derby figurines. Had she really done it? Had she really agreed to become a man's mistress? She blinked back unwitting tears and carefully removed her riding hat, placing it next to her on the bed. Then she stood up abruptly. This was no time to be missish, she told herself. What was done was done. She had given her word and there was no going back. Besides, she had had no choice in the matter. She had struck a bargain and now she must fulfill her part in it.

Moriah walked briskly into her dressing room to the massive oak armoire that housed her none-too-plentiful wardrobe. She pulled open the doors with the intention of selecting a morning gown, but instead found herself wondering what she ought to wear this night. As such—well, assignations were outside of her experience, she could not be sure what was proper. She supposed a woman experienced at this sort of thing would wear the lowest cut evening gown she possessed. Moriah did not possess a low-cut gown, however, and besides, she had no desire to look like a—like a woman accustomed to—to doing what they were about to do. She did not wish to arrive at his lordship's hunting box half naked. His pointed, suggestive gaze was quite unnerving enough when she was fully covered in her riding habit.

She felt a queer fluttering in her legs and her stomach as she realized that far more than her décolletage would be revealed to the viscount before this night was through. She felt herself blush thoroughly, even though she was alone. She remembered now how she had felt when he had taken her in his arms and kissed her. She'd felt weak, as if her limbs had no power to resist or move away, yet curiously alive in a way she'd never felt before. She did not know what it meant; she only knew that she was not dreading this evening's encounter. Nor was she looking forward to it, she told herself firmly, and turned her mind once more to her wardrobe.

She supposed she ought to wear an evening gown—it would be evening, after all. But she would have to ride all that way; even with a cape she would be quite exposed to the night air. And how would she explain to Lizzie why her gown was crumpled and smelling of horses?

No, she decided resolutely, better to do the sensible

thing and wear her blue riding habit. No one would question what it smelled like, and it would be the most comfortable to ride in. If the viscount was less than pleased—well, she had told him she was no beauty. It made little sense to show off charms she did not possess.

That particular decision duly disposed of, she pulled her plum-colored muslin morning dress from its hook. She wondered distractedly just how she would occupy her mind until this day, which loomed interminable, finally ended. She was still most concerned about Papa, but since Finch had rather reluctantly presented her with the key to the pistol cabinet yesterday, she could be somewhat easy in her mind, at least for now. Tess had just this week been imploring Moriah to intercede with their father for the necessary funds to provide her with several new dresses. For once Tess was not being frivolous. It was amazing how much she'd grown these past few months, and her figure seemed to blossom more with each passing day. But this was not the time to purchase new gowns.

Suddenly it occurred to Moriah that a visit to Mrs. Grimes would be most opportune. She and Tess could bring her a stack of linens to mend, and she knew that a trip to the Grimes cottage would put her own problems into perspective. Come what might, Moriah reminded herself, she would never starve, nor did she have a parcel of frightened children who mightn't have shoes in winter.

She laid her morning gown carefully on the primrose velvet chaise, wondering where Lizzie could have got to. Surely Mrs. Trotter would have informed her by now that Moriah was in need of her. With a sigh, Moriah began unfastening the front buttons of her riding habit and then slipped out of it. She stood in her petticoats looking down in mock dismay at the muslin morning gown. It was quite absurd that she could not dress herself, she mused, not for the first time. She had two perfectly good hands and was not a child, after all. But, alas, current fashion rendered a lady helpless without her maid; only a contortionist could correctly do up the myriad buttons that seemed to run up the back of every gown deemed worthy of the name. It was as well she had decided to wear her riding habit tonight. Lizzie would insist on helping her prepare for bed, and Moriah would have to dress herself once the household was asleep. Her habit, she realized, was the only garment she possessed that fastened in the front, and thank goodness for it. It would not do at all, she thought, to arrive at Lord Roane's hunting box with half the buttons of an evening gown undone.

Unaccountably, she felt herself blush again and thought it the outside of enough that Lizzie chose this moment to make her belated appearance.

Roane was not in the best of humour when he arrived back at the Court. He closeted himself in his study, giving strict orders that he did not wish to see anyone nor do anything but sip a glass of brandy. He did not sip it, however, for such was his agitation that he downed it in two strong gulps and quickly poured himself another. He marched across the oak plank floor to a large picture window and stared out at the formal gardens below.

She wouldn't come tonight. Of course she wouldn't. It was unheard of. But what if she did? He would send her away, of course. But would he? Could he, if she arrived at midnight, breathless from her ride and quite willing to—to—

He was startled by a knock at the door and a muffled, "My lord?"

"Dammit, Finley, what is it?" he barked, turning around. "I thought I gave orders to—"

"Justin, old chap! Never say rusticating agrees with you. Well, and if you don't look the picture of countrified elegance. When did you have time to replenish your wardrobe?" came the familiar, all-too-enthusiastic voice just as his young cousin burst into the room.

"Well, good Coz, welcome," said Roane, his annoyance tempered by a good bit of amusement at the typical harum-scarum entrance of his cousin, Andrew Wainsfield, son and heir of the Earl of Westmacott. Andrew's red hair was windblown, his usually tawny skin was flushed pink from the sun, and his travel garments looked as though they sported every bit of mud that had splattered from London to Herefordshire. "And to what do I owe the rather—er—sudden pleasure of your company?" he asked as Finley closed the doors.

"Oh, I had a hankering to see Roanbrooke again. Been a long time, don't you know. Besides, thought you might want company, country quiet not being exactly what you're used to and all," Andrew replied in his usual rush of words, and then added rather sheepishly, "Oh, and—er—I've a message from m' father."

"Ah, have you, indeed," Roane murmured, trying to keep his lips from twitching at this feeble attempt to camouflage the real reason for Andrew's descent upon Roanbrooke. Roane set his glass of brandy down and waved his cousin to the well-worn leather sofa before seating himself in the adjacent tufted leather wing chair. "And what does my esteemed uncle have to say, may I ask?" he continued, once

Andrew had sprawled comfortably on the sofa.

"Uh, well. Let me see if I can remember his exact words." Andrew's face became serious and his blue eyes a bit glazed as he put himself to the task. "The earl says to—uh—" —here Andrew paused and his voice became deeper, in imitation of his father's firm, blustering tone—"to tell that rakehell nevvy of mine it's about time he decided to remember his responsibilities. Let him be quick about setting Roanbrooke and the farms to rights; no doubt it's all but fallen into ruins." Andrew smiled ruefully and, seemingly relieved at Roane's answering grin, continued in his own tone of voice. "And then you are to take yourself a wife and set up your nursery, because—er—let me see if I can quote him exactly "—he took a breath and resumed the earl's tone—"because Heaven knows that graceless son of mine has no need of your fortune and lands; he'll be disgracefully rich *enough* some day."

The viscount could not help chuckling and Andrew joined him, for it was well known that the earl held them both in great affection. And, of course, what he'd said was true. Andrew, though he was the viscount's nominal heir until Roane produced a son, certainly had no need of a second inheritance. "Well done, Drew, well done," Roane declared. "Was that *all* my uncle had to say?"

"Er—no, Justin, 'fraid not." Here Andrew's face became serious again and he leaned forward in his seat, then crossed his legs in a futile attempt to hide his unease. "The earl said that—er—when you've finished all that—it won't take above a month, so he said—then you may—er—take your seat in the Lords."

"Ah. So, we come to the crux of it. Well, best get on with it. I have the uncanny feeling that the worst is yet to come."

"Yes, well, Fa' has a special . . . mission that he—er—wishes you to embark on. Says he needs you. *England* needs you. And after this mission, why, what a maiden speech you'll deliver! The peers'll all stay awake, for once. That and an advantageous marriage—need a good hostess, well-connected, even political family, all that sort of thing—will set you on your way. Why you'll be a political institution afore your fourth decade!"

Andrew was becoming a bit too involved and impassioned in his monologue and Roane was becoming annoyed. "Enough, Drew. You know perfectly well I've no desire to be a 'political institution,' and I certainly have no intention of marrying one. Now, I do enjoy your company, Coz, but I rather think you've been the earl's messenger for long enough. Shall we—"

"Justin, you mistake me," interrupted Andrew firmly. Roane's eyes narrowed at the determined set to Andrew's jaw. Now when had the young pup acquired that? Andrew was twenty-two years old, six years Roane's junior, and he had worshipped Roane as an older man for so long that the viscount did not know quite what to make of this change in tone. "It's true Fa' sent me, but I *wanted* to see you. And—and besides that, more important than that, I agree with him."

"You what?" demanded the viscount, skepticism evident on his face.

"Devil take you, Justin! Don't look at me like that. I may not be the sort of chap to deliver fiery speeches—don't have the drive to commit m'self to politics—but that don't mean I don't see and hear what's going on, y' must know. Fact is, the country's in a bad way. Riots all over the North, y' know. We need you; the earl is right, Justin."

Roane simply stared at his cousin, quite amazed at the earnestness of his speech. And then it dawned on him that sometime over the past year, Andrew had grown up. He was no longer offering Roane a moonling's adoration; rather, he was offering friendship. Roane was a man with numerous admirers and even close acquaintances. But of true friends, confidants, he had few; somehow he found it difficult to entrust his soul to another man. And so he was rather pleased to accept Andrew as his friend. He found himself smiling, a not-too-frequent occurrence, and then he rose from his seat and said, "Care for some brandy, old friend?"

Andrew grinned back and nodded and Roane did the honours himself. When they were each ensconced with a warming glass of brandy in hand, Roane resumed the conversation.

"Why me, Drew? I'm no politician," Roane said softly, thinking he'd said much the same to the earl just over a se'ennight ago in London.

"But you *could* be, Justin. It's in your blood. Your father was damned effective in the Lords to hear tell, and the earl thinks you've inherited his eloquence. It's more than that, Justin. You've a certain — well — magnetism about you, and it's not just the ladies who come under its spell." Andrew's voice lowered at this last and he flashed his engaging smile.

In answer, Roane sipped his brandy and stared at his riding boots, rather uncomfortable under this praise. At length he looked up. "A man who has spent the last six years in the gaming hells and brothels of London is hardly a candidate for revered statesman."

"Gaming hells, White's, Tattersalls — it makes no never mind, Justin. Fact is everyone likes you and listens to you. You've the drive that it takes, Justin; I agree with m' father that it's time you put it to more use than at the tables. And, now I think on 't, what *are* you doing here? Had your fill of gaming for a while now you've made such a coup?"

Roane raised his eyebrows in surprise and clenched his glass tightly in his hand. Andrew, about to put his own to his lips, lowered it and said, "Oh, come now, Justin. Must know it's all the talk in Town. You and the baron that night. Tell me, Coz, what are you going to *do* with the Abbey? Seems to me you've got quite enough to do right here at Roanbrooke."

"I do not wish to talk about it, Drew," replied Roane severely, his jaw rigid. "And, by the by, word has not yet reached this little corner of the world. I should like to keep it that way for a bit."

It was Andrew's red eyebrows that shot up this time. "Whatever you say, old chap. Don't know but what — " His eyes narrowed and he studied Roane carefully. "Well, it don't signify. Fact of the matter is — "

"Er — how long were you planning to stay, Drew? You are most welcome, of course, but I — I should like to inform the staff," interrupted Roane, not really wanting to know the answer but wanting even more to shift the subject.

"Well, Fa' wants me down in Kent to see to the estates in 'bout a fortnight. Till then I'm all yours, Coz," Andrew replied with his usual good-natured enthusiasm.

Roane resisted the urge to groan and instead took refuge in his brandy. Hadn't he enough complication in his life just now without having to amuse Andrew as well? And come to think on 't, how the devil was he to make good his escape tonight, when he knew Andrew would expect him to stay up with him well past midnight, helping him to perfect his game of piquet or somesuch? "Well, this is indeed a surprise, Drew, but I shall enjoy some company here in the wilds," he managed to say, however unconvincingly.

Andrew grinned and sunk deeper into the leather cushions. "Surely there must be *some* amusement to be had here, Justin?"

The question did not please Roane, but he knew he had best come up with a suitable reply. Andrew had a very probing mind. Besides, he wanted to be certain his cousin was effectively diverted from the subject of Uncle George. Roane did not think he could handle a discussion of riots in the North Country today. He had enough problems here in the Midlands. "Why—er—yes, now you mention it, I am to be honoured by Sir Hugo and Lady Crowley at a ball Tuesday next. You may be sure you will be included," Roane said at length.

Andrew crossed his legs. "Ah, Sir Hugo. Yes, pleasant-enough chap. Good deal of influence in the Commons. Wife is rather a dragon, ain't she?"

"A veritable viper," murmured Roane, his lips twitching. "Oh, by the by, the viper has a daughter. No less reptilian, though she hasn't yet grown all her scales. Fair warning."

"Thanks Coz. Any other local—er—lovelies I should know about?"

Roane felt his face become thunderous. "No," he retorted, too sharply. "There's no one of interest here. No one at all."

Chapter 11

Moriah had been most distressed just a few moments ago to discover that her midnight-blue riding habit was nowhere to be seen. She supposed that it *had* needed laundering, but still, she felt that Lizzie's timing was quite reprehensible. Moriah had fumbled through her wardrobe in the near darkness — she dared only light a single taper, for one never knew who might still be stirring late at night — searching for a gown without too many buttons. It was only then that she discovered, behind an old lavender evening gown, her rather worn dark brown riding habit. She hadn't had it on in quite some time; in fact, till that moment she'd completely forgotten its existence. With a soft sigh of relief she'd pulled it from its hook, and now she was struggling to fasten the last two buttons at her chest. Though she was finally successful, she had to admit that the garment no longer fit her. Damn! she thought. She seemed to be blossoming as much as Tess, and at her age that was quite absurd.

Roane paced the sitting room floor in his hunting box, retracing the same path across the carpet that he'd trodn seven dozen times this half hour past. He'd long since loosened the perfect folds of his snowy white cravat, unbuttoned his deep green waistcoat, and rumpled his hair as his long fingers swept nervously through it time and again. The waiting and not knowing whether she would come was, in a word, agonizing.

He'd had the deuce of a time convincing Andrew to retire early. He'd nearly forced the poor boy to drink himself into a stupor in the attempt. But at last Roane and his best claret had persuaded Andrew that he was really more tired than he knew after his arduous days of traveling, and his cousin had reluctantly taken himself off to bed.

The viscount thought it perfectly ludicrous to have to sneak out of one's own house in the middle of the night, but there it was. The servants, were they to become privy to such nocturnal comings and goings, would merely be amused. But Andrew was likely to ask whether his latest light o' love had a sister or friend. Roane had slammed the stable door shut a bit too loudly at that thought, and then as he'd mounted his stallion, another thought had come to him. Moriah Landon would likewise have to steal out of her house, and no one, were her absence discovered, would be the least bit amused. At that point Roane had kicked his horse furiously and headed for his hunting box.

It now lacked but several minutes to midnight. The Viscount poured himself another brandy, took one gulp, and then banged it down on the sideboard. He'd drunk far too much already, he knew. What with trying to render Andrew bosky and his own nervousness, he'd lost count of how much liquor he'd consumed this night. He was not drunk by any means; his gait was steady and his thoughts all too clear, but there *was* a certain fuzziness in his head that he wished very much would go away.

The door opened before she had a chance to sound the knocker a second time. It was dark, but she could make out his frame in the moonlight. He must have been waiting just beyond the door, she thought, and suddenly felt her heart begin to pound in her chest.

"Miss Landon! I—good—good evening. Come in," he said, seemingly flustered, even surprised to see her, though why that should be, she could not think.

Moriah stepped silently into the vestibule and followed him into the sitting room. She felt momentary panic as she realized she had not the slightest idea of what one was supposed to say or do in such a—a situation. But then she willed herself to calm down. He would explain everything, she told herself, if he had one ounce of gentlemanly instinct in him, for he would know she had never, was not accustomed to . . . Oh, dear, what *was* the proper way to refer to such an event?

He led her to a place near the sofa and turned to stare at her. The flickering lights from the candelabra danced across her solemn, beautiful face. Her eyes met his and he felt that intense warmth again. He swallowed hard; his hands felt wet, clammy. His breathing was irregular. He moved closer to her and tried to open his mouth to speak. She had not yet said a word and he had no idea what to say to *her*. How absurd, he thought, that at his age a female should be able to render him tongue-tied, but somehow it was not at all unpleasant. He let his eyes drink in the sight of her face and figure. My God, what a figure! The dark brown riding habit she wore might have been painted on, for all it hugged every delicious curve she possessed. He longed to trace her silhouette with his hands but refrained. There would be time enough for that later. Or would there be?

What was he going to do now she was here?

Belatedly, he remembered his manners. "Please, sit down," he said softly.

"Uh, no. No thank you," she replied in her husky voice. She lifted her chin a trifle and clasped her hands at her waist. It was as if she wanted to meet the enemy head on. By God, but she had pluck.

Your move, he told himself. What comes next? He let his eyes course over her again and chuckled inwardly at the thought of her riding habit. Every other woman would have worn the most enticing evening gown she possessed. But not Moriah Landon. If she were going to ride, then riding habit it would be! He had not seen this particular one before, and he frowned slightly when he realized that it barely fit her. It angered him that her father's recklessness had reduced her to such a state of penury.

And dammit, what was she doing here? She should have had a London Season. She should be wearing magnificent low-cut ball gowns. What the devil was wrong with Landon? And how could Roane add grief to her already troubled life? How could he take her upstairs? A voice at the back of his head reminded him that if she hadn't had a Season, at least she had life. That was more than little Nell'd had.

But that has nothing to do with Moriah Landon, he silenced the voice. For Godsakes, she wasn't even born when all that happened! He had to send her home, quickly, before it was too late.

"M—my lord, what—what do you wish me to—to do?" she stammered, her voice startling him out of his reverie, her question startling him even more. How could she ask such a question? And how the hell was he to answer it? She was gazing at him through wide, luminous amethyst eyes that held more curiosity than fear. How like Moriah Landon. Any

114

other female would swoon at the thought of sharing a man's bed for the first time, be he bridegroom or no. But Moriah Landon simply and calmly asked for instructions! And all *he* could seem to do was gawk like a silly schoolboy. Oh, Lord, where was that eloquence Andrew spoke about, now when he needed it so badly?

"Would you—er—care for some refreshment?" was all the eloquence he could manage. He gestured for her to precede him toward the sideboard, upon which sat a plate of cheeses, a large bowl of fruit, and a carafe of wine. They crossed the carpet in awkward silence and she seemed to stop abruptly when they reached the sideboard. She looked down at the food and then up at him with eyes narrowed in distress. For a moment he was confused; this certainly seemed like enough food for a midnight repast. And then he realized what had upset her. He moved close to her and smiled reassuringly. His voice was soft when he spoke.

"My valet is the only servant who ever comes here. He is never here at night; he is utterly loyal to me and exceedingly discreet. You need not worry."

She seemed to relax visibly and smiled faintly for the first time. Her red lips parted slightly, and they looked even more inviting when she smiled. He wanted very much to kiss them, but instead he asked if she would care for some fruit.

"No, I—no, thank you. I am not very hungry. Some—some wine would be nice," she replied.

Not hungry and in need of a glass of wine. Not indomitable after all, he mused, as he poured her a glass of the rich, deep red claret. He refrained from pouring himself any. Of course, he was completely sober, he assured himself, but he had the uncomfortable feeling that his head was not quite functioning

115

properly. He knew he must somehow talk her into leaving, but the words just did not seem to reach his tongue.

Her gloved hands were shaking as she took the long-stemmed goblet from him. He watched her take a slow, steady swallow.

He knew she would refuse to sit down and so did not ask. But he searched desperately for something to say. "Are you—er—cold from your ride, Miss Landon?" he inquired, thinking as soon as he'd spoken that she could not possibly be cold when it was so bloody hot in this room.

"I—no. It is a warm night, my lord. And it is rather . . . warm in here, is it not?" she asked ingenuously, the husky voice at odds with the innocence in those eyes.

"Why do you not remove your gloves, Miss Landon?" His own voice was very low and his eyes caressed her face. He realized for the first time that she was not wearing a hat. Had she forgotten, or had she weighed the options and decided it was not necessary to wear a hat when paying a midnight call?

She set her glass down, gazing at him uncertainly. Then she very slowly drew off one glove and then the other. She looked down at her naked hands and then back up at him. Her eyes were wide, a deep violet in the candlelight. She stood there, not a foot away from him, clutching the black gloves in her tiny hands. She was breathing rapidly but otherwise seemed incapable of movement or speech. He was tired of trying to speak himself.

He stepped toward her. Gently, he disengaged the gloves from her hands and set them on the sideboard. And gently, ever so gently, he took her into his arms. He bent his head and lightly touched his lips to hers, but the soft kiss he'd intended never materialized.

116

For her lips felt hot and moist and he felt a fire inside him that he did not know if he could ever put out. She closed her eyes and her lips parted tentatively; he felt her hesitation but he could not wait. He pressed her closer and kissed her with a hunger he did not know he possessed. His hand stroked her back and he felt her body become pliant, relax against his. His hand came to her breast and caressed it gently. She moaned softly, but in the next moment she stiffened and tried to draw back. Her eyes opened and he gazed into their depths, the full impact of her innocence suddenly hitting him. He took a deep breath and stepped back from her, placing his hands gently on her shoulders. Somehow he had to maintain some physical contact with her.

"My lord, I—I forgive me," she rasped. "You—you must think me very foolish. I—"

"No!" he breathed, almost angrily. "I think nothing of the sort. But I *am* reminded, however, painfully, that I am a gentleman. And that this—this is wrong." He took another deep breath and steeled himself for what he knew he had to say. It could not have been less painful than preparing to cut off his arm. "You are a very beautiful and desirable woman, Miss Landon. But you must see that I simply cannot—that it would be wrong of us to—to"

He struggled for words and she pulled away from his grasp. He could see her trying to compose herself and succeeding. He told himself that was a good thing, but he was disappointed, nonetheless. "My lord, we—we had a bargain," she began with great dignity, her hands clasped at her waist in what he was beginning to believe the proverbial posture of complete composure. "If you wish to break your word, have the—the goodness to respect me enough not to dissemble regarding physical attributes we both of us know I do not possess." She paused, and it pleased him to note that she was still breathing rapidly. His eyes stole down to her breasts, rising and falling heavily against the thin brown fabric that hardly looked as if it could hold her. He looked up when she spoke again. "I realize that I—I lack the knowledge and—and wherewithal of an experienced woman, but still, I had thought you a man of your word, a man of honour."

Blast! he thought. This was all becoming hopelessly twisted. If he sent her away, she would think him a worse scoundrel than if he let her stay. But dammit, that was no excuse for seducing her! Lord, but that last brandy must have muddled his mind more than he knew. Almost involuntarily he stepped close to her again. His fists were clenched at his sides as he fought not to touch her.

"I assure you I am a man of my word, Miss Landon," he retorted in a voice more heated than he'd intended. Wasn't it his blasted honour, in the matter of a gaming debt, that had got him into this in the first place? "But that has nothing to say to the matter. I—"

"Did we not have an agreement, my lord?" she interrupted, her lower lip protruding in an adorable pout he did not think she was aware of. He looked down again at her breasts, which nearly grazed his chest every time she breathed. She smelled of lush roses, and he felt heady from the mere proximity of her. He was trying, really trying, to remember his code of ethics, and she was doing everything she could to make him forget.

"Are you trying to seduce me, Miss Landon?" he blurted, hardly aware of the words until they were out. "Don't you give a damn about *your* honour, your virtue?" He was angry now, his voice raised, but though she seemed to pale, she replied in a low, steady voice.

"You do not understand, my lord. You do not have a family. You do not have a beautiful little sister who—"

"You're damn right I have no sister!" he growled, cutting off her sentence and pulling her to him savagely. He felt engulfed in a wave of intense fury mingled with desire that would not be denied. His family was gone, and by God, he would take now what her grandfather had taken twenty years before. He ground his mouth brutally down onto hers, telling himself it was his right to take her. He held her in an iron grip, his lips bruising hers as he felt the fire sear through him. Part of his mind warned him to stop, that he was too befuddled with drink and the sheer need for her to think clearly, but he shut out all thought.

His hands massaged her back insistently as his mouth pressed hers, demanding her surrender. She held herself rigidly and her eyes were open; she seemed almost shocked. And then her eyes closed, her lips parted under his, and she became soft in his arms. The kiss went on and on, his hands caressing her sides, her back, her full breasts. He felt as if he were drawing a response from deep within her, and when one delicate hand stole to the back of his neck, he knew he was awakening senses she did not know she possessed. And somehow, he realized that his anger had dissipated. In its place was only a fierce desire and something even stronger, something he did not quite understand. He felt a deep longing to possess her, to bind her to him in the most elemental way possible. He knew that he could not let her out of his arms, let alone his house. There was no turning back now.

His mouth left hers; he kissed her eyes, her nose, her chin. He willed himself to slow down; he did not want to frighten her with his passion. Besides, it would not do to take her on the floor of the sitting room, like a common serving maid. She deserved better than that. He disengaged himself from her, stepping back and then taking her hands in his. His hands were hot and moist, his breathing ragged. The trip up to the bedroom would cool his ardour, if only a bit, and he thought that just as well, for he wanted to be gentle with her.

She looked at him with uncertain eyes. Did she fear what was to come next, or was she still afraid he would send her away? Probably the latter, he thought. "We'll go upstairs," he rasped, finding any speech at all difficult. He saw her eyes clear as she nodded mutely. Amazing woman, he thought, as he lifted her easily in his arms and carried her to the spiral stairs at the back of the house.

"My lord, you can't possibly mean to carry me all that way," she said when they reached the foot of the stairs. Her voice was so incongruously matter-of-fact that he was taken aback.

"I do assure you it is not all that difficult," he managed to reply, realizing as he did the absurdity of the conversation.

"Oh, I was not questioning your strength, my lord. It merely seems an unnecessary expenditure of energy and quite inefficient. I am perfectly capable of walking, you know," she said, even more matter-of-factly. Where was all that passion of a moment ago? It had not been *her* ardour he'd wanted to cool. But it *would* take quite a bit of energy, he reflected, light though she was. He chuckled inwardly at the thought of her concern that he conserve his strength. She really could have had no idea what she said.

With a faint smile he set her down on her feet. He took her hand in his and ascended the first step. "Come, my dear," he said in a low, husky voice. Her hand tightened on his and she swallowed hard. He could not tell, at that moment, if her eyes held desire or fear. She seemed to square her shoulders and thrust her chin up just a trifle. She gathered her skirts in her free hand and looked up at him, her beautiful face calm and solemn.

"I am ready, my lord," she whispered. Amazing woman, he thought again, as together they ascended the winding stairs.

Chapter 12

Slowly, Roane drew Moriah into the master bed-room, which was dominated by the massive oak canopy bed. He stopped at the foot of the bed and turned to face her. The lingering flames of the firelight cast intermittent shadows across her face. Her eyes were deep, dark pools as she gazed up at him. He stepped close to her; neither of them spoke. He lifted his hands and gently cupped her face, kissing her softly, briefly, on the lips. The fingers of his right hand traced the line of her jaw and then fell to her throat in a long, sensual movement. Slowly he began to unbutton the bodice of her riding habit. She was breathing rapidly but her eyes were full of inno-cent bewilderment. He unfastened just enough but-tons to see her rounded bosom rise above the line of her petticoats. He gasped at the sight of her.

"God, but you're beautiful," he breathed roughly. He drew her into his arms and his lips covered hers again. His hand shook as it cupped the smooth, golden skin of her breast. She moaned and grasped his neck tightly. He felt intoxicated, whether from drink or from the feel and scent and sheer nearness of her, he did not know. He felt he would go mad with desire, but he determined to take his time and savour every minute, for both their sakes.

Gently, he drew his lips from hers and slid his fingers once more to the buttons of her dress.

He had unfastened only one more button when her husky voice eclipsed the golden silence surrounding them. "My lord I —" She paused and her hand came up to stay his. He looked down into her eyes, the smoky passion of a moment ago now replaced by uncertainty. My God, he thought, she couldn't mean to back out now!

"My lord, I —" she began again, "I do not — do not know how — how to go on. You must . . . tell me . . . that is —"

Relief flooded through him as she groped for words. He even chuckled inwardly, despite his heated state. So, it was instructions she wanted, once again. Such a practical little miss she was. It would be his greatest pleasure to make her a little less so. "Relax, little one," he murmured throatily. "You are doing just fine. There are some things, you know, which are simply not enhanced by conversation and a book of instructions." And without allowing her to reply, he kissed her again, slowly and softly.

Her response came naturally and he felt absurdly happy. He held her close to him, kissing her brow and her hair, and then began to disengage the pins from the full bun at the nape of her neck. He longed to see her dark hair flow freely down her back. Several thick, lustrous locks came tumbling down and he wound them through his fingers, luxuriating in their silky feel and rose scent.

"My lord, I . . . please —" she began again, stiffening a bit.

Oh no, what was it this time? Did she wish a point-

123

by-point agenda? "What is it, little one?" he asked, bemused.

"The pins. My hair pins. Where are they?"

Hair pins? What in the world—? He let her hair slide from his fingers and took a step back from her, mild shock on his face.

"Pins," he repeated. "I—well, I suppose they've fallen to the floor. Really, my dear, I cannot see—"

"Oh, but my lord, I—I shall need to—to put my hair back up after—er—that is, later, when I—when I must return home," she stammered.

This time he chuckled aloud. "Oh, my little pragmatist, pray do not trouble yourself." He took her into his arms and a soft smile suffused his face as he looked down at her. "I do promise to help you retrieve them—er—later. And so, do you suppose you may contrive to forget such practicalities for a time?" His hand caressed her back as he spoke and his voice was low and intimate. He bent to kiss her throat and let his lips wander downward for a moment.

"Y—yes," she breathed finally, smiling tentatively, her voice unsteady.

He smiled in return and then brought his mouth to hers again. There was no hesitation in her this time. The fire he had felt between them seemed to burst into flames as she molded her body to his and moaned softly, involuntarily, in her passion. She was warm and willing, and he felt a strange surge of joy as he swept her into his arms and carried her to the bed.

The last vestiges of rational thought were swept away from Moriah as the viscount lowered her to the massive oak bed. She did not understand what was happening. She knew only that every inch of her body was aflame as she responded to his touch, his voice, his masculine scent. She felt as if she were seeing it all through a golden haze. Her dress was off, then her petticoats, his shirt. When? How? He seemed to be taking his time and she desperately wanted him to hurry, though she did not know why. He kissed her; his hands explored every part of her. She clutched at him, feeling an urgency and she did not comprehend. And then they came together. She felt a stab of pain; he held her tightly, murmuring into her ear. And then there was no more pain, only an intense heat and a wondrous pulsing sensation that rose steadily until she felt that she would shatter into myriad tiny pieces. Then suddenly she cried out, clinging to him for dear life as he stiffened and matched her cry. And finally they were still. The only movement in the room was the tiny dancing flames in the hearth, the only sound their occasional crackle.

"You are so lovely," Roane murmured after several moments and kissed her brow tenderly. He edged himself from her and turned onto his side, gently pulling her against him. "Go to sleep now, Miss L— Moriah," he whispered, correcting himself as he realized the utter absurdity of such formality.

"Mmm," she murmured in reply and curled up like a contented kitten, her back pressing against his chest. He pulled the coverlet over them and gazed down at her. He did not think to sleep and lay wide awake, listening to her soft, even breathing and savouring the feel of her.

The tiny flames in the hearth danced lower and lower. Roane thought she slept, and he felt once more that strange joy. He felt replete and completely sober as well, which he was not quite suire he *had* been just a while ago. He gazed again at the beautiful woman beside him. Moriah Landon, little pragmatist. He knew that he had finally pierced that formidable composure, and it had been a joy. And he realized something else. He had told himself that it was his right to take her, but he had been wrong; no man had such a right. She had thought to pay her father's debt, as it were, but now he knew that he was in *her* debt. Somehow, he felt she had given him a rare gift, and he felt curiously humbled.

He became aware of a slight tremor coming from her and realized that she was not, after all, asleep. He touched his hand to her bare shoulder. "Cold?" he murmured, but she shook her head slowly. He sighed contentedly and nestled himself closer to her. He was startled from his pleasant repose a moment later, however, when he felt her tremble again and then heard a single muffled sniff. She was crying, he thought. Damn!

"I'm sorry, little one. Did I hurt you so much, then?" he asked gently, though inside he was furious with himself.

She shook her head vehemently and he wished very much that he could see her face. She sniffed again, quite audibly this time. "No. No, you — you didn't hurt me at all. I mean . . . not after . . . not really," she whispered.

Then what in the world—? She was not, instinct told him, the sort to cry over spilt milk, as it were, especially not when *she* had made the decision to spill it. No, it must be that he'd hurt her. Damn! He held her tightly, as if he could stem the tide of her tears, and ran his hands along the smooth skin under her eyes and on her cheeks. Her face was streaming with tears that she was no longer trying to check. He cursed himself inwardly for a cad and a brute.

"Moriah, I — I would have given anything not to have hurt you. . . ."

"Truly, my lord, you did not. It — it is not that," she said quietly, choking on a sob.

126

"Then why—" he began but stopped abruptly, for suddenly he knew exactly why. She tried to squirm away from him, but he held her fast.

After a moment he asked gently, "Would you be less distressed if you had suffered, Moriah? If you had not . . . enjoyed our . . . time together?"

The sobs subsided into a whimper. "Absurd, isn't it?" she asked, and he was relieved to hear a bit of humour in her voice. "I—I did not expect that I would react so—so—" She struggled for words and finally whispered, almost inaudibly, "I know it was very wrong of me." He felt the tremor run through her again and knew she was quietly crying once more. She curled herself more tightly into a ball, pulling further from him. He let her go and stroked her shoulder as he spoke, his voice soft.

"Come here, little one. I am told that I have a very broad shoulder. You must never cry alone. You must always come to me."

He raised himself up slightly and then very gently but firmly turned her to face him. He stretched out on his back and pressed her head on to his shoulder, pulling the coverlet nearly up to her chin. She lay still, but he could feel her warm tears on his chest. "I will not debate with you the morality of what we have done," he murmured after a moment, his fingers lightly stroking her cheek and tracing the curve of her ear. "But as to the rest—well, you may not yet realize it, little one, but you are a very warm, passionate woman."

She stiffened in his arms. "What you mean is that I am a wanton," she retorted. Her voice was muffled, but he could hear the bitterness in it.

"No, dammit! That is not what I mean. And don't ever let me hear you say that again. You are unquestionably a lady, Moriah," he exclaimed, his grip on her tightening as he tried to keep the anger from his voice.

"Miss Billingsley would not agree with you," she murmured, her voice becoming clearer. He was relieved that she had stopped crying.

"Miss Billingsley?" he inquired.

"My governess. She spent a great deal of time instructing me in how to be a lady. My behavior this night was not—that is, a lady does not act like—well, in such a manner, even with her own husband," she said, finishing in a whisper.

"Oh? And just how does a lady act with her own husband, may I ask?" Roane was beginning to be amused.

"I—I have not thought much on it, my lord, but of a certain, she does not act with such—such—that is—"

"And your Miss Billingsley—your—er—expert on such matters—is no doubt a maiden lady, is she not?" he interrupted quickly, wishing to save her further explication.

"Yes, of course."

Roane chuckled rather lecherously, letting his hand slip under the coverlet to caress her back. "And has it not yet occurred to you, little one, that perhaps your Miss Billingsley simply did not know what she was missing?"

She lifted her head, her mouth open, her expression hovering somewhere between shock and merriment. He felt sure that merriment would win out, though that would probably distress her even further.

He pressed her head back down onto his shoulder before she had a chance to say anything. "I do not know," he mused, his hand rhythmically stroking her arm, "whence comes the nonsensical notion that a man wants some kind of saintly snow maiden in his

128

bed, but I do assure you that any man who takes a passionate woman to wife is a lucky man indeed." His voice had become impassioned as he spoke and his hand tightened on her arm. He wanted to add that any man who took her to wife would be many times blessed, but he found that the prospect of another man marrying her did not please him at all. And then he remembered that after tonight no man *would* ever marry her. And, of course, *he* never could, she was a Landon and it was out of the question. Suddenly he was seized by a cold fury and his body became rigid all over. He was furious at himself for what he had done, and even more angry at Landon, at her grandfather, at all society and its rules. Images of Landon, little Nell, his father, tumbled before his mind's eye, only to be replaced by the image of Moriah, her eyes smoky with passion just a few moments ago. He forced his body to relax, determined not to think of the future, not even to think beyond tonight.

Moriah had not said anything, which was just as well, for he no longer wished to talk. She had relaxed against him and was breathing peacefully now. He kissed the top of her head. "Go to sleep now, little one," he breathed, certain she had nearly drifted off and feeling rather sleepy himself.

"Oh, no, my lord," she said, her matter-of-fact tone once more jarring him in its incongruity. "I—I must not sleep. After all, I must return home before—that is, when it is appro—"

"Do not worry, Moriah," Roane interrupted, restraining a chuckle and not wishing to engage in a discussion of what was customary in such circumstances, a discussion he knew she was perfectly capable of pursuing. "I am, I assure you, a very light sleeper. Experience has taught me to be so."

"Oh. I see. Yes, of course," she said in a flat tone, one of such distress that he almost laughed aloud. It was uncanny the way he could read her mind, and he found it most interesting that the thought of his experience with other women should overset her.

"I meant . . . experience on the Peninsula, little one. During the *War*," he stated pointedly.

"Oh, yes, of course, the War," she replied, not troubling to disguise the relief in her voice. He found himself enchanted by her complete lack of guile. "I — I had not realized that you fought in the War," she continued, and he detected a note of concern in her voice. "Was it — was it very dangerous? Is that why you became a light sleeper?"

"Yes, Moriah. One always had to be alert to — But we shan't speak of it now. Go to sleep and I shall wake you."

"Very well, my lord. Good night," she whispered, burrowing comfortably into his shoulder.

He smiled in the near darkness. "Good night, Moriah. Ah, there is just one thing more."

"Yes, my lord?" she asked sleepily.

"I should be honoured if you would dispense with the formality of my title, as I have done with yours, Moriah," he replied, his hand moving softly over her shoulder.

"I — er — oh, I suppose it *is* a bit foolish, under the — er — ah — circumstances," she said in that matter-of-fact tone of hers. "Very well — ah — Roane. Good night."

He frowned and moved his fingers to trace the line of her jaw. "Roane" was what his friends, and even some of his female companions, called him. But that was still his title, and somehow, it sounded grating coming from Moriah. "My name is Justin, little one," he said in a low, intimate voice.

130

She moved her head as if to look at him. Even in the dim light he could see the curious look in her eyes. "Justin," she whispered, as if trying out the sound on her tongue. "Justin," she said again, nestling her head against him once more. He held her close, and he was never sure who fell asleep first.

Chapter 13

It was ten o'clock in the morning when Lizzie finally woke Moriah, who was even more surprised than her maid that she'd slept so unaccustomedly late. She sat up in bed, her eyes still heavy with sleep, and it was not until she began to sip her chocolate that the memories of the past night came rushing toward her.

Alone in the room, she felt herself flush, and it was not a flush of embarrassment, as she knew it most definitely should be. Instead her body felt warm as she recalled the events of the previous night. Well, not precisely the events, she amended, for in truth she could not recall the details of what had transpired. But the feelings were etched indelibly in her mind and on her body. Even now she felt a delicious ripple of sensation run through her and she realized that she was very much looking forward to her visit to the hunting box this evening. And then suddenly she flushed again, this time with shame. Whatever had come over her that she looked forward to giving herself so dishonourably to a man who was a virtual stranger? Was she, indeed, a wanton?

She did not know; she did not understand herself. She had accepted what she'd had to do; she'd known it was wrong but it could not be helped. But to react as she had, and for those feelings to be with her still . . .

Moriah recalled that when she had been considering Lord Ro—ah—Justin's offer (was it only three days ago?) she had known, somehow, that if she accepted him she would never again be the same. And now she understood why. For he had awakened feelings that she did not know it was possible for her—indeed, for any woman—to have. And now for the first time she understood the full consequences of what she had done. It was not only that she had risked her good name and ruined her chances for marriage. It was that he had taught her what it meant to be a woman, in the most elemental sense. And since she was not the sort of woman to allow herself to be bandied from man to man, it meant that when he was gone, she would be alone, more alone, she knew now, than she had ever dreamed possible.

She drained her chocolate and slammed her cup down on her bedside table. Damn him! she thought. If he had been callous, unfeeling, or repulsive, she would not have to deal with her outraged conscience nor her betraying body.

And damn him for a libertine, a hardened rake! Gentle he may have been, but what sort of man would so cavalierly bed a maiden of birth and breeding? He was hateful; he had no respect for her whatever. And yet, she could not help recalling his tenderness, his complete understanding of her distress, his concern for her, which seemed so genuine. And then, when it had been time for her to leave, he had treated her with the utmost courtesy. He had allowed her privacy to dress. And, true to his word, he'd collected her hair pins and then, laughing softly with her about playing lady's maid, helped her twist her hair back into its customary bun. He had ridden with her as far as he dared onto her own land, saying he disliked the idea of her riding alone at night. And when finally they had parted, he had kissed her chastely on the brow, a kiss totally at odds with his request that she meet him again this night.

Damn him! she thought again, rising abruptly from the bed. The man had no decency in him! "Justin" indeed! Had he not brazenly taken advantage of her situation, not to mention her innocence? She hated him with all her being, and she must not allow herself to forget it!

She walked determinedly into the dressing room and flung open the doors of the wardrobe. Her attempts to divert her mind from its disturbing thoughts were helped along by a cursory knock at the door.

Not a moment later Tess bounded straight into the dressing room, quite dressed and ready for the day. "Why, you slug-a-bed!" said her lovely sister. "Thank goodness you are not ill. Mrs. T. and I were more than a bit worried, I can tell you. But now you are up and about, I take leave to reprimand you sharply," she continued good-naturedly. "What mean you by leaving such important correspondence lying about without a word to me?" Tess let the card with the Crowley crest flutter in her hands. "A ball, Moriah! And *I* am invited! My very first ball! How *could* you not tell me!"

Tess was fairly jumping up and down in her excitement, and Moriah sank down onto the velvet chaise, a mixture of emotions darting through her. Not the least was guilt, for she had indeed opened the Crowley invitation yesterday. But so distracted had she been, contemplating her upcoming meeting with the viscount, that she had tossed it aside with nary a thought. And, well, she amended, if she *had* thought on it, it was that she could not possibly attend and face Lord Roane after—after—

But now she looked up at her sister's expectant face and knew there was no hope for it. It had been very kind of the Crowleys to include Tess, who was at least a year away from the time when most girls made their come-outs. She squelched the uncharitable thought that it must have been Sir Hugo's idea—she had never thought his wife particularly kind. At all events, Moriah knew she could not disappoint Tess; who knew when, circumstanced as they were, she would ever attend another ball?

Besides, it would look odd, indeed, if the Landons were not to attend, and Moriah knew it was imperative for her scheme that they all carry on as if nothing untoward was afoot. That reminded her that she must bring up the matter of her father this night with the Viscount. Somehow, they must contrive a way for Papa to retrieve his markers honourably. She found distasteful the thought of discussing the matter with Justin—Lord Roane, she corrected herself—and of having to ask something of him. But she immediately reprimanded herself sharply. That was the whole reason she'd gone to him in the first place!

She forced her mind back to the ball but found those thoughts no more comforting. For the thought of seeing Lord Roane at such an event dismayed her terribly, though not for the reason she had anticipated. It was not, Moriah realized, that she would feel embarrassed to face him, for she knew instinctively that she would not. It was rather that neither she nor the viscount would be able to publicly acknowledge their acquaintanceship. They would have to meet as strangers and act as such, and that would be very difficult to bear.

She was not attending to Tess's animated monologue, but she realized, at the end of it, that she had agreed to rummage in the attic for one of Mama's ball gowns for Tess and then to a trip to the village to purchase various trimmings to refurbish it. Ah well, she thought resignedly, it was just as well she had something to occupy her mind this day. Perhaps it would pass more quickly. Now, whyever should she wish that? she demanded of herself harshly. She hated the Viscount Roane and was certainly not looking forward to another encounter with him. She was dreading this evening, she told herself determinedly, just as was proper.

Moriah had not expected to enjoy foraging for gowns in the attic, nor had she given much thought to her own attire for the ball. But somehow Tess's enthusiasm communicated itself to her and Moriah found herself quite excited when her younger sister found a white muslin edged with plaited yellow ribbons that would do just perfectly. And when Tess urged Moriah to find something for herself, the older sister did not demur. It was not, she assured herself, that she disliked the thought of appearing before the viscount, at a ball in his honour, in one of her two slightly worn, somewhat ill-fitting gowns. It was merely that she counted it a foolish waste to allow Mama's perfectly lovely gowns to languish in the attic. As such, she chose an ivory satin gown trimmed with large silk roses of a deep violet to match her eyes. Though she would have preferred a deeper, more striking color than ivory, she knew that this befit her nineteen years, and she could ill afford to flout convention. But, she reflected, she could not go so far as to wear white, and she thought it just as well that white was not particularly flattering to her golden skin. At all events, she was certain that with a bit of alteration the gown might be updated and

136

made to fit reasonably well.

Tess insisted that they set off for Much Henley straight away in search of whatever ornamentation might be found there. Moriah agreed, with little reluctance, determined to put aside her distressing thoughts, at least for a while. What was done was done, she reminded herself, and no amount of bemoaning the fact would ever change it.

Moriah and Tess set off in the family gig, which was always used for local trips. It was becoming a bit rickety with age, and Moriah had thought fleetingly of taking her father's closed carriage. But she'd overheard the groom telling Cook that the carriage had arrived from London much the worse for wear and so she thought it more prudent to use the gig. Hodges, who had been groom at the Abbey for many years and who much preferred Herefordshire to London, seemed to approve her decision, for he appeared in high spirits as he mounted his box to drive the young ladies into the village.

Tess chattered happily about the delights that awaited her at her first ball. Moriah thought it charming that Tess could muster as much excitement for this as she might for a London come-out and reflected that in some ways her sister was quite unspoiled. Moriah, for her part, could not seem to squelch an image of herself in ivory satin, circling a grand ballroom in the arms of the Viscount Roane.

But Moriah plummeted quickly back to reality as the gig encountered a huge pothole that caused the axle of the aging vehicle to scrape gratingly over the ground. She groaned inwardly as Hodges steadied the gig, thinking that any severe damage was something they could ill afford.

"Village up ahead," the groom called back to them, and as the vast meadows yielded to clusters of timbered cottages, the last vestiges of Moriah's pleasant daydream faded. Instead she thought of the village and villagers and what would happen if anyone were ever to find out what had transpired last night.

Tess fairly jumped down from the gig as soon as Hodges reined the horses to a halt, but Moriah found that her own enthusiasm had suddenly disappeared. Rather, she felt acutely uncomfortable, having no desire to encounter any of her neighbors and even less to attend the Crowley ball.

Much Henley was not a very large village, any major shopping having to be accomplished in the city of Hereford. But it did boast a better than passing milliner, a pleasant tea shop, and a reasonably well-stocked though small establishment that had the audacity, or imagination, to call itself Endicott's Dry Goods Emporium.

It was to Endicott's that Tess immediately headed, with Moriah trailing somewhat wearily (or was it warily?) behind. Really, she must not slink about like some felon who feared to be transported for his latest highway robbery.

"Oh, Moriah, do have a look at this lace! Would it not be just the thing for my new gown?" Tess exclaimed, as she carefully fingered an exquisite piece of white Brussels lace that was wedged between a delicate bit of gold netting on one side and a bolt of crepe lisse on the other.

They stood in one of the rear corners of the shop, behind a rather high display of feathers — ostrich plumes and boas, streams of osprey and peacock feathers — that completely obscured them from the view of anyone else in the shop. Moriah let her eyes scan the table before them, laden as it was with beautiful, intricately woven fabrics and lace, and

138

could not repress a wistful sigh. Tess had excellent taste, and Moriah dearly wished she might have the wherewithal to indulge her. Tess was perfectly right about the Brussels lace she was now holding so lovingly, and Moriah did not relish deflating the girl's dreams.

"Oh, but I am certain it will prove exceedingly expensive, Moriah," she heard Tess say, breaking into her reverie. "We might ask Mr. Endicott, of course, but if it is so, I am persuaded we might contrive with some silk ribbons and perhaps a small rosette or two. You know, just under the high waist. Do you not think so?"

Moriah stared at her sister with genuine amazement, and then smiled warmly. So, Tess was not quite like their mother, after all.

But further thought on this subject was forestalled as voices were heard just the other side of the feather display. It was not Moriah's habit to eavesdrop, but she was instinctively quiet and cast a look at Tess, which caused the younger girl to follow suit.

"Oh, Mama, everyone is well aware that I have already had a Season. I simply do not see why I must wear white muslin to the ball. I declare the color is quite insipid, and I do not show to best advantage in it," came a rather high-pitched, petulant voice that Moriah recognized as that of Olivia Crowley.

"What utter fustian! You are a very beautiful girl, Olivia, no matter what you wear. And I deem it of prime importance to emphasize your youth. You may be past your first Season, but it does no good at all to remind the world of it, particularly as you are yet unattached. And why you failed to bring the Marquis of Rexford up to scratch is beyond me." Lady Crowley paused for breath and Tess stifled a giggle. Moriah knew it was reprehensible to eavesdrop, but she, too, was amused, and so they kept silent as Lady Crowley continued. "I cannot help but think that if you had exerted yourself more with Rexford—not but what that's water under the dam by now. Well, a viscount is not a marquis, but Roane will suit admirably nonetheless."

At this last Moriah froze and could only hope Tess did not notice how rigidly she held herself.

"But you must know, Mama, that he is not hanging out for a wife," interjected Olivia. Moriah felt unaccountably relieved at her words and then was immediately annoyed with herself for caring one way or another. What had Roane's matrimonial plans to do with her? "And everyone says—" Olivia went on, but her mother stopped her.

"Don't interrupt, Olivia. It shows a lack of breeding that is most unbecoming. And I deplore the use of slang!" snapped Lady Crowley, and then she continued. "I have worked very hard to bring this about, and I insist you be guided by my better judgment. That he is not precisely searching for a wife is quite irrelevant, I assure you. You will be a vision in pure white, my dear, and though you are a very comely girl at all events, I have been very—shall we say—selective with the guest list so that you will not have much competition. The viscount stood up with you several times in London, so he cannot have been indifferent. And he will have no choice but to do so again Tuesday next, several times. Then it will be up to you to fix his interest."

"You seem to be forgetting the Landons, Mama."

"I forget nothing. Of course I had to invite the important county families, but you need think no more on 't. Moriah Landon cannot possibly interest the Viscount Roane. A girl with no looks to recommend her, whose father has nearly dissipated the family fortune—truly, Olivia, I think your wits have gone a begging."

At this, Tess's hand went out to grasp Moriah's in sympathy, but the older sister merely shook her head and tried to smile. It was all no more than the truth, after all."

"Tess is very beautiful, Mama."

"Perhaps, but she is the veriest child. Roane is a sophisticated man for whom only a woman with polish and address will do. No, I think we may discount Theresa as well, though I will own I was a bit miffed that your father insisted on inviting her; he has strange notions of kindness at times, I must say. Besides, I have reason to believe the viscount will wish to be very well connected indeed in his marriage."

"But he already is quite—"

"You see," continued Lady Crowley, as if Olivia had not said a word, "I—er—overheard your father saying that the Earl of Westmacott—Roane's uncle, you must know—is desirous that his nephew take his seat and become active in the Lords. And what better political sponsor than your own dear Papa? No, Olivia, I insist you wear the white muslin, and I should like to add some lace to the skirt. Oh, and I believe I shall purchase several ostrich plumes for my new toque. Let me see, my gown is purple and—"

"Oh, Mama, I declare I am fagged to death with all this shopping," Olivia fairly whined, and Moriah wondered how much shopping they could have done whilst standing here. "Could we not take tea first? And that wretched carriage ride has quite given me a headache. That landau may only be two years old, but I cannot see why Papa refused to have the springs seen to. . . ."

Moriah and Tess had to suppress a cascade of

141

giggles, and Moriah was most relieved, for several reasons, when mother and daughter moved off toward the front of the shop, arguing the whole while.

Moriah waited until they had exited the shop before murmuring, "Well, Miss Billingsley always said that eavesdroppers do not hear well of themselves." But she saw a look of such sympathy on Tess's face that she had to laugh. "Oh, it is not that I mind *what* they said, about either of us, merely that it is so disconcerting to be discussed in the manner of cattle put up for auction. But come, let us not refine too much upon it," she added, and urged Tess to concentrate on the choices before them. Moriah found it difficult to do so, however, and had to keep reminding herself that Roane's political and marital ambitions did not signify to her in the least.

It was just as they stepped out into the sunlight, a little while later, that they encountered Mrs. Shoup. Moriah had not seen her in quite some time, and she returned that lady's warm smile with pleasure.

"Moriah, Tess," said Mrs. Shoup in her soft, lilting voice. "I do hope you go on well." She was a petite, slender woman and had to look up at them as she spoke.

"Oh, yes, everything is lovely," bubbled Tess, but Moriah merely nodded, her eyes lowering and her smile becoming tremulous. She wondered why she should find it harder to deceive Mrs. Shoup than her own sister or housekeeper.

"Moriah, you are—that is—" Mrs. Shoup began, concern in her voice, and Moriah forced herself to look up.

"I am right, Mrs. Shoup," Moriah answered slowly, and forcing a lightness of tone, added, "That bonnet looks charming on you. You look wonderful in pink, you know." It was true, thought Moriah.

142

The color brought a glow to her clear pink complexion. Her heart-shaped face, though not beautiful, had a soft, almost girlish look to it, despite her middle years, and such few wrinkles as she had were laugh lines around her mouth and eyes. Her sandy brown hair was caught in a topknot, the escaping curls adding to her girlish look. There was no sadness about her, despite her precarious social position and the persistent rumours about her long-term liaison with an unknown nobleman. Instead, hers was a face in repose, and suddenly Moriah realized that the rumors about her were true. For Moriah saw what she had never seen before—Mrs. Shoup was a woman who loved and was loved by a man.

"Thank you, my dear," Mrs. Shoup was saying. "You girls look intent on your errands and I know I must not keep you, but I *am* delighted to see you." Moriah knew the lady's delight was genuine, but Mrs. Shoup moved aside to let them pass nonetheless. It had happened before, and though they never spoke of it, Moriah was aware that Mrs. Shoup wished to protect them from unkind tongues should they be seen conversing together. It had always saddened Moriah that Mrs. Shoup could be cut by her own neighbors, but now it made her furious.

"What a charming lady," Tess said as they moved off toward the gig. "I cannot imagine that any of those dreadful stories about her are true," she added with the assurance of the young that everything in the world is either black or white. Moriah felt suddenly very gray.

Chapter 14

Roane had driven his horse hard once he had seen Moriah Landon onto her own land in the middle of the night. It was as if he had wanted to drive his own turmoil of thoughts from his mind for, indeed, once Moriah had gone, he could no longer keep those thoughts at bay. He had slept surprisingly deeply when she'd been in his arms, something that he rarely did with a woman in his bed. But when he arrived at the Court and slithered between the silk sheets in the imposing master bedchamber, he found he could not sleep at all. All he could think of was Moriah, warm and soft in his arms, and of the fact that no man who called himself gentleman would ever have done what he had this night. And then memories of the past rushed headlong into his mind, reminding him that there was poetic justice in what he'd done. He'd meant to ruin the Landons, and so he had.

He must have drifted off to a troubled sleep some time after dawn, for he next became aware of Andrew, standing by his bed with an absurdly young grin on his face, even for his twenty-two years. Roane let out an unseemly epithet and told his cousin to go to the devil, but Andrew merely chuckled.

"Come on now, Justin. I'm the one with the fuzzy head, not you. This is the country, remember? Time to get up. Why, it's past ten o'clock. I confess I do feel rather wretched, but nothing a nice hard ride over the hills won't cure." Andrew punctuated his cheerful statement with a vigourous shaking of Roane's tired shoulders. And Roane, unable to tell his cousin that what ailed him would not go away merely because he managed to get his rump into a saddle, reluctantly rose from his bed.

Roane was right, of course; the ride did him no good at all. Andrew's good-natured banter and questions about the surrounding countryside and its inhabitants were even less soothing.

"Never known you to be such a bear before breakfast, Justin," Andrew said at one point. "Did you, perhaps, shoot the cat after I'd gone to bed?" Roane smiled and assured his cousin that he'd not made any further inroads in his supply of claret last night. He refrained from adding that he'd been drunk nonetheless, intoxicated in a way he'd never thought possible.

Needless to say, breakfast did not improve the viscount's humour one iota, and he could only be grateful that Andrew's vigourous consumption of several helpings of the eggs Benedict, buttered toast, and everything else in sight prevented his cousin from talking too much or asking too many questions.

Roane welcomed the surprise rain shower that began to fall in the early afternoon and declared his intention of retiring to his study to work for a few hours. He said he was sure Andrew could amuse himself for a while and resolutely ignored the doubtful look on his cousin's face as his host took leave of him.

Once safely closeted behind the heavy oak doors

of his study, Roane headed immediately for the brandy decanter, but he banged it down on the silver tray with a force that nearly shattered it and sent its contents sprawling. He had no intention of raddling his brain again this day. He must think very carefully and probably, if he knew Andrew, very quickly. His cousin would undoubtedly come bounding in in a short while, happily declaring that Roane had buried his head in his stuffy books quite long enough. In the meantime, Roane had to make some sense of what had happened last night. And he had to decide what to say—and do—tonight. In a few hours he would be confronted with Moriah Landon again and his senses would reel, all notions of honour and morality suddenly ceasing to exist.

But he could not let that happen, he told himself as he headed for his desk. He was a gentleman, after all. He stopped short before the large burr walnut desk and stared down at it, as if wondering what it was there for. Then he turned about and began instead to pace the Oriental carpet with the rapid, almost jerking motions of a panther ready to strike.

He'd had to tell her to meet him again this night. He'd known that if he hadn't, she would probably have assumed he was—well—not quite pleased with her in some way. And, if he were completely honest with himself, he'd told her to return because—because he wanted to see her again, dammit! But she was a Landon; what right had he to want to see her again? And besides, what would he do with her when—that is, he could not allow a repeat of last night, much as he might wish it. He was a gentleman; he had forgotten himself once, and he must not do so again. But then what the devil would they do together? They could not very well spend the night playing piquet. And not that he wouldn't enjoy talking to her; he might very well, but it simply wasn't practical. Not when she looked like that, and they were all alone in the middle of the night.

Roane stopped pacing long enough to run his fingers through his hair, and then stalked to the large picture window. He stood for a moment, looking out over the formal gardens, surveying his estate. The well-kept lawns looked especially rich, bathed in sunlight even as the light, steady rain continued to fall. He was avoiding the real dilemma and he knew it. He was a man of honour. He had taken the virtue of a young woman of breeding, and every code of decency demanded that he marry her. But she was no ordinary woman. She was a Landon, and the Landons had dishonoured *his* family, had in fact been responsible, in one way and another, for their untimely deaths. How could he marry such a woman without further besmirching the honour and the memory of his family?

He cursed inwardly at the sound of the hearty knock that could only herald Andrew's arrival. True to form, his cousin entered a moment later, the usual cheerful spring to his walk. Blast! thought Roane. He'd only been here a half hour or so. Could Andrew not amuse himself longer than that?

"Well! Glad to see you're so busy, Coz!" exclaimed Andrew, his eyes flitting from the viscount to his desk, where it was quite obvious that not a paper had been touched, not a missive opened. "You've been here for nigh onto three hours, don't you know, Justin. I—"

"Three hours! Why that's impossible!" Roane exclaimed, but even as he spoke his eyes followed Andrew's out the window to the lengthening shadows on the lawn and gardens. Amazing that he hadn't noticed, he thought, as he turned back to Andrew

147

with a rueful look that was almost a smile.

"Helped m'self to a light nuncheon—hope you don't mind," Drew continued. "Didn't want to disturb you, but the rain shows no sign of a letup and I reckoned you'd—er—*worked* enough." Andrew stared rather dubiously at Roane, and the viscount quickly offered him some brandy. Anything to divert his young, curious mind. Besides, much as he might wish Andrew at Jericho at the moment, he *was* a guest in his house.

Roane poured Andrew a generous glass of brandy and watched his cousin settle himself comfortably in the soft leather sofa. He poured himself a glass as well, merely to avoid raising Andrew's suspicions should he not, but he resolved not to drink it. He sank down into an adjacent leather wing chair and swirled the brandy in its goblet, hoping his dark thoughts did not show on his face. He listened to the steady stream of the rain on the rooftop and was suddenly very angry with himself. A man should be able to enjoy an afternoon such as this—a soothing summer rainshower, a warming glass of brandy, good company. Dammit, was he *never* to have any peace?

Andrew stretched his buckskin-clad legs out and made himself comfortable, so comfortable, in fact, that Roane knew that, unless the rain stopped, they would probably be closeted in this room the whole of the afternoon. And when, after a few pleasantries, Andrew introduced the topic that was obviously uppermost in his mind, Roane knew there was no hope for it.

"Er—by the by, Justin, have you—er—been thinking about—er—what m' father said?" Andrew inquired, his tone leaving no doubt that it was such ruminations that he hoped had occupied the viscount all afternoon. Roane did not disabuse him of the notion but merely smiled enigmatically.

"Look here, I know army life didn't satisfy you, Justin," Andrew continued. "Here's a chance for you to really do something worthwhile. Serve your country and all that. Now the—"

"I've said before that I have no doubt the country will survive without my efforts, Andrew," Roane interrupted dryly.

"But, Justin, you haven't even heard what the secret mission is," blurted Andrew, reminding Roane, at that moment, very much of a child being denied a request. There was more than a bit of romanticism in his cousin, and he wondered why Andrew simply didn't undertake this "secret mission" himself.

"My apologies, Drew. Just what sort of—er—secret mission does my esteemed uncle have in mind?" asked Roane, trying not to sound amused.

Andrew put his drink down on the sofa table, cleared his throat, and sat straight in his chair. Roane had the feeling that he was about to be treated to a well-rehearsed monologue. "Well," he began, "daresay you may know the Secretary's been sending secret committees to the north country. All those riots, machine breaking—General Ludd and his sort, don't you know."

"If there *is* such a person," Roane murmured.

"Yes, well, daresay you know more 'bout it than I do, Justin. That's why you'd be so good at this, y' see. At all events, fact is, Sidmouth's pretty well convinced, after all those committee reports, that there's an organized rebellion afoot. Widespread, 'smatter of fact. Hunt and Cobbett and the rest—they've got the people yellin' for Parliamentary reform, stormin' the factories, and I don't know what all. Most of the ministers think it's one step away from a full-scale revolution, Justin."

149

"Merely because people want food in their mouths and better working conditions hardly means to say they want to see the end of king and country. I daresay reform is an idea been put there by outsiders—Hunt and his ilk. But what does all this have to do with me? Sidmouth's got his reports *and* his emergency powers, not that it's made a difference, I don't suppose. They simply can't transport every man who gets up to make a speech, can they?"

Andrew suddenly laughed aloud and slapped his knees. "Oh, that's famous, Justin."

"What the hell is so funny, Drew? You know as well as I do the Home Office isn't about to start a Reign of Terror. No more do I believe every hosier in Leicester wants to see my head roll. They want to feed their families, though they've got to know breaking machines is not the way to go about it. And as to Parliamentary reform, well, I suppose a few minor changes—"

"I tell you it's famous, Justin," repeated Andrew. "That's exactly what the earl said you'd say. That's why he wants you to go to Lancashire. The government needs a moderate voice like yours. Fa' wants you to follow in his footsteps and—"

"Follow in his footsteps? Good God, Drew, you're his heir, not I. You go to Lancashire. And what the bloody hell would I do there?"

"Oh, no, Justin, I can't go. Why, you understand all this better than I, and the earl's been drillin' me for days! No, he wants you to go, unofficially, you know. Talk to people. Draw your own conclusions. *Then* you'll come to Parliament in January and—"

"No, Drew," interrupted Roane. "I told you before I've no intention of taking my seat, and as to Lancashire, with all due respect to the earl, I'm afraid it's out of the question." Roane placed his untouched drink on the sofa table and rose from his seat. Andrew opened his mouth to protest but Roane forestalled him. "The rain's let up, Drew. You might enjoy a ride now, you know. There's nothing to match country air after a rain shower. As for me, I've some work to do. So if—"

"The earl won't be best pleased, Justin. He's like to post down here himself, if I don't miss my guess," Andrew warned, grinning and rising reluctantly.

"You leave the earl to me, Drew," countered Roane with a confidence he was far from feeling. About all he needed right now was a visit from his all too astute uncle—and his uneasiness had nothing to do with Parliamentary reform.

Deftly, with the utmost politeness, Roane maneuvered his cousin to the doors of his study and presently found himself alone, having promised to meet Drew for a drink before dinner.

Roane closed the doors securely behind his cousin and stalked to his desk. He yanked the chair back and sank into it, burying his face in his hands simultaneously. Andrew had distracted him briefly, but he could not longer evade the dilemma besetting him. And what the hell was he to do? It was all a question of honour, as it had been from the beginning. Angrily, he jerked his chair back and stormed over to the sideboard. He splashed more brandy into an empty goblet, clenched it tightly in his hand, and strode to the hearth. He bent his head and fixed his eyes on the empty grate, his free hand coming to rest on the mantel.

Honour, always honour. It was honour that had got him into this coil in the first place. Landon's debt of honour, his own honour, and that damned offer that he really never made, and now the honour due his parents' memory versus his honour as a gentleman. He took a sip of his brandy and then remembered his resolve not to drink today. He stared at the crystal goblet in his hand, his eyes narrowed in an angry frown. And it was still more complicated, as his discussion with Andrew had reminded him. For there was the earl to consider. Roane had spent nearly as much of his boyhood with his uncle and cousin in Kent as he had right here. That the earl loved him like a son he did not doubt, and he knew Uncle George would be bitterly disappointed should he ever become aware of last night's events, especially did Roane not do the honourable thing by Moriah. Suddenly Roane remembered his uncle's last words to him. "Vengeance most hurts those who reap it, Justin," he'd said. How could he ever convince the earl that he had not deliberately set out to ruin Moriah Landon? Never, he thought; he never could.

Damn and blast it all! And damn his blasted honour! he thought savagely, and suddenly, without thought, he hurled his goblet into the grate. He watched it shatter into myriad pieces, the brown liquid splattering against the walls and trickling over the brass andirons.

He stared dumbly into the grate, hardly able to believe he'd broken an antique piece of crystal. No more could he believe what he'd done last night. He ran his hand through his hair, and then he thought of Moriah. Those deep amethyst eyes rose in his mind's eye, and he remembered the feel of her warm, lush body in his arms. He had never before seriously considered marriage, and now, for one moment, he allowed himself to think of what marriage to Moriah Landon might be like. The nights, he knew, would be most delightful, and he hardly realized that the frown had left his face as he pictured Moriah in his bed, her eyes smoky with passion as they had been last night.

But as to the days, well, he could only conjecture, for in truth he did not know her very well. She was certainly a very practical young woman, and he had little doubt that she could run his household quite efficiently. She was also, he guessed, rather strong-willed in her quiet but firm way, and that would not be at all to his liking. But she was also possessed of a great courage and a strong though unusual sense of honour that he could not help but admire. It occurred to him fleetingly that many men in his position would consider her morals quite below reproach for what she had done. But Roane knew it was as much his fault as hers, more actually, for she was such an innocent. He could not help respecting her for her courage and determination, although he thought, smiling wryly to himself, that those very qualities in a wife might well drive a man crazy.

A wife! What the hell was wrong with him? The deep frown descended onto his face as quickly as it had lifted. How could he consider marrying Moriah Landon? He had spent the last six years of his life trying to destroy her family. Could he suddenly negate everything he'd believed in and striven for ever since he was old enough to understand?

For the first time since he'd been standing there he raised his eyes to the mahogany framed mirror above the mantel. His face looked haggard; the lines around his eyes and mouth seemed deeper than usual. How, he wondered bitterly, could he face himself in the glass every morning, how could he retain his self-respect if he so forgot family feeling as to ally himself with a Landon? And yet, how could he live with himself if he did not?

He dropped his eyes and rubbed them with a hand that he realized was actually shaking. Until Moriah Landon had walked into this house the world had seemed black and white; everything had been so clear. He opened his eyes once more and stared into the glass. The eyes that gazed back at him did not look their usual clear blue. They looked suddenly very bleak and very, very gray.

Chapter 15

Moriah could not stop the pounding of her heart as she hammered the knocker softly against the door of Lord Roane's hunting box. The moonlight had illumined her way and now, as he opened the door, she could see him quite clearly. He was clad in an open-necked cream-colored silk shirt with wide sleeves. There was a slight breeze in the air and she wondered why the sight of him should make her feel suddenly so warm. He wore comfortable brown breeches and looked every inch the country gentleman, but she could not help thinking, as she had once before, that he reminded her of a pirate. He lacked only the patch over one eye. His dark brown hair looked a little less perfectly coiffed than usual, almost as if he'd run his fingers through it in anxiety over something. Though what could possibly trouble him she did not know. His eyes looked tired, she thought, and for a moment seemed to pierce her until finally he ventured a glimmer of a smile.

"Good evening, Moriah. I trust your ride was pleasant. Come in, please." He took her arm this time and led her to the sitting room, initiating, as they walked, a conversation of pleasantries that almost made her think he was nervous. But that was absurd. She did not imagine the Viscount Roane was ever nervous about anything.

He waited for her to remove her gloves and then helped her off with the light wool cloak she'd worn. Then he seated her on one of the green and gold love seats near the hearth, with the same courtesy he might extend a debutante in the supper room of her first ball. Moriah gratefully accepted the glass of Madeira he offered her, but she noted that he himself did not take any. Nor did he sit down. Instead he began pacing the deep green carpet in front of her, passing in and out of the shadows cast by the tapers on the mantel. His square jaw looked most determined, his blue eyes dark and rather fierce, and his hands were thrust behind his back. She could not help seeing the firm muscles of his thighs as he moved, and she felt her pulse quicken, though she did not understand why. She looked down and sipped her wine, but her eyes raised themselves again. He had not said a word nor did she speak, but merely watched him. Even in his pacing he looked lithe and elegant, and she could not decide whether he reminded her more at that moment of a pirate pacing the deck or a panther preparing to strike. Either way, the sense of power and strength he emanated was never so evident as at this moment, and she felt a shiver run through her. It was not, she was painfully aware, a shiver of fear.

She could not take her eyes off him. He halted in his tracks and looked in her direction once; their eyes locked and held for a moment with an intensity she'd felt before but still could not fathom. Then he abruptly resumed his pacing. Moriah sensed that he was in the throes of some very powerful emotion, but she waited silently, somehow certain that he would explain himself presently.

Roane could not seem to stop pacing up and down nor could he open his mouth to say what he knew he had to say. He did not know why he should be so apprehensive — it was all quite simple and straightforward, after all. He did not imagine that anything could go wrong. He forced himself to stop before her and stand still.

He looked down at her and saw that she was gazing up at him expectantly. He felt that intensity between them again, and a sudden warmth. Their eyes held; hers were wide and curious, his searching, demanding. It was, he realized, as if there were some kind of magnetic pull between them. And, as if in response to that pull, she slowly rose and stood facing him, her eyes never leaving his.

They stood very close, not a foot apart, and he tried to ignore the heat in his loins as his eyes searched her face. Had he noticed before that it was heart-shaped, with high cheekbones, a perfect canvas for the beautifully shaped red lips and large amethyst eyes? And those eyes—of a certain they looked different tonight. There was something about them, a certain softness perhaps that surely was new. His own eyes slowly travelled the length of her as he fought to keep his hands from doing the same. Tonight she had exchanged her riding habit for an evening gown and she had even removed her gloves without prompting. Roane could not help smiling inwardly. His little pragmatist was becoming a little less practical and proper, was she? The gown, though not cut too low across the bosom, yet bared her throat and shoulders and seemed to cling to every delicious curve of her body. But Roane frowned as he realized that was because it probably had not fit properly for several years. Nonetheless, she looked delectable, the particular shade of lavender accenting her eyes, the soft silk fabric moving in a fluid, sensuous motion when she did. She was beautifully proportioned, he thought, not for the first time, his eyes caressing the full breasts that seemed to strain for release from inside that gown. He ran his tongue over his very dry lips and tried to make himself speak. Why was it suddenly so difficult?

She stood very erect, her hands, as always, clasped at her waist. He marveled anew at her composure and at the fact that, despite her petite size, she achieved an elegance of carriage and grace of movement that few women ever did. She cocked her head to one side, her lips parting slightly in a soft smile. The tapers on the hearth cast a golden glow across her smooth, bare shoulders, and it was with the greatest difficulty that he restrained himself from taking her into his arms. The task was not made any easier by the fact that her own breathing was quite rapid. Amazing, he thought, that his desire for her was no less for having once been sated, was perhaps even greater. But he did not even reach out to take her hand. Somehow he knew that if he did, all rational thought and speech would desert him.

He took a small step back and kept his hands firmly planted behind him.

"Moriah," he began, surprised at how unsteady his voice sounded, "I have done a good deal of thinking this day past, about—about our—er—situation. We, as ladies and gentlemen of birth and breeding, live by a certain code of behavior, as you know, and—and you and I have—have broken that code." She frowned and he held up a hand as if to forestall a protest, but she remained silent and he continued. "You must know that I—I do not hold you to account, for I understand your motives. But as for my—my conduct, I—well—" Roane stammered for words and finally let his voice trail off. Then, seeing a familiar look of distress descend onto her face, he hastened to add, with a somewhat rueful smile and a voice softer than it had been, "That is not to say that I—I regret what transpired, for it was rather a . . .

wondrous delight." He was barely aware that his hand had come up to caress her cheek as he spoke this last and he let it fall as he added, "But—but—well—" Here he drew himself up and his voice became firmer. "What I am trying to say is that I wish very much that you will do me the honour of—of becoming my wife." There, he thought, he'd said it. But he felt compelled to add, "It it really is the best thing for us to do in the—in the circumstances, Moriah, and I am certain we shall get on well enough. In some ways, very well indeed." He murmured this last and his hand came up once again to brush her cheek.

But he withdrew the hand quickly as he realized that her reaction was not at all what he had anticipated. Her eyes went wide with shock and she took a step back, one small hand uncharacteristically leaving her waist and going to her brow. Good Lord, he thought. What a cad indeed she must have thought him to be so astounded that he would do the honourable thing by her. She looked as if the idea had never occurred to her.

"Moriah, surely you must—" he began, but she shook her head, forestalling him.

"My lord, I—please, I—I beg a moment to compose my thoughts," she said in her calm, husky voice. And, taking her own forbearance of a few moments ago as example, he decided to remain silent, however difficult it be.

She turned from him and walked slowly toward the hearth and stood before it, her head bent. He watched the candlelight dance across her long neck and shimmering black hair and decided suddenly that marriage to Moriah would have its good points, however much his conscience troubled him at the thought. But what the devil was she pondering so

159

deeply? How difficult could it be to find the words to accept his proposal? Of a certain she could not refuse, and so . . .

Moriah's head was whirling, despite her outward calm. His words had completely taken her by surprise. Never, ever, had she expected him to offer for her. She had suddenly to revise her opinion of him as an unprincipled though highly attractive blackguard. And she had to admit to herself that the idea of marriage to the Viscount Roane was a very attractive proposition, in more ways than one, though she was not as certain as Roane claimed to be that they would go on well together. Something about the intense energy and determination he exuded led her to believe he would not be an easy man to live with. But life, she thought, would certainly never be dull. No, the days would not be dull, and the nights — she felt herself flush at the thought that the nights would be very pleasant indeed. And then there were more practical matters to consider. Marriage to Roane would solve so many of her problems. She would have no more financial worries. Tess could have her come out, and Moriah was sure the viscount would take her father in hand. She sighed softly to herself as she thought that it would be so wonderful to have someone to lean on, to be stronger than she. For nearly as long as she could remember, *she* had had to be strong for everyone around her.

She straightened her bent head and stared directly at the silently burning tapers. She knew that she dare not look at Roane, for every time she did, she felt a certain weakness in her loins and she did not want her judgment impaired. She knew full well that a more impulsive person might throw caution to the winds and say yes to him at this very moment. But the years had taught her to be prudent and practical, to weigh her options carefully. And so, having considered the positive, her thoughts flew now to the negative.

She and Roane hardly knew each other, despite their—their intimacy of the night before. She could not even claim friendship between them, let alone affection, nor had he mentioned either one. And she supposed, sighing now to herself, that there was very little respect between them either. And so there could be only one reason for the viscount's sudden surge of nobility. He was offering for her out of a sense of honour and duty, and perhaps pity as well. She shuddered inwardly at the thought. She wanted no man's pity nor did she want to be any man's albatross, the duty with which he had been forced to bind himself. That pity, that sense of honour could turn to anger and then hate all too readily, she feared.

Oh, she knew he desired her, very much in fact. But she instinctively felt that even the desire would wane eventually. He would tire of her, perhaps in a se'ennight, a month, a year, but the time would come. Had he not said it was customary for a woman to remain under a gentleman's protection until he tired of her? And while a mistress could walk away with her dignity and independence, a wife could not. No, as a wife she would be his chattel, she would be his to command, beholden to him, dependent upon him. She would have to stay hidden at whatever country seat he chose, while he betook himself off to the pleasures of London. And she would be that sad object of pity and even scorn, the neglected wife of an unfaithful husband. And well she knew the humiliation that would entail, for did not her friend Sarah have to bear that very thing? Oh, her husband did come home now and again, a duty call, as everyone knew, when he would alternately bellow at his wife and then regard her with an icy, indifferent civility that Moriah found even more distressing. And he would only briefly acknowledge his children and then be off again to "business" in London. Many was the time Moriah had comforted Sarah after such an episode, and she knew she could not bear such a life for herself. At home at the Abbey, she might have creditors dunning her at every turn, but at the least she was her own mistress, an independent being who answered to no one and was respected by servants, family, and neighbors alike.

As Lord Roane's mistress she would be able to retain her self-esteem. For some reason—she could not say why—she felt that at least for the duration of their—their liaison, she would be the only woman in his life. And when he chose to end it, she could walk away with her head high, knowing that she had saved her family. As a wife she could never walk away nor even hold her head up. The possibility that anyone might become privy to their relationship she refused to consider. They were both exceedingly discreet; they simply would not let it happen.

No, Moriah did not doubt for a moment that he would tire of her, perhaps even grow to hate her eventually. He was, after all, a confirmed and reputed rake, and he was not likely to change. Long, sad experience with her father had taught her that a leopard simply did not change his spots.

She took a deep breath, as if to let resolve fill her. It had seemed, for a fleeting moment, a very appealing proposition indeed. But she knew it could not be. She straightened her shoulders and thrust her chin up, and only then did she turn and venture a look at the Viscount Roane. He stood where she had left him, his eyes dark and rather piercing, his hands clasped behind him, feet planted widely apart, his full head of hair just a bit tousled. She let her eyes roam the length of him and come up to gaze at the square, resolute jaw that defined his face. How she admired strength in a man, for she had seen so little of it. Moriah mentally shook herself and kept her voice as calm as she could. "My lord, I—I—"

"My name is Justin, Moriah. Have you forgotten?" he asked in a voice that made her feel weak all over. But she knew her resolve must not weaken.

"J—Justin. I—I am sensible of—of the great honour you do me in—in asking me to be your wife, but I—I must decline your offer. I—I am afraid we should not suit."

He was beside her in two long strides. "What the hell are you talking about, Moriah?" he demanded, towering over her. "And don't give me that blather about a 'great honour' and 'we should not suit.' I should have thought we were beyond that nonsensical sort of formality, you and I." His voice had softened at this last, and she found it difficult to meet his eyes.

"Nonetheless, Justin, I—I cannot marry you," she repeated.

"Why the devil not, Moriah? You were willing enough to—to come to my bed. You do not, I venture to say, find me all that repulsive," he murmured and took her hands in his.

Moriah felt a flush course through her, but with it a surge of anger at his ungentlemanly reminder of—of certain things. Still, he *had* offered, and perhaps she owned him some explanation.

"You—you know very well that I—I do not find you re—repulsive. But you also know that marriage entails more than—"

"Oh, for heavensakes, Moriah, I had not thought you one of those silly romantics who consider undy-

163

ing love the only prerequisite to marriage. Surely you must see that we two should wed. It is the only honourable course open to us, and I need not add, I am certain, that you would have no further cause for worry over money or your family. Besides, I — I do not think it would be all that unpleasant, you know." As before, his voice softened at this last, having become almost a caress, and his thumbs had begun rhythmically massaging the tops of her hands. She was finding conversation increasingly difficult.

"I am *not* addicted to the Minerva Press novels, my lord. . . ."

"Justin," he corrected, not letting go her hands.

"Justin. I am not a silly romantic, but — but despite those aspects of marriage that — that would be rather — ah — pleasant, I — we — we do not know each other very well. And I suspect we should find ourselves at loggerheads rather more often than not," she managed to say, not quite sure if it were true, but needing desperately to convince him. Her voice sounded a little too breathless in her own ears, and when he relaxed his grip briefly, she gently pulled her hands away and stepped back from him. "You are being very noble, J — Justin," she continued in a stronger voice, "but I believe your nobility is misplaced. We had a bargain, you and I, with terms and conditions. I have begun to meet mine and — and I am certain you will meet yours. That — that is all that is required. This nobility — "

He took a step closer to her, an angry step, and this time his large hands gripped her elbows. "I am not in the habit of seducing unmarried ladies of quality, Moriah, and I — "

"You did *not* seduce me, my lord. I came of my own volition," she interrupted firmly.

"You felt compelled, Moriah," continued Roane,

his voice slightly raised. "And that is hardly the same thing. No, as the man I must take full responsibility for—for what happened and I wish to make honourable amends."

Honour! thought Moriah, becoming rather wrought up and trying unsuccessfully to wriggle from his grasp. It was always honour! So important that a man would kill himself or another over it.

"Oh, you men and your damned honour!" she blurted. "Honour is paramount, is it not, and everything and everyone else bedamned! Well, this is *not* your responsibility, my lord. It may come as a shock to you, but we of the so-called weaker sex *are* capable of standing on our own two feet and making our own decisions!" She stopped abruptly, as if hearing her own voice for the first time. Why, she sounded positively shrewish! She lowered her voice and her eyes at the same time. "At all events, my lord, I wish not to discuss this further. You needn't worry about me. I shall be right. I thank you for—"

"I think you ought not to decide just yet, Moriah. Perhaps—"

"No!" she said quickly. She must not allow herself time to change her mind. "No, my lord, I—"

"Justin."

"J—Justin. I—my decision is final. I shall come to you here, as I said I would, but I—I cannot marry you."

What an extraordinary woman she was, Roane thought. He was baffled and angered, but he could not help admiring her nonetheless. Any other woman would have jumped at his title and his wealth; the man involved would have been, he thought cynically, nearly irrelevant. But Moriah Landon, with a great deal more compelling reason to accept him, yet scrupled to do so. And just what were those scru-

165

ples? he wondered, as it dawned on him that she had not given him one good solid reason for refusing him. His grip on her changed to something of a caress as he let his hands slide up her bare arms.

"You baffle me, Moriah. You claim you are not given to romantical notions. You are, in fact, a most practical young woman. And yet, you resist this most practical of all solutions. I do not believe we should be at 'loggerheads,' as you put it, for I do not believe you to be an argumentative woman. What exactly *is* it that you would wish in a marriage, Moriah?" he asked gently.

"I do not plan to marry, my l—Justin, as I told you once before. But if I were to do so—well, I—I have very few illusions about life, you must know. But one is that marriage, if not based on love, should be based on mutual respect and—and at least some affection."

"Affection can grow, Moriah. And—well, you must know that I have a great deal of respect for you. I—"

"Oh no, you do not, my lord," she interjected firmly. "You do not respect me at all, else you should not have made me an improper offer at first stop."

Oh, lord, the viscount groaned inwardly, abruptly stepping back and running his fingers through his hair. Back to the offer that was never really an offer. Well, he certainly had no intention of running round in circles over *that* one again!

"Be that as it may," he said wearily, "do you think on it, Moriah, and—"

"No, Justin, please. I—I beg you will take me at my word," she whispered, her eyes imploring.

How did she always contrive to make him feel like a worse cad for doing the proper thing than he would for doing the improper?

"Very well, Moriah," he said with a sigh. He came close to her again and brushed a stray hair from her cheek, and his voice grew very soft. "I do not understand you, little one. But—but I will always be here if you need me. And—and my offer stands, if you—if you should change your mind." Now, why had he said that? He had offered and been most emphatically refused. His honour was intact, as was his family's. Why, then, was he not immensely relieved? She shook her head slightly and his eyes scanned her face. He thought her eyes looked suddenly moist but she quickly lowered them. She did not reply and he wondered what to say next. Or even what to do. He knew what she had come here for, but much as he might wish to, he simply could not take her upstairs. After their discussion tonight that would be even more reprehensible than his behavior last night had been. He could not simply send her away now; he knew she would be distressed did he try. Besides, he didn't want to, blast it all!

And then, thankfully, he remembered his instructions to his valet this afternoon. He put his forefinger under her chin and gently lifted it. "Would you—would you care for some supper, Moriah?"

Relief was evident in her eyes, but her outward calm was belied by the rapid pulse at her throat.

"I should like that very much, Justin," she replied, her voice husky once more. He felt his own pulse beat rapidly at his temples and knew of a certain that his troubles with Moriah Landon were just beginning.

Chapter 16

Roane seated Moriah at the oak table in the small dining room at the back of the hunting box. The tapers burning on the sideboard and in the wall sconces illumined the bare skin of her shoulders and throat with a soft, golden glow. As he bent over her to gently push her chair to the table, a whiff of her rose scent assailed him, and he had all he could do not to kiss the lovely, smooth curve between her neck and shoulder.

He walked to the sideboard, to somehow steady himself, and asked if he might fill her plate, to which she tendered a rather breathless, "Yes, please." He had instructed Norris to provide a light supper, but the repast that greeted his eyes seemed more in the nature of a banquet. He filled a plate for each of them with various cheeses, fruit, cold salmon, capers, and a slice of bread and, having carried these to the table, made great ceremony of filling their wine glasses. When he could delay no longer, he took his seat next to her, wishing very much that Norris were not so knowledgeable about romantic tête-à-têtes. It would have been so much easier if he had set their places a formal distance apart. As it was, it was hard to keep his knees from grazing hers under the table, impossible to keep his eyes away from her breasts, so

168

firm and rounded as they pressed against the table when she leaned forward to take her wine goblet in hand.

"Th—thank you, my lord," she said after several moments. "The supper is—ah—lovely." She was not a woman given to small talk and he wondered what *she* had cause to be nervous or uncomfortable about.

"Yes," he replied, striving for lightness of tone and slicing a piece of cheese, "Norris has quite outdone himself."

"Yes," she echoed in that flat, toneless voice he was coming to recognize. He made haste to correct her misapprehension.

"That is not to say that Norris is—er—accustomed to doing such things. His services are usually more in the nature of agonizing over the crispness of my cravats and the shine on my Hessians." Seeing the distress still evident on her face, he continued. "My reputation where women are concerned is not stainless; you know that. But I am not, you must know, in the habit of bringing women here. I have not been in residence at Roanbrooke much of late, but when I am—well, I use the hunting box as a sort of retreat, a place to come and think, away from a house full of too many servants."

Moriah's face seemed to relax, and Roane watched her take a sip of wine and then pop a wedge of cheese into her mouth. "Where do *you* go for solitude, Moriah, when you merely want to think about something?" he asked, leaning back in his chair. He determined to concentrate on the conversation and ignore the way the light played on her black hair and bare shoulders.

She smiled faintly. "Well, I do *not* have a house full of too many servants, you must know. I use the cloisters as my retreat, when I want to ponder some problem, just as the monks of old did. Of course, what remains of the cloisters is now more in the nature of a picture gallery, but still I think the ancient atmosphere lingers. And there is a lovely rose garden just outside; I do so love roses," she declared with an almost dreamy look in her deep amethyst eyes.

It struck him that a woman with eyes like that and one who loved roses ought to have fewer problems to ponder and more illusions than she did. He tried to repress the angry thought that he had gone a long way toward shattering any illusions she might have had. And he squelched the impulse to reach out and caress her face, to pull her to him. God, but a man could get lost in those eyes. He could not help remembering what they had looked like last night, dark and sultry as the heat of passion overcame her. He took a deep breath and grasped the edge of the table, as if to keep his hands still. This kind of proximity to her was a ridiculous test of willpower. In fact, the whole situation was ludicrous. And why the devil, now he thought on it again, had she refused his offer? Really, it would simplify matters so much if — But no, he stopped himself. It was best this way. He didn't really want to marry her, after all; he wanted to bed her, and that was hardly the same thing. He cleared his throat and tried to recall what she had last said.

"And what do you do, Moriah, when you are not called upon to solve the problems of all those around you?" he asked, after a moment, in a rather unsteady voice. He found that he was genuinely interested in her answer; he knew so little about Moriah Landon, despite all.

"Oh, I keep quite busy, I do assure you. I am certainly never bored, and I find that the quiet of country life suits me well. Not that I shouldn't enjoy visiting London, you must know, for I am persuaded I should like it very well. But I should tire of the constant activity and crush of people soon enough, I expect," she replied, seeming more at ease than he could ever recall her being. Then her eyes narrowed slightly and she cocked her head. He watched the fluid movement of her bare throat as she did so. "But I should imagine that for you matters would be quite the opposite. You have spent so much time in London, after all. Does the routine of country life tire you overmuch, Justin?"

Roane tore his eyes from her. He was torn between the desire to speak with her, really speak with her, and the increasing urgency of his need to sweep her into his arms and up the stairs. He swallowed hard, unable to erase the memory of last night. He deliberately picked up his wine goblet and studied it, forcing his mind back to her question. "No, I—truth to tell, I have often longed for the solitude of country life," he found himself saying.

"Then why did you stay away so long, Justin?" she asked softly.

For the first time, he took a sip of wine. Then he sighed deeply. Was it her question or her mere presence that seemed so disconcerting? "It's a long story, Moriah, a *very* long story. But come, you haven't answered my question. How do you spend your quiet hours?"

"Well, I confess I have not had much time of late. I have been rather—er—preoccupied. But I—well, I may condemn myself as something of a bluestocking, I fear, but I have become very interested in the history of—of the abbeys and castles hereabouts," she answered almost sheepishly, and then busied herself with slicing her salmon.

171

"Oh?" he prodded gently, his interest quite definitely piqued. He could not imagine any woman who fit his notion of a bluestocking less.

"Yes. I—I had always been interested in history; Miss Billingsley saw to that." Roane grinned wickedly at the mention of the oh-so-knowledgeable governess, recalling her theories about men and women, but she said nothing. "And then," she went on, "I was approached—oh—two years ago, I suppose, for information concerning the Abbey, for a certain guidebook, you must know. I began pouring through books and old family journals and compiling notes. It's all so very fascinating, and so when I'd finished with the Abbey I just naturally began studying the history of some of the other abbeys hereabouts. There are quite a few, you know. And then there are the border castles. What marvelously colorful stories *they* would have to tell could the ancient stones speak. I have only seen a few, but someday I should like to travel up and down the Welsh border, visiting all the castles and ruins." Her eyes sparkled with enthusiasm, and Roane was enchanted.

"I should love to accompany you," he murmured without thinking, and then immediately regretted his words, for the sparkle flew from her eyes and she looked quickly down at her plate. He cursed himself for an unthinking idiot. Of course he could not escort her to the border castles, nor anywhere else. This was not a courtship; they must never publicly acknowledge any but the most casual acquaintanceship. Damn! he thought. This coil was becoming more complicated by the hour.

The room was silent save for the occasional crackle of the fire. The light cast by the tapers was soft, a muted glow that seemed to surround Moriah and caress her golden skin. He ached to slide his hands down her bare neck, to her shoulders and beyond. But he dared not touch her at all, anywhere. He knew he had to say something, perhaps to change the subject, but he was loathe to do so. He plunged on as if nothing unfortunate had been said. "The simple pleasures of the country elude one in Town. I should like to learn to appreciate them once again," he said as matter-of-factly as he could.

In answer, she raised her head and abruptly stood up, taking her plate in her hand. "May I—ah—refill your plate, my lor—Justin? I—I believe I myself should like more—ah—cheese."

He stood immediately after she did. "You needn't trouble yourself, Moriah. I shall get it for you," he said, his eyes narrowed, perplexed. He moved closer to take the plate from her and in so doing his fingers brushed hers. Her eyes flew to his and for a moment neither of them moved. Her touch sent a wave of heat through his body. Reluctantly, he took the plate, and his hand, away from hers.

"Thank you, Justin," she said, turning to face him, her husky voice rather breathless, her amethyst eyes luminous.

Good God, Roane thought as her rose scent assailed him anew. What the devil was she doing, sidling up to him like this? If he did not know better, he could swear she was trying to—But no, of course not. It was Impossible. And yet, could she really want more cheese? He looked down at her face. It was flushed, and several black tendrils escaped their confines. At that moment only the plate he held prevented him from taking her in his arms. And then he glanced briefly down at himself, at the visible evidence of her effect on him. Damnation! This situation was past intolerable.

"Pray do be seated," he rasped, and then pivoted

quickly so that he was behind her. He seated her preemptorily and made his way to the sideboard. He took several deep breaths and determined to take his time about choosing a piece of cheese.

When he turned back to her, he saw that she was toying with her wine glass. She appeared rather restless, pensive. Nonetheless, when he proffered the refilled plate, she smiled her thanks, sliced the cheese, and began to nibble a small wedge. How could she be hungry at a time like this? His own hunger had nothing at all to do with food.

He wondered whatever to say now, but Moriah, her composure once again restored, spoke first.

"My lord, I—I am reminded of a matter which—which—well, we—we have received an invitation to the Crowley ball, you must know," she said, her eyes meeting his.

"Yes, I had hoped you would," he replied, but she went on as if she'd not heard him.

"And I—I *would* make our excuses, except—except that it might look odd—call attention to—to—and then there is Tess to consider. She would be terribly disappointed if—"

"Moriah, whatever are you talking about? Of course you must attend. And I shall very much look forward to dancing with you."

She looked at him, mystified. "Then you will not mind if—"

"Mind?" he blurted, angry now. Did she think him cad enough to cut her in public? "On the contrary, I shall insist upon it. We needs must keep up appearances. And besides, I wish you to save the first waltz for me. It will be the only thing that will make the evening bearable, I am persuaded," he went on, trying to keep his tone light.

She reached for her wine goblet, seemingly flustered, and as she leaned forward Roane was afforded a lovely view of her rounded breasts. He resolutely looked up at her face. She sipped her wine and then set the goblet down.

"For shame, Justin," she parried lightly. "And here is Lady Crowley put to such trouble just to honour you. But I truly doubt whether she will allow the waltz to be played. Here in the country it is still considered rather fast, you must know."

Roane was pleased to note the humour lurking in her eyes, and he replied in kind. "Ah, but I am a very demanding guest of honour. And if I wish the waltz, then the waltz we shall have!" He punctuated his statement by stabbing two capers with his fork and conducting them to his mouth. She laughed and he was mindful of how infrequently she did so. He wanted to touch her, anywhere, but instead he concentrated on spearing several more capers.

"My lord, there is one—one thing more I would discuss with you," she said quietly.

Roane set his fork down and looked up. Her hands were folded calmly in her lap, her eyes watching him steadily, but he was not fooled. "Do you realize, little one, that every time you become a wee bit ill at ease, shall we say, you revert to using my title? Really, my dear, you do give yourself away," he said with a twinkle in his eye.

Her red lips protruded in a delightful pout. "I am *not* 'ill at ease,' *Justin!*" she protested. " 'Tis merely—oh, I suppose I *am* at that. It—it concerns my father."

He merely nodded and after a moment she went on. "His valet and I have been watching him. We've filched the key to the pistol cabinet, but I do not know how much longer—that is, I—you said we might devise a way for him—ah—"

"Yes, yes I did, Moriah, and in truth I have thought much on it," he interjected, understanding at once her discomfort. Despite all, she did not want to have to ask him for anything, and he was furious with himself for not broaching the topic himself. He had actually given it a good deal of thought while Andrew had prattled on at dinner about tenant problems on the earl's estates in Kent. There seemed only one way for the baron to believe his debt was paid, and that was for him to retrieve his own markers. "I think the best course, Moriah, is for your father to win back his markers. Tell him that you — that you sold your pearls and that you wish him to use the sum they yielded to challenge me to another round of piquet."

He withdrew a wad of bills from the pocket of his breeches and placed it on the table next to her plate. "You will not wish to delay, of course, so may I suggest that he invite me to dine tomorrow evening, with the intention of playing afterward? The baron shall enjoy an amazing run of good luck, during which time he shall recoup his fortune. Well, go ahead, my dear, take the notes. You will need them." Roane smiled at her, but Moriah's eyes were fixed on the roll of banknotes. When she looked up at him, her eyes were narrowed in distress and her voice was barely a whisper.

"My — my pearls could not possibly fetch such a sum as this must be."

"Oh," he countered, relieved that that was all that was troubling her. "Well, in that case, tell him — tell him that you found a sapphire bracelet that had belonged to your mother. And I think you should tell him, after he trounces me — and I will allow him to get just drunk enough to believe that — tell him that you will never forget him if he ever gambles again.

176

Somehow we must—"

Roane stopped himself mid-sentence as he realized that she was not attending him. Her eyes were focused again on the wad of banknotes and her body seemed rigid, unmoving. Suddenly he understood that the worth of her pearls had nothing to do with her distress.

He lifted her chin with his forefinger and spoke very softly. "You really must take the money, little one. It is the best—indeed, I am persuaded it is the *only* way." He leaned over and, taking her hand from her lap, pressed it onto the notes. She looked down at her hand and then back at him with tear-filled, anguished eyes. Her voice was so low as to be barely audible. "I—I know it is best, but I—it makes me feel like a—like a—"

"I know," he interjected, a bit too harshly. "But you are not. Nor do I think of you as one. Do you understand, Moriah?" She nodded slowly and he wanted more than anything at that moment to enfold her in his arms. But he dared not; he knew where they would end up if he did. He was amazed at the turmoil of his own feelings. He was unbearably frustrated and furious at himself, at Moriah, at the whole world. And at the same time he felt protective of her in a way he did not understand. But he wished to God he had not made her pay so dearly for his gallantry. Perhaps he should renew his offer. But no, she had begged him not to. Besides, she was a Landon; why did he keep forgetting that?

He watched her slowly slide the banknotes down into the pocket of her gown. Then she reached for her wine glass and drank, still not meeting his eyes.

"I—I shall have to see to it that Finch—Papa's valet, you know—renders him sober enough to listen to me," Moriah said after several moments, her voice

177

suddenly almost matter-of-fact, her eyes now glued to an apple she was trying to slice. It seemed that the pragmatic little miss had returned. "I shall need him to be too muddled to recall that Mama never possessed a sapphire bracelet, but not so muddled that he won't rise to the occasion of another card game," she added with a twinkle in her eye.

Roane was delighted at this further glimpse of her sense of humour, but he somehow regretted the rapid and complete return of her composure. She was so much less vulnerable this way. Nonetheless, he matched her tone as he said, "I am sure you will handle the matter with your accustomed efficiency and aplomb, my dear." He ventured one further sip of his wine and then added, "Come, let us go."

Moriah nodded solemnly and he went to draw her chair back from the table. He guided her by the elbow back to the sitting room and, once there, reached for her cloak, which he'd draped over one of the love seats. She turned to him with a startled look on her face. Oh, Lord, he thought, dropping the cape, here we go again. He did not pretend to misunderstand that look.

He stepped very close to her and spoke softly, not touching her. "I would like nothing more than to — to take you upstairs, little one. But it is late and — and I am, despite all, a gentleman."

"We had a bargain, my 1 — Justin," she countered implacably.

"You have already fulfilled your part of the bargain, Moriah."

She looked at him askance, her glance clearly telling him that one night's . . . company did not a mistress make. Again he did not pretend to misunderstand.

"You must never underestimate yourself, little

178

one," he murmured, and could not resist taking her face in his hands. Her eyes looked deep, luminous, and sensing her distress, he added, "But you must know, there are different kinds of — er — companionship. I have enjoyed this evening very well, and I — I hope we may repeat it." He told himself he'd said that for *her* sake, but in truth he was not at all sure. "I shall look forward to another evening of conversation, or perhaps — " On impulse he asked, "Do you play chess, Moriah?" She looked at him askance again. And well she might, he thought. Whatever possessed him?

"I am persuaded that mistresses do not play chess, Justin," she retorted, and he was a bit taken aback by her bluntness, when he was trying so hard to be delicate, to protect her sensibilities. But he noted that humour again lurked in her eyes. Really, she was quite amazing.

"I asked whether *you* played, Moriah."

"Well, yes, as a matter of fact I do. But I am afraid my skills have become sadly lacking. I have not had a challenging game this age, not since — "

"Let me guess," Roane interrupted, his lips twitching, "not since the departure of the venerable Miss Billingsley."

"Yes!" she exclaimed. "How ever did you know?"

"Just a — er — lucky guess," he replied drily. "I shall be happy to — ah — tutor you in any skills you may be lacking or that Miss Billingsley failed to teach." The double entendre somehow slipped out, and as had happened once before, her mind was all too quick. She colored and swallowed hard. He thought it was time they were leaving.

He swung her cloak round about her shoulders and pulled her close as he fastened it at her throat. Several locks of her thick black hair came undone and he reached up with one hand to tuck them back into place. But instead the hand went to the nape of her neck and he pressed her to him. He brought his lips slowly to hers, determined to exercise restraint, yet needing, desperately needing, some contact with her. He kissed her softly, lightly. She responded warmly and he could feel her body beginning to mold to his. And then the kiss deepened. His free hand came up to caress her back and bare shoulders, and then little explosions of warning went off in his head. He wrenched himself away from her and looked into her eyes. They were half closed, smoky. "You will be my undoing," he rasped. Then, taking a deep breath, he added, almost growling, "Come, let us go."

She was silent as he guided her out of the house and round back to the stable. He put his hands at her waist, as if to help her mount, but instead his eyes searched her face. "Tomorrow night I shall be occupied with your father," he said.

She nodded. "Monday night, then, I shall come." Her voice was low and husky, yet her words did not seem at all forward. Somehow, it was as if each understood that they would meet as soon as possible. And he wondered, as he lifted her easily onto her horse, if that damned "agreement" she always spoke about was her only motivation. He did not really think so, but could he ever be sure?

And what was *his* motivation, for Godsakes? Whatever had become of him, a sane, rational man, agreeing to play chess in the middle of the night with a beautiful woman he had vowed not to touch? It was madness. Why didn't he simply forbid her to come? Why, indeed?

Chapter 17

Andrew rolled from his right side to his left for perhaps the hundredth time, pummeling the pillow with his fist. Damn! Was he never to get any sleep? He'd been tossing about this bed for hours, with sleep no closer to him now than it had been when he bade Justin good night. He'd *never* get used to country hours! Why, it must only lack an hour till dawn, a time when any sane man was just coming home from his club or home from some nice bit o' muslin. The fact that it was also the time when cows and geese and hens awoke ought to have nothing to do with human beings. He pummeled the hapless pillow again and turned onto his back. Justin seemed to have had no problem adjusting to these ungodly hours, blast him!

Well, then, thought Andrew, kicking aside the coverlet savagely and tumbling out of bed, his dear cousin should have no objection to a predawn ride about the fields. It would get Justin ready for the day and Andrew ready for sleep.

The morning air was crisp but pleasant as Andrew made haste to don buckskins, shirt, and boots. It was that hour when one could not be sure whether it was sun or moonlight that faintly lit the sky, but it was enough light for him to dress by. He closed the door softly behind him and hurried to Justin's rooms. He had no compunction about waking his cousin, but nonetheless thought it wise to do it gently. But several turns about Roane's suite, including a dive onto his bed to insure that the dim light was not deceiving him, finally convinced Andrew that his cousin was indeed *not* in his rooms. Nor, it seemed, had he yet been abed.

Had Justin actually beat him to the stables? Or was he doing something ludicrous, like working or even reading? But no, no one would do such a thing in the small hours of the morning. Still . . . Moments later Andrew was downstairs in Justin's study, which he found quite as deserted as his rooms had been. So it must be the stables, he surmised, and then thought with some satisfaction that if Justin were having difficulty sleeping as well, perhaps he would not insist they retire so bloody early this night!

Andrew's walk was naturally light, and so he approached the stables almost silently. He was about to push open the large wooden door of the first set of stalls when he was stopped short by the sounds from within.

"His lordship out again tonight, is he?" Andrew stiffened as the clear words of one of the stable boys rang through the door.

"Reckon so, Tommy. Been gone a while, too, by the looks of it. I've been here nigh on two hours and the stallion was gone afore I come," replied his companion, and Andrew's eyes widened in alarm. Where the devil was Justin?

"Well, he be back afore dawn, Albie, and we best make ourselves scarce when he does come. Ain't no business of ours he wants to set himself up with some fancy piece t' other side of the village," countered Tommy.

Andrew was at once startled and filled with no small amount of awe. Damned, but Justin worked fast! He'd not even been in the neighborhood above a few days and already—

"Well," began Albie, "my cousin Jimmy says—"

"Never you mind what Jimmy says!" came the authoritative voice of Palmer, the head groom. Palmer must have just come in from the back room, and now Andrew heard scuffling noises, as if the stable boys were scrambling to get on with whatever tasks they'd been neglecting. "Boys, boys! I've told you before I'll not have idle gossip in my stables. Nor idle hands neither. Now, why don't you be brushing down his lordship's mount, Tommy? And you, Albie, you finish those saddles straightaway. Do some work for pity sakes, 'stead o' jammerin' away like a gaggle o' geese," old Palmer scolded in that gruff though not frightening way of his. Then he grumbled unintelligibly to himself for a moment, and Andrew could picture his leathery face contorted in a frown as he tried to look fierce.

"Uh, Mr. Palmer, sir, beggin' your pardon," Tommy interrupted, "but, uh, his lordship's mount— it ain't here, see. We was just talking about—"

"What do you mean, it ain't here? Where in blazes *is* it then?"

"His lordship's gone, Mr. Palmer, sir. That's just what we was talkin' about, Albie and me, when you come in. Last night he—"

"Well, well, never you mind about that. More workin' and less talkin' 'swhat I allas say. Now go— to. Go—to!" snapped Palmer, moving closer to the outside door.

At this point Andrew deemed it time to beat a hasty retreat. He reached the house quickly and darted up to his room. Splashing some brandy into a glass, he sat down in a chair by the empty grate and yanked his boots off.

He took a long gulp of the brandy, his mind whirling. He would not ride out now; he might encounter Justin, and it was clear that his cousin wished his privacy. Andrew frowned, more than a little perplexed by Justin's behavior. This secrecy was not like him at all. If he'd wanted to go off to some light o' love, why did he not just say so? Why the charade of "retiring early, old fellow," "keeping country hours" and what? And the night before. Now Andrew thought on it, Justin had been at great pains to ply him with spirits. Why, to be blunt about it, Justin had got him pie-eyed, clean raddled. His head had ached nearly all day. But Justin had been sober enough to hightail it out of Roanbrooke in the middle of the night.

Devil take it! thought Andrew, downing another swig of brandy. What in blazes was going on? Perhaps, he reasoned, Justin merely wanted to be sure of his turf before letting on. But no, his cousin had always had supreme confidence where women were concerned. Then what the devil —

Andrew did not consider himself the most intelligent of men nor the most logical. But he did have good instincts and he had a healthy respect for them. And his instincts told him that something was not right. And he could do nothing. He certainly could not confront Justin, nor would he question any servants. No, he would simply have to sit back and wait upon events. His natural curiosity and exuberance rebelled at the thought, but then his father was always telling him that he had got to learn patience and forbearance. Andrew supposed now was as good a time as any to start.

Moriah nearly collided with Lizzie in the upstairs corridor, for the maid undoubtedly could not see two feet in front of her for the tears clouding her eyes and streaming down her face. "Is it true, miss? Oh, is it true?" she sobbed, her eyes nearly as red as her perennially red cheeks.

"Is *what* true, Lizzie? What's wrong? Whatever are you talking about?" Moriah asked, grasping the girl by her elbows.

"Cook told me, and she had it from her cousin Ellie, who works over t' the Ashford place. Lady Ashford's brother, he — he come to visit last night and told Lady Ashford. And M — Mary, her maid, you know — well, she heard it all, you see, Miss Moriah." Lizzie collapsed in a new fit of sobbing, which Moriah interrupted. Mary might be a premier gossip, but Moriah seriously doubted Lizzie's storytelling capabilities.

"Cook told you *what,* Lizzie?" Moriah demanded, although she was afraid, very afraid, that she knew the answer.

" 'Bout the baron, miss. 'Bout the Abbey. We done for, miss. Rolled up. Fleet Street. Oh, Lor', what's to become of us?" wailed the plump little maid, and in that moment Moriah knew she had done the right thing by going to the viscount. For it was not just her own family who depended on her, on the Abbey and the living it provided. There were so many others. Lizzie and Mrs. Trotter, Reeves, who was too old to go elsewhere . . .

Oh, Lord, she thought, wrenching her mind back to the problem at hand and realizing that if Lizzie was in this state, no doubt the news had already spread belowstairs, as it had at the Ashfords. By midday not a soul for miles around would be ignorant of the fact that the Baron Landon had finally lost his entire fortune.

She squelched the impulse to break down and rail at the vicissitudes of fate; could not this news have been kept from Herefordshire one day longer? But such thoughts were futile and would avail her nothing. She could not control the frenzy of gossip that would no doubt seize the neighborhood, but at the least she could control her own household. The staff had long since been pared to the minimum, and those that remained were utterly loyal. And so Moriah deemed it prudent to take a chance.

She gave Lizzie a gentle shake, still grasping her arms. "Lizzie, you must listen to me. 'Tis very important, but not a word of this must go beyond the household. We are not yet at our last prayers. I—I have a plan." Moriah whispered this last, hoping to spark the girl's curiosity. The ploy worked, for the sobs abruptly stopped and Lizzie blinked back her tears.

"A plan, miss? What kind of plan?"

"I cannot tell you, Lizzie. And it may not work. But if it does, well, we shall be out of the basket. But, mind you, keep mum. Not a word of this must leave the household, lest it spoil everything." She thought that, where loyalty ended in keeping everyone silent, a love of intrigue would take over. Lizzie looked rather wide-eyed at her mistress and then finally nodded, her sobs now the merest whimper, and Moriah gave an inward sigh of relief.

But there was naught Moriah could do about the news of her father's ruin. Indeed, she'd known all along that it would inevitably come to Herefordshire.

She ought to be grateful the reprieve had been as long as it had. After all, Papa had been home more than a se'ennight. For now, she realized she faced a more immediate problem. She dismissed Lizzie and began a purposeful march down the corridor. It was time, she knew, to prepare for a siege of creditors, Sunday or no.

She heard her name being bleated before her foot had touched the last step of the main stairwell.

"Miss Moriah. Oh, there you be, miss, praise the Lor'. Cook's gone aft 'im with a broom, she 'as, mort o' good 'tis done. Big cove 'e is, just stands there like there be no more'n a fly ter disturb 'im," blurted Millie, the scullery maid and Cook's only help in the kitchen. She was also the only maid from London, and Moriah still found it difficult to understand her after nearly a year.

Moriah did not exactly feel up to calming another incoherent servant in the throes of the vapors. "Calm yourself, Millie," she replied, repressing a sigh. "And tell me what you're talking about. It sounded as if you said Cook is attacking someone with a *broom*. Really, you must speak more slowly and clearly." Millie sniffed, pulling a crumpled handkerchief from the pocket of her apron and savagely attacking her small freckled nose with it.

"That's right, Miss Moriah. With a broom, just like I says. But it don't make no never mind, y' know. 'Imself just stands there a-bellowin'. And such a big cove, take up the 'ole doorway, 'e does."

"Who, Millie? Who is Cook attacking with the broom?" demanded Moriah, becoming exasperated.

"Why Mr. Soames, miss. The butcher, y' know," replied the girl, as if the matter were perfectly obvious. "Come for 'is blunt, 'e 'as. Says as 'ow 'e bain't leavin' without it. Big cove, 'e is, not afeared o' nowt, just stands there like—"

"Very well, Millie," Moriah interrupted briskly. "I shall see to the matter presently. And you must go and wash your face and then return to your chores." Moriah did not repeat what she had told Lizzie. She could not be sure whether Millie had yet heard of the baron's disgrace, and she did not wish to be the one to enlighten her. As to Moriah's own plan, Millie would hear of that soon enough as well. "And you are not to trouble yourself about Mr. Soames or any financial matters concerning this household. I shall handle everything," Moriah concluded.

"Oh, but miss, they all be sayin' belowstairs that the master—that 'e—oh—" Millie began to spurt like a watering pot again, and Moriah tried to calm her own growing impatience.

"Never you mind, Millie. I shall take care of everything. But you shall help me greatly if you will go about your tasks as always and not gossip outside this household about these matters. Is that clear?"

Millie attacked her nose with the rather soggy handkerchief again, bobbed a "yes, miss," and scurried off.

Moriah did not waste a moment in reflection but, gathering up her skirts and her courage at the same time, followed the maid to the kitchens. Under normal circumstances she would have sent someone down there to convey the butcher abovestairs to her. But she could not trust Millie to be coherent. And Moriah instinctively knew Mrs. Trotter would be hidden under a pile of linens in the furthest supply closet. The housekeeper was a gem at stretching a pound note and running a large household on a skeletal staff. But she ran like a frightened rabbit at the sign of any creditor. Reeves was simply too old for this sort of thing, and so as Moriah descended the narrow stairs to the kitchens, she knew that she was very much on her own. Even Millie disappeared somewhere into the shadows, where Moriah knew she would remain till the storm passed.

Millie's description had been apt. The large form of the butcher loomed threateningly in the rear doorway. His stern, craggy face and bloodied once-white apron made him look even more intimidating. And indeed, Cook stood before him, her mob cap askew, her rotund form fairly shaking with rage, as she gripped the broom handle and shook the over-worn straw bristles near the unyielding face of Mr. Soames.

"I'll not be leavin' till I've got what I come for, Mrs. Briggs. Now you just put away that mangy broom and see I gets me blunt. You know 'swell as I what happens t' them as don't pay their debts." It was not so much his words but the contorted rage on his face that was near-chilling in its menace.

Cook staggered back a foot, but she kept the broom aloft. "You'll get your money, Mr. Soames, like you allas do. But I won't be disturbin' the mistress this day, so you go on and take yerself off. Ain't no need to take on so and—"

The butcher frowned prodigiously. "You best go straight away to your mistress and—"

"Good day to you, Mr. Soames," Moriah said as pleasantly as she could, and stepped forward to reveal herself.

The expression on the butcher's face changed so completely and abruptly that Moriah almost laughed. Cook dropped the broom, and her mouth dropped open simultaneously.

"Well, that be better now. Good mornin' to you, Miss Landon," he said magnanimously, tipping the shapeless black cap that sat on his head and bowing slightly. That formality completed, he did not waste a moment in casting a smug, superior look toward Cook.

Cook whirled around to Moriah. "Miss, you oughtn't t' trouble yerself with this. I can—"

"I know, Mrs. Briggs," interrupted Moriah kindly. "And you know how well I value your services. But I *am* here, and so I might as well speak to Mr. Soames myself. However, I do not care to stand about in this manner. Thank you, Mrs. Briggs, for—er—occupying Mr. Soames until my arrival. If you will please conduct Mr. Soames abovestairs to the morning room, I shall receive him there."

The butcher almost smiled and poor Briggs nearly had the apoplexy, but she hastily clamped her mouth shut on the words of outrage forming there and bobbed a cursty, or as much of one as her bulk would allow, to her mistress.

Moriah smiled at them both, and then turned with great dignity and repaired back to the stairwell, and then on to the morning room. She had time only to seat herself at her large mahogany desk and set her face into a mask of composure before she heard Cook's vigourous rap at the door. She bade them enter and within a moment was left alone with Mr. Soames. He stood tall before her desk, but his determined look was belied by the nervous way he fingered his cap. Moriah knew that, Cook's umbrage notwithstanding, she had made the correct decision in insisting they speak abovestairs. Here, she had the advantage of Mr. Soames, for the elegance of the surroundings put the butcher at ill-ease. Regardless of the Landons' financial straits, the highly polished mahogany, the fine Belgian carpets, the air of distinction about the room, could not help but remind him of their rank and station. And the mere fact of his being received abovestairs ought to placate him enough so that at the very least he would remember his manners.

"Pray be seated, Mr. Soames," she said politely. He carefully backed his large form, bloodstained apron and all, into the leather armchair she indicated. His grey eyes were uncertain, but he did not lower them as he waited for her to speak, and his stern jaw was set rather implacably.

"Now then, Mr. Soames," she began, her arms folded on the desk in front of her, "I will not dissemble with you. I well understand why you have come." The butcher eyed her suspiciously but did not dare speak. "But I must tell you that all is not as it seems. We are not, you see, quite at our last prayers." She smiled as she spoke but his frown of disbelief only deepened, causing his face to look even more craggy and not altogether pleasant.

"I only come for me due, Miss Landon. And past due at that," he ventured gruffly, twisting his cap in his large hands. "Meanin' no disrespect, miss, but — well, what with all the talk, a body can hardly be blamed now, can he?"

"No, as I said, I quite understand, Mr. Soames. Now, if you will but hear me out, I think we may come to some accord," she said with far more calm and confidence than she felt. The butcher's expression did not change, however, and he shifted uncomfortably in his chair.

Impulsively, Moriah decided that sitting behind the desk was indeed not the best way to conduct this interview. She rose and walked calmly to the front. Mr. Soames was obliged to stand as well, and they stood facing each other, several feet apart. She had to look up to speak to him, but he seemed more relaxed, which was all to the good. She supposed no man appreciated being spoken to by a woman seated behind a desk. It was quite absurd, but there it was.

She clasped her hands at her waist and continued in a voice that was calm but strong, a voice of authority. "The fact is, Mr. Soames, that I have some funds of my own, put aside for such a day as I might need them." His eyebrows lifted, whether in surprise or disbelief she did not know. She ignored the gesture and went on. "I do not have the money just yet, but I have sent to London for it. And then, you see, I shall have enough to pay you and several others. I assume you will be reasonable enough to wait a mere se'en-night longer, Mr. Soames, is that not so?" She paused for breath, rather appalled that she had so easily been able to tell such an outright clanker.

Mr. Soames drew himself up even taller, but his jaw had rather slackened. He was routed and he knew it. "Well now, miss, if you're certain it's only a se'ennight more you'll be needin' . . . "

"I believe I made that clear, Mr. Soames," she said quietly, any relief at her victory tempered by the knowledge that, for the first time in her life, she had made a promise she did not know if she could keep. "Oh, but there is one thing more you must know. I would that you keep silent about—about what I have told you. You see, my funds are not unlimited, and if word should be got about—well, then, I should be obliged to divide whatever I have amongst several—er—people. And I really would prefer to pay you in full, Mr. Soames, for you have always provided excellent service. You do understand, Mr. Soames?"

The craggy face had broken into a smile. "Oh, indeed I do, Miss Landon. Mum's the word, you know."

Moriah tried to smile in return. She dismissed the butcher as quickly and politely as she could. When

192

he had gone she closed the door behind him and leaned back against it with a deep sigh. It was not one of relief. She had bought time, but that was all. The fact of her father recouping his losses would not put extra money in her pocket. She did not know what she would do about Mr. Soames next week. And as to the other creditors, she fervently hoped Cook and her broom could dispatch them summarily.

In the meantime she had work to do. She turned and yanked the door open. She had got to set the stage, as it were, for tonight. She proceeded briskly down the corridor toward the main stairwell. She had given Finch her orders early this morning and hoped that by now he had succeeded in carrying them out. The poor man had been scandalized when she'd said she wished Papa slightly drunk, but not so pie-eyed that he could not understand what she was saying.

Oh dear, she thought, if that simple request so took him aback, what *would* he say—indeed, what would any of them say—if they knew where she'd spent the last two nights? She shuddered at the thought, but in the next moment she was angry. Dammit all! At least they'd have a roof over their heads! What right had they to judge her actions? But her anger and the bravado that accompanied it soon subsided. No one would understand, she thought. She was not quite sure she understood it all herself.

Chapter 18

It had not been easy for Moriah to cut through the veil of self-pity that her father had drawn about himself and convince him to meet Lord Roane this night. Papa had mumbled about how it was all to no avail. Moriah could not possibly have come upon so much money as another game would require, no matter what she sold, and he was like to lose it again at all events. Moriah had reassured him for several long fruitless minutes that his luck had been down and would in all likelihood change. Finally she had drawn the wad of banknotes from the pocket of her dress.

Papa had stared at the notes and then at Moriah, his eyes blinking with sudden dawning hope. "Where—ah—where did you—what did you say you sold, my dear?" he had asked, swallowing hard.

She had repeated her well-rehearsed Banbury tale about a sapphire bracelet of Mama's, but she realized that Papa was no longer attending. A strange kind of light had come into his eyes, and Moriah knew that he was in his own world, making plans and dreaming dreams. She had given him hope; it pleased her but at the same time rather frightened her. If Papa grew this excited about another game, another chance, how would she keep him from further gaming once he had, in his mind, recouped his fortune? For this time she knew that somehow she must do just that. In a way she knew that deep down Papa would want her to do so, to protect him from himself, as it were.

Now, as she watched Papa descend the wide staircase in anticipation of the viscount's arrival, she gave an unwitting sigh. Papa looked quite dapper tonight in his black coat and knee breeches. If he appeared perhaps too formal for the country, Moriah said nothing. His black and white and gold embroidered waistcoat, though several years old, still fit him perfectly. It was amazing, she thought, that Papa's propensity for drink had never gone to his stomach. But his eyes were another matter, for they were still quite red. Nonetheless there was a gleeful look to them and a smile of anticipation on his lips.

He looked, Moriah reflected briefly, not altogether unlike a child who knew he was about to receive a much awaited present. She sighed again. It was really very difficult to have to be parent to one's own father.

Moriah proceeded her father into the drawing room. The fire had been lit and the tapers burned in the wall sconces that hung between the raised panels along the pale green walls. Moriah's eyes swiftly surveyed the room which, for all of its formality, was given a sense of warmth by the thick mint green and gold carpet that covered much of the parquet floor, and by the profusion of chintz fabric that had been used to adorn the windows and several skirted tables. The room had a certain delicacy about it. The Queen Anne chairs were especially fine, as were the Dresden figurines that stood upon the mantel and the mahogany sofa table. And there was a certain timelessness to the room as well. Moriah guessed that the drawing room had looked very much the same for nigh on to a hundred years. There was an unwritten rule at the Abbey that a new bride might redecorate to her heart's content, but the drawing room was not to be touched except, of course, for occasional refurbishing. And even that had to be done with an eye toward retaining the original look of the room. It was a room, she thought, that spoke volumes about the enduring quality of Wykham Abbey.

Since Mama's death and what with Papa away so much, the drawing room had been little used. She was glad Papa had decided to gather here before dinner. It was, she reflected, appropriate for the viscount's first visit to the Abbey.

At that thought she felt a strange fluttering in her stomach, and with it a wave of mixed emotions that was most disconcerting. Not wishing anyone to see her face, she moved to the great front window, tugged aside the heavy draperies, and stared unseeing into the night. She felt great pride in her home, 'twas true, and she knew that the viscount's coming here tonight would mean that the Landons would be able to keep that home. But she could not help the feeling of sadness and even apprehension that was beginning to creep over her at the thought of meeting Lord Roane like this, as if they were strangers. And sadness, too, that his first visit to Wykham Abbey was for such a purpose as this, and not — not . . .

Her ruminations were interrupted by the sound of the baron's voice ordering the sherry. Moriah turned to see him stroll into the room with Tess on his arm, a smile lighting his face. Moriah caught her breath at the sight of them, for Tess in that moment looked so like their mother that it was quite uncanny. She wore her only dinner gown, a pale yellow jaconet round dress, which set off her budding figure admirably. And then Moriah realized that it was Tess's hairstyle that made the resemblance so strong, for tonight she had eschewed her usual simple way of pulling her hair back with a ribbon and instead had had her blond locks bound up in a series of coiled ringlets not at all unlike the style their mother had worn. Moriah wondered if Papa had noticed.

Moriah shook her head in amazement as she thought of how like their mother Tess really was. For following her interview with Papa, Moriah had steeled herself to speak with Tess. Much as she dreaded to do so, she could not very well allow Tess to hear of Papa's debacle through the servants' gossip. Tess had taken the news surprisingly well, although in retrospect it was not at all surprising, for she had reacted much the way Mama would have. And of course, the imminent opportunity for Papa to recoup had softened the blow considerably.

"Oh, poor Papa! How devastated he must have felt! And I shudder to think what might have happened to us if — oh, but you are a marvel, Moriah. How you contrive as you do, I vow I do not know. To have had that bracelet all these years and never said a word! And then to sell it without a qualm when we most need it — oh, I *know* Papa will win tonight! I am sure of it!" Tess had exclaimed, quite innocently.

Those thoughts aside, what struck Moriah forcibly now, as she watched Tess come forward with Papa, was that her sister was growing up, very, very rapidly. Moriah felt some of the earlier tension leaving her body. She had done what had to be done for her home and family, and she was glad of it.

Nonetheless, she remained at her place near the window when the viscount was announced several minutes later. As Lord Roane strolled into the room, she felt the fluttering in her stomach again. He looked every inch the powerful, confident lord he was. He wore cream-colored breeches and shirt and a coat of dark green superfine that bespoke both superb tailoring and a superb body. She lowered her eyes quickly at that thought and those that followed rapidly. Really, she must not dwell on — on that aspect of her relationship with the viscount, not if she were to meet him socially with any equanimity at all.

Papa stood at the main hearth in the center of the room, with Tess seated just to the side. Lord Roane crossed the wide expanse of room to reach them in several leisurely strides. He had not yet seen Moriah and she remained where she was as Papa extended his hand in greeting.

"Evening, Roane. Welcome to Wykham Abbey," Papa said genially as the two men shook hands.

"Good evening, Landon. Thank you for your invitation," Roane replied evenly, though he was suddenly assailed by a tumble of mixed emotions. He was here at Wykham Abbey for the first time. For years he had anticipated the downfall of the Landons, and now that he had achieved that very goal, he was about to throw it all aside for—for what? What was wrong with him? The sixth baron, Thomas Landon's father, had ruined Roane's mother and killed his father. It was only just that his heir should suffer.

Roane felt stone cold as he shook hands with Thomas Landon and watched a beautiful young girl come to stand next to him. Moriah's sister, Roane surmised, and felt his jaw clench. His own sister Nell would have been much older, of course, but still, would not her hair have been just that color, her features just as delicate? What the devil was he doing here, preparing to virtually hand back the Abbey to—

"May I present my daughters?" Landon was saying, and Roane heard the rustle of skirts in the shadows. He turned and watched Moriah come forward.

Suddenly he felt the cold leave him and in its place a strange warmth seeped through his body. She did not look up but still he knew that her eyes would be luminous, perhaps a bit distressed, in the evening light. He longed to reassure her, to touch her; he wished everyone else at Jericho. Unwittingly Roane found himself forgetting all about the sixth baron. They had made a bargain, Moriah and he, and he would keep it. Then he mentally shook himself, confused. For it wasn't just that damned bargain and he knew it.

Moriah knew that if she didn't hurry, Papa would be forced to introduce his younger daughter first. Papa was a bit of a stickler in his own way, and not wishing to distress him, she glided to the hearth in a rustle of primrose silk taffeta. Besides, she told herself bracingly, it was unlike her to behave so—so cowardly as to hang back in the near shadows.

"Ah, Moriah, my dear, here you are," Papa was saying as she came upon the group, her eyes fixed on Papa. "My elder daughter, Miss Moriah Landon," he said to Lord Roane. "Moriah, this is the Viscount Roane, our neighbor."

Only then, as the viscount took her hand, did she raise her eyes to his face.

"It is my pleasure, Miss Landon," he said in the most polite of tones. His face was impassive, betraying not a flicker of emotion, but when her eyes met his her heart began suddenly to hammer in her chest. She had expected his eyes to be as cool and clear blue as his expression was bland. But there was nothing cool about those eyes. They were warm, a deep dark blue that held hers for one very long, intense moment. And then she caught the faintest glimmer of a smile on his handsome, resolute face. Was it a smile of reassurance? He squeezed her hand for a brief moment before letting it go. As the warmth of his hand left her she realized that she had better say something.

"How do you do, Lord Roane?" she managed in a somewhat steady voice. She wondered whether anyone could hear the pounding in her chest and chided herself for being foolish.

Roane turned as Papa made the introduction to Tess, and Moriah had a moment to compose herself. She was only moderately successful and was grateful when Reeves appeared with the sherry. The company remained in the drawing room chatting idly for no more than a quarter of an hour, but Moriah could not say later whether she had uttered one coherent sentence.

Dinner was, unfortunately, not very much better, although it did not seem that anyone else felt so strained as she did. Certainly one could not fault the surroundings, nor the food. The dining room with its rose damask wallcovering was a lovely backdrop for the fine white Belgian lace tablecloth and the rose-tinted crystal that Mama had loved. Moriah had reviewed the menu with Cook this morning, and she thought the braised goose with glazed root vegetables excellent. Papa, she noted, had made his own foray to the kitchens, adding one more course, the poached turbot, to the meal. Moriah sigh inwardly. They had almost lost the very roof over their heads, but Papa insisted on serving a full and proper meal to their guest, his role in Papa's debacle notwithstanding. Or perhaps it was *because* of his role in Papa's downfall. . . . She supposed it was just one more example of that strange sense of honour peculiar to men.

Yes, here, she thought, were all the elements for a pleasant, relaxed meal. Even the company seemed determined to charm one another. Yet she knew the charm was all on the surface, and she felt anything but relaxed.

Papa played his role as host to the hilt. One would never have known, unless one looked very closely at the bloodshot eyes and the lines of weariness surrounding them, that he had a care in the world. She did not know when she had last seen Papa in such seeming good spirits. And then she realized that it was probably not all an act. No doubt Papa actually believed his luck was about to turn. That hope—the thought that with the turn of a few cards he would be on top of the world again—had been enough to completely revitalize him. Moriah did not know whether to be pleased or horrified.

"And have you found Roanbrooke to have faired well in your absence, Roane? Your man of affairs seems a pleasant enough chap, not likely to have problems with the tenants, eh what?" Papa was saying.

Now, how in the world did Papa know that? Moriah wondered. She wasn't even sure Papa had ever *met* Lord Roane's agent, but in point of fact, he was quite an amiable man. Good thing, too, Moriah thought tartly, for it was up to him to placate tenants distraught over certain much needed repairs that had not been attended to because the viscount was so long in absentia. Immediately, Moriah felt ashamed of such an ungenerous thought. True, there might be some neglect, but things did seem to run fairly smoothly on the viscount's lands. Moriah's eyes shifted from her father to Lord Roane, who put down his glass of claret and proceeded to answer Papa.

"My agent is, as you say, a 'pleasant enough' fellow and, I might add, quite capable of carrying out rather complex and frequent long distance orders." Lord Roane's voice was decidedly civil, his expression bland, his eyes a cool blue, but Moriah sensed nonetheless the intensity beneath his words. He would be unfailingly polite, while at the same time making it clear that he had not, as was generally believed, neglected his home.

Lord Roane seemed to consider his statement the final and definite word on the subject of his affairs, for he very subtly shifted the topic, saying, "I gather that Wykham Abbey had a rather fascinating history, Landon. When exactly does it date from?"

Lord Roane neatly sliced a piece of his braised goose and awaited a reply. Moriah was grateful that he was exerting himself to be such congenial, even charming company. She knew well that he had little liking and even less respect for Papa, and so she could only conclude that Lord Roane was a consummate actor. She found the idea most disconcerting.

Her train of thought was immediately diverted, however, when she glanced across the table at Papa. He had become very tense, and she realized why. He reached unsteadily for his wine goblet and downed nearly all the claret in one gulp. He had been riding on a crest of blustering confidence all evening, dashed only now as it suddenly dawned on him that the viscount might have been asking about Wykham because it was soon to be *his*.

"Ah—Wykham, d—did you say, Roane?" Papa fairly stammered, and downed more of his wine. He glanced quickly about the room, then at Moriah and Tess, and Moriah thought he seemed to relax a bit. His eyes took on a faraway, almost dreamy look for a moment, and then he turned to Lord Roane. She did not know whether it was the wine or a resurgence of hope as he contemplated the coming card game, but when next he spoke, he was once more the carefree host.

"Truth is, Roane, Moriah's the family historian.

She could write tomes about Wykham, I'll wager. Worked on one of those guidebooks, you must know. It was thirteenth century, was it not, my dear?" he concluded, looking proudly across to where she sat at the foot of the table.

Moriah was flabbergasted. Papa was always chiding her for her "unladylike" interest in local history, and here he was positively boasting of her accomplishments! She mentally shook her head. Male honour and pride again, she supposed. There were some things she would *never* understand about men.

The Abbey was usually a subject upon which Moriah could speak most eloquently. But she found that she had to take a sip of wine to fortify herself. It was the viscount's eyes, she decided, that so disconcerted her, for they became a very deep, warm blue whenever his gaze fell on her. And that had happened rather too often for her own peace of mind this evening. His mere presence, and especially those piercing eyes, had the strangest effect on her heartbeat. It was difficult enough to deal with him in private, but in public it positively unnerved her. He was gazing at her very intently right now, and she detected that glimmer of a smile again. She realized that he had asked his question deliberately to draw her into the conversation.

"It was indeed thirteenth century, Papa," she began, as steadily as she could, and then directed her gaze to the viscount. "Wykham was founded by the Cistercians, my lord. It was abandoned at the Dissolution for nearly a century, as were most all the abbeys in the region. We have every reason to believe that the Landons have been here ever since."

"It would seem that the Landons have preserved as much as possible of the original Abbey. That was a portion of the gatehouse I saw out front, to the left of the house, was it not?" he asked with keen interest.

Moriah answered in the affirmative and was grateful when he next turned his attention to Tess. Moriah did not wish to become involved in an earnest discussion with the viscount, nor did she wish to give him the opportunity to request a guided tour of the Abbey. She glanced momentarily at Papa, who was regarding her with a most speculative glance. Oh, Lord, she thought, she hoped Papa would not suggest such a tour.

"And you, Miss Tess, do you share your sister's interest in history, or do you find other occupations more to your liking?" Lord Roane asked. Moriah marveled at the softness of his tone, calculated, she knew, to set Tess at her ease.

Actually, Moriah thought Tess was acquitting herself rather well this evening. Pleased to have a dinner guest for the first time in a great while—and a gentleman guest at that—she seemed to be quite enjoying herself. She had answered the viscount's gentle compliments very prettily, and Moriah thought her remarkably poised for one so young. Nonetheless, Moriah was not quite prepared for the fluttering eyelashes nor the decidedly languorous tone with which Tess answered the viscount.

"I am afraid I have not a fraction of Moriah's energy, my lord. I declare we are all quite in awe of her, for she runs the household and sees to the tenants, and *still* has time to read all those musty journals. I fear my accomplishments are more in the nature of playing a tune on the pianoforte. And I am told I have a fine hand with a needle, my lord," she concluded demurely.

Oh Lord, thought Moriah, she's flirting with him. It was not Tess's words that distressed Moriah.

204

Though the same words uttered by one such as Olivia Crowley might be catty, and even caustic, Tess's voice was sweet and Moriah knew that her sister genuinely *was* in awe of her. No, what distressed Moriah was the realization Tess was going to be very difficult in the next few years if she was not able to meet eligible young men.

The Viscount Roane was *not* eligible, of course, but at all events Moriah had no fear that he was taking Tess seriously. The compliments that he had paid her in the drawing room and once at dinner might well have been uttered by a fond uncle to his niece, and he was regarding her with a bemused look on his face. His gaze shifted a moment to Moriah, and she caught the unmistakable twinkle in his eye meant, she knew, only for her. Their eyes locked for one moment, and there passed between them a look that was profoundly intimate in the shared under-standing it conveyed.

That look was nearly Moriah's undoing. She felt that increasingly familiar warmth course through her body and did not see how she could continue to carry on polite conversation. She was greatly relieved when the pastries and trifle were removed, for that was the signal for the ladies to leave the gentlemen to their port. Now, Moriah hoped, as she and Tess took their leave, the evening could begin in earnest. That is, she hoped Papa would remember what this evening was all about and broach the subject of cards with the viscount. She gave her father a speaking look as she departed, carefully avoiding Lord Roane's eyes alto-gether.

Once in the Blue Saloon, Moriah sipped her coffee distractedly while Tess chattered away about the vis-count.

"So elegant of manner, Moriah, do you not think

205

so?" she asked enthusiastically. "And he must have been very good-looking when he was younger, I should think."

Moriah nearly spilled her coffee at this last statement, but merely murmured something noncommittal, reminding herself that at Tess' age, anyone over twenty seemed ancient. Tess seemed unaware and continued prattling about the viscount. Moriah knew, though, as she listened, that Tess was in no danger of losing her heart. She was merely enjoying her first flirtation, and a very mild one at that. Moriah sighed almost imperceptibly. It was just as well that she herself would never have a Season. Light flirtation was not, she was certain, her forte. But as for Tess . . .

It was a few minutes before the gentlemen joined them, but they declined coffee, as she'd known they would. Papa informed them, as nonchalantly as he could, "The viscount has agreed to play a few rounds of piquet, eh what?" and she and Tess rose as if on cue to leave them to their play.

Moriah assiduously avoided the viscount's eyes as polite "good nights" were said all around, but he insisted on holding the door for them. Tess exited first, and as Moriah passed through the doorway, Lord Roane murmured, so that only she could hear, "Good night, little one. Sleep well." The intimate words sent a ripple of warmth through her body, and her eyes, as if of their own volition, flew up to meet his. The look he gave her made her feel very weak, and she knew that she would definitely not sleep very well, if at all.

Chapter 19

In the event, it was not just the strange sensations that the viscount evoked which kept her awake. She had feigned tiredness when Tess had invited her to her room for a "comfortable cose," for she did not feel at all like company. And she had remained impatiently silent as Lizzie helped her prepare for bed. She bade Lizzie leave her hair loose, not having the patience to sit and have it plaited. Finally, the maid slid her scooped neck ivory lawn nightgown over her head and held out her beautiful rose silk dressing gown, the one that had been Mama's, for Moriah to slip into.

Moriah breathed a sigh of relief once she was alone, but she could not relax. Pulling the sash of the dressing gown tight, she found herself pacing her bedchamber floor, unable to stand still, much less climb into bed. Moriah was, to put it mildly, rather worried. What if Papa discovered the ruse? What if he played so poorly that Lord Roane could not possibly let him win? What if . . .

Oh, this was ridiculous! Moriah chided herself. She determinedly sat down on the violet satin coverlet of the bed and took several deep breaths. She would make herself ill with such frenzied speculation. What she ought to do was to go downstairs, quietly, just to be sure that all was going well. She sprang up and walked to the door and opened it a crack. She could still hear movement in the corridors and she fancied she heard whispered voices coming from somewhere downstairs. Servants' voices. She could not imagine why they were still there—the dining room ought to have been cleared by now. And then it hit her that perhaps she was not the only one in the household who couldn't sleep. She had seen several startled looks today as it became known among the servants that the viscount was coming for dinner. For they knew well that it was he who had won the Abbey from Papa.

And now that the two men were once again engaged in play—well, she thought, it was a wonder the servants weren't all lined up in the corridors outside the Blue Saloon this very moment, their ears pressed to the door. Actually, she could not imagine dignified old Reeves stooping to such undignified activity. Nor the no-nonsense Mrs. Trotter, for that matter. And Finch was such a stickler, but still, where the master's welfare was so closely concerned . . . And as to the others, she had no trouble at all picturing Lizzie and Cook and Millie, even Hodges from the stables, unabashedly eavesdropping.

Resolutely, Moriah closed the door and marched herself to the Hepplewhite chair near one of the rear windows in her chamber. She, of course, would never for one minute consider eavesdropping. It was simply not done. And yet, she certainly could not sleep, not with so much at stake.

The floral curtains were open, as was the window, for it was a warm, breezy night. Moriah pulled the chair close to the window and sat down. She stared out into the night, letting the soft breeze waft over her face and her throat, bare where her dressing gown gaped open. She was being silly, really. Lord Roane would not let her down. No, he would not mean to, but what if . . .

No! She would not allow her thoughts into that direction again. She focused them instead on the viscount, on Justin, on his firm, square jaw, his expressive blue eyes, his broad shoulders and muscular torso . . . Oh dear, she thought, as that increasingly familiar feeling swept through her, better not think about *that* either. She was a well-bred young lady, after all.

I'll read, she decided, and jumped up to fetch a book and a taper from her bedside table. She settled herself near the window once again and there remained for some time, but she could not, at each turn of the page, recall a word of what she had just read.

She did not know how much time had passed before she became aware that the house was very quiet. Very quiet indeed. She put down her book, rose slowly from her chair, and softly crossed the room. Once again she opened the door just a tad and listened. Silence. Neither movement nor voices. Gathering her dressing gown close to her body, she tiptoed into the corridor, careful to close the door behind her.

She did not allow herself to think as she silently and carefully trod the stairs, glad that the wall sconces were still lit, since carrying a taper would have gone a fair way toward announcing her arrival. She would not eavesdrop, she assured herself as she moved along the main floor corridor. She would simply ascertain that all was well, and then she would go to sleep!

The house was eerily silent and only faintly lit as she crept toward the Blue Saloon. She was only a few feet away when she became aware of voices. She darted closer, cocking her head to make out the words.

"A very good claret, Landon," the viscount said smoothly. "My compliments."

Papa mumbled something unintelligible in reply, and Moriah knew he was rather in his cups. At least that part of the plan had come off all right. She realized, as she leaned against the door, that her body was completely stiff, and she willed herself to relax. She could not, after all, maintain such a rigid body pose for long, and she had not yet heard what she wanted to.

It seemed that she waited for a very long time, surrounded by complete silence. She kept shifting her weight from her right foot to her left to keep from cramping, and rubbing her arms to keep at bay the cold that had crept into the corridor. Why didn't they speak loud enough for her to hear? Why must they play in muffled whispers? Damn! But the only intelligible sound from within was the occasional slapping down of a playing card on the table or the crystal wine decanter clanging onto the silver tray. Her mind was too occupied for her to sleep, her body too uncomfortable, but she felt as if a kind of stupor descended over her as she waited and waited . . .

The voice that finally broke the silence was smooth and assured. "I'm afraid the rubber is mine once again, Landon." Her body jerked itself into an alert, tense position at the viscount's words. Something was wrong, dreadfully wrong. It was too late in the evening for the viscount still to be winning. The tide should have long since turned to Papa's favour.

Lord Roane's next words did not dispel her unease one iota. "Care to double the stakes, Landon?" he asked in a cold voice that was very unlike the voice she had come to know.

"Double s—stakes," echoed Papa, sounding like he had a mouthful of marbles. "Why not? Cap'tal idea. Cap'tal idea. I sh'll win, y' know. Double s—stakes it is." Oh Lord, Moriah thought, Papa was truly foxed, beyond sense and beyond caring.

"We shall see, Landon, we shall see," replied Lord Roane with a silkiness that was somehow chilling.

Moriah shivered and ran her hands up and down her arms. An agonizing silence followed the viscount's words. She pressed her ear to the door but heard nothing save the shuffling of the cards. My God, she thought, whatever was going on in there? What was the viscount doing? Her common sense told her that he would not betray her, that all would go according to plan. After all, the viscount had nothing to gain by winning again; it was all his money in the first place. And the game—the whole ruse, in fact—had been his idea. Besides, though he had taken her as his mistress, something no decent gentleman would ever have done, he was simply not the sort of man who would betray her. Somehow she knew that.

But even so she could not still the stirrings of anxiety that were constricting her chest, nor could she move from where she stood. She *had* to hear more, had to be certain that—

"And Cook said as I was ter look for the soup tureen, she did, Lizzie. Says as 'ow mayhap 'twere left in the dining room, don't you know." The scullery maid spoke in a whisper that was rather too loud, and Moriah felt herself freeze. That was *not* the voice she'd wanted to hear, and she realized that the maids were just around the corner, rapidly approaching the Blue Saloon.

"Well, I might just help you then, Millie, seein' as

211

how I be still up and about. Soup tureen, did you say?" responded Lizzie with an eagerness she rarely applied to her chores.

Soup tureen indeed! thought Moriah, exasperated. They must all be awake belowstairs, sending minions up on fictitious errands, one at a time, to spy on the proceedings within the Blue Saloon. It was positively Gothic, she thought.

Millie and Lizzie left a good deal to be desired as spies, though, for their footfalls were none too light, and as they drew closer, the light of a single taper announced their approach. At this point Moriah forced her stiff joints into action. It would simply not do for the servants to find her here doing exactly what they had come to do! Quickly she stepped back from the door and fairly flew down the corridor away from the approaching light. Her slippers made nary a sound on the wooden floors, and she did not think she drew a breath until she had reached the safety of her bedchamber.

She leaned back against the closed door and took a deep breath. Really, she was behaving absurdly. Everything would be fine, and she ought to go to sleep straight away. She stepped away from the door and took a step toward the canopied bed. But then abruptly she turned around and pulled the door open several inches. She did not know what she expected to hear, but she simply could not go to sleep as if nothing were afoot. She thought she heard faint whispers and the rustling of skirts. Lizzie and Millie, she thought. The soup tureen spies. With a sigh of resignation she backed away from the door and slowly, her limbs beginning to feel heavy with fatigue, she crossed over to the empty hearth and glanced at the hand-painted porcelain clock that sat on the mantel. One-thirty in the morning. Oh, Lord, how long would they play?

She climbed onto her bed but did not allow herself the luxury of snuggling beneath the satin coverlet; she did not wish to fall into a deep slumber. She curled up at the side of the bed, her limbs by now aching but her mind as alert as ever and her ear cocked to the open door. She must have dozed, for she did not hear the soft chime of the clock, announcing the second hour of the morning. She was awake for the single chime of half past the hour, however, and then the treble chime of three o'clock. It was soon after this that she thought she heard scuffling noises, perhaps the bump of a chair against the wall. In one swift, fluid motion she uncurled her body and sat up, her feet, still in her slippers, falling to the floor. She darted to the door and thought she heard voices, muffled male voices. She slipped out into the corridor and crept toward the stairwell. The house seemed darker now, and she moved silently and carefully. She was nearly halfway down the stairs when she heard the viscount's voice.

" . . . old fellow. Up you go. There's a chap now." The viscount seemed to be straining under some physical exertion and in a moment she realized what it was. For she next heard Papa's voice, his words completely garbled but clearly indicating his very drunken state. No doubt he was having as much trouble walking as talking, and Lord Roane was attempting to assist him.

With Papa so completely raddled she realized she need no longer tread stealthily, and besides, at this juncture she surmised that her help might be needed. She pulled her dressing gown more tightly around her and hurried down the stairs.

"All right, old chap. Have it your way. I suppose you . . . " she heard Lord Roane say, and then his voice trailed off, as if they had moved farther away. She hurried along the corridor to the Blue Saloon. The doors were open and several tapers still flickered. Her eyes went immediately to Lord Roane, who was bending over the blue chintz sofa. The back of the sofa faced the door and Moriah surmised that Papa now lay there. The viscount stood up, his eyes still on the sofa. He shook his head and rubbed his brow with his left hand. Then he raised his eyes.

"Moriah!" he blurted in a loud whisper. He came to her in several long strides. "What the devil are you doing here?" he demanded, his hands lightly grasping her upper arms. "You should have been abed hours ago. And you—you—you're not dressed!" he fairly exclaimed, seeming to take a deep breath and holding himself rigidly.

Moriah was not quite sure if he was angry, just merely surprised, or something else. And she did not yet know what the outcome of the game was. She determined to ignore the warmth of his large hands on her arms and the piercing look in his eyes. "I—I couldn't sleep. I heard noises, and I thought perhaps I might be of some help."

"Well, I suppose you can at that," he said, seeming to relax a bit. "Your father is—er—rather—er—"

"Foxed, my lord?"

He frowned at her. "Yes, rather. I was reluctant to ring the bell at this hour, but perhaps you know where his man might be found. I did walk him several paces down the corridor, but I despaired of ever getting him near the stairwell. So, I brought him back here."

"Yes, of course, I shall summon Finch," she said, noting that his eyes gazing down at her had darkened. "But I—ah—the game, my lord? Did everything—"

"What? So formal again, Moriah?" he asked, his voice suddenly husky, his eyes searching her face and then travelling to her throat and beyond. She swallowed hard, realizing that her hair was loose, her dressing gown had quite gaped open, and her thin lawn nightgown with its wide scooped neck was very revealing. His hands had tightened on her arms and he had somehow drawn her closer.

She tried very hard to sound nonchalant. "No, Justin, I—er—just wondered about—about how it went."

His eyes had swept the length of her body, leaving a trail of heat in their wake. Her knees suddenly felt weak and unwittingly she moved closer to him. She knew it wasn't wise, wasn't safe for her to be here with him like this. And yet she had to know.

His breathing was rapid and he seemed to struggle to keep his eyes on her face. "How . . . what went, Moriah?" he rasped.

"The game," she whispered.

He put one hand on her back and pulled her against him. "The game," he echoed absently and began to massage her back.

Moriah was torn between extreme agitation on the one hand and a very strong desire to melt in his arms on the other. Suddenly his hand stopped and he cocked his head, his eyes narrowed.

"Of a certain the game went fine, Moriah. Everything went off just as I said it would."

She breathed what she thought was an imperceptible sigh of relief. Justin looked at her curiously and then very gently but firmly put her away from him, a frown descending again onto his brow. "Did you doubt me, little one? Is that what this is all about?"

"No, I—it's just that I—I couldn't sleep and so—well, I—I happened to overhear you say that the

215

rubber was yours again, and then you doubled the stakes and—"

"Why, you little minx," he murmured, putting his hands on her shoulders. "You've been eavesdropping. Well, then, it serves you right, whatever you heard."

"I have *not* been eavesdropping, Justin!" she protested, stamping her foot lightly but making no attempt to move away from him. "I simply came downstairs and happened to overhear you and—and as for doubting you . . . I . . . truly didn't, you know. But I did fear lest Papa should become wise to the ruse."

"Ah, I see then, little one," he mused, entwining one hand in her long hair. "It is not my good faith you doubt, but rather my skill as an actor."

Moriah did not care to be reminded of his consummate acting ability, and she tried to ignore the ripple of his fingers through her hair and the warmth in his dark eyes. Truly, she ought to betake herself upstairs straightaway. She had heard what she needed to hear, so why did she not move? "You—you must admit it seemed strange that you should still be winning at one o'clock in the morning," she ventured, willing her body not to relax under the gentle massage of his hand on her shoulder.

"In future I shall take it very ill if you doubt me, Moriah," Justin whispered. "Of course, I had to win some of the time. I could not very well simply hand him every rubber on a silver tray, now could I? And, as for doubling the stakes, if I hadn't kept doing that I venture to say we would still be at our play, with no end in sight."

Moriah sighed ruefully. "I—well—I—" she began, but stopped abruptly at the sound of a very strange noise, something between a snort and a groan. Justin's hand immediately left her and he took a step back. She tried to ignore the fact that she felt suddenly bereft. They both turned simultaneously toward the sofa. The sound was most definitely coming from Papa, and Moriah decided that it was more in the nature of a snore.

"I think it time we put your father to bed, little one. And it—it really is not wise of us to stand about in this manner," he said in a low, soft voice. He turned to look at her again and her eyes met his. There was that moment of intensity between them again, as if there were some communication she was not really aware of. She lowered her eyes and forced herself to speak. Whatever was wrong with her, anyway?

"I—I shall summon Finch, Papa's valet," she said, trying to summon up some of her renowned efficiency.

"I shall stay, if you like, until he comes. My only concern is that you are not—that is—the servants—" His eyes swept over her and his voice became husky again. "I think, for more reasons than one, that I should go."

Moriah nodded, hardly trusting herself to speak. "I—Finch and I can handle Papa. Come. I—I will show you to the door." She turned and felt the warmth of his hand at her elbow as he drew close to her and fell into step beside her. Despite his nearness she felt a chill filter through the thick walls of the Abbey and she tried not to shiver. They did not speak until they rounded the corner and descended the stairs into the entry lobby.

"Go to sleep now, little one," he said as they stood facing each other, just inside the large double oak doors of the main entrance. He took a step closer to her and brushed a gentle finger along her cheek. "It is late and you are cold. You need not worry. Your father will be quite pleased with himself in the morning. As to the future—well, we must somehow devise a way to keep him from London and its gaming hells." Moriah cocked her head, wondering at his use of the word "we." Since when had Papa become Justin's problem as well as hers? But his next statement diverted her thoughts entirely. "Oh, and by the by, I am afraid I rather lost count toward the end. I had a bit to drink myself, you must know, and I am rather tired and—well, I believe your father won back a bit more than he lost to me in the first place," he said very nonchalantly. She eyed him dubiously, not at all caring for the tenor of this last statement. "Be sure he gives you a hundred-odd pounds to meet some of your household expenses."

Moriah's eyes widened and she opened her mouth to protest, but he cut her short, pulling her close to him and bringing his lips to hers in one very brief, very warm kiss. He pulled away just as abruptly, leaving her dazed and hardly able to voice her suspicions regarding one hundred-odd pounds that he happened to have lost track of.

"Until tomorrow evening, Moriah," he whispered, and then he opened the door and disappeared.

Moriah felt a rush of the cool late night air as she stared into the darkness, unable to move. Then, slowly, she closed the heavy door. She knew she would have to deal with Papa now, and Finch. She just hoped to God she was too tired to deal with her own thoughts. Wearily, she turned and crossed the lobby, feeling a lump rise in her throat. Could he really have lost count? He didn't appear at all inebriated, though undoubtedly he was tired. Oh, damn! She didn't *want* his money. She needed it—quite desperately, in fact. But she didn't *want* it! Didn't he know that? Saving the Abbey was one thing, didn't

he understand? And why did she feel so lonely, so—
so unbearably cold now that he had gone?

Roane found that he could not sleep at all that
night, and it wasn't cold he suffered from. Rather it
was that the ride home had not sufficiently cooled
him down to allow him any peace. Images of Moriah
in her flimsy, revealing nightgown, her black hair
falling loosely down her back, floated before his eyes
and joined him in bed. Damn! He pounded the
pillow for the third time. It had taken every ounce of
willpower he possessed for him to leave the Abbey
with no more than a kiss. He wanted her so much it
hurt. But what troubled him more was that it was not
only in bed that he wanted her. He wanted her
company as well, and that thought rather took him
aback. And it brought him to what he knew, at the
back of his sleepless mind, was really troubling him.

He had done it. He had allowed the baron to
recoup his losses. The fall of the Landons, for which
he had planned and waited for years, was not to be.
He had—he had besmirched the honour and memory
of his parents. It was as if he had abandoned them.
And he had done it because of his own honour,
because of that ignoble bargain he'd struck.

Oh, blast! He pounded the pillow again. It was not
because of that damned bargain. No, not if he would
be honest with himself which, in the wee hours of the
morning, he was wont to be. No, he had done it
because of Moriah. Because she had asked him to,
because she needed him to. Abruptly, he sat up in
bed, swung his feet to the floor, and ran his fingers
through his hair. What had she done to him? Tonight, when he'd first seen her, he'd felt the coldness
leave him, and with it his hatred for the Landons.

Who was there to hate, after all? The sixth baron was long dead, and Moriah's father was merely pathetic. Tess was a complete innocent and Moriah—Moriah . . . He sighed and rose to his feet. He did not at all understand the effect she had on him. Whatever it was, it was like to drive him crazy. He could not bed her again, and she would not marry him. Which was just as well, he told himself sharply, since there was no way this side of heaven he could ever marry a Landon!

Without quite realizing it, he had donned his dressing gown and slippers, and now padded softly to the door. As if propelled by some outside force, he made his way through the corridors, down the stairs, and to the main drawing room. Somehow he had avoided this room since his return from London, and he felt remiss. It was here, in this ornate, little used formal room, that he had always come to renew his anger and resolve to ruin the Landons. For in between the two huge picture windows there hung the full-length portraits of his mother and father. He knew nearly every detail of each one, having committed them to memory years ago in his lonely, confused childhood.

His father looked handsome and aristocratic, as always, his mother beautiful and smiling in her frothy pink dress. But as he stared at the paintings in the early morning light, he frowned. It was strange, but for the first time he noticed how very much older than his mother his father had been. He'd always known it, but somehow it hit him quite forcefully now. Some twenty years had separated them at least, and the portraits did not deceive. He gazed at his father, at the graying temples and the tiny lines around the eyes, and he saw more than his age. There was a hardness to those dark eyes and to the set of his mouth. Roane had oft been told, by older acquaintances, that he had the look of him, and he wondered if he shared that coldness. It was not a very attractive quality. And his mother—what a beauty she had been. How gentle and—and loving she looked. It was in her blue eyes, in the soft curve of her mouth. He found himself wondering very suddenly if his father had accepted her love and if he'd been able to give her the love she needed. He found the question most disconcerting.

And then, inevitably, his thoughts drifted to Moriah. There was a softness about her too and he wondered . . . Damn it all! Suddenly he knew that if she were not a Landon, he would press his suit again.

He looked up at his parents and felt a wave of shame and guilt, as if he were indeed abandoning them. He couldn't. He just couldn't.

But as he turned to leave the room, he had the uncanny sense that this feeling of guilt had nothing to do with this night's, or even this week's, events. No, it was much older that. And then the feeling left him, and there was only emptiness.

Chapter 20

"Ughh!" growled Thomas Landon as he thrust aside the empty mug. "Blast you, Finch! Whatever *do* you put in that vile concoction of yours?" he demanded, falling back against the numerous pillows of his huge mahogany bed.

"Why, my lord, could you be wishin' me to give away all the secrets of my trade? No, I'll wager not," Finch said, smoothly rescuing the mug from the baron's none-too-steady hand and setting it down. "Now come, you'll feel right as rain straight away. Up with you now. You did say as how I was to wake you early. Very particular about it you was, even if you was a bit, well, up in the world last night." Finch folded back the heavy down comforter and reached for the Baron's burgundy silk dressing gown.

"Clean-raddled Finch. Bosky, I was," Landon muttered, his hand automatically going to his temple. Lord but his head ached abominably. Finch held the dressing gown up for him but he didn't move. "Did I happen to say *why* I wished to rise early, Finch?" he asked in a low voice.

"I believe you wished to see your solicitor, my lord," Finch replied, his face impassive, his short wiry frame ramrod straight, his hands still holding the dressing gown aloft.

God bless Finch, Landon thought. Always the soul of discretion, and a master of understatement into the bargain. A bit up in the world, indeed! And as to anything Landon might have babbled last night about his solicitor, he knew not a word would filter through Finch to the servants' grapevine. But at the moment his valet's most valuable asset was the fact that he spoke in a soft voice and had enough sense not to draw the curtains open to let the blasted sunshine pour in. Landon glanced at Finch's impassive face over the top of the dressing gown and smiled despite himself. Finch was a stickler that he'd probably pass the entire morning with his hands in the air, dressing gown poised and ready for such time as the master deigned to rise from his bed.

And so, taking pity on his loyal and proper man-servant, Thomas Landon somehow managed to roll himself out of bed.

There was blessed silence in the dressing room as Finch shaved and dressed his master and applied his very special pomade to the baron's salt and pepper hair. Naturally Finch would never divulge the secret of his pomade. Landon supposed it was another of the man's age-old family recipes, like that vile concoction he always made the baron drink or the boot-blacking that stunk something dreadful but worked wonders on scuffed Hessians. As to the pomade, the baron sniffed deliberately as Finch's deft fingers swept through his hair. He thought he smelled almonds and rosemary, which seemed unexceptional enough, but a second sniff brought the faint odor of mutton suet to his mind, and the Baron decided that perhaps, on second thought, he'd rather not know what was in it after all.

When Finch finally stepped back, pleased with his handiwork, Landon rose from his vanity and allowed

223

his man to shrug him into his coat. Trying to second-guess Finch's recipes had been an effective way to keep from thinking of the matter at hand, but he knew that he had to face reality, and very soon.

"I did it, you know, old fellow," he said quietly as Finch brushed several imaginary bits of lint off the shoulder of his black coat. "I won⸱it all back."

"I know, my lord," replied Finch, matching his own quiet, even tone.

"You know?" he demanded, watching Finch's impassive face carefully.

"Yes, my lord, you—er—told me so. Last night, that is." The valet looked distinctly uncomfortable.

"I was not aware that I was capable of rational speech last night," Landon countered dryly.

"Well, my lord, I—er—truth is, you was rather—er—beggin' your lordship's pardon, but you *was* rather pie-eyed last night. Shot the cat, you did. And you kept—er—mumblin' and jabberin' and I had all I could do to get you into your bed, you must know, and I didn't pay no never mind to what you said. But you kept repeatin' somethin' and tuggin' at my sleeve, 's if 'twere somethin' of import, you know. Then when you was finally all tucked up you sat up suddenly and whispered, clear as a bell, 'bout how you won the Abbey back and how I was t' waken you early so you could see Mr. Fairley today. And then next thing I know you're asleep, peaceful as a babe."

"I see," said Landon pensively. He remembered how, even in his drunken state, certain things had become very clear to him last night. Or perhaps it was *because* of his drunken state. Did they not say that sometimes a madman saw truths that no one else did? Could not the same be said for a man deranged by drink? His eyes slowly encircled his dressing room, taking in the huge wardrobe, the rows of drawers, and the sturdy armchair in the corner. Then he became aware that Finch was regarding him with a strange look in his eyes. He did not think he had ever succeeded in keeping anything from his all-knowing manservant, but this time was different. No one, absolutely no one, must know what was in his head.

The baron smiled and Finch seemed to relax a bit. "May I offer my congratulations, my lord?" Finch actually broke into a grin, and then added, handing the baron his hat and driving gloves, "And I think I might speak for all the staff, your lordship, when I say that we—well, we're all very happy for you and—and mighty grateful, too."

Landon was touched by what he knew to be a sincere tribute, but then his eyes narrowed. "The entire staff, Finch?"

The grin disappeared from Finch's ruddy face and he once more became the efficient manservant. "Come, my lord, I know you don't want to tarry overlong. I've ordered the carriage brought round," he said briskly, but the twinkle in his eyes told the baron what he wanted to know. Though Finch would consider it a point of honour never to gossip about his master's indiscretions or repeat late night rumblings about solicitors or some such, it was clear that good news was not to be considered such privileged communication.

And it *was* good news, Landon reminded himself, and remembered to put a lively trip into his step as he bid his valet good day and sauntered down the corridor.

But Dermot Finch was not fooled for one minute. He knew his master too well, and he knew something was wrong. He hastened to tidy the dressing room and resolved to seek out Miss Moriah as soon as he'd finished.

The baron descended the main stairwell and then turned toward the entry hall, but changed his mind. Hodges and the horses would keep a moment longer, he decided. He had something else to do first. He headed for the morning room, knowing full well he would find his eldest daughter there and not lingering over breakfast as Tess might be. Moriah rose from her desk at his entrance and came forward, a tentative smile on her lips. "Papa," she said simply, but her voice seemed full of emotion. He thought she looked rather well in her primrose pink morning gown, though a bit tired about the eyes, as if she hadn't slept enough.

Landon remembered to put on his broadest smile. "Well, daresay you've heard the news by now, m' dear. Finch seems to have virtually shouted it about below-stairs."

"Yes, Papa, but it's wonderful, isn't it!" Moriah exclaimed, giving him a hug. She refrained from sharing with him her suspicions that the staff had known long before Finch had made his way below-stairs, and she certainly couldn't tell him how *she* knew. She stepped back and looked at his face. Finch had done a good job of repairing the ravages of last night's claret. "I knew you could do it, Papa, I just knew it! We're all quite proud of you."

She hadn't meant to do it quite so brown, but somehow Papa did not look as happy as he ought. Even his smile seemed forced. "You're looking quite fit and dapper this morning," she said. "Are you — are you going out?" She quelled the unreasonable apprehension that began to creep through her. Even Thomas Landon could not find a card game in the environs of Much Henley before ten o'clock in the morning. And he was not dressed for traveling — certainly he was not off to London this day.

"Yes, 'smatter of fact I am. Have some business to attend to in the village. Anything I can fetch for you?"

"No, I don't think so, Papa, thank you."

"Oh—er—'fore I forget, Moriah. I did rather well last night, you know. Won a bit over and beyond what I lost to Roane at first stop." He reached into his coat pocket and withdrew a small purse. "Well, here—here's some blunt, Moriah. Use it to buy yourself and Tess some new gowns, and maybe pay off the nastiest of the creditors while you're about it. Well, I'm off now, m'dear," he concluded in a rush of words, as if he were embarrassed by what he'd just said.

Moriah did not have to feign surprise nor the catch in her throat. "Thank you, Papa," she whispered, and was able only to give him a brief kiss on the cheek before he patted her face and was gone.

Moriah slipped the purse into the pocket of her morning dress and walked to her desk. She sat down, feeling rather dumbfounded and quite perplexed. Never before, that she could recall, had Papa given her money without her having asked for it. Not that he ever would have denied her money for a new gown, but he just didn't think of it, and she made it a point to ask rarely, there being so many more important uses for their limited funds. And as to household expenses, Papa, in his rather childlike, fanciful way, had never considered paying off another tiresome creditor quite as crucial as the chance to win a fortune at a heretofore untried gaming hell.

Abruptly, Moriah withdrew the purse from her pocket and opened it. She slipped the roll of banknotes out and counted it. One hundred twenty pounds. My God, she thought, the viscount had *said* one hundred-odd pounds. This must be everything

Papa had won over and above the Abbey! A deep frown descended onto her brow as she folded the notes and stuffed them back into the purse. Now she was very perturbed indeed. For while she was relieved that he did not plan to take his winnings immediately to the card tables, yet she was most concerned for him. Papa was far too calm for the jubilation she'd imagined he would feel, and his handing over virtually all of his winnings was too unprecedented for her not to feel apprehensive.

Well, she shrugged, forcing her mind back to her paperwork, she did not suppose he could land himself in too much difficulty in Much Henley. And her own energies were best put to deciding just how to use the infamous "hundred-odd pounds" to best advantage. She tried not to think about where it had really come from. Lord knew, she did not want to take money from the viscount and she would tell him so, this very night. But as for returning it, as her pride dictated, she knew that would not answer. She simply could not afford her own pride; too many people would suffer did she let it interfere with her common sense. And then, too, there was Papa to consider. He wanted her to have the money. And though he did not pay much heed to household affairs, he would think it strange, indeed, did he hear rumblings from belowstairs about overdue accounts and persistent creditors.

She had set her hand to her morning correspondence for but a few minutes before Reeves interrupted her to announce that Finch wished to speak with her. So unusual was it for her father's valet to seek her out that she felt a moment's panic. Papa! Something must have happened to Papa! But that was absurd. He'd only just now left her. Still, she felt that rush of anxiety. What it was that she feared she did not know, and she forced herself to calm down as she rose and walked to the front of the desk to greet Finch.

"Miss Moriah, I beg your pardon for disturbin' you, but if I might have a moment . . ." Finch began, coming to stand next to a plum-colored chintz chair, his thin frame bending in a deferential bow.

"Papa? Is — is everything all right?" Moriah could not help blurting.

The valet smiled slightly and nodded. "The baron is even now on is way to the village, Miss Moriah."

Moriah closed her eyes for a moment in relief. "Yes, yes, of course. Well, and how may I be of help to you, Finch?" she asked, regaining her usual tone of efficient composure and clasping her hands at her waist.

"Well, it — " Finch stopped abruptly and turned his head to where Reeves stood in the open doorway, his white head erect and a formal, blank expression on his face. But Moriah knew Reeves was listening to every word they said, and Finch knew it too. Finch waited several moments, standing perfectly still, perhaps four feet from Moriah, until finally both heard a discreet cough from the butler.

"Will that be all, Miss Moriah?" Reeves asked in his most starchy voice.

"Yes, thank you, Reeves," she replied, and Finch turned back to her as the doors clicked shut. Moriah could not help smiling inwardly at Finch's not-so-subtle assertion of what he considered his territorial rights. A butler might be senior servant in the household, but a valet considered himself a breed apart, answerable only to his master. Finch was in her father's confidence, and by that turn of his head and rather pointed pause he had made it quite clear that he would not share that confidence with anyone from belowstairs. His ruddy face seemed to have reddened, and he shifted his feet as he went on.

"Well, it—it *is* the master I'm concerned about, Miss. You see, he—he—well, mayhap I oughtn't to say anythin', seein' as how I've not much more'n a feeling to go on, but he doesn't seem himself at all, miss. Not meanin' to worry you, I'm not, but—well—"

"Yes, of course, Finch. You were right to come to me. Just—just what have you noticed about the baron?" she asked anxiously.

"Well, he—he just doesn't seem so—so cheery as a body might expect, considerin' what he just did last night. He was more . . . quiet-like this mornin', I should say, Miss Moriah."

Moriah did not wish to share her own misgivings about Papa at this point, especially since she could no more define them than Finch could. Nonetheless, she thought a moment and said, "Perhaps he is simply worried about the future, Finch. I think it would be a good idea for the baron to make this an extended visit here at the Abbey," she added pointedly.

Finch understood that Miss Moriah expected him to do what he could to keep the master away from London. And *that* he would be only too happy to do. 'Twas true a valet's consequence could only be increased by havin' his master appear in London society dressed to the nines, his Hessians smooth and spotless, his cravat tied in the latest knot. But it was plain as pikestaff London was a no-good place for the baron. And they'd been together a long time, Dermot Finch and his master, and he'd do anythin' to keep the master well. Anythin' at all. "A very good idea, miss," he replied, nodding his head. "London's a bit spotty of people just now at all events, it bein' so hot and sticky-like."

He was glad he'd come to speak with Miss Moriah. She wasn't like all those other females, allas shriekin' and a-wailin' and havin' the vapors just when a man needed to talk sense. But her next words troubled him just the same, though he wasn't sure why.

"Excellent. I do think Papa would enjoy the country air for a while. And at the least we need no longer concern ourselves with the pistol cabinet. Thank you, Finch, for coming to me. You must feel free to do so at any time."

Finch knew when he had been dismissed, and so he took his leave quickly, but his mind was still uneasy. Well, he would watch over the master the best he could. And as to the pistol cabinet, he knew it was time to put back the key. If only he knew what 'twas troubled him so.

Chapter 21

Thomas Landon directed Hodges to set him down from the carriage just before the edge of the village. He needed to clear his head, and a stroll down the village lane in the sunshine would be just the thing. He did not know whether the servants' grapevine would yet have spread news of last night's happenings, but judging from his own household, he guessed it a good possibility. And so he reminded himself to walk with a jaunty step and forced a triumphant smile onto his face, though he hoped not too many people would be about so early.

All was quiet as the baron made his way past the cottages along the lane, and he let his mind drift to his daughters. Tess had looked beautiful last night—so like Clarissa that Landon might have shed a tear or two had he not been so preoccupied with the need to win the Abbey back. Tess, he realized, was rapidly leaving her childhood. And even Moriah had looked rather fetching, and she certainly was no child. One only had to see how she filled out that gown of hers to know that. Not to mention the fact that she had been mistress of the Abbey for more years than was proper.

Landon raised his eyes toward the sky and sighed deeply. Somehow, while he had been off in London, losing and then trying to recoup a fortune, his daughters had grown up. He had never, until this week, given much thought to their futures, and he could no longer deny to himself that he had been most remiss in this. Moriah was a year past the age when most girls made their come outs. But, of course, there had been no money for a London Season. He himself had seen to that, he thought bitterly. And even now, when he had won the Abbey back, they still had little but the roof over their heads. And a heavily mortgaged roof at that. If only he had poured some money, the few times he'd had it in his hands, into the land, into improvements that would help them turn a profit. Instead he had turned the cards, time and again. Oh, God, how had he allowed it all to come to this?

He blinked back the moisture in his eyes even as two serving girls rapidly approached, whispering and staring surreptitiously at him. They did not dare speak to him, but nonetheless he tipped his hat as they shyly dipped a curtsy and hurried on. So, he thought, almost indifferently, the grapevine had already done its work. Well, now it was time for him to do his. For the world might be impressed, even awestruck, but Landon was not impressed with himself. He was not gloating, did not even feel triumphant. In truth, he did not consider last night's victory *his* at all. It was not even the luck of the cards. No, he knew, deep down inside of him, that the Hand of Providence had reached out to him when he had fallen to the depths of despair. And he knew he must never spurn that Hand, must never again sink so low. And there was only one way he knew to prevent it. And so he would see Mr. Fairley straight away.

Still, Landon did not hurry but ambled down the

dirt road, letting his mind wander back to last night. It had struck him at dinner, despite his preoccupation with other matters, that Roane was a fine figure of a man, one he would not be at all averse to having as a son-in-law. Of course, there *was* that terrible tragedy between their two families, but that had happened so many years ago. Roane had been but a child; Landon could not conceive that he had ever been made privy to the sorry details, and it was highly likely he had forgotten the whole by now at all events. And so, from time to time last night, Landon had observed Roane with his daughters. At first Roane had seemed rather taken with Tess, trying to put her at her ease and offering her pretty compliments. But Landon had quickly realized that there was no fire in Roane's eyes when he looked at Tess. He had, in fact, gazed at her with the same admiring glance one might accord a particularly pleasing watercolor.

But strange as it seemed, his eyes had been rather warm, even intense when they settled on Moriah. And he had appeared quite interested in what she had to say about the Abbey. Still, it did not seem possible that a man of Roane's stamp would be attracted to Moriah. Not that her conversation was not intelligent, but a man wanted more from a woman than knowledge of local history, after all.

Landon absently circumvented a plodding milk cow that had wandered into his path, but he remained intent on his thoughts. Obviously, he sighed inwardly, his daughters would have to look elsewhere for husbands though, of course, the only hope for them would be to marry locally. At least that was possible now he'd won the Abbey back. For in addition to providing a roof over their heads, it gave them a mantle of respectability. And marriage for Tess should really be no problem; as soon as she was a bit older and began to go about in society, she would be besieged by swains. A beautiful face and an ethereal demeanor went a long way toward mitigating the lack of a dowry. But Moriah was another story entirely. Aside from the fact that she was not exactly a beauty, she was too—well—too damned *capable* for the tastes of most men he knew. He shuddered as he wondered whatever would become of Moriah. He had little doubt that she would contrive to marry Tess off creditably, but as for Moriah herself . . .

Well, at the least, he told himself bracingly, she would have the Abbey. Perhaps one day the land would produce enough for the mortgages to be paid off. Yes, the Abbey was in Landon hands again, and he meant to see that it stayed there; hence his visit to Mr. Fairley.

Landon had rounded the bend by now and come to the paved road. He was dismayed to see several carriages already abroad and could only hope that their owners were ensconced in the shops for long enough to allow him to traverse the distance to the brick building that housed Albert Fairley's office. In the event, he had gone only a few steps when he espied Mrs. Shoup stepping out of the milliner's shop. She spotted him immediately and came toward him, and he supposed if he had to meet anyone here, he was glad it was she. Landon tipped his hat and bowed cordially. "Good morning, Mrs. Shoup."

Mrs. Shoup smiled, emphasizing the tiny laugh lines around her mouth. Landon noted with a half smile the sandy brown hair caught up in a topknot, and the fetching green walking dress and matching bonnet. A sight for sore eyes, he thought. There was something so—well—so peaceful about this woman. He could not say why; it was simply a feeling that he'd always had. In fact, had he ever been of a mind to marry again—But he reminded himself that she was taken. And though he did not enjoy listening to gossip, the alleged existence of a man in Mrs. Shoup's life was something he had always accepted, as had those of his cronies who knew her. Many were the wagers that had been placed as to who the man was, but Landon had never taken one up. No one had ever unearthed her secret; he did not suppose anyone ever would. Yes, Mrs. Shoup was spoken for, as it were, and besides, no one could ever replace Clarissa.

"How nice to see you here in the country again, my lord. I hope you are enjoying your stay?" There was a twinkle in her eye, but he was not quite sure if it indicated that she was privy to the recent events in his life. He did not think she was much given to gossip, but if she had chanced to hear something, he knew she was too much the lady to mention it.

"Tolerably well, my dear Mrs. Shoup," he replied, his lips twitching slightly.

"I'm glad," she said warmly, her eyes still twinkling. "By the by, I came upon your daughters the other day, here in the village. They are quite lovely, you know."

"Thank you, Mrs. Shoup," Landon replied, smiling and hoping his anxiety for them did not show in his eyes. "They—they seem to have grown up rather fast," he could not help adding. He did now know why he had confided what was uppermost in his mind, except that somehow it was so very easy to talk to this woman.

And she understood immediately what was troubling him. "I suppose children always do. And it cannot be easy for you, a man alone with two daughters to establish," she said softly. Any other woman would have made the statement while batting her eyelashes and perhaps placing a possessive arm on his sleeve, a not-so-subtle hint that *she* was just the one to undertake the marrying off of his daughters, *her* stepdaughters. But coming from Mrs. Shoup the words were simply a way of saying that she understood his plight. And not by a flicker of the eyelid did she display any disapproval of the way he had thus far handled, or treated, his daughters. Any feelings she might have on the subject she would keep to herself, and Landon reflected that, her reputation notwithstanding, Mrs. Shoup was one of the only true ladies he had ever known. And that somewhere in his majesty's realm there was a very lucky man indeed.

Landon's smile deepened as he replied to her. "You have read my mind, Mrs. Shoup. It is time, I know, to — to —" The baron's voice trailed off and his smile faded. He felt his eyes take on a distant cast and a lump rose in his throat as he contemplated what he must now do. And then somehow he forced his eyes to focus again on Mrs. Shoup.

"I — well — that is —" he stammered, but she came to his rescue.

"Oh, my lord, you must forgive me. Here I am chattering away whilst I am persuaded you must have any number of things to do."

He was immensely grateful for her tact, and he could not help the glint in his eye as he said, "I have much enjoyed talking with you, Mrs. Shoup. I wish you a pleasant day."

"Thank you, my lord. And a good day to you," she replied in her soft, lilting voice, extending her gloved right hand. He brought it to his lips briefly as he bowed. "Commend me to your daughters," she added brightly. "And perhaps we shall meet at the Crowley ball."

The baron's eyes narrowed in puzzlement and then he recalled. Finch had said something, several days ago, about a ball in Roane's honour, but Landon had been too much in his cups to regard it. Besides, he'd known he could not go in disgrace to such a rout. But now, of course, the situation was much altered. Certainly he would go. They would all go. And perhaps, just perhaps, one of his daughters might attract an eligible part. He thought of Moriah and the money he had given her. She could, had she wanted, have commissioned a gown, even on barely two days' notice. But she wouldn't, he reflected. She was too damned practical! Really, there was no hope for her, he thought, exasperated, and then remembered his manners.

"Yes, Mrs. Shoup. I am certain we shall meet there," he said genially. They parted soon thereafter, the baron tipping his hat and watching her petite form glide gracefully away from him.

He registered belated surprise that Agatha Crowley would allow Mrs. Shoup to cross her threshold, but then realized that that must be Sir Hugo's doing. Hmm, he mused, as he continued on his way, this assembly might actually be rather interesting. Ordinarily he found such crushes a dead bore. Or rather, he amended, had found them so these last years, when he no longer had his Clarissa to escort, and dance with, even rescue from over-eager admirers. But he *would* go to the Crowley ball, it being the least he could do for his daughters. And he would do the pretty to all the ladies, even appear appropriately triumphant to the men, although it would not do to gloat. Not at a ball in honour of the man he'd just trounced.

He reflected that it was a good thing Roane bore him no ill-feeling about last night, else it should have been deuced awkward for Landon to show himself at the ball. He did not know precisely how he knew Roane's mind on this, but somehow he did. He supposed it was because Roane knew very well he did not need another estate to worry about, especially one so in need of funds as Wykham.

Landon had by now come to the brick building that housed his solicitor's office. He climbed the steps slowly, telling himself that there was no turning back. And Fairley's reputation for discretion would serve him well now. Not that Landon would let on *everything* he planned to do. Of course not. Fairley would simply be following straightforward legal instructions. No one must know what Landon was really about.

The baron took a deep breath as he crossed the threshold into Albert Fairley's office. He knew what he had to do; he must not let his courage fail him. And he was aware that the course he had elected would cause pain, but he also knew that, in the long run, it was best for his daughters. And as for him, it was the only honourable course left.

Chapter 22

Moriah waited impatiently for the household to settle itself down and fall asleep so that she might dress and be on her way to the hunting box. Not, she hastily assured herself, that she was eager to go to Lord Roane. It was merely that she wished to get it over with. She was propped up in bed, just as Lizzie had left her, her white lawn nightgown buttoned to her chin. Several tapers burned in the candelabrum on her bedside table and she held a book that she was making a futile attempt to read. In point of fact, she was not quite sure which book it was she held, and now she unceremoniously tossed it to the foot of the bed.

No, she reassured herself, she was not looking forward to this evening. As such she tried very hard not to dwell on the Viscount Roane, on the way he had looked at her, spoken to her, held her, the night before. Her body reacted treacherously to those memories, and she squelched them firmly. Instead she concentrated on what she would say to him regarding the infamous "one hundred-odd pounds."

She did not want his money, and she would tell him so in no uncertain terms. They had struck a bargain, and gifts of money, no matter how surreptitiously given, were no part of it. Surely she could make him understand how she felt. The Abbey was one thing . . .

She found her thoughts disturbing and deliberately channeled them in another direction. The Abbey. She had saved the Abbey. Her eyes flew around her pale pink bedroom, resting now on the graceful Georgian highboy and then on the floral curtains that matched the canopy and coverlet of her bed. This was *her* room, had been so ever since she'd emerged from the nursery. And this was *her* home, hers and Papa's and Tess's. For the first time all day, she permitted herself a huge sigh of relief. She had saved her home, and her family as well. She had been so concerned for Papa this morning and so caught up in household matters all afternoon that she had scarce had time to reflect upon it all.

Wykham Abbey was theirs again. It belonged to the Landons, just as it always had. Thank God for that, she thought, and then mused irreverently that God had actually had little to do with it. She had paid a dear price for the redemption of her home, and she felt all the proper remorse, she told herself firmly. Though, in truth, that was not quite the emotion she felt when she recalled, rather vividly, just how she *had* redeemed the Abbey. She could not exactly define that emotion and elected not to try.

She attempted instead to set her mind to devising ways to keep Papa in the country, away from the gaming hells of London. But she found her mind quite wayward, quite insistent, in fact, on dwelling on the evening ahead. Lord Roane — Justin, she amended — had indicated a desire to play chess, and he had been very adamant about not—not—well, not continuing their—their meetings in the manner in which they had begun. Could he really be that fond of chess? One did not, she was certain, forego a significant gaming debt in return for endless nights of playing chess.

In truth, she did not understand Justin at all. He wanted her, but he would not touch her. He kept invoking his honour as a gentleman, which was rather, she thought wryly, like closing the gate after the pony had bolted. He had even gone so far as to propose marriage, when she felt perfectly sure he did not wish to be leg-shackled. And all this from a man who had callously, coldly propositioned her at their very first meeting! Really, she thought again, the male sense of honour was quite incomprehensible.

And her own reaction to him was equally incomprehensible. She must not forget that ignoble proposition, must now allow herself to enjoy his company overmuch. She must not dwell on his quick wit, his tenderness, nor the way he always seemed to anticipate her thoughts. And as to what the mere touch of his hand did to her—oh, Lord, that did not bear thinking of at all.

She noted that the tapers were burning rather low and became aware that the house had grown silent and still. She slipped back the comforter on her bed and quietly let her bare feet slip down onto the carpet beneath. It was time to dress and be on her way, but she knew it was not at all the thing for her heart to be suddenly beating so rapidly.

Roane arrived at his hunting box a full half hour before the appointed time of midnight. He had spent the day—or that part of it when Andrew left him alone—thinking about his parents, and Moriah, and trying to make some sense of it all. He had found himself restless, eager for night to fall, but told himself that that would not do at all. And now here he was.

It had been decidedly easy to escape Andrew tonight, for his cousin had yawned several times at dinner and declared his intention of retiring early. And though Roane was relieved that he had not been called upon to ply Drew with drink again, yet he was uneasy. It had been *too* simple, and now he thought on it, Drew had been casting curious looks his way these two days past. And then there was last night. Roane had been too preoccupied to think much of it, but Drew had hardly cavilled when Roane had deserted him for dinner with the flimsiest of excuses. For a moment he wondered if Andrew might have some inkling as to his nocturnal activities, but Roane dismissed the idea as impossible. Besides, if Andrew did suspect something, he would be sure, in his own inimitable way, to tax Roane with it. As to last night's game, once Andrew had heard about that, Roane was able to satisfy him with the very simple explanation that the baron had invited him to a game and asked him to keep mum. Andrew's main concern on that head had been Roane's loss, but Roane convinced him that it was almost a relief to have one less estate to trouble himself about.

Now dismissing Andrew from his mind, Roane made a rapid inspection of the main floor and was pleased to note that Norris had, as usual, carried out his orders precisely. A cold collation had been placed on the sideboard in the dining room and the table set. The chessboard had been arranged in the sitting room and the fire laid, although Roane did not think it necessary to light it. He had not requested a fire upstairs in the bedroom, for of course they would not avail themselves of that particular room. He shook his head, sighing ruefully and wondering just how long he could keep this up. He remembered the look on his valet's face when he had requested the chessboard. Norris had been totally, completely incredulous, had in fact asked that Roane repeat his order twice before he would believe that the Viscount Roane intended to spend an evening with his mistress playing chess.

He couldn't believe it himself and, besides, she wasn't his mistress, dammit! She was — she was — well, he wasn't quite sure *what* she was but —

He heard the clear sound of the knocker reverberate through the house. She was early, that's what she was, he thought, and despite himself, felt suddenly lighthearted.

"Good evening, Moriah," he said, smiling as she stepped over the threshold. She looked, as always, delectable. She wore the same lavender gown she'd worn two nights ago, and her black cape hung loosely about her bare shoulders. She smiled and greeted him in return, then divested herself of her cape and gloves in what seemed like one graceful, fluid motion. There was none of the former unease in her manner. In fact, she preceded him into the sitting room as comfortably as if it were the most natural thing in the world. And then she turned to him, and he kissed her lightly on the lips, as if he'd been doing it forever. He drew back, a slight frown on his brow. He wondered at himself, and at her. It was not supposed to be this way.

Yet the sense of ease between them continued as he poured them each a glass of sherry and made them comfortable. He motioned her to the green and gold sofa, and without a second thought sat down beside her. He held his glass in his right hand and let his left sprawl across the back of the sofa till it rested just inches from her bare shoulder. She bent her head to sip her sherry, and he watched the candlelight play upon the long nape of her neck and her smooth shoulders. Several curling black tendrils had come undone and fell gracefully down her back. Suddenly the calm he had felt between them turned into a very definite tension. He ached to slide his hands over her soft skin and felt his fingers stiffen in their effort to keep still. Where was the conversation he had determined they should have? She stared straight ahead over the rim of her glass, and he wondered whether she felt the tension as well. And then, as if of their own volition, his fingers found their way to her hair.

"Are you . . . cold?" he asked softly as his fingers entwined themselves in the silky tendrils. "Shall I light the fire?"

"No, I . . . it is quite warm," she murmured, still not looking at him. And then his hand grazed her nape and the hair fell from between his fingers as they began to stroke her bare skin. Very slowly she lowered her glass to her lap and turned her head to face him. Her red lips were slightly parted, her face flushed, her amethyst eyes dark. Her breathing was shallow as she stared at him without saying a word. She was, he realized, completely incapable of hiding her feelings. For what he read on her face was desire, pure and simple. A few days ago she had hardly known such a thing existed, but her instincts were warm and passionate, and she did not attempt to hide the stirrings he invoked in her. He felt a surge of masculine pride that he had been able to awaken her, and with it a fierce desire to possess her again. He wanted her, here and now, and he knew she would not demur. And her surrender would not merely be the be the result of that infernal "agreement" she insisted they'd struck.

He put his sherry glass down on the sofa table and leaned toward her, one hand coming up to trace the line of her lips and her jaw. "Moriah," he whispered throatily.

"Yes . . . Justin?" she echoed softly. She inched closer to him and he could distinctly see the rise and fall of her breasts inside the low-cut gown. My God, he thought, *she's* practically seducing *me* and she has no idea of it.

In fact, she had no idea of the ramifications of any of this. She did not know what her smoky eyes revealed, nor did she have any notion of her effect on men. Dammit, but she was such an innocent. "You are so lovely," he rasped, and then abruptly tore himself away from her. He rose, jerked his sherry into his hand, and strode to the mantel. He gulped half the glass and then turned to look at her. Her eyes were narrowed and her lower lip protruded as if in a pout. Was she disappointed or merely puzzled? Perhaps a bit of each; he could not tell. But of a certain it was not relief he saw on her face.

"How—how is your father?" he managed after a minute. "Is he enjoying his victory?"

She, too, sipped her wine before speaking, but when she did he could see that her composure had returned, full measure. "He's—well, the truth is that I—I am not certain *how* he is. He seemed very quiet—subdued today. Not at all what one would expect. And somehow I cannot be at ease. And even more strange, he—he gave me all his winnings, without my even having to ask. Speaking of which—"

"Er—then what is it you fear, Moriah? It does not seem as if he plans to gamble again, at least not straight away, not if he gave you his money. Are you afraid he may be ill?"

"No, it's not that. In truth I cannot quite put words to *what* it is I fear, but speaking of the money—"

"And—er—the rest of your household, are they suitably triumphant?"

She frowned slightly at his interruptions but answered readily enough, a reluctant smile tugging at her mouth. "Yes, rather. The news spread like wildfire and everyone is enormously relieved and quite in awe of Papa. And he, strangely, seems untouched by it all. But, what of *your* household? Has word reached there as well? I hope this hasn't—well, lowered your consequence before your servants."

He was touched by the genuine concern in her voice, especially when she had so many problems of her own and even though the thought that such an incident could actually lower his consequence was quite nonsensical. "No, my dear, my consequence is still quite intact," he said with a gleam in his eye, leaning one arm on the mantel. "I have to assume word *has* got about, but my servants are ignoring it. Which they might well do, since I have not appeared overly despondent, after all. No, I should say, Moriah, that all is well and that perhaps you worry overmuch. You are too young for such burdens. Oh, I do understand your concern for your father, but still I think you might relax your vigil just a little."

Moriah gave him a rueful smile, leaning forward and placing her glass on the sofa table. "Yes, I suppose I *do* fret about him—and about Tess. But I'm not that young, you know. Somehow it—it all makes me feel very old."

His lips began to twitch, and leaving his sherry on the mantel, he strolled back to the sofa. Then he reached a hand down and helped her to her feet. "I quite agree, my dear," he quipped when they stood just two feet apart. "You are nearly in your dotage. Just exactly how old *are* you, Moriah? Not much above eighteen, I'll wager."

"I'm nineteen, Justin."

"Ah, nineteen. Well then, come, ancient one, let us totter in to supper," he said good-naturedly and, tucking her arm in his, led her to the dining room.

She waited only until he had seated her at the table and turned to the sideboard before attempting to broach the subject he had no intention of discussing.

"Justin, there is something I must say to you regarding the m—"

"Would you prefer chicken or glazed beef, my dear?" he interrupted, eyeing the platter of cold meats.

"Chicken will be fine, thank you. Now Justin, I am well aware that—"

"Breast, wing, or thigh?" he blurted.

"Ah—er—breast, please. Last night—"

"Asparagus?"

"Yes, thank you," she replied and he could hear the exasperation in her voice. He wondered how long he could keep this up. "It is becoming rather obvious, Justin, that—"

"I think I shall try the glazed beef," he interrupted unabashedly, and quickly filling his plate, he hastened over to the table, frantically searching his mind for a more promising topic to divert her thoughts.

"Justin, if you will—"

"I must tell you, Moriah, that I very much enjoyed visiting your home. The Abbey is very beautiful. I am pleased that I was able to arrive during daylight and so to see the front aspect, the gatehouse ruins and all, as I approached. I confess I would have liked to have seen more, but even so, I was quite impressed."

"Thank you, Justin. I do have rather a passionate devotion to it myself," she replied enthusiastically, and then suddenly the expression in her eyes became pained. "Oh, but that is not to say that I—that for the sake of the Abbey alone I would have—that is—my family—"

"Moriah," he interrupted firmly, covering her small hand with his, "will you believe me when I say that you need not explain? I—I *understand,* Moriah. Truly I do."

The eyes that met his were moist, a deep amethyst. "I . . . thank you, Justin," she rasped. "Then perhaps you will understand why I cannot accept—"

"Would you care for more wine, Moriah?" he interjected neatly.

"Ah—yes, thank you. I want—"

"I presume the Abbey is one of the best preserved of the ruins hereabouts, is it not, my dear?" he asked, pouring the wine.

She swallowed a spear of asparagus. "Yes, I would say so, Justin. Though, as I've told you, I haven't seen nearly as many of the old abbeys and castles as I'd like to some day. I have done a good bit of reading, however. It seems a shame that so many of them have fallen into such decay. But, I suppose everything changes, does it not? Even our very way of life . . . "

"What do you mean?" Roane took a sip of wine and regarded her with interest.

"Oh, I do not mean to go on so. 'Tis just that I have only today had a letter from Miss Billingsley—my former governess, you must know."

Roane coughed. Er—yes, I know. You've mentioned her before. I—er—believe she has rather . . . interesting ideas about marriage."

Moriah blushed and sliced her chicken. "Yes, well,

she lives in Lancashire now. She has personally been witness to so much violence, Justin—machine breaking, bread riots . . . I do not know what the end of all this will be. But somehow, with all the factories invading the countryside, with the displaced farmers—well, things will never be quite the same, will they?"

Roane sighed. "Much as I don't like to think about it, you may be in the right of it, Moriah." He paused to sip his wine and then went on in earnest. "And all these demands for parliamentary reform must be addressed as well. We obviously cannot give in to the radicals and yet—"

"And yet we cannot ignore them," Moriah interjected. "Miss Billingsley writes that she has just heard Cobbett speak. He is rousing all the north country with his reform rhetoric."

"I know, Moriah. And, you know, what with all the talk and the outbreaks of violence, there are those in the Ministry who are certain an organized revolution is afoot."

"Yes, I have heard as much. But I cannot truly think 'tis so. Do you, Justin?"

"No, actually I don't, Moriah," Roane replied, and then paused and put his fork down on his plate. Was he actually discussing politics with a woman, and one who looked like this? He was, and worse, he was enjoying it! He smiled ruefully and went on, mindful that certain information he possessed was undoubtedly confidential. "And I know that there are those in the government who do not think so either. My Uncle George for one—the Earl of Westmacott, you must know." She nodded and he continued. "But they are in the minority."

"Oh, Justin, do people really believe that the average labourer wants to see the end of king and country? I should think all they really want is enough food on their tables."

Roane regarded her curiously for a moment. "That is precisely what I told my cousin Drew—the earl's son, you know. He's visiting at the Court just now and—" Roane paused, seeing the stricken look on her face. He knew that look and immediately took her hand again. "I have told you that you needn't worry, Moriah. Andrew is safe in his bed, none the wiser that I have gone out."

"I—I am sorry, Justin," she whispered, her eyes lowered. Roane could not help his eyes sweeping from her face down to her bare throat and lower still. Her hand felt warm in his and he knew their political discussion was over. Somehow, for a few moments before, he'd felt that special tension ease from the room but now it was back; he could feel it throughout his body. He took another sip of wine, knowing it was the wrong thing to do. Then he stood and willed himself to ask Moriah if she'd like a game of chess, knowing it was the right thing to do. He might have guessed she would not make it easy for him.

She rose from the table and uncharacteristically began to pace. "Oh, Justin. You—you are being the perfect host, and of course I should very much enjoy a game of chess, but—but that is not what I—that is, our—ah—agreement was not for you to entertain me. It was—"

He went to her and took her hands in his. "I know well what our agreement was, Moriah, and I refuse to enter into a lengthy discourse about it yet again," he said, a bit too harshly. Then he gentled his voice. "Nor shall we discuss again how much I—er—want you. I intend to behave as a gentleman. Now, will you or will you not give me a game of chess?"

She did, and played rather well, actually, but

251

Roane was aware that neither of them was concentrating properly. He tired to ignore the lovely curve of her lavender gown as it plunged to meet her breasts, tried repeatedly to keep his eyes off her red, slightly parted lips. They talked little but several times their eyes met and he felt that special intensity surge between them. His bishop took her knight, but inwardly he vowed that he would not take *her* tonight. He must not.

Eventually they settled into the game. He decided that she made good initial moves but that her follow-through was weak.

"You were well taught, Moriah," he said as he put her in check, "but — er —"

"But sadly out of practice. I know. Miss Billingsley was a good teacher, though."

"I don't doubt it. And quite a varied curriculum she seems to have devised for you," he murmured.

She looked at him warily but seemed to catch the twinkle in his eye. And then she laughed openly. It was the first time he'd heard her laugh so fully and he was delighted. He felt a twinge of regret, not the first, that she had refused to marry him, but quickly squelched it. He'd made his offer and been refused. It was best this way. Or was it? he wondered as she smiled coyly and captured his pawn.

"You miss your Miss Billingsley a great deal, do you not, Moriah?" he asked, trying to divert his thoughts.

"Yes. Tess is a charming companion, of course, and I do have my friend Sarah, but — well, I used to miss the stimulating discussions we always had, until —"

"Until what?"

She bent her head to the board. "Until? Oh — ah — nothing, really. I — the game is lost, is it not? Here, I shall move my queen, but I fear to no avail."

Roane promptly took it, ending the game, but his mind lingered on her unfinished statement. The game left him most unsatisfied, in more ways than one.

They rose from the table and he helped her on with her cloak. She gave him that look again, but this time he was prepared. "Do not look at me like that, Moriah," he said softly, fastening the cape at her throat. "This is hard enough as it is."

"I do not understand you, Justin," she whispered.

"Sometimes, little one, I do not understand myself. But let us speak no more on 't. Now come, I shall ride part way with you." He began to usher her to the door, but she stayed him with a hand on his sleeve. He might have known she'd not forget.

"Very well, Justin. But there *is* one thing. It's about—about the—the extra money my father seems to have won from you. Justin, you and I know that you are perfectly capable of counting and—and, oh, don't you see that I cannot accept money from you, that it makes me feel—"

"My dear, I cannot think why you have got such a bee in your bonnet over all that. I was half foxed myself, you must recall, not to mention bleary with fatigue and tension. I let the game go on a bit too long and he won a bit more than we'd intended. Why you needs must ascribe ulterior motives so such a simple occurrence, I cannot think. Now, shall we agree to say no more about it?" he said bracingly.

She exhaled a rather exasperated sigh and looked at him through narrowed eyes. Then she slowly nodded her agreement, but he knew very well she had not believed a word he'd said. But he also knew the matter was closed, and at the least she ought to be able to keep her most pressing creditors at bay.

They rode together in silence as far as he felt he

could accompany her. "Tomorrow night is the Crowley ball," she said when they drew rein.

"Yes. You must save me the first waltz, Moriah."

"But I—" she began, and he frowned prodigiously. "Oh, very well, Justin. The first waltz. And then Wednesday night, shall I—"

"Yes, Moriah, Wednesday night," he said. He did not want to hold her to it, but would she not be terribly upset did he tell her not to come?

He leaned over and kissed her briefly on the lips. "Sleep well, little one," he whispered. But as he watched the solitary horse and rider go off into the darkness, he knew of a certain that he would sleep very poorly indeed.

Chapter 23

Emily Shoup awoke near dawn in the throes of a nightmare. It was a recurrent one, a dream of Roland Shoup, her divorced husband. He had been a particularly cruel man, and the divorce had been extremely difficult. It had all been made bearable by one man, a widower with broad shoulders and twinkling blue eyes. One man who had been first her friend, and then her lover, and then, quite simply, had become the most important part of her life. That the feeling was reciprocated she had never doubted. And, as she looked back, life had been quite good to them. They'd had nigh onto fifteen years together and that was, after all, more than many people had. It had never been easy. They'd always had to be very discreet, and there had always been the long periods of separation. But the times when they were together made up for everything.

They had discussed divorce over the years but knew it was nearly impossible for a woman to accomplish. And then Roland himself had sought the divorce, so that he might marry a rich Italian contessa. And so her marriage had ended five years ago. But in all the time since, she had steadfastly refused to marry the man she loved, despite his repeated entreaties. For though she herself bore stoically the scandal and ostracism of divorce, she could not allow him to share it. He was a brilliant statesman, but despite his exalted place in the ton, she knew the taint of divorce would destroy his career. And so they met in secret and loved from afar when they couldn't.

It was hardest at times like this, when she lay sleepless and alone in her big bed. Emily sighed and rose. She would go down and brew herself a cup of tea.

The Earl of Westmacott made his way quietly and slowly on horseback, his path illuminated by the early morning light. She was not expecting him; indeed, he had not expected to come for several weeks. But then he'd had the news from the Continent, and he simply couldn't wait. Now that he was here, he relished surprising her. She would undoubtedly still be asleep and he knew just how he would wake her . . . .

And so he was most surprised, as the sun was barely peeking through the night sky, when she opened the door herself.

"George!"

"Emily. My love, my dearest love," he rasped, and then she was in his arms, and he was leading her through the house and up the stairs.

The morning was well advanced before they felt the need for any intelligible conversation, or food or drink. When they finally rose from the bed, Emily rang for a breakfast tray and the earl went through the connecting door to his own room to retrieve his silk dressing gown.

He reflected wryly that Emily had not needed to specify two for breakfast. The household staff, though handpicked for their discretion on the outside, yet gossiped like magpies on the inside. They'd probably all known of his arrival within minutes, and he knew that breakfast would include the freshly baked rolls he loved. His bed, however, had not been turned down. He chuckled. It was no secret that he would not be using it.

When he reentered Emily's chamber, it was to find the servants setting out their breakfast at the round table beneath the window. It had required not one but three trays to accommodate the sumptuous repast that the servants had conjured up belowstairs this morning, leaving George more certain than ever that his arrival had been remarked from the moment he'd reined in. He and Emily ate their breakfast of warm, fresh rolls, kippers, eggs, and bacon in companionable silence. They smiled, speaking little but gazing fondly at each other, and several times he took her hand across the table and stroked it. It was such luxury to be able to sit here like this with Emily not two feet away. She looked exquisitely lovely as always, her sandy brown hair pulled back softly with a ribbon, a lavender silk wrapper draped about her lush body.

When he had drained his coffee cup for the second time, he slowly rose and crossed to the further window in the room, the one that gave onto the rear garden. He gazed out for a moment and then turned to Emily. "I bring you news, Emily," he said soberly.

"Yes, George, what is it?" she asked with concern, and he turned to face her.

"News from the Continent. Roland Shoup is dead."

He watched her beautiful, pink skin turn pale. Slowly, she too rose from the table and came to stand near him.

"How?" she asked quietly.

"In a duel, several days ago." He stood very still, watching her intently.

She closed her eyes and leaned her head against the window, her back to him. She seemed to be shaking, perhaps crying, and he wanted nothing so much as to gather in his arms. But he sensed her need to have this moment alone and so he waited. Finally she took a deep breath. "Well, thank God for that. It was a long time coming, wasn't it?"

"Yes," he murmured, "long overdue, I should say."

She turned to face him, blinking back the bit of moisture in her eyes. "Just so. And—ah—how long will you be staying, George?"

He took a step closer and gently put his hands on her shoulders. "Emily," he said in a voice that sounded strange to his own ears, "don't you realize what this all means?"

"About Roland? Why, yes. It means that a good many fathers and husbands in France and Italy can sleep more soundly in their beds at night."

"No, Em, I mean about *us*. Don't you see? You are free, truly free! Now even the highest sticklers, those who do not recognize divorce at all, cannot fail to acknowledge that, if not a divorced woman, you are a widow."

She shook her head and started to turn away, but he took her hands so that she had to face him. "Marry me, Em. It's long past the time. I don't want to live like this any longer. It's too hard; it gets harder all the time."

"I know, George, and—and it may be true what you say, but you—you are not an ordinary citizen, not even an ordinary peer. You know what this will do to your career. Why, you'll be named a Secretary next year. Everyone says so. I don't want—"

"Dammit, Emily!" he blurted, dropping her hands and striding several feet away. "I am forty-eight years old and I'm tired of sneaking around in the middle of the night! Why, just—just having breakfast with you is such luxury! It's—it's ridiculous!"

"But George, I—"

"No, Emily. I enjoy my career, 'tis true, but it's *not* the most important thing in my life. *You* are. And truth to tell, I—I should never have allowed you to dissuade me these five years past, except that I knew that you would be subjected to very unkind gossip and outright cuts in London. I did not want to do that to you, else believe me I should have ignored the consequences to my career."

She stood with her back to the window, distress evident in her blue eyes. "You must give me time to—to think on it," she said quietly. " 'Tis all so sudden."

"Sudden!" he exclaimed, dashing back to her. He grabbed her forcefully by the shoulders and pulled her close. "For Godsakes, Em, we've been together for fifteen years! How long a courtship do you want?"

She laughed, despite herself, it seemed. "Oh, George, I love you so," she moaned softly into his shoulder.

"I know you do. And that is why you're going to marry me. I warn you, Em, this time I shan't take no for an answer."

She shook her head and pulled away. He saw the tears in her eyes and hugged her close again. "Sometimes, my stubborn little wench, I think I ought simply to drug you and drag you off to Gretna Green like some overeager halfling."

She blinked up at him in amazement and he smiled. And then he kissed her, long and slowly. When finally he raised his head and they drew apart, she said a bit shakily, "You know—ah—Andrew and your nephew are here, at Roanbrooke. Where—where will you stay?"

He looked quizzically at her but answered readily enough. "And well I know they are here. I sent Andrew up after Justin, to talk some sense into him.

It's time my nephew started doing something worthwhile with his life. He should take his place in the government. He was made for it, born for it. He's just too stubborn to admit it. At all events, I would have given them a little bit more time together, but I—I couldn't wait with my news. But you're right of course, I cannot very well stay here with no one the wiser, not if I'm to see Justin and Drew. And I can't stay at Roanbrooke, not with the hours I intend to keep," he said and favored her with a wicked grin at this last. "So I've put up at the Inn. My man is there even now. And I shall merely tell Justin and Drew that I have government business that may keep me abroad at odd hours."

She cocked an eyebrow at him. "And will they believe that?"

"Oh, Drew will believe anything I tell him. And as for Justin—well, truth to tell, one never knows *what* Justin is thinking. But I daresay he'll keep his counsel, no matter what it is," he replied. "And now, my dearest, we have something of far greater moment to discuss, namely our marriage," he added pointedly, and reached for her again.

She neatly sidestepped him and went to sit on the blue velvet settee at the foot of the bed. "I suppose you've heard the talk about Lord Roane and the Baron Landon?" she asked with great nonchalance.

Now for the first time the earl felt his expression become grim. "Yes, Em, I know," he said heavily. "I know that the baron is done for and that Justin was there to pick up the pieces. I was at White's that night, you see."

"Yes, but that—that is not the last of it, George."

"What do you mean?"

"Well, apparently the baron was *not* at his last prayers. I mean to say, he must have had something else left to gamble, because he challenged Roane to another game."

"Which Justin did not accept," Westmacott finished wearily, leaning against the wall.

"No, George. Quite the contrary. Roane did accept, and the baron won it all back."

"What? Are you sure?" he demanded, straightening up. "I can hardly credit it."

Emily chuckled, smoothing the folds of her silk wrapper with a delicate hand. " 'Tis a nine days wonder, I know, but 'tis true enough. It is all the talk of the village."

The earl ran a distracted hand through his hair. It did not make sense. It simply didn't, he thought, not if —

"I expect it will be all the talk tonight as well," Emily continued. "Oh! I forgot completely about Agatha Crowley's ball. I am promised to attend," she said in a rush of words, and then her eyes twinkled. "But come, you have received a card as well, have you not? It would be just like Lady Crowley to assume you had naught better to do than hightail it up from London to grace her ball."

"*Justin's* ball, Emily. You forget for whom she is doing this," Westmacott replied with a gleam in his eye. He came to stand before the settee. "And though it will further puff up Lady Crowley's consequence, I shall of course attend. It isn't often I have the opportunity to dance with you, my love."

"Oh, George, dare we?" she breathed, looking up at him. "We shall have to be exceedingly discreet."

"And so we shall be," he replied, taking her hand and pulling her up. "For the next few days. After that we shall announce our engagement and —"

"George, dear," she interrupted quickly, "do let us walk in the garden. The flowers are so beautiful at this time of year."

The earl looked stern for a moment, then yielded gracefully. "But of course, my love, do let us walk in the garden," he murmured.

When they had dressed and made their way out to the garden, the earl took Emily's arm and they strolled peacefully along the neat rows of pink and yellow roses. The roses gave way to gladiolas in full and fragrant bloom, and then they came to a small arbour framed by profusions of wisteria. It was a favourite place of theirs, and he seated her on the wicker love seat he'd purchased the summer before.

He strolled a few feet away and absently fingered the delicate purple blossoms of the wisteria. Then he turned to face her. "I am well aware, my love, of how many times you changed the subject before. But I shan't allow you to get away with it, you know. I will have this settled, and very soon." She opened her mouth to speak but he forestalled her. "No, Em. The time has come. 'Tis summer, you know, when the flowers blossom full and open, when the fruit ripens. The time is ripe for us. Do not gainsay me, Emily," he concluded softly.

She rose and came to stand near him. "George, you must not think I mean to thwart you, nor that I wish it any less than you. 'Tis only my love for you, my concern for your career that—"

"Dammit, woman!" the earl exploded, crushing a delicate cluster of wisteria blossoms in his large hand. "I have *told* you that you need no longer concern yourself with that. I don't *want* some damned ministry if I can't have you! Don't you understand that? And stop being so bloody noble all the time. Look at me! I'm a man, not some bloodless pillar of the government! I want a wife. I want to take her to bed every night and wake up with her every morning. I want someone besides my valet to come home to every day! I want *you,* Emily!" he said fervently, wrapping his arms about her.

"Oh, George, if we—if we *did* marry now, it would immediately become known that all along we—"

"I don't give a damn! Not any more," he countered forcefully. Then another thought struck him and his voice was less sure. "Do—do you, Em? Is that what—"

"No! Of course not. It is only for *you* that I—"

"Oh, love," he interrupted, clasping her tightly to his chest. "Do you realize that we have been so bent on protecting each other that we have insured our unhappiness? It is enough, Emily. No more."

She looked up at him with tear-filled eyes. "My dear, I should like nothing better than to be your wife, but I—but I—"

He slipped a finger under her chin and tilted her face up to his. "What are you afraid of, Emily?"

"I? Why I am not afraid of—oh, lord," she sighed. "I—I suppose I *am* at that. Afraid—afraid that you will—will come to regret it. Especially if it means your career will—"

"Hang my blasted career, Emily!" he roared, storming several feet away. He felt his pulse throb at his temple. What the devil would it take—? "I hope I may never see Whitehall again!" he blurted, and then tried to calm himself. "Now, I shall give you but a few days to come to your senses." His face softened and he stepped closer to her. "After that I shall be forced to take drastic measures." His eyes twinkled at the last and her face relaxed into a smile. He held out his arms and she melted into them. He kissed her, very gently, and then not so gently at all.

When he managed to pull away he smiled down at her and smoothed a wisp of hair from her brow. "Oh,

Em," he sighed happily, "do you know you get more beautiful with each passing season? I don't know how you do it."

She peered up at him and laughed softly. "Spoken like a man besotted, my lord. The truth is I see tiny new wrinkles all the time."

"Hmm. Very tiny, I should say," he murmured, tracing circles over the smooth skin of her cheeks. "But it doesn't worry you, does it? Most other woman would fret themselves to distraction over the mere hint of a wrinkle."

"Most women don't have *you,* George," she whispered seductively, her body very close to his.

He stared down at her quizzically. "As you say, my dear," he replied, and then yawned delicately. "I declare, Emily, the fresh air has quite tired me out. I could do with a—er—nap, I should think."

"Could you now? Well, and what of your son and nephew? Should you not—"

"They can wait," he replied baldly. "I'll see them at the Crowleys tonight at all events. Just now I've more—er—pressing things on my mind."

Emily's lips twitched. "To be sure, my lord. But are you—ah—certain you would not like to—ah—practice being respectably married and—ah—wait until nightfall?"

"We'll never be that respectable," he growled, and pulled her closer and kissed her quite ruthlessly.

And then, slowly, the Earl of Westmacott led his lady love back to bed.

Chapter 24

Moriah was most apprehensive about the ball this evening and felt that the day was passing all too quickly. The household was in a flurry of activity as Lizzie and Mrs. Trotter helped Tess and her prepare for the ball. Papa did not emerge from his rooms all day, except for one brief sojourn in his study, and Moriah could only hope that he wasn't drinking too much.

He wasn't, she realized with relief as he joined his daughters in the main entry hall when it was time to leave for Crowley Manor. He looked quite sober and very dapper in black coat and satin breeches, but Moriah was perturbed by the sadness lurking in the back of his eyes.

Nonetheless, he surveyed his daughters with obvious approval. And well he might, Moriah thought. Tess looked absolutely breathtaking in Mama's white muslin gown with its yellow ribbons and the delicate rosettes that Lizzie had painstakingly added. Her hair had been swept up in a topknot with tendrils trailing down her long graceful neck. And Moriah had to admit that she herself looked rather becoming in the ivory satin. It was cut low across the bosom and, with a tuck here and there, had been made to fit her form rather well. The beautiful large violet silk roses emphasized her eyes, and she had added several at the bottom of the full skirt as well. She wore the amethyst earrings that had been her mother's, but no other jewelry save a matching pin that adorned her sleek black hair.

When they arrived at Crowley Manor there was a lineup of carriages ahead of them, and Moriah mused that Lady Crowley must have invited all the gentry from Herefordshire and two counties beyond. Some fifteen minutes later, when they were finally ushered up the stairs into the huge, crowded entry hall, she knew she was right.

As they made their way slowly to the reception line, Moriah recalled that the manor had undergone extensive renovations recently. She'd not been here for several years, however, she and Olivia never having been great friends, and she wondered what changes Lady Crowley had seen fit to make in what had been, to Moriah's mind, a warm, charming country manor house.

When they reached the ballroom, Moriah could not help gasping aloud. For the sweeping, once graceful room had been transformed into what must have been Lady Crowley's concept of a Roman villa. The entire room was done in white marble, with statues and huge pillars interspersed in the most unlikely juxtapositions. But at least the profusion of flowers trellised along the walls and encircling some of the pillars mitigated the coldness of the room.

Moriah's thoughts were diverted as she realized that Papa was already talking to Sir Hugo. The baronet greeted them all warmly, but Lady Crowley smiled tightly, as if she was not sure the Landons warranted more. She wore a purple gown weighted down with oversized encrusted jewels and a matching toque, which might have given her a stately air had not its three large ostrich plumes bobbed up and down into a most comical manner. Olivia, in a white muslin dress that made her look absurdly young, mimicked her mother's grudging smile. And then Moriah found herself face to face and hand in hand with Justin Traugott, Viscount Roane.

But, as at the Abbey, his greeting was smooth and proper, and the extra pressure on her hand and the special warmth in his eyes reassured her. Out of the corner of her eye she saw Olivia watching their little interchange, but her false smile did not falter and so Moriah assumed she'd noted nothing exceptional. Olivia made a point of standing on tiptoe and whispering something in Justin's ear. His face remained impassive but Olivia giggled prettily and Moriah was glad to move on.

As soon as they entered the ballroom, Papa was surrounded by well-wishers and gossipmongers alike. He seemed to be handling them with a quiet dignity that Moriah had never seen in him before, and so when her friend Sarah tapped her on the shoulder she felt safe in making her escape. She and Tess followed Sarah to a quiet corner next to an ornate pillar. A handsome young man in regimentals appeared and Sarah introduced him as her brother. They chatted for a few moments and then the orchestra struck up the first dance. It was a quadrille, and Moriah stilled the pang she felt as Justin led Olivia out onto the center of the floor. After all, she'd known it would be this way. His face was a mask of politeness but Olivia looked smug. The dance floor filled rapidly and Sarah's brother invited Tess to dance. Moriah and Sarah were whisked off soon enough themselves, and Moriah found that for a few moments she could forget her troubles and enjoy the dance.

In fact, she thought, sometime later, she was enjoying herself rather more than she'd expected. She kept a sharp eye on Tess, who was besieged by nearly every young man in attendance. Tess acquitted herself well, flirting prettily and remembering not to dance more than once with any one man. If Tess's dancing feet were never still, what surprised Moriah was that neither were her own. She stood up with two local squires, a widower, a Captain of the Guards . . .

In truth she would have enjoyed herself excessively except for two factors. One was the sight of Justin and Olivia sharing a tête-à-tête several times. She chided herself for this; Justin owed her nothing, after all. And he needs must be polite to his hosts. But then Moriah recalled Lady Crowley's words in Endicott's Emporium about Justin and politics and how advantageous marriage to Olivia might be. She recalled, too, Justin's genuine interest in their political discussion last night, and she felt utterly miserable.

The second factor that marred her pleasure in the evening was more difficult to define. Some of her dancing partners were respectful though friendly, but several others looked her up and down in a manner most inappropriate. She had just now escaped a handsome middle-aged peer, Lord Chilton, who held her entirely too closely and kept trying to lead her out into the garden. He was, she recalled, the same man who had stared so rudely at her outside Mr. Fairley's office. She did not like him; his smile, more a smirk actually, was lecherous. His eyes raked her person insolently, lingering too long on her bosom. But it was not his behavior that shook her so much as his parting comment when Moriah finally struggled free from his grasp on her wrist. "Play your little games, if you like. But I shall come for you again. I

268

know you better than you may think." Then he'd chuckled unpleasantly and departed. Moriah had felt dizzy and had leaned against the nearest pillar to steady herself. Could anyone really tell that she was no longer a—a maiden? No, it wasn't possible, and after all, she reassured herself, everyone else was treating her properly. She must not allow a few men who were obviously not gentlemen to overset her.

She was relieved when Tess came to interrupt her unpleasant reverie and was glad to listen to her sister's enthusiastic chatter. "Oh, Moriah, the evening is quite perfect, is it not? Even Papa seems to be having a good time!" Moriah glanced across the room to where her father stood at the center of a laughing circle of elderly gentlemen. At least she needn't trouble herself about Papa, she thought, and mustered up an appropriate response to Tess. But she stopped mid-sentence as she saw Justin approaching. He wore a chocolate-brown coat and satin breeches, set off by a buff-colored shirt. The clothes were superbly made and fit him to perfection. She watched him stride lithely to her and was reminded, as before, of a panther. That sense of power and strength that she had first noticed about him was still there, and she felt her heart race. In order to distract herself she tried to focus her attention on the handsome red-haired young man accompanying him.

"Miss Landon, Miss Tess," Justin said pleasantly. "How nice to see you again. I do hope you are enjoying yourselves. I would like to present my cousin, Andrew, Lord Wainsfield. Andrew, Miss Moriah Landon and her sister Tess."

Justin's speech gave Moriah a bit of a jolt. She was not best pleased to come face to face with his cousin, but she needn't have worried, for Lord Wainsfield was nearly oblivious to her. Too much so. For he greeted Moriah politely but absently, his eyes fixed all the while on Tess.

"Miss Tess," he breathed, taking her hand. Tess blushed and answered him demurely, and Moriah had the strange feeling that for once Tess was not flirting. The orchestra began a cotillion, and young Wainsfield invited Tess to dance. She followed him onto the floor without a backward glance.

Moriah's eyes flew to Justin's, and for a moment she caught a flash of alarm as his eyes followed the couple. But then it was gone and he turned to her. "Tess looks lovely tonight. And you look beautiful, Moriah. Are you—are you enjoying yourself, my dear?"

"I—I am trying, Justin. I *do* enjoy the dancing."

"I'm glad. I cannot ask you to stand up now, since I am waiting for my waltz, but would you care for a glass of lemonade?"

"Thank you. I'd like that. I own it is excessively hot in here. But, in truth," she added in a whisper, "I suppose we ought not to be seen together too much at all events."

"No, I don't suppose so," he replied, but his face was grim. He procured her the refreshment and found a very public alcove for them to sit. He was painfully aware that Moriah was correct and that they must give all the wagging tongues absolutely no grist for the gossip mills. There was gossip enough tonight and it was none of it pleasant. He'd overheard three different tabbies gleefully spreading it about that Roane had already taken a mistress ". . . and he not here in the county above a se'ennight." No one seemed to have figured out who this supposed mistress was, for which he was profoundly grateful. But he could have strangled the servant who must have lept to conclusions about his nocturnal comings

270

and goings. As it was, he could only hope that Moriah hadn't heard any such rumblings.

It didn't seem so. She was not overly distressed at all events, and he thought he could read her fairly well by now. They sat side by side and spoke, with infinite politeness, of trivialities. There was little else they could do in the midst of all the bustle; he could not take the chance of anyone overhearing any but the most banal of conversation. He cursed all of society for requiring this charade of him, for forcing him to keep his distance from her.

He was, in point of fact, having a miserable time at this ball in his honour. He had to stand by while one man after another approached Moriah, flirted with her, and danced a damn sight too close. She looked as though it bothered her, but he couldn't be sure. And the Crowley woman, hostess or no, was like to drive him to drink with her not-so-subtle hints about her officious daughter.

He rested his eyes for a moment on Moriah, thinking that she had never looked more beautiful. The violet roses on her gown and the amethyst earrings brought out the magnificent color of her eyes. And for once her gown fit her perfectly, in fact emphasized her figure stunningly. He forced his eyes to the dance floor, lest they linger too long on Moriah.

"Tess is enjoying herself enormously," Moriah said.

"She is very charming, Moriah."

"Yes, and truly, I think, quite unspoiled. Especially considering her looks and that fragile manner of hers. I own she can wind most of the household right around her little finger."

"But not you. Am I correct, little one? I am persuaded that you have had a good deal to do with making her such a delightful young lady," he whispered near her ear.

Moriah felt a rush of pleasure and, with it, embarrassment at his words. She strove to change the subject. "And what—what of *your* family, Justin?" she asked, and suddenly his face clouded over, but not understanding why, she went on. "Other than your cousin and his father, the Earl of Westmacott, you have never mentioned anyone. Surely—"

"You are correct, Moriah. I have never mentioned my family," he interrupted coldly.

Moriah blanched at the icy look in his eyes. She wondered at his reaction but hid her confusion by reverting back to the safe topic of Tess. She stared out at the dance floor once again. "I—ah—that is, Tess is—ah—acquitting herself well tonight," she stammered. "I have always thought it a great shame that she would not have a Season, for I own she would take very well," she concluded more steadily.

"Yes, Moriah, she would," he replied, deliberately softening his tone and very grateful that she had not pursued her previous question. He regretted his reaction; he had been cold to the point of rudeness, but he could not help it. His family was simply not something he was prepared to discuss with her. What the devil could he say, after all?

"Do you know, Justin, I do not believe Tess has sat out a single dance," she added in a light tone.

"Nor have you, I daresay," he retorted without thinking. He hoped she did not notice the edge to his voice.

Her eyes flew to his face and he noted her distress. Oh, Lord, not another question about whether mistresses—"Justin, I—it—it is difficult," she began, her voice a mere whisper, her eyes once more on the dancers. So it was not a question, but something else. He waited, and she went on. "I do like to dance,

272

but some of the men . . . I—well, I do not under·
stand why—that is—"

"What is it, Moriah?" he probed gently, keeping
his voice very low.

She tried to smile. "Oh, I—I suppose I am being
silly or fanciful. They are only flirting, after all."

She would say no more, but she didn't have to.
Roane felt all of his muscles tighten in anger. He
could not explain to her that the extraordinarily
sensuous aura she exuded caused men to behave less
than properly. Nor could he protect her; she had
refused him that right.

"Moriah, some men" he started to say, "—well,
unfortunately there are always those who do not
behave as they ought and you—you" She had a
pained expression on her face and he cursed himself
for a poor choice of words. He remembered only too
well *his* behavior the first time they met. He had not
the slightest idea how to go on and was very glad she
saw fit to interrupt him.

"But you . . . are you enjoying this little rout in
your honour? Certainly our hostesses seem to be
lavishing you with attention," she said, and he could
not decide whether her tone held amusement or—or
jealousy. He had not time to pursue that particular
line of thought, for the music stopped and he knew it
was time to relinquish her.

As they stood up an attractive brown-haired
woman in a pale blue gown approached. Moriah
introduced her as her friend Sarah Ashford.

"Ah, Lady Ashford, what a pleasure to meet you,"
Roane said with a smile. "I believe I know your
husband, John, is it not? I saw him in London less
than a fortnight ago," he concluded, and then
watched in consternation as her pretty face paled.

"I—ah—how nice, Lord Roane. I trust he is well,"

273

Lady Ashford replied cautiously. Her tone told him she'd not heard from Ashford in *more* than a fortnight.

"Yes, he goes on quite well." What else could he say? That Ashford was always smiling, with a drink in one hand and a woman hanging on the other? What was wrong with the chap, to leave such a pretty young wife to rusticate by herself nearly all the year? In his bewilderment Roane turned to Moriah, who deftly changed the subject. But before she spoke Roane had caught the look on her face, an expression that spoke volumes. And now for the first time he understood her refusal of his offer. How much did she know of men, after all? Her father was a wastrel; her friend's husband was a rake. And as Moriah herself had pointed out, she hardly knew Roane at all. He cursed inwardly at the thought that what little she did know of him could hardly commend him as a husband.

The orchestra began to play again, and when Moriah's hand was claimed, Roane invited Lady Ashford to dance. He entertained her with amusing anecdotes of the ton and tried to ignore the sadness in her brown eyes even as she laughed.

As the dance ended Roane espied Lady Crowley bearing down on him and he deftly escaped to the card room. He remained only a few moments, long enough to assure himself that Landon was not there, and then sauntered out with the hope that Agatha Crowley would have found another audience for her recital of her daughter's charms. He spotted her across the room in her purple gown that seemed to display half the crown jewels. As always, she had Olivia in tow. Not taking any chances, Roane headed toward the center of the room, where Tess Landon stood with a group of young people. He had meant to stand up with her at all events and was pleased that she was not yet engaged for the country dance just now forming.

Tess was a graceful partner but she seemed troubled, and he inquired as to the cause. She demurred, fobbing him off with some moonshine about her previous partner having trounced on her toe, and then the steps of the dance separated them. When they came together again he pressed her and finally she smiled shyly and said, "I own I do not quite know how to go on with you, my lord. For here we at Wykham have been rejoicing at our good fortune, at having our home restored to us, but it—it is your loss, is it not?"

He smiled down at her. "I am touched by your concern, my dear, but I pray you may be easy. 'Twas a fair game, and besides, Roanbrooke and my other lands keep me quite busy enough, I daresay." He was rewarded with a radiant smile and reflected that she was, indeed, a most refreshing young lady. She seemed without guile or conceit; that and her concern for others were most unusual, given her looks, and he surmised once more that much of the credit went to Moriah. But he also knew that London society would eat such an ingenuous child alive.

It was just as well, he thought, that she was not about to make her debut. As to what London society might do to Moriah—well, he declined to think of that at all.

And he tried very hard, in the ensuing dances with hopeful young daughters of ambitious mothers, not to think of Moriah at all. Instead, he thought of her a bit too much, followed her with his eyes a bit too often. And when the strains of the first waltz rose from the violins, he crossed the floor toward her a bit too quickly.

He thought he heard a collective murmur arise as he clasped her hand and pulled her to him. But he ignored it, just as he ignored the curious sea of eyes and blur of faces surrounding them. It was good, so good, to hold her in his arms again. It had been so long since he'd done so. She smelled of roses, and her body felt warm and pliant. She seemed to relax against him, as if she'd been holding herself rigidly until now.

"I love you in that gown," he whispered.

"Mmm. Thank you, Justin," she murmured dreamily.

For a few moments he held her close, marvelling at how well she fit in his arms and how well they moved together across the floor. And then, as if by mutual consent, they moved a respectable few inches apart. He certainly had no intention of giving the tabbies anything further to gossip about. Still, he kept his hand firmly on her back, and she tilted her face up to his. He swept her gracefully, skillfully, around the dance floor, and for those precious few moments he could forget that there were any other people in the room. She seemed to forget as well, her eyes taking on a rather smoky cast that made him long for the hunting box. He felt the desire rise in him and knew he had to distract himself. This was simply not the time. . . . And then he noted that Moriah's expression had changed. She was gazing across the floor with a decidedly worried look. His eyes followed hers.

"Damn!" he muttered softly. "Drew ought to know better. I'll have a talk with him. Do not trouble overmuch, my dear. I realize it's their second dance, but this *is* the country. I do not think it will be much remarked."

"Perhaps, Justin, but a waltz! Tess should know

better as well. Why, she's only sixteen. And—and I am afraid they have been much in each other's company this night."

"I cannot think what Drew can be about, but I will attend to him later. For now, I have a beautiful woman in my arms and I intend to enjoy her." He smiled at her intently and was delighted to see her flush. He gently pushed her head onto his shoulder and, increasing their pace, twirled her about the floor.

It was over too quickly and he had no choice but to relinquish her to her next partner. He slowly kissed her hand and her violet eyes locked with his; again he felt that intensity between them. He was loathe to give her up but, having no choice, decided he'd had quite enough of the overcrowded, stuffy ballroom. Why Lady Crowley needs must fill a room meant for fifty people with several hundred was beyond him. He strolled out onto the terrace, a rather large affair now festooned with flowers and almost too crowded with refugees from the ballroom.

"Lord Roane, how nice to see you," a pleasant, lilting voice from behind his shoulder said.

He turned and smiled. "Mrs. Shoup. Good evening, ma'am. I see that you, too, are in need of some air."

She chuckled, leaning back against the wooden railing all but hidden by cascades of trailing white roses. She looked lovely, as always, in a mint-green chiffon gown with long flowing sleeves. "I should say so," she answered. "Although one might have known that Agatha Crowley would comb half of Britain to create a shocking squeeze. Oh, but I am being discourteous, am I not? They have all come to honour *you*, after all, my lord," she said with a twinkle in her eye.

He replied in kind. "But, of course, Mrs. Shoup. The fact that I know but half of my esteemed guests does not, I assure you, discommode me in the least."

She chuckled again and then they spoke for some minutes about London. She asked interesting questions and listened avidly to his description of the parade of aspiring young dandies on Rotten Row of an afternoon. She laughed at his report of the latest musicale, during which he had discovered a hidden talent for sleeping in a straight-backed chair. And she wanted to know what the latest exhibits at the British Museum were. Were the Elgin marbles as impressive as 'twas said, and was there anything else that the ton deigned to consider of interest?

At that *he* laughed, and he found himself wondering why she never went to London, for surely she would enjoy it immensely. He knew, of course, the stories about her longtime paramour, but of a certain that must not preclude an occasional visit to the metropolis. No, she must have reasons of her own and he thought it tactful not to ask. As to her lover, he had suspicions of his own—an imprudent comment passed now and again by a certain personage in London, but he would keep such speculation to himself. It was none of his affair, after all.

"You and Miss Landon look quite handsome together out on the dance floor," Mrs. Shoup was saying, and his eyes narrowed slightly. "She is very beautiful, is she not, my lord? A very unusual girl, I should say."

"Yes, Mrs. Shoup, she is both," he replied cautiously. There seemed to be a purpose to her words but he could not think what.

She turned to gaze into the ballroom. "My lord, I—" she began, her voice suddenly tentative, "forgive me if I presume, but I believe her father is much occupied with friends just now and—well, I mean to say . . . perhaps you might—ah—keep an eye peeled for her, my lord. I believe she needs someone to do so."

Her words, so kindly spoken, rendered him speechless for a moment. That she should have read the situation as he had with regard to Moriah and some of her dance partners was amazing enough. And he could not help but be flattered that she'd had such faith in him as to seek him out as Moriah's "guardian." But the irony of it shamed him greatly, and then, too, he felt uneasy. Why had she chosen him after all? Was there something in his manner toward Moriah that suggested they were any but the most casual of acquaintances? Mrs. Shoup continued to gaze inside, strolling now toward the French doors. Clearly she would say no more, and he could not ask.

He cleared his throat, feeling suddenly like a schoolboy who'd been given a gentle rap on the knuckles by the headmaster. "I—er—you are very perceptive, Mrs. Shoup. I shall not take your words lightly." And with that they stepped into the ballroom, parting amiably as she went off to chat with several friends.

He could not locate Moriah, such was the swirl of color and crush of people before him, but he did espy Drew and remembered his resolve to speak with him. He made his way to the far side of the ballroom, where Drew stood with a group of young people, among them Tess Landon. Roane made polite conversation for a few moments and then succeeded in disengaging Drew.

Andrew hailed a passing footman and, securing two glasses of brandy, followed Justin toward the corridor. It was just as they neared the threshold, in

279

fact as they were passing between the statues of two Roman goddesses, that the voices reached them. The words were unmistakably clear, and Andrew turned to see two dowagers, whose names he could not recall, deep in conversation, quite oblivious to the throng around them. They were turned just enough away so as not to see Andrew and Justin pass.

"I do think Agatha had ought to set her sights elsewhere. Roane does not at all appear to be hanging out for a wife," declared the wide one in the chartreuse gown. Andrew's eyes darted to his cousin, who gave no indication, other than a narrowing of the eyes, that he'd heard anything. He continued to wend his way through the crowed, but still Andrew could hear the other woman's reply.

"I am persuaded you are right, Drusilla. Why, I hear tell he has already found himself a mistress here in the country. Though I own he is very discreet about it. Absolutely no one seems to know who she is or where he found her."

Andrew could hear no more and was relieved when he and Justin finally attained the corridor. There was a fierce scowl on his cousin's face, but Andrew squelched the urge to make reference to what they'd just overheard. Justin took a long, slow sip of his brandy. It did not seem that he would refer to it either. Instead, the words he did utter caught Andrew by surprise.

"Tess Landon is a taking little thing, is she not?"

Andrew's ears perked up, his body tensed. "Er — well, yes, I suppose she is," he replied, hoping to sound casual.

Justin's expression was unreadable. "She is very young, you know, old fellow. She could easily lose her heart — and be hurt or hurt someone else. And a man must have a care for a young girl's reputation.

Forgive me, Drew, but two dances is rather—well, it does rather set them all to talking. And a waltz—"

"Now see here, Justin—"

"No, Drew, *you* listen. A girl of sixteen has no business dancing the waltz. And if *she* doesn't know it, then you sure as hell ought to. And in any case— well, step lightly old chap. She really is too young for—for anything, you know."

Andrew stiffened. "You're out there, Coz. 'Smatter of fact, can't think what all the fuss and bother is about. I realize she's very young—hardly out of the schoolroom I should say. And—well, I suppose the waltz *was* inadvisable, but as to the rest—well, just helping the chit to ease into society, don't you know. Can be rather frightening, a girl's first ball."

Justin looked at him sideways, then smiled. Andrew breathed a faint sigh of relief. "I'm glad to hear it, Drew. Always knew you were a sensible chap," his cousin said, and the two men repaired to the card room in perfect amiability. But Andrew was visibly shaken. He had no idea he'd been so transparent, and what the devil was he to do now?

And he also wondered at Justin's unprecedented concern for Tess Landon's reputation. Not that he wasn't a gentleman, but still it was unexpected, considering his cousin's recent dealings with the Landons. And, come to think on it, there was something else that had jarred him just a while ago. It was, he had to admit, perfectly acceptable for Justin to waltz with Moriah Landon, even if they *had* only just met, and even if Justin had just won and then lost the baron's fortune, such as it was. No, what disturbed Andrew, in a way he could not define, was something about how his cousin had looked at Miss Landon when they were dancing. Or something about the way they'd looked at each other, or—well, he did not truly know. And then Andrew's thoughts were diverted as they attained the card room.

"Well, Roane, good to see you, old chap. And young Wainsfield, is it not?" exclaimed a dapper, superbly rigged-out Lord Clivehurst. They made suitable replies and then again when Sir Jeffrey Storch, very obviously in his cups, joined the group. Andrew knew that Clivehurst and Justin ran in the same set, but he thought his cousin did not much care for Sir Jeffrey.

"Care t' try your hand at faro?" Sir Jeffrey asked, his speech somewhat slurred. He seconded his invitation with a broad, unsteady sweep of his hand that sent some of the contents of his drink sloshing onto the floor.

Andrew jumped aside to avoid being sprinkled with brandy. Clivehurst moved into the breach. "Don't think they'd be interested, Sir Jeffrey. Leastways not Roane. Ball in his honour, after all. Got to do the pretty to all the ladies, eh what, Roane?"

"As you say, Clivehurst. But the ballroom does get a bit stuffy now and again, wouldn't you say?" Justin replied good-naturedly.

"Yes, rather. Especially when there are certain ambitious mamas raking one up and down with acquisitive mother-of-the-bride eyes," Clivehurst retorted, and Justin laughed aloud.

"Well, Roane certainly ain't interested in leg-shackling himself, are you, my lord?" Sir Jeffrey asked with a leer. "Too busy — and too successful — with his doxies for that, daresay? Care to share your latest, Roane? After all, ain't 'nuf bits o' muslin to go around here in the country."

Andrew watched Justin stiffen and his jaw clench. He was making a great effort to control himself, but still Drew was relieved when Clivehurst once more intervened. "Bit stuffy in here, Sir Jeffrey, eh what? You look a little peaked, old fellow. Why not take a turn out on the terrace; I'll join you in a trice."

"Peaked, you say? Well, and no won'er. Frightfully hot's what it is," Sir Jeffrey mumbled, and then bowed unsteadily. "Servant, gentlemen. Think I'll take a turn 'bout the garden."

He sauntered away, propping himself against the wall every so often. Andrew sighed with relief.

"Sorry, old man," Clivehurst was saying. "Shot the cat again; drinks too damned much. Not but what— well, can't expect the world to ignore your latest conquest, Roane. And though nothing can excuse Sir Jeffrey's crudeness, still, everyone here tonight is wondering how you've contrived to set anyone up in so short a time. It'll be a nine days' wonder, you know. Now, I'm not asking, mind, but any time you'd care to share your secret . . ."

Clivehurst was relaxed and smiling, and so was Justin. And that was why his cousin's next words so astounded Andrew. "Always happy to help a fellow out, Clivehurst, surely you know that. But fact is that this time the tattlemongers have brewed a tempest in a pot of tea. Since I've been up from Town I've concerned myself with nothing more romantic than the mildly handsome face of my estate agent and his prosaic pile of ledger books. However, if you—er—should hear of any high flyers in the vicinity, why I'd be much obliged."

Justin spoke so casually, so pleasantly, that Clivehurst, after his initial shock, had no choice but to believe him—or at least pretend he did. Andrew, who could do neither, took refuge in his drink. The nine days' wonder, he knew, was not that Justin had so quickly found a mistress, but that he was so carefully protecting her. The identity of a man's mistress was

283

simply not a well-kept secret. It usually added to a gentleman's consequence, but even if Justin cared not a whit for that, still, to refuse to tell a good friend or his very own cousin . . .

Andrew was relieved when their little group broke up, and as he and Justin wandered back to the ballroom, his head was full of unwanted conjecture. Justin was entitled to his privacy, after all. But Andrew could not help wondering. . . . Was she a respectable widow or the wife of someone not at all complacent?

Chapter 25

It was just as he and Justin rounded the corridor toward the ballroom that Andrew gasped. They both stopped short, Justin mumbling a shocked, "What the—?"

"Fa—Father!" blurted Andrew. "Whatever are you *doing* here? And—and where have you been all night? And your—your bags—well, I mean to say . . . have you just arrived? Father, whatever are you *doing* here?"

"Whoa, halfling," countered the earl, holding up a hand in protest and laughing softly as he approached. "I believe we are here in honour of Justin, are we not?" His eyes twinkled and he bowed slightly. "Evening, nephew, Drew."

"Good evening, Uncle," Justin replied evenly. Westmacott had the feeling that Justin was not best pleased to see him and wondered why.

"Fa, you know I don't mean, 'What are you doing at the ball!' I mean, 'what are you doing in the country at first stop?' "

"Why, I came to see you two, especially Justin here, as you both must know," the earl replied smoothly.

He did not miss the reproachful look Justin cast toward Andrew. "Don't look daggers at *me*, Coz; *I* never wrote him a word!" Drew exclaimed, and both young men eyed him curiously.

"Well, fact of the matter is, I would have given you two a bit more time but that I had other business out here in these parts. And so—well, here I am."

"But—but where have you been?" Andrew asked. "Why haven't we seen you? Surely you are staying at—"

"I am staying at the White Feathers Inn, Andrew. You must forgive me, Justin, but my business may keep me abroad at odd hours and I did not wish to disturb the routine at Roanbrooke. At all events, I am only just arrived today," Westmacott said calmly.

"Oh, but I'm sure Justin wouldn't mind if you came and went at odd hours, would you, Justin?" Andrew pressed eagerly. His father sighed inwardly. He might've known Drew would not make this easy. But it was Justin's response that rather unnerved him.

His nephew looked at him quizzically out of shrewd blue eyes. "No, of course I wouldn't mind," he said very softly. "But then, you must do as you wish, Uncle George."

There came a bustle from the direction of the ballroom and then, to the earl's relief, several people appeared in the corridor.

"Oh, there you are, Lord Westmacott," Agatha Crowley trilled in a voice too brittle. "There is a country set just now forming and the ladies are all asking for you. Mustn't hide in the corridor, you know." She took his arm and he cast a rueful glance at his grinning son and nephew. But he went quite willingly, for the moment preferring his hostess's sharp voice to his nephew's sharp eyes.

Andrew drifted off and Justin elected to join the country set along with his uncle. But when the

286

orchestra next struck up a waltz, Justin retired to the sidelines. There was only one woman with whom he cared to waltz, and they'd already had the one dance propriety allowed. He was not best pleased to see Clivehurst lead Moriah out, and distracted himself by hailing a footman for a brandy. Damn! he thought. His uncle's appearance only complicated his life further. It was one thing to keep things from Andrew . . . But then, perhaps Uncle George was hiding something as well, and that might help matters somewhat.

He reflected that the earl never waltzed, and wondered where he would have gone off to. He wondered, too, whether the enlightened guess he'd made some time ago was true. His uncle's unexpected visit and that farrago of nonsense about government business and odd hours made him think it was.

Justin had often wondered, once he was old enough to understand such things, why his uncle had never remarried. And why, as the on dits had it, the earl took such pains to be discreet about his mistresses. A chance word here and there had made Justin think that perhaps there was only *one* mistress, and the impression that his uncle had been to Herefordshire more often than he cared to admit had rung bells in his head. Of course, he couldn't be certain, but . . .

"I say, Justin. There you are," Andrew piped up from behind him. "Been looking for you. I vow it's a nine days wonder! Look over there, Coz. M' father is actually dancing the waltz! Never thought I'd see the day!"

Justin's eyes turned toward where Andrew was discreetly pointing. And it was there, at the edge of the ballroom, that he saw the Earl of Westmacott gracefully executing the turns of the waltz with a lovely lady in his arms, a lady named Emily Shoup. "Well, fancy that, Andrew. Fancy that," he murmured.

The earl was not at all enjoying himself. He had loved dancing with Emily but found it near torture having to watch other men dance with her, a damn sight too closely. If she wore his ring they would keep a respectable distance, one and all. As it was—well, he could not help overhearing whispers about Emily Shoup and her mysterious lover, and he knew such talk gave men ideas. Sir Hugo Crowley was dancing with her now and there was a look in his eyes that the earl could not like. Her last dance, with a rather bosky sir Jeffrey Storch, had been even worse. Well, the earl told himself, very soon he would have the right, the public right, to protect her from such as he.

He turned away, deciding he'd had enough of the ballroom. He was passing behind a huge bouquet of flowers when a snippet of conversation arrested his attention.

"And I still say, Margaret, that Agatha has put her eggs in the wrong basket. Why, Roane is no more interested in the parson's mousetrap than I am," said a shrill female voice.

The earl could not see the women, nor did he care to. But he stayed where he was.

"Now, Arabella, how can you know? He has been very attentive to Olivia tonight," said the one called Margaret.

"Merely doing the pretty, my dear. And you must know that he has a new mistress, here in Herefordshire."

"What? Already?" Margaret was duly shocked.

"Oh, my dear Margaret! Where *have* you been all

night?" came the smug reply. "Yes, *already*. And close as wax about it, too. They say even his best friends don't know who she is! A real high flyer, I'll wager."

"Hmm. How very mysterious. Still and all, a man must marry and set up his nursery. He could do worse than Olivia Crowley." The earl's body was tense. He did not know whether it was Justin's behavior or the fact of the gossip that vexed him more.

"That's as may be. But I own he could do better. 'Tis in Town he'll find his future bride, you may be sure of that. Why, my very own niece will make her come out this year, you must know. A veritable beauty, she is. *And* the daughter of an earl. My sister married the Earl of Carnby, you may recall."

"Yes, Arabella, dear, how could I forget? Ah, tell me, this story about Roane and his—ah—mistress, how has it got about so fast?"

"Oh, my dear, the servants, of course. One of the grooms is cousin to a Crowley footman. Or to the upstairs maid. I really can't recall, but it doesn't signify. And it's only to be expected. Servants are dreadful gossips, Margaret. You must always beware. The lower orders do so enjoy that sort of thing, you know."

The earl nearly choked at this last and made good his escape. There was much he and Justin had to discuss, and now was as good a time as any to start. He ran his nephew to ground in the card room and was relieved to find him merely an observer. He disengaged him easily and they wandered off to a small saloon with several tapers burning.

"You are looking well, Uncle," Justin said when they'd settled into two comfortable chairs.

"Thank you, Justin. As are you. But enough beating about the bush, my boy. Don't know how long we can remain here uninterrupted, and we really ought to talk. You are, you must know, the center of a good deal of gossip tonight."

"Ah, well, the ball is in my honour, after all."

"Gammon!" the earl exclaimed, and decided to tackle that which seemed, at the moment, the easier topic. He leaned forward and lowered his voice. "Why did you give the baron another game, Justin?"

Justin sighed, his lips curling slightly. "So. You've heard. Well, it—it seemed only fair, you know. The man found himself with some extra funds, after all."

"Had second thoughts did you, Justin?" the earl pressed. His nephew looked decidedly uncomfortable but the earl knew he must get to the bottom of this. Justin must put aside his obsession with the Landons once and for all and get on with his life.

"You—er—might call it that," Justin replied, his hands gripping the sides of the chair.

"I see. And, how is it that he won everything back? Recouped entirely? I can hardly credit the gossip, but there it is, and Landon himself seems in good spirits."

Justin looked even more discomforted and moved to loosen his cravat. "What would you have me say, Uncle? I suppose I was drinking a bit much and—well, things rather got away from me."

"I have never known you to over-imbibe nor to play imprudently, Justin. Though why you should want Landon to win after all the time you spent—"

"Really, Uncle, you refine too much upon it," Justin interrupted, suddenly rising and going to stand next to the mantel. "It was a fair game and 'tis over with. Landon has his home restored to him and that is an end to it," he said with finality.

The earl too rose and regarded his nephew

measuringly. Justin was a grown man and Westmacott knew he ought to respect his privacy, but still—

"And you, Uncle," Justin continued rather pointedly, "what sort of—er—business brings you all the
way out here?"

The earl strove to keep a flicker of surprise from
his face. So, he would go on the offensive, would he?
It was clear that Justin was hiding something. But it
was also uncomfortably clear that his question had
not been merely a ploy to change the subject. It had
not been an innocent question at all. He recalled
Justin's reaction to his staying at the Inn. Damn! He
couldn't possibly suspect . . . could he?

Westmacott looked his nephew in the eyes. The
younger man's expression clearly said, "You keep
your counsel, and I'll keep mine." The earl had been
outflanked, very deftly, and he knew it. And as to the
talk of Justin's mistress—well, this was simply not
the time to bring it up. Not the time at all.

Lady Crowley had made it known to Roane, with a
not so gentle hint, that he was expected to take Olivia
in to supper. He led her out for the supper dance
with a decided lack of enthusiasm. Then he escorted
her into the refreshment room, listening with only
half an ear to her chatter about various well-known
personages of her acquaintance.

A large buffet had been set up at the far end of the
room, with rows of long, narrow tables arranged to
accommodate the maximum number of people. The
room was already crowded, but Roane spotted Moriah just ahead of them and was surprised and
pleased to see Drew escorting her. But then he
frowned. Tess would be most likely to sit with her
sister. Drew was either hopelessly naive or very clever.

He guided Moriah to a table and Roane advanced rapidly through the crush of people until he was able to maneuver Olivia and himself to Drew's table.

"Ah, Justin, how capital! We shall sup together. You ladies of course know each other, do you not?" Andrew said jovially, and then he and Roane seated the ladies. "And I believe Captain Bradley comes our way. Oh, and Miss Tess is with him. We shall be a pleasant sextet, shan't we, Justin?" he asked as Tess Landon and young Bradley approached.

Very naive or very clever, Roane thought again as greetings were exchanged and Tess was seated.

He and Bradley then made their way to the buffet while Drew stayed behind to entertain the ladies. Bradley was very much a military type but seemed pleasant enough for all that. They'd been introduced earlier tonight, and Roane knew him to be Sarah Ashford's brother. He wondered how young Bradley felt about Lady Ashford's situation, and his eyes, even as he heaped a plate with lobster patties and cold poached salmon, drifted to Moriah momentarily.

He and Bradley filled one plate and then another, requiring several trips from the buffet to the table, until everyone seemed provided for. Roane found himself seated next to Olivia, with Drew to her right. Across from Roane sat Tess, and then Bradley and Moriah. The pairing and the seating arrangement were certainly not conducive to romantic tête-à-têtes, and so conversation was general and spirited. Roane was relieved but he sensed that Olivia was more than a little miffed.

"Your home is very beautiful, Miss Crowley," Captain Bradley was saying gallantly.

"Thank you, Captain Bradley. I own my mother has done an excellent job of renovating Crowley

Manor," she replied, and then turned pointedly to Roane. "My lord, do try the lobster patties. Our chef is quite without equal, you must know. And the cold glazed pheasant is Mama's own recipe."

Roane dutifully sampled a lobster patty. "I vow I must agree with you, Miss Crowley. The lobster patties are quite without equal," he remarked with studied gravity, careful not to look down the table at Moriah, who seemed to be choking on her wine. "Ah, Miss Tess," he continued, "have you tried the salmon?" Olivia's mouth tightened in annoyance. Tess answered in the negative, and Roane urged her to correct her omission.

"My lord, are you planning any renovations at Roanbrooke? I am persuaded it is most pleasant to live in a house that can claim all the modern conveniences, not to mention the latest styles," Olivia interjected quickly.

"Well, I might agree that our kitchens could do with a bit of updating, Miss Crowley. But as to the rest, I think not," Roane replied easily. "I rather like the old place as it is. What say you, Andrew?"

His cousin chomped on a piece of glazed pheasant and quickly swallowed it. "Oh, quite agree, Justin. Yes, I do. Can't tamper with Roanbrooke, Miss Crowley. Been around since Cromwell, don't you know. Got to preserve the old houses, eh what?"

"Oh, I should say," chimed in Captain Bradley. "My sister tells me Wykham Abbey is quite an interesting structure, Miss Landon. Dates from . . . what . . . the fourteenth century?"

"Well, the thirteenth, actually," Moriah responded, setting down her fork. "And there are several other abbeys hereabouts. Castles as well. Would—"

"Of course, it is most edifying to view the ruins of previous centuries," Olivia interrupted in a superior tone, "but one's own home must be as comfortable as possible, do you not agree, my lord Roane?"

No, he did not agree, nor did he care for her rudeness. Moriah seemed more taken aback than anything. "I consider my home, antiquated though it be, quite commodious," he drawled.

"Oh, I'm certain it is, my lord. Indeed, I should simply love to see it one day," Olivia purred demurely.

Roane blinked at such forwardness but otherwise kept his expression bland. "Thank you, Miss Crowley, but I daresay you might find it a bit drafty, you know," he replied, and then, before she could protest, he added quickly, "Tell me, Captain Bradley, will you be with us for long, or are you posted away?"

" 'Smatter of fact, my unit's been posted up north. Leaving in the morning, don't you know," Bradley answered genially. "Daresay m' sister won't like it, but there 'tis."

"Why are you being posted up north, Captain?" Moriah asked with interest. "Or is my question indiscreet? If so, pray forgive me and—"

"No, not at all, Miss Landon. It is no secret, after all, that there've been violent outbreaks all over the north country."

"No, it isn't," Miss Landon replied. "Why, I have only lately been discussing the very same with—with a friend. And my former governess writes that the situation is quite unfortunate."

"It is at that. Roane, you are lately up from London. Have you heard the rumblings there? More than a bit of concern, daresay," the captain said.

Andrew listened in amazement as a lively discussion ensued on the very subject about which his father had sent him to Justin at first stop. Why, it simply wasn't the sort of thing a chap discussed at

294

supper with ladies present! But there was Bradley, warming to his subject, and Justin, though ever so discreet, replying in kind. Drew noted his marked interest with satisfaction, and then turned to Miss Landon. Now if that didn't beat all! She, too, was participating in this conversation! Machine breaking was not, he thought, the sort of topic women generally found of interest, much less one they were able to speak upon with any intelligence whatever. Tess, he was comfortably certain, would have no notion at all who General Ludd *was*. He could not help glancing down the table momentarily to smile at her. Then his eyes went back to Justin, who did not seem at all surprised at Miss Landon's knowledge of the turmoil up north.

In fact, Justin was rather enjoying himself. Andrew eyed his cousin speculatively, and then noted Miss Crowley's decided frown. It was time, Andrew knew, to shift the topic. And since Justin seemed not to have realized it, Drew took it upon himself to ask Miss Crowley if the delicious oranges had come from the Crowley hothouses. She flashed him a brilliant smile and waxed enthusiastic about the superiority of not only the Crowley hothouses but the gardens and grounds as well. Justin gazed at Andrew curiously for a moment, then nodded almost imperceptibly and agreed with everything Miss Crowley said. And so continued the discourse until supper, mercifully, had come to an end.

Chapter 26

The Earl of Westmacott found himself feeling restless and wished this infernal ball would end. Actually, he amended, he cared not a whit whether it went on all night, but *he* wanted to go home—to Emily. And since he could not openly claim her and say, "Come, love, it is time to bid our hosts good night," he could do naught but wait for a sign that she was ready to depart. And even then, they could not leave together.

"Damn it all, I'm too old for this!" he muttered as he scanned the ballroom in vain in hopes of catching her eye. A passing footman offered him a brandy, which he downed in two strong gulps. And then he decided to take a turn about the garden, it being preferable to becoming bosky in Agatha Crowley's ballroom.

Moriah had, much to her surprise, actually enjoyed the supper interlude. While she and Justin had had to maintain a formal distance, yet they had contrived to have an interesting conversation. And, in fact, she had several times had the uncanny sense that they were conversing quite alone. As she danced a country dance now with a man whose name she was hard put to recall, she scolded herself for being fanciful. Dangerously so, for, as she reminded herself, there was nothing between Justin and her but a business agreement.

Nonetheless, when the dance ended, she could not keep her traitorous eyes from searching for him. She was well aware that he could not ask her to dance again, but still she could not help feeling disappointed when the orchestra struck up and he did not appear. She admonished herself that her preoccupation with Justin was highly improper and foolish in the extreme, and finally decided that it would be best to quit the ballroom altogether. As such, she made her way to the veranda outside the row of French doors at the rear of the ballroom. The veranda, however, was quite crowded and she gazed longingly at the beautifully kept formal gardens. Moriah knew very well that she oughtn't to descend to the gardens. It was not at all the thing for her to wander there alone, but she was suddenly overcome by a desire to *be* alone. Assuring herself that there were too many people about for anyone to notice her, she quietly slipped down the steps to the ground below.

Roane had been enormously relieved when supper had come to an end. Olivia Crowley's blatant attempts to fix his interest had begun to grate, as had the necessary formality between Moriah and him. He knew he had ought to keep an eye on her but was finding it increasingly difficult to watch her dancing with other men. He was of half a mind to disappear into the card room but first scanned the ballroom for Moriah. A cotillion had just ended, and he watched her take her leave of her partner and then move toward the French doors leading outside. In need of some air, he thought, as was he. Roane debated the wisdom of following her, of perhaps contriving a moment alone in the garden with her. He knew well that such would be the height of foolishness and was about to turn heel and head for the card room when something stopped him.

He was not sure at first what it was—merely a prickling, a warning sensation at the back of his neck. He stood some fifty feet from the French doors, and despite the crush of people, he had clearly seen Moriah exit to the veranda just moments ago. And then as he'd stood there, debating which direction to take, he'd watched but casually as others sauntered out the doors. There were two elderly dowagers, obviously in the throes of exchanging very juicy on dits. Then came a young man in regimentals accompanied by two attractive young women, then another man, Lord Chilton, if Roane was not mistaken. Didn't at all care for the fellow, he reflected. Rather arrogant and possessed of a nasty temper. And not above poaching on another man's preserves if some high flyer had taken his fancy. Suddenly he felt that prickling sensation again and then he recalled the look on Chilton's face just now. He'd seen several men look at Moriah that way tonight. Actually he had no idea whether Chilton even *knew* Moriah, but still—

The card room could wait, Roane thought as he quickly darted through the crowd toward the French doors. Of course, it was entirely possible that Chilton merely wanted a breath of air. Roane hoped so but doubted it. He had seen that look before and he knew what it meant.

Moriah relished the fresh air and the sweet smell of

honeysuckle as she trod one of the gravel paths laid out so symmetrically in and around the various gardens. Lanterns twinkled in the trees, and ahead she espied a group of some six people strolling as she was. So, she was not the only one in need of a bit of air, she thought. But their number gave them respectability, and she knew she would do well not to be seen here alone.

As such, she turned down a narrower pathway. It wove its way past a rose garden and then a grove of hedges that seemed, in the moonlight, to be sculpted in the shape of animals. And it was then that she first heard the footsteps. They were heavy, surefooted steps that crunched the gravel with purpose, some fifty feet behind her. A man, she knew instinctively, and then hurried on, lest she be recognized. But the footsteps hurried after her, and when she stopped abruptly, there was silence behind her.

Moriah felt panic rise in her throat. She was being deliberately followed. There was no other explanation. She stood frozen to the path, unable to move, and then, as suddenly as it had come, the panic lifted. Of course there was another explanation. Who else but Justin would follow her? He had obviously seen her leave the ballroom and had followed, perhaps hoping for a private word with her, something quite impossible in the ballroom. And of course he could neither approach her nor call to her, lest anyone be about. Her spirits soared immeasurably and she hastened down the path in search of a secluded arbour where they might be safe from prying eyes.

Justin followed at a discreet distance, and she smiled to herself as she led him down three different paths and finally to a small, cozy arbour nearly surrounded by tall hedges and boasting a very pretty stone bench. She stood beside the bench, a soft smile on her face as she listened for the approaching footsteps. They came rapidly, the crunch of the gravel unmistakable. Then she heard nothing for several moments, for the arbour was surrounded by grass. His quickness of pace pleased her, as if—

Her thoughts ceased as his hand appeared to draw the hedges aside. And then her eyes widened in terror and her hand flew to her mouth, so to keep from screaming. For the man who stood now before her was not Justin. Not Justin at all, but Lord Chilton, who had eyed her so insolently in the ballroom. She had not realized then quite how tall he was, but his presence now loomed large and threatening, seeming to fill the arbour.

"So, my dear, I see you are as eager as I," he said as he slowly approached.

"My lord, I—you—you are mistaken. I merely came out for a breath of air," she said in a strangled voice.

"Oh, come now, Miss Landon, you must do better than that. To a delightfully secluded enclave such as this, merely for a breath of air?" he said unpleasantly. "No, I think not. Ah, but perhaps you were expecting someone else? Well, no matter. A woman who is willing for one man is always willing for another, eventually," he drawled.

His smile, more an insolent smirk, the same she'd seen in the ballroom, sent a chill down her spine. She stepped back as he came nearer. "I—I do not know what you have imagined, my lord, but you are quite wrong. Now, I should like to return to the ballroom," she replied, raising her voice to give it more authority than she felt. She took a step forward this time, trying to appear nonchalant, as if there were no question but that he would let her pass.

His large hand sprang out to grasp her wrist and he was no longer smiling. He seemed huge, standing in front of her, his gray eyes dark with intent.

"Do not toy with me, Miss Landon," he said harshly. "We both know why you came here. Let us not waste precious time whilst you act the outraged maiden."

She tried to twist from his grasp and back away from him, but he tightened his grip. Her breathing became shallow as she looked desperately behind him, searching in vain for help. "There is no one there, my dear, nor will there be. You so conveniently provided for our privacy, did you not? I assure you that no one will find us."

Moriah tried to speak but he forestalled her, suddenly grabbing her bare upper arms and pulling her close. She struggled fiercely now but he held her firmly, one arm snaking around her waist as he lowered his head to hers. She turned away, desperate to avoid his lips.

"No!" she screamed. "Leave me be! You have no right—" He clasped her chin and turned her to face him, bringing his lips to hers. She wrenched her mouth away. "No, I tell you! Let me—"

"Ahem. Oh, excuse me," came a familiar voice in the darkness. "I seem to be interrupting something." A blessedly familiar voice, Moriah thought, as Chilton's hold on her relaxed just a bit. She felt her fear leaving her and twisted to free herself entirely.

"Take yourself off, Roane. This is none of your affair," growled Lord Chilton. Moriah opened her mouth to speak, but at a look from Justin remained silent.

"Forgive me for bringing the matter up, Chilton, but I believe the lady is less than willing," Justin drawled, his voice casual, but Moriah could see his

301

fists clenched at his sides.

"Hah! She's no lady, Roane. And she's mine for tonight. Now I suggest—"

"No, Chilton, *I* suggest you step aside and allow the lady to return to the ballroom," Justin said firmly, stepping closer to emphasize his words.

Lord Chilton let her go and she darted back, out of his reach. "Are you all right, Miss—ah—Landon, is it not?" Justin asked.

"Yes, I—ah—I am fine," she managed to say.

"Your concern is misplaced, Roane. I tell you she's no lady. I know. I've had all kinds," Lord Chilton spat derisively, then eyed Moriah up and down in that leering manner of his.

Moriah could see Justin's jaw go rigid and prayed he could hold his temper and still get rid of this odious man. They must keep up the charade. They simply must.

The Earl of Westmacott had been strolling along in the night air, trying to contrive a discreet way to get a message to Emily. Suddenly he'd halted in his tracks, the sound of a woman screaming piercing his reverie. What the devil? he wondered, even as his feet turned and headed in the direction of the woman's cry.

"I suggest, Chilton, that you apologize to the *lady* for your—er—overeagerness, and then take yourself off. Far away from her. Is that clear?" Roane said with icy, controlled calm. Steady, old boy, he told himself. He knew he couldn't call Chilton out or even land a blow to his jaw, not without giving all away. And so he clenched his fists and waited.

Chilton shrugged. "No use kicking up a riot and

rumpus, Roane. The jade ain't worth it, you know, old fellow."

Roane felt his blood boil and took a menacing step toward him. "Very well, Roane. Very well. I shall be off. You can have her. To say the truth, she's more trouble than she's worth." Roane glowered at him and then Chilton turned to Moriah. "My apologies, my *lady*," he drawled, assaying a low, mocking bow. And then with a curt nod to Roane he straightened his coat and sauntered off as if nothing untoward had occurred.

Roane stared after him just long enough to assure himself he'd really gone, and then he turned to Moriah. Her anguished face made him wish he had broken Chilton in two. He started toward her. And then, suddenly, she was in his arms, sobbing.

"Oh, J — Justin, he tried to — to . . . he wanted — he —" she cried, her body shaking.

"Hush, Moriah. It's all right. I'm here now," he rasped, holding her tightly, one hand stroking her dishevelled hair even as he tried to control his own raging emotions. The thought that another man had dared — He crushed her even closer and her hands clutched his back.

"You needn't fear, Moriah," he heard himself whisper, "for it will never happen again." Even as he said the words, he knew them to be true. He could never again allow such a thing to occur. He *must* protect her, and that meant only one thing. He would renew his offer and this time give her no opportunity to refuse.

"Oh, J — Justin, if you hadn't come, I shudder to think what —"

"But I *did* come. He — he didn't hurt you, did he?" Justin asked urgently, putting her just enough away from him to look down at her. The deep amethyst

303

eyes were rimmed with tears that trailed down her cheeks.

"No, no, I am right," she replied.

"Thank God I came when I did," Roane said, his voice unsteady. "I followed you and Chilton, but then I lost you and . . . Moriah," he paused, his hands tensing on her shoulders, "why the devil did you come out here at first stop?" he demanded roughly. "And then to venture so far and to so secluded an arbour. I cannot imagine what you were about!"

Moriah gulped but did not flinch from his gaze. He was right to be angry. "I—I needed a breath of air, and I *knew* it was imprudent, but I did so wish to walk in the garden. And then—and then I heard footsteps and I thought—well—"

"Yes, Moriah?" His voice was almost a whisper and his dark eyes held hers.

"I—I thought it was you," she whispered back, and then was immediately shocked at herself. Had she really said that aloud?

"Ah," he breathed, "I see." His whole body seemed to relax. He gently pushed her head onto his shoulder and began to stroke her hair again. Oh dear, she thought, he did see, perhaps far too much. But there was such tenderness in the soft touch of his hand on her head, and she felt so safe in his arms that for a moment she didn't care. She only knew that when he enveloped her like this she felt as if she were home, as if she belonged here and always had. Then immediately she chided herself for such foolishness. She looked up at him and caught a strange light in his yes.

"Well, I—I must confess, little one, that when I saw you leave the ballroom I had half a mind to follow. But I knew it would be . . . indiscreet. And in fact, I suppose we *hadn't* ought to stay here much longer."

"Yes, but why then *did* you follow—?"

"I saw Chilton leave after you and I—well, I didn't care for the look on his face. Instinct, I suppose, no more than an impression . . . And dammit, Moriah, you—you ought to know better!" Roane scolded, his voice suddenly harsh, his body rigid once more. He knew he ought to shake her till her teeth rattled. "A young woman simply does not go wandering off by herself—and especially one who looks like you do!" His arms tightened around her but he didn't shake her, and his tone grew unwittingly soft. "You're too damned tempting by half. Oh, little one, whatever am I to do with you?" he murmured with a gentleness that he hardly recognized. This was not the first time she had turned his anger into something else entirely. Never had he spoken so tenderly to a woman.

But then, Moriah was no ordinary woman. And soon she would be his wife. But much as he wished to, he would not renew his offer now. She was overwrought and neither the time nor the place was right. It was too clandestine, for one. He did not want her to throw their infernal agreement up at him again nor to accuse him of merely being noble. No, it would be best to court her properly at the Abbey. She was not indifferent to him, of that he was certain. But tonight she would miscontrue his reasons.

Indeed, he did not precisely understand them himself. He looked down at her, at the wrinkled dress and tearstained face, and a fierce resolve coursed through him. He did not know all of his reasons, nor did he care to delve into them. He only knew that he must protect her, lay claim to her in such a way that no man would ever again dare to touch her.

Immediately an image of his parents rose to mind,

and with it the agonizing guilt of abandoning them. And then, as before, came that fleeting sensation that he had abandoned them a long time ago. But the image faded, and he let it go. They were dead and gone; he could do no more for them. But Moriah was very much alive, and so was he.

He took her face in his hands and the expression in her eyes—a strange mixture of confusion, trust, and something else—made his breath catch in his throat.

"Oh, Justin. I—I know I should not have ventured so far, but still I—I do not understand why he—" she began, and he could resist her no more.

He bent to kiss her brow, her cheek, and then he was kissing her lips. Somehow, their arms slipped around each other and he was kissing her passionately, deeply, his mouth plundering hers in a kind of desperation. A desperation born of that strange guilt mingled with a longing for her that was like to drive him mad.

Moriah felt shaken by his kiss. She looked up at him in the moonlight, at the firm square jaw and the dark blue eyes intense with emotion, and suddenly she knew. She had fought herself at every turn, but still it was there, the truth she did not want to acknowledge, but which was as real as the passion that hung in the night air between them. She loved him, this man who had ruined her father, and then ruined her. Against all odds, she loved him. And he—what did he feel? He was so tender one moment and almost savage in his desire the next. Was it only desire? She couldn't believe that, yet she knew that there was no future for them. True, he had offered once, but out of duty. Men did not marry their mistresses if they could help it, wellborn or no. And she did not want a man who felt he *had* to marry her.

"Ah, little one," he rasped, "I don't think you have

any idea what you do to me." The look in his eyes sent a special warmth coursing through her, and she knew that if he were to offer for her right here and now, she would not refuse.

This is not the time, he told himself firmly, and to distract his wayward mind, he said, "I do not think Chilton will trouble you again."

"But—but he *knows,* Justin," she said, and he saw that distress had replaced the smoky look in her eyes.

He kept his hands draped lightly on her bare shoulders. "No, my dear. I can assure you Chilton knows nothing of the kind."

"But—but he *does,* Justin. You heard what he called me. And he is right. I am *not* a lady. I gave up my—my claim to that distinction when—well, you know when. He can tell, and I—I am persuaded that others can too," she stammered, her voice catching on a sob.

A white hot fury gripped Roane and he silently cursed Chilton, and himself, for bringing her to this. She tried to turn away, but he stopped her, his hands going taut on her slender shoulders. "Moriah," he growled, "look at me! I won't have you talking that way. You are unquestionably a lady! I have told you that before." She shook her head, stifling her tears, and Roane's tone softened. "And as to the other, I must assure you, my dear, that he cannot possibly know anything of the sort. A woman simply does not—er—appear different after—well, that is—believe me that—"

"Then why—why did he follow me, Justin?"

"Oh, my dear," Roane murmured, pulling her close again. "How can I explain it to you? I tried to before, in the ballroom. You are very beautiful, Moriah, and—and alluring. Who knows better than I what the sight of you can do to a man?"

"I—I do not understand, Justin. And I—I am frightened. I—"

"You needn't be, little one," Roane said, and kissed the top of her head. "Our secret is safe, and I will keep you safe. And perhaps we ought not to continue—"

"No, Justin," she declared, looking up. Her eyes were suddenly clear and he could see her customary composure returning. "We have a bargain and I—"

"Very well. Very well, my dear," Roane chuckled. "I have more sense than to argue that with you yet again." She smiled in return and he added, "But you *will* be more careful in future, will you not?"

"Yes, of course I shall," she replied, her husky voice strong now, the tears gone. "I am right now, Justin."

"Good. Now I think it most sensible that we get you back to the ballroom straight away." Roane put her gently away from him. "But first we must see to your hair." He turned her around and expertly began to pin the fallen black locks back into place. Then he turned her back round and deftly smoothed the flowers at the shoulders of her gown.

"Thank you, Justin," she murmured, and he produced a handkerchief for her to repair her face.

"You're welcome," he replied, and brushed a gentle finger along her cheek. "Until tomorrow, little one," he whispered, thinking of the morning, when he would set all to rights.

"Until tomorrow night," she echoed, and then in a swish of skirts, she was gone.

He felt a rush of cold air as soon as she'd gone and shook his head ruefully. How unlike him. He did not understand himself at all. Slowly he turned to leave the arbour.

"A very touching scene, my dear Justin," came a

308

voice in the darkness. Roane froze. He knew that voice all too well.

"Very touching indeed, Nephew," his Uncle George said in a low, dangerous voice, and then the earl stepped into the arbour.

Moriah walked slowly back toward the manor house, her mind a jumble of emotion. She loved him! It was extraordinary, it was foolish and futile and would only lead to despair, but there it was. And she knew he cared for her, though not enough to. . . She sighed, her hands going up to readjust her gown. How she wished that they had met under any other circumstances. Then perhaps . . .

Suddenly her left hand began groping at her shoulder. There was—there was a flower missing! Justin might not have noticed, but some eagle-eyed dowager assuredly would. A young woman emerging from the gardens with part of her attire missing was certain grist for the gossip mills! Without a thought, Moriah turned and hurried along the path. She had not gone far and hoped she would find the arbour easily.

But as she approached it she heard a raised voice that she did not recognize. Wondering if she had indeed mistaken the location, she tiptoed closer, keeping herself hidden by the hedge. And then came the answering voice, and she stiffened as she recognized it.

"How long have you been here?" Justin demanded.

"Long enough," the man said grimly.

"You surprise me, Uncle. I would not have thought it of you. To eavesdrop like that—" Uncle! Moriah stifled a gasp. That must be the earl. Oh, God, what had he heard? What must he be thinking? She knew she hadn't ought to eavesdrop either, but she found that her legs would only carry her a few steps, to where she could peer through the hedge, unseen and unheard.

"It is not a customary pastime of mine, Justin, but a woman's scream drew me here and I watched in approval as you rescued a lady in distress. And then I grant you, I should have left, or revealed myself, but that there rapidly unfolded a scene so incredible that I thought my eyes and ears had deceived me. And when I realized the enormity of it all, I stood appalled, quite frozen in my place."

Moriah too stood appalled, hardly daring to breathe. The earl, though not so tall as Justin, was powerfully built and looked like he was barely controlling his fury.

"Now look, Uncle George—" Justin began.

"How *could* you, Justin!" interrupted the earl in a cold, furious voice. "How could you do it? I knew you wanted revenge on the Landons, but *this*—I never thought you'd go this far." Oh, my God, Moriah thought. Whatever—whatever—

"What the devil are you talking about, Uncle?"

"I'm talking about the fact that you weren't content merely to ruin Thomas Landon for something that happened twenty years ago. You—"

"I told you Landon orchestrated his own fall," Justin said in a low, smoldering voice.

"Maybe so, maybe so, my boy, but you were deliberately there to pick up the pieces. You cannot deny that, can you?" demanded the earl. Moriah stopped breathing, awaiting Justin's answer.

He looked down at his feet, then back at his uncle. "No," he mumbled, and with that single word, Moriah felt a cold knot form in the pit of her stomach. "You know well that I cannot. But then—"

"But that wasn't enough, was it?" the earl pressed.

310

"Oh no, your little drama had a second act, didn't it?"

"I don't know what you're talking about! And I hardly think this is the time or place to discuss it." Justin's face was taut with controlled anger and some other emotion.

"On the contrary, Nephew, we have a great deal more privacy here and now than in a house full of servants. And what I have to say cannot wait. Don't come the innocent with me, Justin. I know what you were about! You needed justice, didn't you? 'An eye for an eye'—isn't that how it goes?" The earl was fairly shouting now. "A Landon ruined your mother and so you had to ruin a Landon, a *female* Landon!" Moriah suddenly felt as if she couldn't breathe. She clutched at her throat, desperately afraid to listen to another word, knowing that she had to. "Isn't that the way it was, Justin?" No, she thought, no, it couldn't be.

"No, dammit, that's not—"

"And I'd say from the looks of things, you've done a damned good job. That poor girl is beside herself; she's terrified! How could you do such a thing?"

"You don't understand, Uncle. It wasn't like that at all," Justin countered, and Moriah felt some of the cold leave her. To ruin her father was bad enough, but surely Justin wouldn't—

"Wasn't it, Justin? I remember the look on your face in London not a fortnight ago. I said you needed a mission; I wanted you involved in politics. You looked into the card room and said perhaps you already had one. Oh, yes, you did, all right, a mission of vengeance. I thought it would end with that night at White's. But then I came up from Town and found myself bombarded with the latest on dit— that Landon had won Wykham Abbey back. You're

311

far too clever to allow that to happen, to allow all these years of burning hatred to go in one night of drunken gambling." Burning hatred? Oh God, Moriah thought, horrified. "Not you," the earl went on. "You're not a drunk and you are, in the end of it, not a gambler either. I've told you that before. I couldn't understand it. And when we spoke earlier tonight, I knew you were hiding something."

"Uncle, please, allow me to—"

"You will hear me out, Justin. You owe me that courtesy at least. Sit down, dammit!" the earl exploded, but Justin remained where he was, facing the earl, his body tense.

"I didn't understand, until I stumbled on this touching little scene. You never meant to keep the Abbey, did you? That was just bait, wasn't it?" Bait? What did he—?

"What in hell are you—?"

"Silence, Justin! I will say my piece!" the earl barked. "The Abbey was merely a way to get what you really wanted—the ruin of Thomas Landon's daughter. Your mother for the old baron's granddaughter." Moriah felt bile rise in her throat as waves of mortification swept over her. She groped for the nearest branch. She mustn't be sick here. Now now. "Isn't that how it was?" the earl's tortured voice rang out.

"No, I tell you! I never—"

"You have violated the very essence of the code by which we live, Nephew. I am deeply ashamed. I am utterly, utterly shaken." The earl turned away from Justin, his body hunched over.

"You are wrong, Uncle," Justin said quietly. Yes, Moriah prayed, let him be wrong. "Wrong about how this began, and wrong about my feelings toward—"

"Do not lie to me, Justin." The earl whirled back

around. "You may delude that poor child, who seeks false comfort in your arms, but not me." Moriah's face burned with humiliation. "I know you too long and too well, Nephew. I remember you in shortcoats, sneaking an extra fruit tart past the cook. Oh, no, you cannot lie to me." Perhaps it was the weariness in the earl's tone, or perhaps his next words, which caused the last spark of hope to die within her. "You planned this all so carefully, Justin. You would never have given up Wykham Abbey once you'd got it, not unless you wanted something else entirely. And now, are you satisfied, or is there more that you intend — "

"Enough, Uncle! I see it is useless to defend myself. I thank you for your faith in me," Justin said bitterly, his fists clenched, his jaw rigid.

The earl came forward and faced Justin. "We shall speak of this again tomorrow. Good night, Nephew," he said, and then turned and was gone.

Justin stared after him, then went to the stone bench and sank down, his head in his hands. Oh, Justin, she cried inwardly, how could you? But she knew he had. She recalled now, too late, how she'd thought it a great coincidence that Papa had lost the Abbey to their neighbor. And she had never understood why he'd wanted *her* instead of the Abbey. Now she knew. She felt another wave of nausea and squelched it with a hand over her mouth. She could not leave here until he did, lest he hear her. She could not face him now. She could not face anyone.

Chapter 27

Somehow, Moriah had stumbled back to the ball-room. She had found Tess and told her she was ill, which was no more than the truth, and then somehow she'd found herself alone in her bedchamber, her hair plaited and nightgown on.

But she had not gone to bed. She had sat by the window, staring out, unable to cry, unable to sleep. And now as the first shafts of morning light crept across the sky, she sat there still, stiff and drained and trying to comprehend it all. That the man who had been at once so tender and so passionate could have been so filled with hate as to set out to destroy her family — she still shuddered when she thought of it. Indeed, had she not heard it all with her own ears, she simply would not credit it.

But there it was. It had all been a sham. His attempts to dissuade her from coming to him at first stop, his gallantry last night, his every gentle whisper, every soft touch of his hand. Oh, what a marvelous actor he was, she thought bitterly. But then, she had always known that. Only his desire for her had perhaps been real — and how convenient for him *that* was!

She dropped her face into her hands but felt so empty that she could not even cry. And she cursed herself for being ten times a fool. Not for falling into his hands—he was too diabolical for her to have avoided that. But for falling in love with him. Where was the practical, sensible Miss Landon, who went about her business with unemotional efficiency? She was gone; he had changed all that. He had lit a flame in her soul and left her with ashes.

Damn Justin Traugott! Damn his villainous soul to Hell! How dare he toy with other people's lives! And for what? To avenge someone long gone? Why that—that was little short of evil! And just what was it that had occurred all those years ago? The most she had collected thus far was that her grandfather had ruined his mother. Not very noble, but his mother had been married, after all. It need not have ruined her life. Surely it wasn't cause for a lifetime of revenge? Suddenly she recalled his reaction when she'd asked about his family. She'd known his parents were long dead and that there had been a sister as well. Now she wondered . . .

But what had *that* to do with *her* family? And besides, it didn't signify, for nothing could excuse Justin's behavior. He was a hateful, devious, unforgiving man, and slowly she began to feel her love for him dissolve into a cold, determined anger. She rose from her rather uncomfortable chair and took a deep breath.

Very well. Lord Roane had his revenge. He had ruined her, and he had even caused her to fall in love with him. She recalled how obvious she'd made her feelings last night, and was furious at herself and at him. Oh, how he must be laughing at her! Damn the blackguard! But she brushed aside her agonizing thoughts. She would deal with all that later. For now, she must deal with the coming day and, more important, the night. For as far as Justin was concerned, nothing had changed; he would expect her at the hunting box.

For a moment she wondered what would happen if she simply did not go, but then thought better of it. She did not think it wise to let on that she was privy to his machinations. For he could still hurt her and her family. He had ruined her, but it had not become known. And now his promises of discretion meant nothing. She suddenly felt a chill as she recalled the earl asking what more Justin planned. My God, could he mean to make this public? But no, that would blacken his name as well. . . . Yet, the earl knew his nephew well, and Moriah feared that there was indeed another act to be played in the terrible vendetta. She wondered at his seeming gentleness. He was leading her on, relaxing her defenses, until what?

She paced restlessly about her room as the first sounds of the awakening household could be heard. She would have to go tonight; there was no help for it. Besides, she told herself bracingly, they had made a bargain and she must keep her word, even if *he* had not a shred of honour. Yes, she would go, but there would be no intimate talk over supper, no friendly repartee. It would be a purely business arrangement, as it was meant to be. She would do whatever he required, but never again would he touch her heart. Lizzie came in shortly thereafter with fresh water, and as Moriah went silently about her morning toilette, she let the cold resolve fill her. At all costs, she would maintain her dignity; it was all she had left.

She ate very little at breakfast, grateful her father and sister were still abed, and then went to the morning room to attend to her correspondence. But despite herself, she could not help thinking of Justin—the Viscount Roane, she amended. What manner of man could harbour such hatred for so many years and then destroy innocent people? She shivered. Really, she did not know the viscount at all. And dammit, she fumed, throwing down her quill, how dare he try, convict, and punish her for something she'd had no part in and, indeed, knew nothing about! Oh, how she would like to rail at him tonight! But she wouldn't; it was beneath her dignity.

And just what *had* happened twenty years ago? Abruptly, Moriah rose from her desk. It was only fair that she know why she had been condemned. But whom could she ask? Certainly not Lord Roane, and she did not think it at all wise to ask Papa. Nor Mrs. Trotter, for that matter; the housekeeper was far too shrewd. But perhaps, if the right opening presented itself . . .

But it didn't when Mrs. Trotter came to speak to her of some housekeeping matters. And then Tess came round all eager to review every exciting moment of her first ball. And Tess had not been gone five minutes when Reeves knocked discreetly and informed her that she had a caller. It was still a bit early and she wondered who it might be.

"Well, now, he asked for the baron first off, miss, but the baron not bein' about, he asked to see you. Dressed up to the nines, he is," Reeves said. He became a bit flustered when she asked the gentleman's name and he could not seem to recall it. Reeves had put him in the Red Salon and, rather curious, Moriah followed the butler out.

Roane had been very pleased with himself as he strode into Wykham Abbey and greeted the aged butler. He had come to court her properly, as he should have done these several days past. And if his sleep was plagued by dreams of his parents, of Nell, and visions of the overturned carriage — well, he told himself that nonetheless he had made the right decision. His guilt might plague him but not having Moriah would be worse.

The butler had returned to say that the master was not at home, whereupon Roane had asked to see Miss Moriah Landon. But, he'd added, with a twinkle in his eye, that he would like to surprise her if Reeves would oblige him by not revealing his identity. The retainer had narrowed his eyes, then nodded almost imperceptibly and conducted him to a small, very formally appointed salon. Roane cast his eyes about the stiff red and gold furnishings and decided this was not the ideal setting for his proposal. But then, he had wanted propriety.

He shook his head and stared out the window. His dreams last night flashed through his mind again. The last had been particularly haunting and he did not know why. It was something about the carriage. He had been with his mother and Nell and the carriage had stopped. And then—and then . . . He was sure there was more but the image blurred, the dream and his memory of the event both fading into nothingness, even as the door clicked open.

He turned as Reeves ushered Moriah forward with a bow. She stopped short on the threshold and he thought she gasped, with anything but delight. Nonetheless he smiled and stepped forward, bowing and taking her hand under the watchful gaze of the butler.

"Good morning, Miss Landon. I trust I find you well."

"Good morning, my lord Roane," she countered, equally formally. Then she threw a dark look at the butler, who quickly bowed himself out of the room.

"Moriah," Roane said in a low voice, taking both her hands. "How lovely you look. The mauve gown

318

brings out your magnificent eyes. But you are a bit tired, are you not?" He brushed a fingertip across her cheek. "My poor dear, last night was not very pleasant for you, was it?" He gathered her into his arms and stroked her hair. "I would give anything to have been able to spare you that—that dreadful incident. And I shall, in the future," he murmured, then tilted her face to his, smiling warmly at her. It was only then that he realized that there was no answering smile in her eyes and that she was stiff in his arms. He also realized that she hadn't spoken.

"Moriah, what is it? What's wrong?"

"This is a rather unprecedented visit, my lord," she said in a voice devoid of emotion. "May I inquire as to its purpose?"

"Its pur—Moriah, the butler is gone. 'Tis all right. No one can hear us," he said gently.

"I ask you again, my lord. What is the purpose of this visit?" she asked woodenly, her face an impassive mask, her body taut.

"My lord?" Roane echoed, frowning. He dropped his hands and stepped back from her. "Moriah, what has come over you? I came to see you, of course. And—and if you must know, to see your father."

"In regard to what?" Her tone was cool, her chin raised. She folded her hands at her waist in that pose he remembered well from their very first interview.

"In regard to . . . never mind. Come here, Moriah, and sit down." He led her to the red damask sofa and then sat down beside her. He smiled and draped his arm across the back of the sofa, near, but not touching, her shoulders. "I merely thought it was time I courted you openly and properly, little one."

"What for?" She was so stiff that Roane was completely taken aback. He did not know what kind of game she was playing, but it was time to end it.

And he knew just how to do it.

"What for?" he repeated, moving closer to caress her shoulder. "I should think I made that rather obvious last night," he said huskily. But she was rigid in his arms. He pivoted to face her and grasped her by the shoulders. "Dammit, Moriah, what's wrong with you? Why are you acting like this?"

She stared at him stonily. "You have not answered any of my questions. What do you want with my father?"

"Moriah, please, stop this!" he exclaimed, shaking her gently. But she did not react. Something was dreadfully wrong. Not even at their first meeting had she been this cold. It was as if she had built a wall of ice around herself and he couldn't break through. "Little one," he said very gently, his hands caressing her arms now, "did something happen last night, after we parted?"

He caught a rather unpleasant glint in her eye, but she quickly masked it.

"You wished to speak with my father, my lord. Is there any message which I may—"

"Oh, for pitysakes, Moriah!" he blurted, dropping his hands in exasperation. Somehow he must jar her out of this terrible state. "If you must know, I came . . . to—to . . . ask his permission to—to pay my addresses to you."

Moriah's eyes widened and she jumped up and darted away from him. To pay his addresses? What kind of game was he playing? He'd set out to ruin her, and that most definitely did not mean marriage.

He was beside her in a moment, placing his hands gently on her shoulders. "Moriah, I . . . please do not shut me out like this. Whatever it is that troubles you, whatever has happened, please talk to me. Let me help you. Look at me, Moriah." He turned her to face him and pulled her close. "Surely you must realize how deeply I care for you. I didn't know *how* much until last night. I—I wish you to be my wife, little one, and that is why I came here this morning." He bent his head to kiss her but she twisted out of his arms, turning her back on him.

What does he want of me? Moriah screamed to herself, feeling sick to her stomach. He could not possibly want to marry her—this was all an elaborate act. But to what end? Unless . . . She remembered the earl's final words: "Are you satisfied, or is there more?" Oh, God, could Justin have some horrible fate in store for her once she became his wife? Was this his ultimate revenge? To marry her and slowly destroy her? For marriage was a two-edged sword. It could offer a woman love and protection, or . . .

That's ridiculous, she scolded herself, surprised at being so fanciful. And yet, was it any more fanciful than plotting the ruin of the Landons over so many years? And hadn't she known Sarah Ashford long enough to know that, for a woman, there was no hell on earth like that of a miserable marriage? Sarah's cold, forbidding husband alternately ignored and bullied her, humiliated her by flaunting his mistresses but, as Sarah herself had pointed out, a man could do far worse. For a wife was totally in her husband's power. Any fortune she might have—her possessions, her very person—were his to do with as he pleased. He could desert her, beat her, or lock her away in some godforsaken castle. . . .

No! Moriah's practical sense asserted itself. Justin was not such a monster. But then, who was he, this man who had harboured his hate for so long? She didn't really know him at all. She could hear his rapid breathing behind her and she shivered. Sarah had once tried to run away, but Lord Ashford had come after her. And then he'd got her with child, and now there was no escape. As there would be no escape for Moriah if she married Justin. He'd proposed once and failed, and so he'd set about to woo her. And how well he had succeeded. She shivered again when she thought how close she'd come. If he'd asked last night . . . And even now, if she'd not overheard what she had, she'd be in his arms. . . .

She took a deep breath and straightened her shoulders. Then she turned back to him. There was a hurt, baffled look in his eyes as he waited for her to speak. Oh, what an actor he was, she thought bitterly. "Lord Roane, I believe we had this discussion once before. I told you then, and I tell you again now, that I believe we should not suit. Nothing has changed." She nearly choked on the last words. Everything had changed. Everything.

"Moriah, what game is this?" he demanded, grabbing her again. She wished he would not. Even now, despite all, his touch warmed her. "How can you say nothing has changed? Can you discount all that has passed between us? Surely you cannot pretend indifference to—"

"What has passed between us is an agreement—a business arrangement. I am prepared to honour that. Nothing more," she said coldly.

Roane sucked in his breath, releasing her. "I see," he said, but he didn't. He didn't understand any of this, but he meant to get to the bottom of it. But it was clear he would get nowhere with her now. Not here. The room was too damned formal, and that ancient butler was like to come in at any moment offering tea and cakes. "Very well, Moriah. We shall keep to our agreement. I shall see you tonight at the appointed time," he said coolly and bowed.

"As you wish, my lord," she replied frigidly, and

322

watched him take his leave.

She walked slowly out of the room and up the stairs to her bedchamber. She locked the door and threw herself on her bed. And then, finally, the tears came, small cries that grew into loud, racking sobs until she fell, mercifully, into an exhausted sleep.

Roane stalked into his house, much in need of privacy and a drink. And so he cursed quite profusely when he heard the booming voice of the Earl of Westmacott emanating from the family drawing room. He slapped his gloves into the outstretched hand of the impassive Finley and darted up the stairs, knowing there was no help for it. But lord, how could he deal with his uncle now?

He found his uncle and cousin comfortably ensconced in the plush mint-green room.

"Oh, I say, Justin! Where've you been all morning?" Drew blurted, and Roane relaxed. Small talk would actually be welcome now.

But the earl rose, took a long sip of his brandy, and somehow very smoothly convinced his son that he was much in need of a ride over the hills. In but a few moments Roane faced his uncle, glass in hand, the expanse of half the room between them. Neither man felt like sitting.

"Justin, you are a grown man," the earl began. "I have no wish to engage in a spate of recriminations. I believe I made my feelings clear last night. But what's done cannot be undone. It can only be mitigated, and to that end I know you must agree that there is only one honourable course. You—"

"Uncle, please, one moment," Roane said with forced calm. "I am fully prepared to meet my responsibilities, but I must first ask that you do me the courtesy of allowing me to explain about last night. Things are not always what they seem, Uncle."

He could see the earl stiffen. "I believe enough was said last night, Justin," he said sternly. "Pray do not humiliate either of us, Nephew, with spurious explanations for what can, in the end, never be excused. It is simply too painful for me to discuss further."

Roane stared stonily at his uncle. That the man who had been like a father to him could have so little faith in him, could condemn him so readily . . .

"The important thing now is that you must marry the girl," his uncle commanded.

Roane took a deep breath. So be it. "I see, Uncle," he said icily. "And I thank you for reminding me of what honour demands, else I should not have realized." He tried to keep the sarcasm from his tone. Then he slapped his drink down onto the sofa table. "Oh, and by the by, it may be of some interest to you that I have twice offered for the lady and twice been refused. Good day, Uncle," Roane snapped, and strode from the room.

He was shaking by the time he reached his study and bolted the door. He downed a glass of brandy, and then threw himself into his large leather chair, his head sinking into his hands. First Moriah, and now this. Good God, what would this night bring?

Chapter 28

Moriah arrived promptly at midnight, and as Roane ushered her into the hunting box, he felt again that rush of warmth. But her expression was decidedly cold.

"Good evening, my lord," she said without a glimmer of a smile.

"Good evening, my dear," he responded pleasantly, taking her cloak and gloves.

She was wearing her brown riding habit, as she had the first night. This time he was not amused. He took her elbow to guide her into the sitting room and felt her stiffen at his touch. Puzzled, he seated her on the green and gold love seat. He offered sherry, which she refused, but he poured two glasses anyway. "Drink this," he said firmly. "I think you need it."

They sat on the love seat, silently sipping their sherry, his knees almost but not quite brushing hers. For though he longed to touch her, at the moment he did not dare. The wall of ice was still there. The wine did not seem to be melting it, and he wondered whether *he* could. Suddenly he wished that he had lit the fire, but it had seemed absurd; it was such a warm summer night. He took another sip of his wine.

"Moriah," he said softly, "we are alone now. There

is no one to interrupt us, nor to overhear. I wish you will confide in me. It is plain that something happened between the time I left you at the ball and this morning. Won't you tell me what has overset you? I am persuaded I may be of help."

Her face seemed to grow even more rigidly composed. "You are quite wrong, my lord. There is nothing."

"There is noth—oh, for pitysakes, Moriah, don't you even realize how you're acting? Why you—you don't even call me by name. You—"

"I shall call you by whatever name you wish, my lord," she countered impassively.

"Dammit, Moriah!" he burst out, slapping his drink down. "That's not the point. You—you're so distant. Last night I held you in my arms and—"

"If you wish to do that again, my lord, I shall have no—"

"Stop it, Moriah!" He did not mean to raise his voice but could not seem to help it. He *had* to get through to her. "That's not what I mean and you know it. What has happened? Did you have any further difficulty at the ball, or is there some problem with your family?"

"No, my lord," she said stonily, but her stomach was churning. Oh, God, could he not leave her be? What more did he want of her?

"Well then, surely—surely it cannot be that *I* have given offense?"

Moriah's eyes widened unwittingly. Oh, the gall of the man! And what an actor he was, his eyes now a warm deep blue and his stern, square jaw softened in concern. Suddenly she felt her tenuous composure slipping away. She began to laugh, a loud, bitter laugh. "Given offense? You? Why, of course not, my lord Roane. How could you even think such a thing?" she mocked, and felt tears at the back of her eyes. She rose and walked jaggedly to the empty grate, keeping her back to him.

He followed immediately and his long tapered fingers gently grazed her shoulders. She felt that familiar warmth and mentally shook herself. She would not let him do that to her again.

"Little one, please," he murmured. "I care for you very deeply. I—I cannot bear to see you this way. Please trust me." No, she cried inwardly, unable to bear the tenderness in his deep voice. "If, indeed, I have done something to—to trouble you, pray tell me and I shall endeavor to set all to rights."

She squeezed her eyes shut to squelch her tears. Set all to rights? Oh, how he taunted her! She knew she must end this conversation, else she would blurt everything. She took a deep breath but could not face him. "My lord, I pray we may terminate this discussion. I—you may recall that we have an agreement, and that is why I am here. If you wish to go upstairs—"

He clamped his hands tightly on her shoulders and whirled her around. "That is quite enough, Moriah," he said through clenched teeth. "I do *not* wish to go upstairs. I wish to understand why—" Suddenly he stopped and stared piercingly at her, at the fiery amethyst eyes and the firmly set red mouth. "Good God, you *are* angry at me, aren't you?" he asked incredulously, and then softened his voice. "Oh, my dear, I would not for all the world hurt you. Pray tell me—"

"Oh, for Godsakes, stop this playacting!" she shouted, twisting from his grasp and storming toward the window. "I cannot bear it! I am here, is that not enough for you? Must you degrade us both with this ugly pretense?"

He strode to her, feeling his pulse throb at his temple, willing himself to calm. "Ugly pretense?" he demanded, seizing her arms. "You may recall that I asked you to marry me, not twenty-four hours ago. That offer still holds."

"Oh, yes, I'll wager it does," she spat disdainfully.

"And just what the hell does that mean?" he growled, his fingers tightening on her forearms.

She managed to disengage herself and stumbled back against the window, then raised her chin and folded her hands at her waist. She spoke coolly but he heard the tremor in her voice. "And to—to what do I owe the honour of this proposal, my lord Roane? To Uncle George?"

"Uncle George?" he echoed, bewildered. "What the devil has the earl to do with—"

"No? Well then," she retorted, her voice barely audible, "perhaps it is simply . . . the ultimate revenge."

Roane blinked and now his voice, too, was quiet. "The ultimate . . . I—Moriah, I don't know what you're talking about."

She laughed painfully and turned her head away. "Don't you? Even now you cannot tell me the truth."

"Moriah, I—" He took a step forward but checked himself when she turned back to him. For her eyes held such a mixture of hatred and despair that he could only gape.

"Oh, how clever you were, my lord," she seethed. "The Abbey was merely bait, of course. And I obligingly took it. But no more. For I, like the earl, have also wondered what next you have in store for your little vendetta."

"The earl!"

"Now I know," she went on, her voice trembling. "When a woman marries a man she signs her life

328

away. Oh, yes, so very clever, my Lord Roane. There is no better revenge, I am sure. But I won't—"

"Oh, my God!" he rasped, a horrid light dawning. "Last night. You—you were there!"

She stared at him and he saw tears in her eyes. "Yes," she said dully. "I was there."

"But—but how—?"

"What does it signify? A—a flower came off my gown and I—I went back to retrieve it."

"Oh, God," he groaned, "you—you don't understand. Neither does the earl." He moved to take her in his arms, but she was so rigid that he dropped his hands. "Moriah, it isn't at all what—"

"Stop it! Stop it, damn you!" she yelled, her eyes closed and her hands clutching at her head. "I can't bear to hear any more of your lies!"

Roane felt as if he had descended into a bizarre nightmare. He had twice had this same conversation with his uncle. But now he had so much more at stake. "Moriah!" he said feelingly, grabbing her hands and forcing her to look at him. "I am sorry for what you heard, but the earl is wrong. I never meant to hurt you. If you will allow me to explain—"

"Explain? What is there to explain? That for twenty years you allowed your hatred to fester whilst you plotted your sordid revenge? Revenge for some long-forgotten scandal that—"

"I hardly consider the untimely deaths of my parents and sister a mere 'long forgotten scandal,'" he interjected coldly, and was rewarded by an appalled look on her face.

"Oh, so, you do not know all of it, do you?" he asked grimly.

"I—I don't understand. I know nothing save what I heard last night, and that I have been tried and condemned for something that happened before I was born."

"Moriah," he said gently, "come and sit down. It is time I told you the whole." A parade of emotions flittered across her face but she did not reply and he led her to the sofa. He refilled their drinks and sat down beside her.

"It is not a very pretty story and I am far from blameless, Moriah, but I am not the monster you paint me," he began. She inched away from him and stared down at her drink. He took a sip of his own, his fingers tense on the glass. "My memory of that long-ago time is hazy, of course; I was but eight years old. I remember the night before it all happened. My parents had a terrible row, so loud that I could hear them shouting in the nursery. I remember doors slamming and my mother crying." Abruptly he rose and stalked to the hearth. "My mother woke Nell, my sister, and me before dawn and bundled us into the carriage. Said we were going on a trip. But I knew she was lying. We were running away. Father, she said, had business to attend to, but I knew that was a lie too. And I sensed he was in danger, though I don't know why. Perhaps I heard the servants talking." He paused and drank again. She said nothing, did not look at him. "My recollections after that are jagged. . . . There was the overturned carriage, but I do not recall the accident. And then they told me Mother and Nell were . . . dead. She was so pretty, little Nell. With hair like Tess's. She—she was only four." He whispered this last hoarsely and finished his drink.

"I—I'm sorry," Moriah said softly. "And you— were you hurt?"

Roane frowned, perplexed. "No. I am certain I was not. And—and strangely, I do not even think I was there—in the accident, that is. And yet, I must have been." He felt an odd prickling at the back of his neck, and then that terrible guilt of having abandoned them all washed over him, but he shook it off. He would deal with that later. "It was horrible," he went on grimly. "Everyone was crying, and then—then they told me about Father. He was dead, too. Shot through the heart. The same day, Moriah. Who would want to shoot Father? I remember asking. But no one answered me."

Moriah watched the anguished face of this tall, powerful man and felt tears prick her eyes. It was all such a nightmare—then and now. She had never dreamed the cause of all this could be so—so terrible. She wanted to go to him, to touch him, but she couldn't. Not after all that had happened. She dashed the moisture from her eyes and he continued.

"For two years I became very withdrawn. Hardly spoke to anyone. A maiden aunt came to stay and Uncle George tried to help me, kept me with him as much as possible. But then Andrew's mother died in childbirth and the earl went away for a long time." He sighed deeply and turned to stare at the empty grate. "It wasn't until I was ten that I learned the truth of it all."

His voice had grown very cold and suddenly Moriah knew with a sickening dread what he would say next. "I overheard the stable boys talking and somehow I understood. Understood that the Baron Landon, your grandfather, had seduced my mother. My father found out and challenged him to a duel. My mother was running away from both of them, I think. My father was—was killed at dawn," he finished softly.

She rose and went to him, unable to stop herself. She put a hand on his arm and he turned to her. "I—I am truly sorry, Justin. It was a terrible tragedy. B—

331

but nothing can justify what—"

"Do you know what that means, Moriah?" he demanded, grasping her shoulders harshly. "To have your whole world suddenly come to an end at the age of eight?"

She winced and he relaxed his hold on her, softening his tone as well. "Don't you see, Moriah, it was the knowledge of what really happened that saved me. I now had a reason to live. I felt that I owed something to my family. I had survived, and somehow I had to make it up to them."

"And so you chose vengeance," she said quietly. It was not an accusation, merely a statement of fact.

He did not release her but met her gaze squarely. "Call it what you will. I never saw the Landons after that, any of them, but I knew that one day I would ruin them. You *must* understand, Moriah. All those lonely years, with only their portraits to give me strength." His eyes bore into hers, his fingers once more clamping the soft flesh of her arms. She wanted to understand, desperately.

Her eyes welled up again and she blinked the moisture back. He went on talking. "You once told me your father could no more help what he is than a wounded man could help crying out from pain. And you forgave him. I was wounded, Moriah, very deeply. I—I had to do it. It kept me going." He paused and searched her eyes. She said nothing. "All those years on the Peninsula and then in Town. I planned and waited. When Landon wanted a game, I was there. But—but I never played unfairly with him. Never even plied him with drink. He did that himself."

"I—I know that," she mumbled.

He drew her close and brushed his lips across her brow. She felt a wave of heat, wanted so much to melt into his arms. His navy blue coat was open and she could feel the strength of him, his muscles taut beneath his cream-colored shirt. "But when I finally won the Abbey, I—I felt empty. There was no joy in my victory. And then—then you walked into my house and—and everything changed."

She stiffened and pulled away. "Did it?" she asked guardedly, turning her back. He had almost made her forget her part in all this.

She felt his large hands on her shoulders again. "Yes, my dear," he breathed softly into her ear. "I tried to hold onto my hate, but it crumbled away. I tried not to want you so much. Not to care. I was tortured by guilt—as if I were betraying my family. But nothing matters except you. Marry me, Moriah, and let us put the past behind us."

Oh, God, she wanted so much to believe him. But the earl's words echoed in her: "The Abbey was just bait . . . your mother for the old baron's grand-daughter." Yes, she had been part of his plan from the beginning. But, she silenced the voice within, once they'd met, he—he changed. He *does* care; perhaps he has even from the beginning, she thought, remembering his initial proposal of marriage. And *that* was why he'd renewed his offer now, not out of some Gothic desire to exact further revenge. Truly, she had let her imagination run away with her on that head. And could she now, indeed, put it all behind her? His breath on her neck sent a delicious warmth rippling through her and, unwittingly, she felt her body lean back against him.

His hands slid down her arms to encircle her waist. "Mmm. That's better," he murmured. "You know, little one, it was quite unnerving to discover that Landon had a full-grown daughter, but now I find I am all out of mind delighted."

He's *lying!* she screamed inwardly, and felt herself go icy cold. He'd known about her all along—the earl had said so! And here he was, proposing marriage in one breath and unabashedly lying to her in the next! How could she possibly trust him, let alone marry him, a man capable of such hatred and duplicity, such sordid revenge? Who could say of what else he was capable? As to marriage, *was* that part of his vendetta, after all? She did not know, but she could not take the risk of finding out.

She flung herself out of his grasp and whirled around to face him. She saw his surprised expression and reminded herself what a superb actor he was. She took a deep breath, trying to regain her composure. She would cry later. "Yes, my lord, let us put the past behind us. I am sorry for your family. And you have had your revenge. Or at least part of it. But my decision holds. I will not marry you."

"Why the hell not? And just what the devil do you mean, 'part of it'? You know very well that—"

"What I know, Justin, is that you're lying to me," she said icily. "You would never have given up Wykham unless you'd wanted something else entirely. I was that something else. And perhaps you still want—"

"Dammit, Moriah, those are the earl's words, not mine," he exploded, striding to her. "I imagined you still in the schoolroom, gave you nary a thought, I tell you." He took her hands and pulled her close. "And I never meant to make you a dishonourable offer. It—it just slipped out." His voice had softened and his eyes, a deep dark blue in the candlelight, pierced hers. "You have no idea how desirable you are, little one. And now it is so much more than that. You haunt my dreams, Moriah. I want you with me always. Give over, my dear. I am not the blackguard you paint me. And we both know you are not indifferent to me. I see it in your eyes, I feel it in your touch, even if you will not say the words." He kissed her eyes and her brow. She shivered, whether from fear or desire she did not know. But how could she still feel desire when — ? She must get away from him. He could hurt her, very badly. And yet, when he held her that way, spoke to her like that, she could not pull away. "I am sorry for all that happened in the past but not that we — we came together," he said in a husky voice, bringing his mouth close to hers. She felt her lips burn, even before he touched them. "You are mine, Moriah. Always and forever."

His lips came down onto hers but his words chilled her. She was his, in his power. "No!" she screamed, tearing herself away. She must not succumb to him.

"Moriah! Little one, what is it?" he pleaded, but she bolted away, behind the love seat and then out of the room.

"Moriah! For pitysakes, come back —" he called, following her.

She heard no more, for she wrenched open the front door of the hunting box and darted into the night. She must get away, must get to her horse. She didn't trust him, and she didn't trust herself.

The air was hot and still as she ran to the stable in back. She heard him pounding after her. She yanked the door, but it was stuck. "Damn, damn!" she wailed, and felt tears coursing down her cheeks. She tugged again, but he was there, his breath on her neck, his arms enveloping her.

"It's all right, little one. It's all right." He turned her around and crushed her to him. "Why are you running away from me, Moriah? You must know I will never hurt you."

The tears came freely now and all she could do was

335

shake her head, pressed against his shoulders. "Whatever happened to that intrepid lady who first walked into my house? Why are you so afraid to trust me? Or is it that you do not trust yourself?"

That intrepid lady was an innocent dupe, she thought, and she is gone forever. She mustered her resolve and raised her head, trying to fight the panic rising in her.

"I cannot," she cried. "I cannot marry you. Do not ask me again. I will *never* marry you. I have seen what John Ashford has done to Sarah. I will not—"

"What have the Ashfords to do with us, for God-sakes? I—"

"No, Justin! You have ruined me, but you will not destroy me. Leave me be! Or if you wish a mistress, I will be that. Be content with that, damn you!" she ranted. "Your mother for the old baron's grand-daughter! An eye for an eye, Justin! Isn't that how it was? Well, here I am. Take me if you will, but stop the lies, the pretense. I cannot bear it. And I will *never* marry you! *Never!* Do you hear?" she was shrieking now, struggling to free herself from his grasp.

"Stop it, Moriah, stop it!" he yelled, shaking her violently. "You're hysterical! You don't know what you're saying!"

She fought him, but he held her in his arms, her back pinioned to the stable door. "Oh yes I do! I will not marry you! No matter what you do to me, no matter how much I—" She stopped herself and blinked at him.

"No matter how much you what, Moriah?" he asked breathlessly.

"Nothing! I hate you!" she hurled back, and then thrust at him with all her strength so that he stumbled and loosened his grip. She shoved his arm away and ran off into the woods. The moonlight filtered through the trees and she ran blindly ahead.

"Moriah! Come back! You'll get lost!" he called, rushing after her.

The air was thick and humid. She felt as if she were choking as she skirted the trees, tears streaming down her face.

And then his hand caught hers, and she was pulled into his arms.

"Moriah! What must I say to make you believe me? If this is your own revenge, then you have made a good job of it! I have been tormented since the day I met you. First with wanting you and knowing I had no right to take you. And then with wanting to marry you and fearing I was betraying my family. And now this. Answer me, Moriah! What must I say?"

She broke away from him, her chest heaving and face contorted in anguish. "Why? Why should I believe you, Justin? Why? When your own uncle does not?" she lashed out.

"Because—because I love you, God dammit!" he shouted back, and she gasped. Suddenly they were both silent, his words hanging between them in the still, sultry night air. He'd said it. Until that moment he hadn't even realized that he loved her. Had been afraid to put the name to his feelings. But, of course, there was no other way to define them. And now . . . what would she do?

She shook her head fiercely and her face convulsed in tears. "Damn you, Justin!" she ranted. "You don't love me. You don't know the meaning of the word! You only know deceit and hate and—"

"That's enough, Moriah!" he roared, lunging forward and seizing her. His blue eyes searched hers and he pulled her against his chest, his arms encircling her. She looked up at him with an anguish that mirrored his own. He could not bear it, this estrangement. "Trust me, little one. Do not be afraid," he breathed hoarsely, and then he bent his head and began to kiss her.

His kiss lit a fire in her, a fire that had been smoldering but would not go out. And then his hands were caressing her sides and covering her breasts and she moaned into his mouth. No, she thought. She must not let him do this. She must not want him so. She still did not know if—

He was unbuttoning her riding habit with one hand, massaging her back with the other. He kissed her throat and then her mouth again, and she returned his kiss, her own hands clutching the back of his neck. Then he was pulling the pins from her hair, letting it fall loose and free. He whispered her name and pressed her against the hard length of him. She felt his strength and power as waves of pleasure coursed through her. She ought not to feel this way, yet she would die if he let her go. The air was hot and moist; her clothes felt oppressive.

Somehow he shrugged himself out of his coat and dropped it onto the ground, pulling her with him. He held her hips; she gripped the hard muscle of his back. He was tugging her dress open; she felt his warm hand close over her breast, and she moaned. There was no more thought, only feeling.

This is madness, he told himself, as they sank to the ground, his coat a bed upon the moss. It wasn't right, not here, not now, when she did not yet trust him. But then he touched her bare flesh, and he knew he was lost. She moaned, and his last rational thought was that perhaps this *was* the best way to convince her, after all.

He kissed her hungrily, desperately, with all the suppressed emotion of the last days. His hands pushed her dress down; he wrapped his legs around hers. She clutched at him wildly; her need as great as his. The summer air was unbearably, unusually hot. She smelled of roses; he could not get close enough. He tore at his cravat and his shirt with deft, frenzied fingers. Together they moved on the soft ground, peeling each other's clothes off frantically. When at last he freed her golden body from the confines of its clothes, he wanted to savor her, to taste her softness and run his hands gently over every contour. But his breathing was jagged, his caresses no less so, and she writhed and clasped him with an urgency that told him she had no need of gentleness. He flung off the last of his own garments and ground his mouth onto hers as he rolled her beneath him. He brought them together in one wild, swift thrust. She arched to meet him, and they surged together in the desperate, thrashing dance of love.

"Moriah, oh God, Moriah," he rasped, and she answered him, his name on her lips becoming a cry as she began to shudder, her body convulsed in spasms. Her release broke his control and with a piercing groan he plunged into the abyss of shattering pleasure.

For endless moments they were still, as still as the sultry night air. And then he eased himself from her, cradling her in his arms as he lay beside her. And then he eased himself from her, cradling her in his arms as he lay beside her. She gazed at him out of smoky eyes, too spent for thought, or emotion, it seemed. She brushed limp fingers through his hair, and then let her hand float to the ground. We are both floating, he thought, wanting the sweet languor to last, afraid that it would not. He kissed her eyes softly. "Sleep now, little one," he murmured, and pulled his discarded shirt up to cover her. She closed her eyes and turned her head into his shoulder, and he wrapped a strong arm about her waist just as he, too, fell asleep.

He awoke first and peered down at her in the moonlight. He marvelled anew at her beauty, his eyes caressing her face and her lovely body, only partially covered by his shirt. As if his eyes had truly touched her, she stirred. Her eyelids fluttered open.

"I — what — I do not understand," she whispered, still in the haze of sleep.

"There is nothing to understand, love," he uttered softly, smiling and stroking her brow. "We have known great joy together, and it is only the beginning."

"No, I — it — I didn't mean for this to happen," she mumbled, almost to herself, putting a hand to her eyes and shaking her head.

"I know that, little one. Neither did I. But you see that I cannot resist you." He grinned and kissed the tip of her nose.

She gave no answering smile, but her eyes narrowed in distress. She tried to sit up, but he would not allow it, his arm draped firmly across her waist. Instead she turned away from him, curling up on her left side and pulling the shirt up to her shoulder. He dropped his arm and made no further move to touch her. She needed time to collect her thoughts.

They lay still, together yet apart, the warm, humid summer air blanketing them. And then he saw her body quiver and heard the unmistakable sound of muffled sobbing. Smiling ruefully to himself, he touched a hand to her shoulder. "You know, little one," he said softly, "if you mean to make a habit of crying each time we make love, I warn you I shall

340

take it amiss. It is not precisely a compliment, you know, to my — er — masculine abilities."

"There will — will not be another time, my lord," she stammered between sobs.

"As you wish, love," he replied imperturbably. "But come, I told you once before that you must never cry alone." Very gingerly he turned her to face him, pleased that her resistance was minimal. He pushed her head down onto his shoulder and stroked her hair back from her face. "I'm afraid your hair pins are quite lost to us, little one. We shall have to stock an endless supply once we are married," he said lightly, and then held his breath.

She tensed and tried to pull away but he held her fast, his arms encircling her. "I — I have never said I will marry you."

He paused and, deciding he must keep this discussion light, said, "No, you haven't. I believe you said you would *never* marry me."

"And so I shan't," she retorted, her normally husky voice muffled by his chest, for he refused to let her move.

"Come, love, do give over. Surely you must admit, in your heart of hearts, that we belong together."

She lifted her head just enough to gaze up at him. "I will grant that there is a rather pleasant — ah — physical attraction between us. Which — which is all to the purpose, since I *did* agree to be your mistress, not your wife."

"A rather pleasant — " he gasped. "You are *mistress* of understatement, little one, that is certain," he chuckled softly, and watched her blush. "But the fact is that I no longer wish a mistress, Moriah," he continued calmly. He relaxed his hold and she sat up, pulling the shirt with her. He stroked her bare back as he went on. "I wish a wife. A sensuous, dark-haired woman with violet eyes and a very practical turn of mind."

"No, Justin, I—"

"No? Well, perhaps you are right. Perhaps a more biddable woman, one who will jump at the chance to be a viscountess," he ventured genially, propping his head upon his elbow. "Someone with political connections. I have been toying with the idea of a career in the government, you must know. Yes. I do believe Olivia Crowley will suit admirably. Of course, there *is* the problem of her mother—a veritable viper, I'm afraid. And then there *is* the problem of physical attraction, but what has that to do with marriage, after all? One may have a mistress for that. Yes, Olivia—"

"Oh, Justin, do cease!" she cried, pivoting around to glare at him. "You wouldn't—you couldn't—that is—would you?"

Roane laughed aloud. "I think, love, that I shan't answer that question. But I am mindful that I ought to go to the Abbey tomorrow and declare myself to your father. And I would you will not refuse me then, else I shall have to apprise him of certain—er—interesting facts, so that he might help convince you."

"Justin! You—you wouldn't!" she whispered, horrified.

"No? Well, I declare it preferable to acquiring a viper for a mother-in-law."

She shook her head, appalled. "Justin, you—you promised—"

"Calm down, love. I'm only quizzing you. You must know I would never violate the privacy of what is between us. But I do think it is time for you to admit your own feelings and accept me."

She jumped up, suddenly heedless of her naked

state, or his. *Was* he quizzing her? She didn't know anything any more. Didn't know what to believe, or what he would do. "Justin, I—I must go now." She bent to retrieve her chemise and slipped it over her head. "Pray do not come to my father tomorrow," she continued, as her dress followed, and then her stockings. "I shall come here at midnight, as per our agreement, and—"

"Stop, Moriah! Enough!" he commanded sharply, springing up and yanking on his breeches. "I have heard all I care to about that infernal agreement." He took both her hands and looked her full in the eyes. "I *love* you, Moriah. You keep saying you do not understand what happened. Well *I* do. You wanted me as much as I wanted you, and it has nothing to do with some damned agreement!"

"No!" she retorted. "And it doesn't signify. Please, I—I need time. I—"

"What are you saying, Moriah?" Roane dropped her hands, recoiling. "That after all that has just passed between us you still do not trust me? Do not believe me?"

It was Moriah's turn to recoil in horror. "Is that what all this was about?" she whispered brokenly, pointing to the ground where they had just lain. "Was it all just a calculated way to—to convince me of your so-called innocence?"

"I never said that I was innocent, Moriah. Only that I love you, and I never meant to hurt you," he said softly, reaching for her, but she backed away. "Dammit, Moriah!" he snapped. "Whose word will you take—the earl's or mine?"

"I—I don't know, Justin. I *want* to believe you, but I—oh, give me time, please!" she choked, then turned and broke into a run.

He stood paralyzed for a moment, hardly believing

343

that she would really go like this, that he had failed to convince her. And then, coming to his senses, he sprinted after her, heedless of his bare chest and feet. This time she managed to wrench open the stable door before he reached her.

"Moriah!" he yelled, bounding in after her. But she ignored him, and before his eyes could adjust to the dark, she had mounted her mare and bolted out.

Cursing fluently, he lunged onto his own stallion and spurred him out. He could see her hair flying in the moonlight as he galloped after her. He urged the stallion on, the sultry air clinging to his naked chest and his bare feet digging into the stirrups. But finally he slowed his horse, making no attempt to catch her, only to see her safely onto her own land.

There was nothing more he could do now, he thought in agony. Tomorrow, he would go to see her father. And then, somehow, he must bring her to trust him. But suddenly he recalled the words of the earl in London — was it only a fortnight ago? "Vengeance most hurts those who reap it, Justin." Good Lord, what had he done?

Chapter 29

Moriah awoke with red eyes and awracking headache, but not wishing to call attention to herself, she rose at her accustomed hour and went down to breakfast. She managed little more than a cup of coffee and a piece of dry toast, and then quickly repaired to the morning room.

She tried very hard to work, and then to read. Anything to distract her from her confused thoughts. For every time her mind wrenched itself back to last night, she could feel her eyes burn with tears. And that she must not allow.

She was somewhat startled when Papa came in to visit sometime about mid-morning. He rarely disturbed her work. She had often mused that he probably wished to avoid, as much as possible, any grim reminders of their straightened circumstances. But here he was, looking a bit tired but rather . . . serene, actually, which was most unusual. So was the conversation he initiated.

"Good morning, my dear," he said genially, coming forward as she rose to greet him.

"Good morning, Papa. You look well." She came round the desk and took his hands.

"Thank you, Moriah. You look—you look beautiful in that violet color. It—it brings out your eyes."

"Why, thank you, Papa," she replied, genuinely touched and more than a little curious about this visit.

Papa cleared his throat. "You—ah—may be wondering about this little—ah—visit. Fact of the matter is, Moriah, I—I just wanted to tell you that I—I'm proud of the fact that you are so independent and capable. And that—that I—I love you very much," he concluded hoarsely.

"Oh, Papa," Moriah began, reaching out to him, but he patted her cheek, smiled a strange smile, and then turned and left the room.

Moriah stared after him, dumbfounded. She did not know which was more astonishing, that Papa had openly expressed his affection for her or that he had praised her "independence and capability," qualities she knew he'd always viewed with great misgiving. Of a certain she must speak to him, but not now. He would not wish it, and besides, she could not, at this moment, trust herself to utter two sentences without her voice catching. Justin had tried to destroy this man. She must never forget it.

Roane had not slept at all and so did not demur when an energetic Andrew suggested an early morning ride. They breakfasted together afterwards, and then about mid-morning Roane excused himself, claiming estate business. It was time to call at the Abbey, he thought with a grim determination. He had no idea what Moriah's reaction would be, and for the first time he did not know what he would do should she refuse him again.

He was tempted to take his stallion, but then thought better of it. He needs must observe all proprieties—and a morning call was most definitely paid in a carriage. But he'd be damned if he'd suffer his coachman's cheerful "good mornings" and comments on the countryside, and so he donned his driving gloves and took the reins himself.

The ride seemed interminable, but when the Abbey came into view he felt, rather than relief, a growing apprehension. Moriah's home sat proud and quietly regal on this still, sunny morning. Determinedly, he wended his way past the ancient gatehouse and turned into the drive. But in the next moment his emotions froze, to be replaced by a cold shock of horror. For it was right then that he heard the shot explode and pierce the morning air. He sat momentarily stunned on the box of the carriage, then jumped down and cursed himself for not bringing his coachman to see to the horses. And where the bloody hell was the groom?

Moriah had just opened her third letter when the shot rang out, causing her heart to thud in shock. Good Lord, whatever—Oh, my God! Papa!

She thrust her chair back violently and bounded out of the room. She heard Reeves and she didn't know who else panting behind her as she raced down the corridor to Papa's study. Shoving the doors open, she lunged inside, then stopped short.

"Papa! No, Papa!" she screamed, and ran to him. His head had fallen on the desk, blood now oozing all over the blotter. She could smell the smoking gun but did not see it on the desk.

Her first impulse was to cradle him in her arms and give way to violent sobbing. Oh, why ever would Papa—? But then her practical sense prevailed and

347

she reached down and felt at his neck for his pulse. "He—he's still alive!" she choked, for the first time looking up. "Reeves! Send Hodges for the doctor. Quickly!"

She turned back to Papa, vaguely noting that Tess had come into the room, Mrs. Trotter on her heels. The blood, she thought. Oh, my God, I've got to stop the blood! Savagely she tore at her petticoat and wadded together a piece of the linen, then pressed it to his temple.

"Oh, Moriah, whatever happened?" Tess cried, and Moriah looked up to see her sister turn deathly pale.

"Mrs. T., see to Tess!" Moriah snapped, and saw the housekeeper catch her sister just as she fainted.

The linen was all red now, soaked through, and Moriah eased her hand away just long enough to tear another piece. She wondered whether she ought to move Papa, lay him down perhaps, but thought she dare not, not till the doctor came.

"Oh, no! Oh, Miss Moriah!" came a wail all too recognizable as Lizzie's. "Oh no, miss. Is he— is he—?" Lizzie drowned her own voice in a sob.

Moriah looked up at her for only a second before saying more sharply than she'd intended, "No, Lizzie, he is not. And it is best now for the entire household to be calm. We—"

"Miss Moriah! Oh, Glory be! I was afraid o' this! Here, let me help!" came Finch's anguished voice as he darted into the room.

Moriah breathed a slight sigh of relief. Here at least was someone who could be of use. "He—he's still alive, Finch," she rasped.

He merely nodded and came round to feel the pulse at Papa's neck. Then he actually smiled. " 'Tis faint, but he'll do," he said. "That's the ticket, Miss

Moriah, got to stop the blood. Now, if you'll hold tight to the linen, I'll see if I just can't carry him to the sofa and make him comfortable."

"Oh, Finch, I don't know if we ought. The bullet—"

"Now, now, he'll be right, Miss Moriah. I've seen worse than this, you know," the valet said softly. And then, very gingerly, despite his small frame, he scooped the baron into his arms. Then, with Moriah pressing the linen to the wound, Finch conveyed him to the plush leather sofa.

Moriah bent to sit next to him, but Finch forestalled her. "I'll do it, miss. You need to rest a bit. Just some more linen, I think." Moriah nodded, yielding her place to Finch. Then she unceremoniously flipped up her skirt and tore again at her petticoat.

"O—o—oh! The poor Baron! Oh, miss, what are we—?"

"Oh, Lizzie! Cease yer caterwaulin' this instant, pray do!" hissed Mrs. Trotter.

At that Moriah's head snapped up. Mrs. Trotter glared at Lizzie, then bent once more to Tess, who was crumpled in a corner armchair. Moriah had forgotten them altogether, and now she addressed the maid. "Lizzie, fetch strips of clean linen. And—and a basin of water. Quickly now," Moriah commanded, trying to keep her voice calm. Lizzie blew her nose, then bobbed a curtsy and nearly collided with Reeves as she exited the room.

"Hodges has gone for the doctor, Miss Moriah. Took off like lightning. How is—?"

"I—I don't know, Reeves," Moriah replied, her eyes on the baron. "I pray the bullet has not gone too deeply. Oh, poor Papa," she breathed, her voice cracking.

Suddenly she felt two strong hands grasp her arms. With a start she whirled around. "Oh, J—Justin!" she exclaimed, relief flooding her. And without thinking, she collapsed in his arms. "Oh, Justin," she cried softly. "Papa . . . he—he . . . tried—he—"

"Hush, Moriah, 'tis all right," Roane murmured, clasping her tightly to him. "He's alive, and they've sent for the doctor."

She clung to him, and over her head Roane caught the eye of the baron's manservant. He mouthed the words "How is he?" and received a reassuring nod in reply. He felt some of the tension leave his body. Then his eye wandered the room and he saw that the butler was regarding him with one raised white eyebrow while the housekeeper gaped in blatant astonishment. O dear, he thought, he would deal with all of that later. For now, Moriah needed him, and that was all that mattered.

Presently, Moriah lifted her head and tried to wipe her eyes. "Finch, P—Papa's valet, you know," she said, indicating the manservant, "moved him from the desk. He was all—all slumped over. Is there—is there nothing more we can do for him until the doctor comes?"

"I doubt it, little one. But I will see. Why don't you come sit down over here?" he asked gently, pointing to a chair next the sofa.

"No, I—"

"Come, Moriah," he said firmly, and led her to the wing chair.

Then he went to the sofa and bent to the baron. His pulse was rapid and faint, and the linen Finch held to the wound was full of blood. He turned questioning eyes to the valet. "Shock?" he asked.

350

"Yes," Finch said in a low voice. "And he's lost a good bit o' blood. But still an' all, I don't reckon he's harmed himself beyond repair."

Roane wondered at the quiet assurance in the valet's voice, but further questions were interrupted by a bustle at the door.

"I ran all the way, Miss Moriah," came a weepy, breathless voice. "Miss Moriah? Oh, there you be." Roane straightened up and regarded a plump maid scurrying forward, water basin and linen in hand. "I'm not too late, am I? Oh, Lor', I—"

"No, no, Lizzie," Moriah answered, rising shakily from her chair. "Just bring everything to Lord Roane."

Roane took the linen and water and bade the servant fetch a blanket. He handed the materials to Finch and watched the valet attempt to bathe the wound. But there was still too much blood. "The bullet?" he asked, bending low.

"I—I don't rightly know, my lord. Doesn't seem— well, 'tis possible there was no penetration at all."

Roane nodded, satisfied Finch was doing all that could be done, for now. He glanced over at Moriah, smiled reassuringly at her, and then went to the desk. The green leather blotter was stained with blood that was still wet. There were droplets on nearby papers and the chair. Roane's eye scanned the desk top for the gun; he found it, a moment later, on the floor. As he picked it up he found himself shaking. The sound of the gunshot had jarred something deep within him. He could not think what; he'd heard the sound often enough, especially in the War. Sighing deeply, he allowed his eyes to flit about the room. Tess was apparently still in a faint, and Mrs. Trotter was patting her hand and waiving a vinaigrette at her nose. The old butler was slowly pacing the floor and Moriah had gone once more to her father; she was kneeling beside the sofa.

She had been right all along, he thought, his eye now going to the open door of the pistol cabinet. She had come to him because she feared for her father's life, and she had been right. Landon *was* suicidal. But—but why now? His gaze fell once more on Moriah. There was such naked pain in her eyes. Oh, God, how he wanted to shield her from pain.

He forced himself to look down at the gun. His eyes widened as he examined it, and then he almost smiled. Well, well, he thought. No penetration indeed. He placed it on the desk and then noticed, for the first time, a letter partially tucked under the desk blotter. He tried to wipe two spots of blood from the edge of the writing paper and then pulled it out. It was marked "For Moriah and Tess." With a grim expression he put it in his pocket; Moriah would want to read it later, in privacy. For now, he did not want anyone else to find it.

A clamour in the corridor arrested his attention and this time he strode to the doorway, five paces ahead of Reeves. Lizzie, still weeping copiously, was followed by an even more hysterical scullery maid and a rather large woman in a white apron whom he took to be the cook. All three opened their mouths to speak at once, and he silenced them with a raised hand.

"Now, now, the baron will be all right. His breathing is regular and the doctor is on the way. It is best that you each return to your duties," he said calmly, and took the blanket from Lizzie's arms.

Then he bade Lizzie come in and help Mrs. Trotter convey Tess upstairs. The stalwart housekeeper could not seem to decide whether to be grateful or piqued at his intervention. Reeves, however, was decidedly miffed when Roane instructed him to stand guard outside the study. But he bowed deferentially and his butler's mask slipped only a little when Roane closed the doors behind him.

He went to the sofa and handed the blanket to Moriah. He watched her lovingly cover the baron. Then he raised her up and, holding her gently by the elbows, smiled at her. "He'll be all right, Moriah. He's suffering from shock, but there were blanks in the gun."

"Blanks?" she whispered, her eyes welling up anew. "Is it possible?" He nodded. "Oh, thank God," she breathed, and he wrapped his arms about her as she clung to him. She raised her head a minute later. "But, Justin, whoever—"

"I do not know," he replied. "Finch? Can *you* shed any light on this?" he asked blithely, looking intently down at the ruddy-faced valet.

Finch did not meet his eye. "Blanks you say? Well, fancy that. And praise be to the Lord, that's all what I say, your lordship," Finch answered gruffly.

"Indeed," Roane murmured dryly, and caught a flicker of a smile on the servant's lips.

"B—but, Justin, the explosion," Moriah said with a tremor in her voice. "Can it not still ki—?"

"Yes, my dear, it can," he answered gravely, wishing her mind were not quite so agile. "But I do not think it will."

She nodded, trying to smile through her tears and succeeding only in shedding more. With one more glance at the baron, Roane led her to the window and gathered her in his arms.

They stood thus, a silent tableau of four people,

for what seemed an endless span of time, until Reeves finally announced the doctor. That elderly, bewhiskered gentleman hurried in, tried to mask his surprise at seeing Roane and Moriah entwined at the window and, with a nod in Roane's direction, bent to the patient. Moriah would have spoken to the doctor, but Roane ushered her out of the room instead.

In the corridor they were met by a lineup of servants alternately bawling and wringing their hands. With a protective hand at her elbow, Roane tried to guide Moriah past them, but she stood firmly, facing the rather rag-tag group. "Thank you all for your concern. We think the baron will be right. The doctor is with him now," she said with that same composure that had so unnerved him—Lord, was it only a se'nnight ago? He noted ruefully that she did not bother to order them back to their chores.

"Oh, Lordy, Miss Moriah, whatever did 'appen to 'him? 'Imself looked right as rain when I see 'im come in from 'is ride this morning', 'e did," blubbered the scullery maild.

"Is it true, miss? Oh the poor baron!" wailed Lizzie. "Is it true he tried to—to—?"

Roane could feel Moriah tense beside him, and he stepped into the breach. "The baron has had an accident. He was cleaning his pistol, but we believe that the—ah—bullet has not entered the head." This pronouncement was greeted with a chorus of "Praise be's" and fresh tears, and Roane steered Moriah away.

They settled in the morning room and sat together on the plum-colored sofa. They hardly spoke, but he kept on one hand firmly about her shoulder and with the other alternately stroked her cheek and held her hand. She seemed to draw strength from him, and he thanked God that he was here. He did not know if she would have sent for him. Likely not, for that would have required forethought. And once she began thinking, she would remember last night. As it was, she seemed to have momentarily forgotten. And she appeared totally unaware that his behavior toward her, and her acceptance of it, were tantamount to an announcement in the *Gazette*. Just as well, he thought, and wondered what she would do when she realized it.

Countless minutes ticked away. He considered showing her the baron's letter but thought it would be less painful for her to read once the doctor had confirmed that the baron would survive. And so he held his peace and then, finally, the doctor quietly knocked and entered the room.

Roane and Moriah stood to face him, and Roane could feel the tautness of her body as he held her gently by the elbow.

Dr. Desmond gave them both a belated and most cordial greeting and then spoke clearly and briefly. The baron was suffering from shock. There had been no bullet, no penetration. The wound would heal and the blood loss had not been sufficient to do him harm. At this Moriah expelled a deep breath and bent her head. She whispered, "Thank God," and Roane could feel some of the tension leave her. She looked up and the doctor continued to say that what the baron needed now was to be kept warm and quiet. He was already being conveyed abovestairs and had to have three days of complete bed rest.

Moriah listened carefully, nodding and smiling despite the telltale moisture in her eyes. Then, with that amazing composure of hers, she invited him to

355

stay to luncheon, which he declined. He did agree to a brandy, however, and Roane summoned Reeves to bring some for them all, insisting that Moriah needed a glass as well. He also commissioned the butler to report the good news of the baron's condition to the staff.

Once the brandy had been served, Roane seated the doctor in the chintz wing chair, Moriah and himself on the sofa. He watched Moriah take her first sip of brandy. She made a face but otherwise suffered no ill effects, and he turned his attention to the doctor. "We have given out to the servants that the baron had an accident while cleaning his gun." The doctor nodded his understanding, his gray eyes sympathetic. "Very wise, my lord."

"I take it you know that there were blanks in that gun. Someone obviously knew the baron very well."

"Yes," Moriah said, "but who—"

"Aside from the occasional wife, only one person can know a man so well as all that," Roane interjected. Moriah looked puzzled and the doctor smiled. "A man's valet, my dear," Roane continued.

"Finch. Of course," Moriah said in wonder. "I recall that he—he came to see me. He was so worried. Oh God, if he hadn't—"

"But he did, Moriah," Roane interrupted firmly, putting an arm about her.

Dr. Desmond cleared his throat, rising and setting his glass down on the sofa table. Roane and Moriah rose as well. "Am I—er—to assume," began the doctor, a trifle red-faced, "that I may—er—wish you both happy, my lord, Miss Landon?"

Moriah nearly choked on her brandy this time and Roane slid the glass from her hand. Recovering, she gaped at the doctor. Oh, no, thought Roane, and spoke before she did. "We—ah—would appreciate your—ah—keeping our little secret for a time, Doctor."

"Oh, I—er—I see, of course," said the good doctor, who then gave them both a broad wink and, after a few more words, took his leave.

As soon as the door closed behind him, Moriah rounded on Roane, her eyes flashing. Her hair was slightly mussed, and he thought she looked beautiful in the violet dress that emphasized those eyes. But never mind that for now. "Just what did he mean, Justin?" she snapped. "And you—why ever did you—?"

"Moriah," he interrupted, praying for inspiration, "you must realize that our—er—being together—er—here, in this manner, gives rise to—er—speculation. And I do think—"

"Oh, my God," Moriah blurted, and felt sick. How could she have been so—so weak as to allow herself to—to—and to forget all that—She took a deep breath and stepped away from him, behind the sofa. "So, I am to assume that because I—I turned to you in a moment of weakness, I have—have compromised myself."

Her voice was husky and he so wished he could sweep her into his arms and make her forget all the bitterness between them. But he knew it would not answer; he had tried that and failed. And so he let her continue. "Or is it—" she went on, frowning and seeming to consider her own words, "is it rather that you, taking advantage of that weakness, have made a declaration which I have appeared to accept?"

He did not like the tone of this conversation at all. He took several steps toward her. "Moriah, I did nothing of the kind. I simply went to you because I

357

knew you needed me."

Moriah's eyes widened as another thought struck her. Lord above, what could it mean? "Just what *are* you doing here, Justin?" she demanded.

Oh, Lord, here it comes, he thought. He had better handle this right. He smiled at her, then came round the back of the sofa. "I was coming to call on your father, little one, just as I said I would."

"I see. This despite the fact that I asked you not to," she countered. It was a statement, not a question.

He placed his hands gently on her shoulders. "Yes, love, for despite all, I believe—"

"Yes, I see," she repeated imperiously, squirming from his reach. She felt her indignation begin to build into fury. "And you just *happened* to arrive as the shot was fired," she added sarcastically.

"As a matter of fact, yes," he replied, and felt a spark of anger within himself. "Just what are you intimating, Moriah?" he asked very quietly.

"It was quite a coincidence, was it not, your coming at that precise moment?" He did not like the disdainful twist to her mouth.

"Yes, it *was* a coincidence. What of it, Moriah?" She turned and strolled toward the bay window behind the desk. Then she whirled around to face him. "It has been my experience that coincidences never *are* such. You weren't just coming, were you? You were just *leaving*. You told him, didn't you, Justin?"

"Told him? What are you—oh my God!" He reached her in several long strides and this time his grip on her shoulders was none too gentle. "Of course I didn't tell him, Moriah. I told you I would never—"

"You told him!" she shouted harshly, her eyes fierce. "You told him and that's why he shot himself!"

"Moriah, that's preposterous!" he exclaimed, shaking her lightly. "You don't know what you're saying!"

"Oh, you are diabolical, sir! It was not enough to ruin him—*and* me. No! You had to insure that I would marry you—and you would go to any lengths to see I did. And, of course, you warned me last night that you might tell Papa—"

"Dammit, Moriah, I was quizzing you when I said that, and you well know it!"

"Or is it that you knew what he would do? What man could bear to think that for his sake his daughter had—had—? Was this all part of your plan, my lord? Did you all along—"

"Moriah!" he said, his fingers digging into her shoulders. "Your accusation is—is odious in the extreme! Not to mention convoluted and—oh, hell! I've not been a saint, but that you would honestly assume that I had any part—why, for heaven sakes, Moriah, he left a note!"

He relaxed his grip and was about to reach into his pocket, but her scathing voice stopped him. "A note! How convenient! And I suppose you just *happen* to have it in your coat pocket!"

He wanted to shake her till her head rolled; he wanted to kiss her thoroughly. But neither would help. And so he dropped his hands, his eyes bleak. "Yes, Moriah, I do," he said quietly. He withdrew the folded writing paper. "I retrieved it from his desk, not wishing a servant to espy it and thinking you would wish to read it in private." He could see her entire body seething with rage. "Here, it has your father's seal, and surely you can recognize his hand.

And it—" he gentled his voice, "it has his blood on it, little one."

He saw her flinch, but then her face went rigid again and she refused to take the letter. "I see," she said icily. "How convenient that *you* were the one to find it. Or did you do more than find it?" Good God, did she think he forged the damned thing? "I shall not deign to ask how you contrived—"

"Oh for Christ's sake, Moriah!" he exploded, seizing her again and pulling her close. "I *love* you! Can't I make you understand? I want to care for you, protect you, *and* your family. Blast it all! I'll even support your father's gaming habit!"

"How very generous of you, my lord Roane," she said distantly, her shoulders taut under his hands. "And now, I should like to be alone. If you will kindly leave my home . . ."

"Moriah! You cannot expect me to leave you like this. Not when—"

She wrenched herself from his grasp and then raised her chin, hands clasped at her waist. "You are mistaken, my lord," she interrupted with controlled, smoldering calm. "I not only ask, but demand, that you leave my home." He took a step toward her. "No! Do not touch me again." She marched to the bellpull and yanked on it. "You are not welcome here, my lord. You have done your damage," she said contemptuously. "Now take your wretched letter and *leave* my home. It *is* my home, you may recall. I paid for it, very dearly." He heard the tremor in her husky voice at this last, but nonetheless she squared her shoulders and exited the room with heart-wrenching dignity.

He did not try to stop her; there was no more he could say or do. Nor did he attempt to force the

360

letter on her. In her present state she was like to tear it to shreds. Once she'd gone, he pocketed the letter. Then he slowly left the room, not at all caring to be dismissed by some overprotective butler.

The baron's letter seemed to burn a hole in his pocket all the way home. God dammit! If only she'd read it! Or he should heave read it to her! He drove his horses too hard in his agony, and then, immediately contrite, slowed them to a normal pace. It wasn't just the letter and he knew it, painfully well. She didn't trust him. It was that simple. And it looked as if she never would.

Chapter 30

The morning's dire events had quite put the earl from Roane's mind, but he might have known his uncle would be awaiting him at Roanbrooke. He did not bother to change his clothes but went directly to the family drawing room. He desperately wanted to get this interview over with and, besides, nothing could be worse than what had just transpired with Moriah.

The earl rose at his entrance, drink in hand. "Good morning, Justin," he said gravely.

Roane nodded. "Uncle," he said noncommittally, crossing the plush green carpet toward the earl.

The earl reseated himself in the wing chair and Roane sank into the mint-green velvet sofa. "I came here, Justin, because I think we need to—to talk." The earl's words might have been conciliatory but his tone was not.

"I see," Roane said remotely. "Where is Andrew?"

"Took off like a bat out of hell not ten minutes past. Headed for Wykham Abbey. It's all over the servants hall that Landon had an accident with his gun. Shot himself in the head, though they say he'll do." The earl studied Roane's face intently. "Why should my son hightail it to the Abbey, Justin?"

Roane sighed. "I'm surprised I didn't see him. I

362

have only just come from there. And I suspect what he is racing to is not the Abbey but one of its inhabitants. The baron's younger daughter, Tess. A very taking little thing. Sixteen years old," he added pointedly.

"Good God!"

"Just so. They met the other night at the Crowleys and—well, Andrew was rather taken with her. I—I thought it prudent to remind him that one so young can easily lose her heart, or her reputation."

The earl raised an eyebrow, and his stern expression relaxed just a bit. "I am much obliged, Justin. I see I shall have to keep a sharp eye on the young pup."

"He meant no harm, and he is a gentleman, but still I did not wish him to forget himself. I told him she is much too young—for anything."

The earl cleared his throat. "Indeed, Justin. Which puts me in mind of her sister, who isn't."

Roane sighed again, deeply. "No, she isn't," he said grimly, then rose and went to pour himself a brandy.

"How *is* the baron, Justin?"

Roane filled his glass, then turned to face his uncle, leaning back against the mahogany side table. "He's in shock, but quite alive. He—ah—well, we are giving out that it was an accident but, between us if you please, he—he tried to kill himself."

"Tried to—Good God!" The earl sat bolt upright. "But why?"

"Would that I knew, Uncle. And the only reason he failed is that his valet filled the gun with blanks."

"God bless a gentleman's gentleman. And how is—er—the family, Justin?"

"When I left, Tess was undoubtedly still in a swoon and—and Moriah had—had recovered sufficiently to order me from the premises."

The earl cocked his head. "What were you doing there, Justin?"

"I went there to—to ask the baron's permission to pay my addresses to Moriah," Roane said tautly, then took a long swig of the drink. "There, are you satisfied?" he demanded bitterly. "Though I must admit I never got to see him. I arrived just as—as the shot was fired."

"A terrible business, Justin. But you did the right thing. You have no choice but to marry the girl."

"Blast it all, I don't *want* a choice! I told you I'd already offered for her twice. Now I think the count is up to four or five. She won't have me. And now—dammit, Uncle George! You've been like a father to me. Won't you at the least make the effort to understand? Won't you allow me to explain?" The words wrenched themselves from Roane's throat and he whirled around and leaned heavily on the table.

"Did I love you less than a son, Justin, I would not be so disappointed," the earl said quietly. "You may say what you like, but nothing can change what I heard and saw. It was painfully obvious that—"

"God dammit, Uncle George!" Roane exploded, slamming his drink down. "Nothing was obvious! No more is it obvious that you and Emily Shoup—" Roane stopped short and froze. My God, whatever had possessed him? For several long moments there was a tense silence.

"What did you say?" the earl asked finally, very softly.

"Oh, dammit! Have another drink, Uncle." Roane sloshed more brandy into a fresh glass and marched to his uncle and handed it to him.

The earl took the glass but made no attempt to drink. "I think you'd better continue, Justin." His voice was ominously calm.

"I . . . forgive me, Uncle George," Roane said, sinking into the sofa again. "I should not have spoken. 'Tis none of my affair. I—I think she's a charming lady."

"So do I, Justin," the earl responded, his lips twitching faintly. "But I do not think that is quite the point. Just where did you get the idea that Mrs. Shoup and I—er—well—"

Now Roane felt his own lips twitching. Perhaps it was better to get it out in the open at all events. "I have suspected for some time, Uncle. A chance word here and there; I know you well, after all. And now—government business, indeed!" The earl looked alarmed, but Roane ignored him. "But I didn't know of a certain until—well, until the Crowley ball."

"The Crowley—but—"

Roane smiled for the first time. "You danced the waltz, Uncle."

The earl sighed resignedly. "Ah, the waltz. Always said it was a scandalous dance. Never know what trouble it may get one into," he said gruffly, but Roane caught the smile lurking at the back of his eyes. "Er—tell me, Justin, did anyone else share your—er—perspicacity with regard to the waltz?"

Roane chuckled. "No, Uncle George, even Drew is still woefully ignorant. May I—ah—ask *you* a question?"

"I suppose so. It can hardly signify now." His uncle leaned back and crossed his legs, resting his drink on his knee.

"How long have you and Mrs. Shoup been—well—"

"Fifteen years," the earl replied quietly.

"Fifteen years! Christ, Uncle George! Why don't you marry her?" Roane blurted, then felt himself redden. "Forgive me," he mumbled sheepishly. "None of my—"

"No, it's not," his uncle interrupted, then sighed again. "The lady has only been—well, shall we say, free, these five years past. Since then she has stead-fastly refused me." He paused and took a long drink. "Trying to save my reputation and my career from the taint of divorce," he said wryly. "Women have the damnedest notions of nobility at times. But this time—well, events have so transpired that I will not take no for an answer," he concluded forcefully, and then rose and strode to the hearth. He stared down into the empty grate, his back to Roane.

"You love her very much, don't you?" Roane whispered.

The earl turned to face him. "Yes, I do."

" 'Tis hard to believe that the lady would refuse you—you, a peer of the realm and a man with whom she—well, I mean to say—And just how many times did you say you'd offered?" Roane teased, trying to keep his expression suitably grave.

The earl eyed Roane fiercely, then suddenly broke into a grin. "Ah, hoist on my own petard, am I?" He went back to his chair and sat down, peering intently at Roane. "You—you really *have* offered for Miss Landon, several times in fact, haven't you?"

"I have never lied to you, Uncle."

The earl sighed and leaned forward in his chair, his hands between his knees and head bent. His nor-mally booming voice was low and gravelly as he spoke. "Justin, I—I've behaved like a damned prig through all this. I don't know what came over me. I—no, that isn't true. Perhaps I do know. It was—it was seeing that girl, that lovely girl, so frightened and—and realizing what society can do to a woman." The earl's eyes were bleak and he ran his hand across his brow. "It—it made me think of—of Emily and

I—I suppose I was angry at myself. For all these years when—well, I guess what I am trying to say is that I—I'm sorry, Justin."

"I understand, Uncle. And I think, you know, that it is not too late. Well, I mean to say, surely you can persuade her to marry you. Why, career or no—"

"Hold, Justin, hold!" the earl interrupted, grinning. "I thank you for the vote of confidence. And as I said, this time will be different." He paused and his voice grew sober. "But I think that perhaps, for you, it is not so simple, is it?"

"No, Uncle. 'Tisn't simple at all." Roane sprang up and began to pace the floor. "It's so bloody complicated that I—I don't know how to unravel it all," he said desperately.

"Would you . . . care to tell me about it, Justin?" the earl asked softly.

Roane barely heard him and kept pacing, running a distracted hand through his hair. "Moriah will not even—" he began agitatedly, then stopped abruptly. He took a deep breath and stalked to the sofa, flinging himself down. "I suppose I *had* better tell you the whole, Uncle," he sighed. " 'Tis the damnedest coil and, well, at this point Moriah will not even speak to me, much less marry me." Roane covered his face with one hand and heard his uncle rise from his chair.

"Here, I think you need this, Justin," the earl said a minute later, and Roane finally looked up. He took the fresh glass of brandy from his uncle and drank liberally.

The earl sat down and peered at Roane expectantly. Roane's knuckles whitened as he clutched the brandy snifter and forced himself to speak. " 'Tis but a se'ennight since I first met Moriah, Uncle, for all it seems a lifetime ago," he began in a constricted voice. "I—I am not proud of my behavior since then, but I am not the complete bounder you—you implied. "I—oh, damn and blast it all," he railed, "I shall never—"

"Justin," the earl interrupted gently, leaning forward. "Why don't you—ah—tell me how you—ah—met Miss Landon?"

"How I—yes, perhaps—well, it—it was a very . . . interesting meeting, Uncle," Roane mused, a glimmer of a smile touching his lips. He took another drink and slowly began his narrative.

Some parts were easy, others devilishly tricky. "So you see, Uncle, I never meant to make her an improper offer at first stop," Roane said at one point, shifting uncomfortably on the sofa. "But somehow I could not retract it. That is, I mean to say, not that I did not wish to, but that each time I tried to she—well, she somehow contrived to make me feel a cad, quite ungallant and . . ."

Roane went on, knowing he had to tell his uncle the whole, or at least as much as a gentleman could speak of. Nothing else would answer, but he wished to hell this interview were over! It seemed to get harder as he went along, and the earl did not help one iota, merely regarding him with faintly twitching lips and waiting for him to continue each time he faltered.

"And what the devil was I to do, I ask you?" Roane burst out a few minutes later, springing up and beginning to pace the floor. "There she was, in my hunting box, at *midnight,* for pity's sake, quite willing and—and expecting me to—to . . . and—and I'd had too much to drink and—well, dammit, Uncle George, *you've* seen her! If that isn't extreme provocation, then I don't know—well, what in blazes *was* I to do? I'm not a bloody saint, for Christ's sake!"

Roane exclaimed, running a hand through his dark hair, then flinging himself back down onto the sofa and drinking deeply. He glanced at his uncle over the rim of his glass and was not best pleased to see that gentleman suppressing a decided grin. Roane pressed on with as much dignity as he could muster.

"And so I—I took her—er—upstairs, and I knew immediately afterwards that—that she was someone very special to me." The earl regarded him intently now, and Roane recounted his bout of conscience, his initial proposal of marriage, his game with the baron, his subsequent nights with Moriah.

"You cannot mean to say you actually played *chess?*" the earl demanded incredulously. It was the first time he'd spoken since Roane had begun.

Roane felt himself relax and smiled ruefully. "Yes—er—yes, Uncle. I am, after all, a gentleman."

"Do you mean to tell me that in all this time only once did you—ah—well—"

Roane's smile faded, and he felt himself redden. "Er—well, no, Uncle. There was—there was last night, you see." The earl frowned prodigiously and Roane's voice became urgent. "I—I love her desperately, Uncle George! I didn't know *how* much until the night of the ball—I suppose when I saw Chilton threaten her. And now—oh, God!" He took another drink, then rose and stalked across the room in agitation. With agony in his voice he told his uncle—his mentor and the only father he had—of his feeling for Moriah and the terrible words they'd had last night and this morning. When he was done, he felt spent and sank dejectedly into the sofa. "What am I to do, Uncle George?" he asked bleakly.

His uncle heaved a sigh. "Lord above, what a nasty coil. And I—I am deeply chagrined for my part in it. I should never have stayed to witness such a private moment. But having remained, I should have immediately recognized the nature of your feelings. As I look back, they were—were perfectly obvious. And I—well, I believe that Miss Landon returns your regard. It pains me greatly that she overheard us, that I have been the cause of so much—"

"No, Uncle. While it is true that, had this not occurred, things might have come about quite differently, the truth is that if not from you then she might well have heard sometime else, certainly about—about the tragic scandal, and perhaps more."

"Possibly, but I—well, if it will help, I would gladly speak with her."

Roane shook his head. "I think not, Uncle. In her present state I believe it actually might worsen matters. Besides, this is between Moriah and me. It—it is a matter of trust, you see."

"Yes, I do see. But for now, Justin, give her time. Much has happened these few days past and she is overwrought. And despite her self-possession, she *is* young. Go and see her this afternoon if you wish, and again tomorrow. I am persuaded that she will come round eventually." The earl stood up and put a comforting hand on Roane's shoulder. "Be patient, Nephew. All is not lost. And in the end—well, *I* shan't take no for an answer and neither should you."

"B—but Uncle George, *you've* waited five years!" Roane exclaimed in horrified accents, rising to face his uncle.

The earl's jaw tightened. "My—my circumstances were quite different, Justin. Miss Landon, as an unmarried lady, cannot—" He paused, then shook his head ruefully. "Oh, devil take it, Justin, you don't need me to tell you that. But you—you needs must have faith, lad. She—she loves you. She *will* come round, you know."

Roane grinned crookedly. "Very well, Uncle George," he said quietly. "You convince your lady, and I shall convince mine."

The earl smiled in return, the familiar twinkle back in his eyes.

Chapter 31

Roane felt immeasurably better after his talk with the earl. But whatever optimism that interview engendered was immediately dashed upon his visit, that afternoon, to Wykham Abbey.

The baron, according to Reeves, was sleeping fitfully but appeared to be recovering. Miss Landon was not receiving visitors. Roane requested that he be announced nonetheless, as she might wish to see *him*. Reeves masked his disapproval and complied, but returned to inform my lord smugly that Miss Landon *especially* did not wish to him *him*.

Roane cursed under his breath, his gaze on the wide staircase. She could play this game for days, and there was little he could do. Storming up to her bedchamber would hardly add to his credit. Nor could he send the baron's letter up and risk her tearing it to shreds. "Please send my compliments to Miss Landon," he said loftily to the butler after a moment, and then added pointedly, "and tell her I shall return in the morning."

He *would* return in the morning and insist she read that letter, he vowed, striding out of the house to his waiting carriage. But as it lumbered out of the drive, he reminded himself that it wasn't just the letter or what had happened this morning that was keeping them apart. She didn't trust him. It was as simple, and as complicated, as that.

The Viscount Roane spent a sleepless night but nonetheless presented himself at Wykham Abbey promptly at ten o'clock the next morning. Reeves tilted his nose up a notch higher as he repeated almost verbatim his words of the previous day. This time Roane cursed a little more vocally, but Reeves was unmoved. Miss Landon was not receiving. Roane eyed the staircase speculatively before stalking from the house.

"Damn!" he exploded once he'd attained the privacy of his study. How long would she keep hiding from him? It wasn't like her to hide from anything, and he felt a sharp pang as he realized that her doing so now was a mark of how deeply he had wounded her.

He strode to the window, then to the sideboard and splashed some brandy into a glass. He felt an agitation rising in him and drank too much in one gulp. "Blast it all!" he exploded, then slammed the glass down onto the table. He was drinking too damn much lately; he paced the room instead.

Unlike his uncle, Roane did not believe that time was in his favour. If he did not see her, he feared that the passage of time would allow her anger to harden into hatred. And then it would be too late. He needed to speak with her, touch her, remind her of everything good that was between them. Fighting a sense of panic, he resolved that, come what may, she *would* see him this afternoon, and there would be reckoning.

But the afternoon brought only the relentlessly proper face of the white-haired Reeves, repeating his instructions. No, Roane thought, she must not hide any longer. They must have a rational discussion, and somehow, some way, he must get through to her. He peered intently at the butler. Reeves had seen Roane and Moriah together; he could be made to understand that Roane was friend and not foe, and that his intentions were honourable. But Reeves was unmoved.

"Be that as it may, my lord," he replied woodenly, "Miss Landon was quite clear on that head. She—beggin' your pardon, your lordship—she said she was particularly not home to—ahem—the Viscount Roane."

Roane's patience was at an end. He was not about to spend the next week riding back and forth twice a day between the Abbey and Roanbrooke in the vain hope that she might relent. "Where is she, Reeves?" he demanded, all trace of civility gone.

"Miss Landon is not at—"

"Is she in the morning room, or is she hiding upstairs?" he persisted, his voice raised, hands on hips.

"Beggin' your pardon, my lord, she is indisposed—er—in her chamber, you must know. And now I must ask you to—"

"You will take this message to your mistress, now, man! Tell her I shall await her in the morning room. I shall give her exactly five minutes to make her appearance, and if she does not, then *I shall come after her!*" Roane thundered, towering over the suddenly ashen-faced butler.

Reeves beat a hasty retreat and Roane took himself off to the morning room. It was not Moriah who appeared several minutes later, however, but an even paler butler. "I am sorry, my lord, but she—she refuses to—ah—that is—"

Reeves looked slightly ill, and Roane felt his temple throb. Good God, but she was stubborn! He strode from the room and back to the entry hall, Reeves in his wake. "Which is her room, Reeves?" he asked ominously.

"My lord, I—I beg you—"

"Which room, man, or must I search them all?" he shouted, fists clenched to keep from strangling the man.

"Er—ah—oh dear," Reeves stammered, then added almost inaudibly, "second landing, third door on the right."

Roane bounded up the stairs, his long legs taking them two at a time. He marched down the corridor and knocked at Moriah's door. When no answer came he turned the handle. What the devil—? He tried again, but it was locked.

"Moriah," he called, rather gently. There was silence.

"Moriah!" His voice was less gentle, and by the third time he was shouting. "Moriah! Open the door! You cannot hide from me forever!"

Still no reply, but he could hear movement within. Damn it all! He'd make sure she never locked a door to him again! He grasped the handle and shook the door, pounding it with his other hand. "Open the door, Moriah, or I swear I'll break it down! *Now,* Moriah!" he roared.

"I pray you will not, my lord," came a cool, imperious voice, "else you'll rouse the entire house, probably Papa as well. I believe you have done enough harm already. "Now *leave* my house!"

Cursing fluently, Roane took a deliberate step back and turned his shoulder to the door. He rammed it once, then again. On the third try the latch gave, splintering part of the jamb with it, and Roane charged into the room.

She was seated at the window in a pink high-backed chair. At his entrance she turned, raised an eyebrow, then slowly rose. "So," she said, imbuing the word with such calm, icy disdain that he froze in his tracks, "you have made your point. You have proven the superiority of your masculine strength. But then, I believe you have done so before, quite recently, have you not?"

His eyes blazed at this reference to their last night together, but he did not fail to notice the tremor of her hand as she clutched the chair back. "Moriah, how can you—?"

"Do not bother, my lord. I am persuaded we can have nothing to say to each other. Nothing that signifies. And now if you'll excuse me . . ." She raised her chin and swept regally past him, pausing at the door and turning to him. "Do not follow me, my lord. I can already hear the servants buzzing in the corridor. And unless you wish to provide entertainment worthy of a circus, I pray you will not break through any more doors."

Roane wanted to throttle her, but he did not move. "Very well," he replied in a quiet, angry voice. "I shall not detain you. But know that I shall return tomorrow and the next day, and the next. You are behaving like a child, Moriah, and my patience wears thin."

She whirled around and flounced out of the room, slamming the door behind her. Roane cursed again, rubbing his suddenly aching shoulder. Well, at the least he had finally pierced that unnerving composure of hers. He strode from the room only to find three pairs of eyes trained on him. Lizzie clutched a feather duster and regarded him with unabashed curiosity. Mrs. Trotter scowled at him, hands folded implacably at her chest as she let forth a loud "harrumph!" And Finch regarded him with, amazingly enough, something like bemusement.

Roane did the only thing a peer of the realm could do in such a briarpatch. He smiled. "Good afternoon to you all. Ah, Finch, how does the baron?"

Finch blinked, then replied genially, "Well enough, my lord. Awake a bit of the time but don't recall aught o' what happened. Head hurts him somethin' awful, and the doctor give him drops to make him sleep, don't you know."

Roane made a suitable reply, and then with all the dignity of his station, betook himself off.

Moriah was at that moment in a most *un*dignified posture, having escaped to the linen room and collapsed, shaking, onto one of the rickety chairs. She had shed enough tears for him and vowed she would not cry again. Instead she tried frantically to think of what she must do. She had to get away. She could not stay here, waiting for the panther to stalk his prey.

But how could she leave now, with Papa still not fully recovered? True, Finch hardly allowed her in the sick room, but still . . . Moriah propped her elbows on the plankboard table and sank her head into her hands. She sat thus for a long time until, finally, she had come to some resolution.

Finch notwithstanding, there was little she could do for Papa now. She could not talk with him yet, and he needed sleep more than nursing. So she could, in all good conscience, leave the Abbey for a while. She would give out to everyone that she'd gone north to Lancashire. Poor Miss Billingsley had been taken gravely ill, and with Papa on the mend, of course she had to go. If the whole household believed it, the viscount would have no choice but to believe it as well. And if enough time passed, he would finally give up and leave her be.

Of course, she would not really go north, Miss Billingsley presently enjoying excellent health and Papa quite the opposite. She would go to a neighbor, to someone whose friendship she instinctively knew she could rely on and whose household was discretion itself. She knew of only one such place. She would send a note round today and leave tomorrow morning, very early, before a certain personage had even breakfasted. Only Finch would know her true destination, so he might summon her if need be. And she could even sneak back at night to see Papa—heaven knew she had enough experience with nocturnal outings, she thought bitterly.

She rose from the table, hoping she would not have to stay away long. Damn Justin Traugott for bringing her to this pass! She was running away—from home, from him, and from herself. She knew it well, and it was not at all her accustomed way. Yet nothing else would answer.

Roane had gotten halfway home when the idea had come to him. He had only one ally at Wykham Abbey, and he would do well to use him. He'd turned the carriage around and startled Reeves with his request to see, of all people, the baron's valet. Roane had given the baron's letter to Finch, explaining how he had come by it and adjuring him to give it to Moriah. He had alluded to his intentions regarding the mistress of the house, conveying to Finch without explanation—a man could abase himself just so far—that it was critical she read and not shred the letter. And then, satisfied with Finch's sincere acquiescence though vexed with the twinkle in the manservant's eyes, the Viscount Roane had once more headed home.

He found himself exhausted after two sleepless nights, but yet sleep came only intermittently. His mind and body ached for Moriah; he could find no peace. And when he finally pushed her from his mind, it was only to replace her with images more disturbing. He lay in bed, in that stupor that exists somewhere between sleep and wakefulness, and heard again the gunshot. It had jarred him, reminded him of something. He heard it again, only this time it came not from the Abbey but from a meadow. There were men in the distance, and suddenly one of them crumpled and fell. Father!

With a start Roane jerked up to a sitting position, sweating and shaking violently. He took several deep breaths and shook his head. No! It wasn't possible. He hadn't been near the meadow—he'd been in the carriage with his mother and Nell. They'd already gone past the village. He could never have heard that shot. And yet—and yet . . . Roane rubbed his eyes, then slowly climbed out of bed. He had no wish to attempt sleep again this night.

It was near dawn that the answer came to him, in spite of, or perhaps because of, the brandy befogging his brain. It was all to do with the axle. He was in the carriage with his mother and Nell, and then Peter Coachman had stopped to check the axle. And that was when Justin had bolted. He'd begged Mama not to leave. Not yet. Father was in trouble. He could feel it. But Mama wouldn't listen. And so he'd run, run all the way to the meadow, heedless of the nursemaid panting after him. But he'd been too late to save Father. And then later—later they'd brought news of Mama and Nell. The axle had been broken after all, and the carriage had tumbled down a ravine.

He was shaking and his face was wet with tears as the full realization of what it all meant hit him. The viscount now might know very well that none of it was his fault, but the child Justin had believed very differently. He had abandoned Mama and Nell, left them to die. And that terrible guilt had oppressed his soul and turned his grief into hatred. And now the hatred was gone, but too late, it seemed. Would Moriah ever understand?

Chapter 32

Moriah sat quietly at the delicate escritoire of the lovely guest bedroom she now occupied. She had been here since early morning and her welcome had been everything she'd known it would be. Mrs. Shoup, who insisted she call her Emily, had been kindness itself.

They'd had a comfortable cose just after breakfast and Moriah had found Emily very easy to talk to. In fact, she'd found herself, with little prompting, gratefully telling Emily the whole. It was so good to share the burden, and Emily had offered comfort without pity or judgment. She had understood, had even seemed to know some of it before Moriah had spoken, although, of course, that was impossible. And then, when Moriah was done crying, Emily had asked softly, "You love him very much, don't you?"

"No!" Moriah retorted, too quickly. "That is, I—I thought I did, but I was mistaken in his character. And so—and so I cannot truly love him, can I?"

Emily had cocked her head and smiled. "That remains to be seen, my dear," she'd said in her lilting voice, and then had sent Moriah upstairs to rest.

And so here she was, at the escritoire with a letter in her hand that she knew she had to read. She had put it off since yesterday, but she had promised Finch she'd read it, and so she must. But it angered her that the viscount had involved a third party and had been able to convince him of the letter's authenticity. Damn Justin Traugott! He could charm the snakes right out of Ireland!

She stared at the unopened missive. "To Moriah and Tess" it said. The hand certainly looked like Papa's, and for a moment she was most anxious to open it. But then she thought of Lord Roane and the lengths to which he would go to achieve his ends, and she had to restrain herself from tearing the thing to pieces.

Finally, she took a deep breath and broke the seal. And from the moment she began reading she knew that it was Papa speaking to her.

Dear Moriah and Tess,

You will never know how much I love you both, and I pray you will find it in your hearts to forgive me for what I have done. I came so close to destroying your lives — I could not allow myself to do that again, nor could I be certain I would not. The lure of the gaming tables in London is just too great. Your mother would have understood; I hope you will. I have taken the only honourable course left to me.

Moriah, I pray you will see Tess settled in a good marriage. She is so beautiful, so like Clarissa. And as for you, my dear, I know that you can take care of yourself. But I pray you will not look askance at the idea of marriage as well. In your own way, I believe you are a diamond of the first water.

Your loving father,
Thomas,
Seventh Baron Landon

The paper was stained with her tears when she'd done, and she could not stop them. She cried for the agony that led Papa to this, and she cried because, if not for Finch, he might well have been dead when she read this letter. He had certainly intended to be. Her handkerchief was well drenched before she ceased crying. She blew her nose and walked slowly to the bed, sinking down onto the mauve satin coverlet.

It tore at her heart that he'd actually thought there was no other course open to him. No *honourable* course, she amended, and felt an accustomed stab of anger at the male sense of honour. She would never understand it. She had certainly never understood Justin's, but then she'd found out he *had* no honour, or if he did, it was well hidden!

She did not wish to think of Justin—Lord Roane, she corrected herself—but she knew she must. She had wronged him terribly; he'd had naught to do with her father's attempted suicide. Her accusation had been monstrous, and now she found herself agitatedly pacing the blue carpet. She was chagrined at her behavior. To have assumed he would actually forge a letter, plan the whole—why, it was preposterous!

She sank down onto a powder-blue chair and sighed deeply, forcing herself to consider the question now uppermost in her mind. For in truth, was it any less preposterous to assume he had ruined her father with the deliberate intention of luring *her* into his trap? And that marriage would be for him the ultimate revenge? He had denied it all, and she wanted so much to believe him. It would be so wonderful if—

She rose and paced anew, her practical sense forcing her emotions aside. For she could not ignore the damning evidence. He had harboured his hatred for twenty years—he'd admitted that much. And any man who could do that . . . Besides, she had not "assumed" that the Abbey was just bait, that *she* was his ultimate victim. Rather, the earl had *said* so. Who would know Justin better than the man who raised him?

No, she told herself firmly. She was right in her resolve. She could not risk marrying him, and so she must not see him. She would stay here, in Emily's warm and welcome cottage, for as long as necessary. But her resolve brought her no peace, only a terrible sense of loneliness.

Emily had entreated her to rest until luncheon, but no longer able to endure her own thoughts, Moriah went belowstairs well before time. The butler having informed her of Emily's whereabouts, she called out even before entering the sitting room. "Emily, would you care to—Oh!" she exclaimed, freezing on the threshold. For there on the sofa, with his back to her, sat a man unabashedly clasping Emily's hand.

"Moriah!" Emily responded a trifle nervously, rising quickly. "I thought you were asleep."

"No I—oooh!" Moriah gasped, eyes wide with sudden comprehension as the man stood and turned to her.

"I do not believe we have been properly introduced, Miss Landon. I am George Wainsfield, Earl of Westmacott," he said genially, his gray eyes crinkling at the corners.

He strode to her and took her hand. "Y—yes, I—I know" was all she could think to reply. "That is, I—I am pleased to meet you." Suddenly, she felt a rush of mortification, remembering all that he had seen and heard at the ball. "Ah—I shall be going now if you'll—"

"Nonsense, child, come in and sit down," blustered the earl, guiding her forward. Emily looked a bit doubtful but the earl smiled adoringly at her. "Now, my love, Miss Landon was bound to find us out, staying here as she is. And I am persuaded she is a most discreet young woman."

"Of course she is," Emily responded. "Forgive me, Moriah, 'tis merely that I am so used to—to—"

"Yes, and it is time you become *un*used to it, love," he interrupted. Then, seating Moriah in a chair next the sofa, he said to her, "It is my intention to persuade your friend to marry me, but she is being decidedly stubborn. Now why do you suppose a woman would refuse to marry a man she truly loves?" he asked smoothly, taking a seat beside Emily on the sofa.

"George!" Emily admonished, and Moriah felt herself go quite red.

"Ah, forgive me, ladies; I spoke out of turn," the earl retorted, but his lips were twitching.

Moriah squirmed in her seat, for no matter whose marriage the earl referred to, she was decidedly uncomfortable. Any hope of a quick escape was dashed as the earl said, "Join us for lemonade and biscuits, do. Actually, I'm drinking brandy. You look as if you could use some."

"No. No thank you. Lemonade is fine," she said weakly, noticing for the first time the tray on the sofa table.

Emily busied herself with the tray and the earl launched into easy conversation, as if this were the most commonplace of morning calls. Moriah felt quite dizzy.

"Emily tells me you've come to stay awhile. Deuced good idea, I think" he declared.

"It—it is?" Moriah was confused.

" 'Course it is. What with my nephew plaguing you so. Only thing to do. And you'll see, my dear. Time works miracles." As he said this last he turned to gaze intensely at Emily, and Moriah felt very much de trop.

Sensing her discomfort and perhaps sharing it, Emily launched into an amusing discussion of village gossip. The earl joined in with all good humour, and then at some point she realized he had quite shifted the subject.

"Oh, yes, I do enjoy the north country. Pennines are breathtaking, you know. Quite a bit of trouble up thereabouts these days, though. Breads riots and— oh, don't let me start on that; I shall bore you to tears, I'm afraid," Lord Westmacott was saying.

"Oh, on the contrary," Moriah protested, setting down her lemonade. "I find I am quite interested. My former governess lives in Lancashire, you see, and she . . ."

Moriah found herself engaged in a lively discussion of one of her favorite subjects and was unaware of anything exceptional about it until she caught Emily eyeing the earl with a speculative gleam. The earl rose and went to refill his brandy snifter. "The government, I believe, is quite off the mark in all this," he continued, sitting down again. "I'd hoped to persuade my—er—nephew to go to Lancashire to observe for himself what's afoot. Then to take his seat in the Lords. I believe he would make a valuable contribution were he to do so. He possesses the kind of honourable, sound judgment we need more of. But alas, my powers of persuasion seem, of late, to have deserted me." He glanced at Emily, then looked piercingly at Moriah.

She had the feeling he was trying to tell her something, and she did not much like it. The Viscount Roane is no concern of mine! she wanted to shriek. But of course, she did not. The earl had said nothing untoward, after all. However, she did wonder, as she excused herself to freshen up just before luncheon, at the earl's words. He had certainly not considered Lord Roane of "honourable, sound judgment" that night at the ball. Had he had a change of heart? Or had Lord Roane bamboozled him too? Somehow the earl did not seem a man easily deceived.

"Why do you not tell her the truth about Roane?" Emily asked when Moriah had departed the sitting room. "She is suffering terribly and, from what you say, your nephew is too."

"It will not answer, Em," Westmacott said, letting an arm graze her shoulders. "They have to work it out for themselves. Else he will always feel she did not trust him. She must come to that herself."

Emily sighed and sipped her lemonade. "I suppose so. You did try to help a bit, though, didn't you?"

"Just a bit," he answered, eyes twinkling. "Now, there is another matter—"

But luncheon was announced before the earl could make yet another attempt to secure the hand of his ladylove.

Roane had called at Wykham Abbey at what was becoming his usual hour of ten and was greeted with the disturbing intelligence that Miss Landon had departed early this morning for the north country. Lancashire, to be precise.

"Lancashire!" Roane exclaimed. "A clanker if ever I've heard one, Reeves. Now where is she? I believe your mistress is expecting me." He *must* speak to her, especially after last night.

"That's as may be, my lord. But fact of the matter is that Miss Moriah left this mornin' with her luggage in tow. I—I'd be happy to convey you abovestairs, so's you might see for yourself what's missin'. Or you could ask Miss Tess or—"

"That—that won't be necessary, Reeves" Roane said, suddenly very weary. Something in the butler's tone told him he was telling the truth. She had gone; she had run away from him. But it didn't make sense that she would leave now, not with her father so ill. Or was that simply a measure of how desperately she wanted to escape him, of how much she hated him?

"Where has she gone, Reeves?" he asked quietly.

The butler seemed to breathe a sigh of relief. "Lancashire, my lord."

"I know that, man!" Roane snapped. "Where in Lancashire? And why the devil did she go up *there?*"

"Her—her former governess took ill, my lord. In a bad way, she is. And what with the master on the mend—well now, off she went. Not but what—"

"Miss Billingsley?" Roane asked, more to himself than to the butler.

"Aye, my lord, that be the one," Reeves replied,

but Roane barely heard him.

Any last glimmer of hope that it was all a hum, that she had merely barricaded herself abovestairs, was gone. For he had no doubt that, with her father stable enough, she would answer the summons of her precious Miss Billingsley.

Damn and blast it all! he cursed inwardly, but he schooled his face to calm and inquired, "And—er—where exactly does Miss Billingsley reside, Reeves?"

Reeves did not miss a beat but replied in what seemed all honesty, "As to that I couldn't say, my lord. We none of us know her exact direction, you see, 'ceptin' the baron, and we wouldn't want to be disturbin' him just now. But Miss Moriah will write from the first postin' inn, I'm persuaded. Still and all, your lordship, I don't rightly know if she'd want you—well, I mean to say—"

"Never mind, Reeves!" Roane glowered. "You know, in your different ways I think you and my butler Finley would get on famously!" And with that he stormed out the door.

He tried not to think as he drove home, and he actually sneaked through his own house to avoid being seen by any well-meaning relatives or servants. He bolted himself in his study and began pacing the Oriental carpet with the coiled energy of a caged animal. He could well have used a drink to calm himself but refrained. Right now he needed a clear head above all.

She had gone to Lancashire to nurse that blasted governess of hers. He knew very well how devoted Moriah was to Miss Billingsley. Did she not invoke her name at the oddest moments? And, of course, she would want to be with the woman in her hour of need. It was simply damned unfortunate that that hour had arisen when—

No! He stopped short and ran his hand through his hair. What was it that Moriah had said—coincidences never *are* such! It was a little too convenient that Miss Billingsley just happened to fall ill now. In fact, it was Roane's guess that the former governess was in the pink of health. And as to Moriah, he would wager anything that she was no more on her way to Lancashire than he was!

Breathing a sign of relief, Roane threw himself into the nearest chair. How could he have been such a gull as to believe she'd gone north? It was true she was devoted to Miss Billingsley, but how much more so to her father! Roane frowned as he thought of what Moriah had done for the sake of her father. No, she would never leave him now.

And yet—Roane rose and walked slowly to the large picture window—and yet he could have sworn Reeves was telling the truth. Suddenly he whirled around and stalked back to the chair. Of course, Reeves *was* telling the truth—the truth as he knew it! Moriah had indeed left the Abbey—"with her luggage in tow" as the butler had said. And she'd told the entire household that Banbury tale about her governess, knowing, clever girl that she was, that if *they* believed it, the Viscount Roane would have no choice but to do the same. And he had—for about one-half hour. But now he'd stake his very name on the fact that wherever she was, it was no more than the ride of an hour or two away from her father.

And just where *was* she? And how the hell was he to find her? he ranted to himself, and this time went to pour a drink. It was at this inauspicious moment that Finley came in to announce luncheon. Roane cursed aloud. About the last thing he cared to do now was entertain Andrew over Dover sole or some such. But upon being informed that Lord Wainsfield had gone out some time ago, Roane, much relieved, requested that a tray be brought to him. He did no more than pick at his food, though. It *was* Dover sole and quite delicious, but he was simply not of a frame of mind to enjoy it.

Where the devil was Moriah? he pondered, pacing the floor again. Finally, he sank down into his favorite leather chair and let a glass of brandy soothe his taut muscles. A voice at the back of his head told him that her whereabouts didn't signify — she'd be no more amenable to his suit now than yesterday, or the day before. Last night's revelation wouldn't matter. Why, even her father's letter hadn't made a difference, if she'd read it at all. She'd gone off anyway. And he couldn't very well go breaking down doors in someone else's house, now could he?

But he silenced the voice and a glimmer of a smile touched his lips. If he'd needed any further proof that she returned his regard full measure, this mad flight was it. A woman did not go careening about the countryside to run away from a man to whom she was indifferent. Oh no! Only from a man she could not trust herself to be near. Ah, Moriah, you little fool, he mused. Let me love you, and I will teach you to trust. But first I have to find you. Dammit! Where *are* you?

"I'm right here, Justin. Right here!" came his uncle's voice and Justin jumped high out of his chair. Good God, had he spoken aloud? The heavy oak doors opened and the earl entered. "You *were* calling *me*, were you not?" he asked, a glint in his eye.

"Er — no, Uncle, not exactly. But — er — no matter. C — come in. I — I guess I — that is, I have been wondering—er—"

The earl closed the doors behind him and sauntered forward. "I came in at 'dammit, where *are* you?' Justin, but perhaps I can guess the rest. I have only now encountered my son, who has just returned from the Abbey."

"Oh?" Roane asked guardedly and then, at a look from his uncle, relaxed and shook his head ruefully.

"And how is it that I seem to miss him each time? Do you suppose he is avoiding me?" Roane asked, actually glad of the distraction. He motioned the earl to the leather sofa near his own chair and poured him a drink.

"I would not doubt it, considering that he knows well how you, and I, feel about his—er—interest in Tess Landon," the earl replied, sitting down.

"She is much too young, Uncle." Roane handed the brandy to the earl and took his own seat.

"Well I know it, Justin. But his behavior has been, shall we say, most honourable and—er—circumspect."

Roane sighed. "And neither of us is in a position to cast stones. Yes, I take your point."

"He is quite smitten, Justin. And now I believe we must wait upon events. But that is fair and far off the mark, is it not?"

Roane signed again. "She is gone, Uncle. She has run away from me."

"I know. Gone north, so Tess informs Andrew."

"Ah. So Tess believes it too," Roane murmured, more to himself than anything.

"What are you implying, Justin?" the earl asked carefully.

"Simply that I do not for one moment believe Moriah has left Herefordshire nor has any intention

392

of doing so," Roane replied, and proceeded to explain his reasoning to his uncle.

It seemed that the earl took a long time in replying, and when he did he kept his eyes on his brandy snifter. "I see. Well then, where—ah—do you imagine she might be?"

"I do not know, Uncle. I have thought of her friend Lady Ashford. But her husband is currently in residence, and somehow I doubt Moriah would wish to—well—add to her friend's—er—difficulties just now. But perhaps"—Roane paused as the idea registered in his mind—"yes, perhaps she confided her destination to Lady Ashford. She must have told someone, after all. Mayhap I ought—"

"Er—Justin," the earl interrupted, leaning forward. "If you will permit a bit of advice from one who is older though not necessarily wiser. Perhaps it would be better not to try to find her just yet. That is—now don't go getting on your high ropes, Justin! You know what they say: Absence makes the heart grow fonder and all of that."

"That's as may be, Uncle. But in this case—well, I believe that 'absence' only gives her ample opportunity to harden her heart, to—"

"But you cannot say for certain, Justin, can you, not having seen her today nor even—er—knowing where the lady is."

"No, but I must make her understand why I—"

"Why don't you give it time, Justin? I am persuaded she will return home within a few days. And then—well, perhaps—"

"I—I miss her damnably, Uncle," Roane interrupted, his voice low. He set his drink down and sank his head into his hands.

"I know you do, Justin. And I—I believe she

misses you as well."

"Hah!" Roane jerked his head up. "If you only knew the half of it, Uncle George, you'd not be so sanguine."

"Indeed" was all the earl would say in reply. And then Andrew burst in on them, with the intelligence that he had missed Dover sole for luncheon and could not help but wonder what culinary delights awaited them at dinner.

Chapter 33

"George!" Emily exclaimed some time later as they sat on the wicker love seat in the garden, "I cannot credit it. Do you really mean to say that you sat there all that time without saying a word about where she — well, I mean to say, my dear, that poor girl cannot sit still a moment, for all her agitation."

"Nor can Justin. But I thought we had agreed, love, that it was best not to interfere, that they needs must work it out for themselves." The earl's voice was gentle, his head bent close to Emily's.

"Which they can hardly do if they do not even meet, George!" Emily retorted with asperity.

She jumped up and circled the gracious arbour, the wisteria blossoms grazing her sandy brown hair. The earl could not help admiring, as he always did, her lithe and girlish figure. She looked delectable in her pale pink gown and he thought of all the ways he would rather spend the next hour besides in earnest discussion. But he *was* deeply troubled about his nephew and so schooled his wayward thoughts back to the matter at hand.

"You know, George," Emily was saying, a troubled frown marring her beautiful brow, "in all the time we—we've been together—and with all our difficulties—the one thing I never doubted was my love for you and—and yours for me." At this the earl could not refrain from springing up and taking Emily gently in his arms. Her body yielded, as it always did, but she looked, if anything, even more distressed. "But—but I look at Moriah, having those very doubts, and it tears at my heart. George, I think—I think you ought to tell Justin she is here."

"To what end, Emily?" The earl dropped his arms and shook his head. "So she might take it into her head to run elsewhere? Justin does not seem to have had much luck—er—persuading the lady before, has he?"

"No," she replied, smiling faintly. "Did I tell you he stormed up at her chamber and broke through the locked door?"

"Did he?" George chuckled. "Well, there is more reason for hope than I thought."

"George, do be serious!" She pushed playfully at his chest and he caught her hands in his own. "Will you not tell Moriah the whole?" she asked, her voice soft. "Or allow me to do so? To tell her that you were mistaken in—"

"No, Em! Not that. Justin would never brook that kind of interference. In truth, he expressly forbid it. But as to the other—" The earl slipped his arms around her waist and drew her close. "I might reconsider telling him where she is if—well—but no. How can I possibly help him when I myself am no fit example? When *I* have been singularly unsuccessful in a similar quest?"

396

"In a similar—George, whatever can you mean?"

"Tut, tut, Emily. Don't come the innocent with me. You see before you a gentleman who is neither wed nor even betrothed, not, I take leave to remind you, for want of trying."

"B—but George, what does that signify?" She tried to pull away but he would not permit it, and she went on. "We are not speaking of us. We—"

"Ah, but you're out there, love. *I* am speaking of us. Just how badly do you want to help those two young people?"

"Just what does—George, what are you saying?"

The earl deliberately stepped away from her. He fingered a delicate wisteria blossom and did not look at Emily as he spoke. "My nephew fears that with each day that passes Miss Landon's resolve against him will only strengthen. And then, of course, there is always the possibility that when her father is well again she *will* fly north, and then who knows if they'll ever—"

"Oh, George! You don't think it will come to that, do you? Why, of course we must do something! Just—just tell Roane that she's here. It's—"

"As I said, my love, I do not think I can do that, unless I myself can set a proper example." Now he looked keenly at Emily but did not move to touch her.

"Oh, I see. 'Tis like that, is it, my lord?"

"Aye, my lady. Blackmail, pure and simple," the earl replied, grinning. He sauntered close to her and reached into his coat pocket. "This was my mother's betrothal ring, Emily," he said very softly. "Will you do me the honour of wearing it?"

"Oh, G—George, you know how I—"

397

"Will you, Em?" he persisted, and slipped the ruby ring onto her slender finger. Then he curled her fingers into a fist, so she could not remove it. "It belongs to you, now, my love. Do not refuse me yet again," he said solemnly.

Emily stared at her hand and then up at the earl, and her blue eyes were moist. "I do so love you, George, and I—I will be honoured to—to be your wife. I only hope—"

But Emily's only hope was silenced as the earl crushed her against him and kissed her, very thoroughly. When at last he raised his head, he said huskily, "As soon as possible. St. George's, Hanover Square."

"St. George's?" Emily stepped back. "Surely you cannot mean that. Why, I should think a small wedding, here in the country—"

"No, love. We'll not behave as if we've something to hide. We'll do it up all right and proper, as befits the Earl of Westmacott and his future countess. The ton will be hard put to gossip about us when they are all invited to the wedding."

Emily shook her head, but her eyes sparkled. "Very well, George," she said at length. "I can see that you will be quite the martinet as a husband, and I have no choice but to obey. But I take leave to issue one order of my own."

The earl's eyebrows shot up. "Which is?"

"That you take yourself off to your nephew straight away and put him out of his misery. But—er—tell him I have only just completed numerous household repairs and I should not like to have my doors splintered apart."

The earl chuckled and drew her close again. "I

shall do your bidding, love. And tell Miss Landon—well, tell her something, but not too much." And then he kissed her again and was off.

The earl having departed soon after Drew's arrival, Roane had tried his level best to pick his cousin's brain. Surely there must be some hint as to Moriah's whereabouts. But Drew knew no more than Tess, which was precious little. Tess was rather overset by her sister's abrupt departure but was, according to Andrew, putting a brave face on it. Mrs. Trotter was in a pelter, as usual, Reeves kept muttering something about Roanbrooke being a mite too close to the Abbey, and the maids had turned into watering pots. Only Finch, it seemed, had maintained his composure. Of course, Roane thought. Finch knew the baron's condition better than anyone and—Suddenly Roane's eyes widened in dawning revelation. He fairly jumped out of his chair and tried to dismiss Andrew rather peremptorily. But his cousin was not quite so compliant this time.

"I say, Justin," Drew protested, "you've been acting—well, rather oddly of late, not to put too fine a point on it. And Tess says—"

"Yes, just what *does* Tess say, Andrew?" Roane interrupted imperiously, recalling only too well that Tess had seen him with Moriah the morning of the shooting.

"Oh, well—er—never mind, Justin. It—it doesn't signify. We can—we can talk about it another time." Andrew retrenched under that gruelling stare, wishing to avoid being raked over the coals for calling on Tess at first stop. Though, from Tess's account of the goings-on at the Abbey lately, Justin was in no position to cast stones.

Drew looked decidedly uncomfortable and Roane felt a pang of remorse. "Drew, I — I realize I've been something of a bear lately. A dreadful host, in fact. I've a rather pressing — er — problem just now, and once I've worked it out I — I shall tell you all about it. For now I — well, there is something I must do straight away."

Andrew smiled. "Very well, Coz, I understand, and I shall make myself scarce." He sauntered from the room, but turned on the threshold and said over his shoulder, "Do not trouble yourself overmuch, Justin. She'll come back soon enough, I expect." And seeing his cousin stiffen with shock and fury, Drew beat a hasty retreat. But he chuckled once outside the door. He'd suspected something was in the wind at the ball, and recent events had borne him out. And he realized that those rumors about Justin's supposed mistress were so much flummery. Justin was much too busy with his determined, though deuced unorthodox, courtship. Drew whistled as he made his way down the corridor. The next few days should prove no end amusing, and he wished his cousin luck. From what he'd seen, Justin and Miss Landon should suit admirably. And, of course, once they were riveted, Drew could see Tess whenever he wanted. It would all be in the family, after all.

Roane cursed audibly once his cousin had gone. How could Drew possibly — and how much did he — ? Suddenly, Roane checked himself and smiled reluctantly. He could not very well break down doors and expect his interest in Moriah to remain a secret. Besides, within a short time he hoped to be able to shout it from the rooftops.

Which brought him back to the matter at hand. To Finch. The man closest to the baron, the man to whom Moriah would, of a certain, have confided her destination. And the man who was, Roane thought thankfully, his one and only ally at Wyckham Abbey.

With no further thought he dashed from his study and made for the stables. He was well on his way, astride his chestnut stallion, before he realized that he was attired in his morning clothes. He had taken the carriage for his previous visit to the Abbey. He frowned, but then a smile tugged at his mouth. His own valet would cluck in disapproval, but he reckoned Finch wouldn't mind a bit.

He was right. The baron's valet evinced more amusement than anything at the disarrayed state of the viscount's garments and no surprise at all at being summoned to his lordship's presence, though Reeves had been most put out. When the butler left them alone in the blue salon, Roane smiled engagingly and put forth his question to Finch. The manservant did not answer immediately, however, but eyed the viscount in a most disconcerting manner.

Dermot Finch looked his lordship up and down, takin' his measure. So, he'd figured out that that Lancashire business was all a hum, had he? Well, and about time. Finch hadn't told the mistress so, but he hadn't thought the viscount one who could be gulled. And now here he was, askin' for her. And what was Dermot Finch to do? His loyalty to the mistress was unquestioned, but he was not sure he'd be servin' her a good turn by keepin' mum.

His eyes flicked over the young man. Come ridin' neck or nothin' over here in his mornin' clothes, had he? And yesterday he'd up and broke down Miss Moriah's door. But there was the mistress sayin' as how she wanted no part of him and runnin' off this mornin' like a scared rabbit. Now it was one thing obligin' his lordship by givin' her that letter, quite another to cry rope on her. Finch peered at the viscount's eyes—you could tell a mort about a man by his eyes, the valet had al'as thought. These eyes were deep blue, and just now so fierce and overset like he never did see. But Finch had also seen those eyes soft with concern and crinklin' up with laughter. He was a right one, was his lordship, strong and dependable.

Still an' all—Finch paused and stroked his chin. The viscount did not move nor say a word. Any other cove would have raked him down for starin', bold as brass, at his betters, but Lord Roane understood that Finch could not answer lightly. There was no mistakin' that Finch liked the viscount very well. The question was, did Miss Moriah? She certainly give out as how she never wanted to clap eyes on him again. She would take it in very bad part were Finch to wheedle the scrap. She had told no one else, and she'd been so insistent that no one was to know, 'specially not a certain gentleman with a penchant for breakin' down doors and shoutin' the house down.

Finch sighed. He'd known Miss Moriah from the cradle. How could he betray her now? And then he remembered the mornin' of the terrible shooting. Everyone a yammerin' and a wailin' . . . but not the mistress. Kept her head, she did, ministerin' to her Papa. And then when Finch come and took over, she let her tears come. But it wasn't to Mrs. Trotter nor Reeves she turned, for all they'd been with the family for years. Nor to Miss Tess, her own flesh and blood. No, thought Finch, his face relaxing in a soft smile. It was to this strong, powerful lord she'd turned, natural as could be. Why, she'd collapsed in his arms right enough and had stayed there. And Lord Roane comforted her as if — as if he'd been doin' such for years.

Well, Finch thought, it was all right, then. Miss Moriah had simply taken some hubble-bubble notion into her head, the way females were wont to do, and loped off. Not but what she'd be in high dudgeon when she found out Dermot Finch had let fall the truth. But he remembered the way the Viscount Roane had held the mistress in his arms, in full view of everyone, and he smiled broadly at his lordship. "Well now, my lord, I hadn't ought to be tellin' you naught 'bout where the mistress be, 'ceptin' that she's gone to Lancashire," he began. His lordship merely raised an eyebrow and Finch went on. "Yes, well, I might ha' *told* her you wasn't no gudgeon as 'ud believe that. But — well, fact of the matter is, she was very particular that it was *you* — beggin' your lordship's pardon — that she didn't want — oh, the devil take it — You — you'll take good care of her, won't you, my lord?"

"You have my word on it, Finch," the viscount replied gravely.

"Well, then, my lord, she's — she's gone to — to Mrs. Shoup's, over 'tother side of the village."

"The devil you say!" his lordship exclaimed, and then grinned. "Mrs. Shoup's! Well, fancy that," he mused, "and I'll wager she has no idea about — well, never mind that. Finch, you are a prince among men!" And with that, the Viscount Roane pumped

Dermot Finch's hand heartily and then bounded out of the house in a manner most unbefittin' his exalted station in life.

Roane fairly jumped onto his stallion and galloped out of the Abbey drive posthaste. He was all for riding at breakneck speed to Mrs. Shoup's—Good Lord, why hadn't he guessed—when he glanced down at himself in chagrin. He hadn't changed since morning and was actually riding a horse in trousers and halfboots. There was no way, he well knew, that he could present himself anywhere in such condition. And so, cursing fluently, he headed home.

He cursed even more resoundingly when Finley informed him that the earl was awaiting him. "Send him up to my chambers, Finley. I must change my clothes," he called, and bolted up the stairs.

It was only when he reached his dressing room, cravat and coat already removed, that the thought struck him. If she were at Mrs. Shoup's, would not Uncle George have seen her? But no, she'd probably keep herself hidden. At least, Roane hoped so, for if the earl had known her whereabouts this morning and for some misguided reason had not told him, Roane would . . .

"Afternoon, Justin," the earl called jovially, coming into the dressing room. He sat himself down and engaged Roane in light conversation as his valet repaired the day's ravages and helped him into his newest riding habit. When Norris departed the earl's face became serious.

"Justin, I—I've discovered Miss Landon's whereabouts."

"You have?" Roane asked, swinging around in his vanity chair, trying not to look suspicious. Had the earl just now found out, or was it that he'd just now decided to tell him? His uncle's reply left that particularly question unanswered.

"Yes, I—I've just seen her. She's at Emily's, Justin."

"Is she, by God?" Justin asked, feigning surprise. Then he rose and, grinning ruefully, clapped the earl on the shoulder. "Thank you, Uncle. Fact is, I—I knew. Just found out, actually, from—well, from the baron's valet."

The earl did not seem at all amused by this intelligence. He stood and cleared his throat. "Oh, I see. Very—er—resourceful of you. Well—er—I say, Justin, I'd be obliged if you wouldn't let on to Emily that it was not *I* who informed you."

"Oh? And—er—why is that, Uncle?"

"My reason cannot signify, Justin. 'Tis merely a favour. I ask your discretion in this matter."

Roane's eyes narrowed with a glint of deviltry. "Very well, Uncle. As you wish. But—er—tell me, did you only now encounter Miss Landon, or have you known all day where she was?"

The earl looked uncomfortable. "Oh, well, of course I—oh! I plumb forgot, Justin!" he exclaimed, his face relaxing. "I've wonderful news. Emily's decided to have me, after all!"

"Oh, Uncle, that *is* wonderful!" Roane declared, pumping the earl's hand warmly. "I am so happy for you. However did you contrive it?"

The earl coughed. "Pure—er—masculine charm, Justin. You've got plenty yourself. Go ahead and use it."

"I believe I will, Uncle," Roane replied, and then, his face suddenly taut, asked, "What—what state of

405

mind is Moriah in?"

"She is very agitated, Justin and, according to Emily, very unhappy," the earl said soberly.

Roane answered with a grin. "Well now, that *is* encouraging," he mused, and then promptly took himself off. He was well on his way to Mrs. Shoup's before he realized that the earl had never answered his question.

Chapter 34

As soon as George had left, Emily had gone up to see Moriah. She did not know what she would say to the girl. She could not speak in defense of Lord Roane; George had made that very clear. But she must say *something*, and how could she advise Moriah when Emily herself was so beset by doubts about marriage? Yet she had made her decision, and she could at the least share that with Moriah.

She did just that, and her announcement was greeted by a wide smile, the first she'd seen on Moriah's face since her arrival. "Oh, Emily, I am so happy for you both!" exclaimed Moriah, hugging Emily warmly. "I cannot think what took you so long, Emily," Moriah said, her eyes twinkling, and Emily knew that was just the opening she needed.

She smiled softly and patted Moriah's hand. " 'Tis a long story, my dear. Would you like to hear it?"

"Oh, Emily, forgive me. I did not mean to pry."

"Nonsense, my dear," Emily said, "I would like to tell you."

They were seated side by side on Moriah's bed as

Emily narrated a somewhat abridged version of her life these fifteen years past.

When she was finished, Moriah surreptitiously brushed away a tear and murmured, "It—it is so beautiful. To have a love like that, that can withstand so much over the years."

"Yes, I count myself fortunate, though it has never been easy."

"Emily, what—what made you change your mind? About marriage, I mean. You were so adamantly against it."

"Yes, I was." Emily rose and strolled to the window. She knew that what she said next would be important for Moriah, and she realized, as she began speaking, that she was explaining it as much to herself as to her young friend. "The earl believes I finally—ah—capitulated because—well, let us just say he was not above a bit of blackmail. But, of course, it was no such thing. The truth is—" she sighed and came to sit once more on the bed, "the truth is that George and I have each been afraid of what marriage might do to the other. But then George decided he'd had enough—the time had come. But I—I was still unwilling to take that risk. And then somehow, in the last day or so," Emily went on, now gazing pointedly at Moriah, "I began to realize that—that one has to take risks in life. Else one is only half alive. 'Tis true George and I may still be in for rocky waters. But I don't know that of a certain. What I *do* know is that we shall be blissfully happy together. I love him with all my heart, and it has taken me five years to decide that that is worth all the risk. Happiness is well worth fighting for, my dear. I have been running away, and I can no longer do so. And when all is said and done, my fears may be groundless, after all."

Moriah was no longer looking at Emily but was staring down at her clasped hands. Emily could see tears in the girl's eyes and she waited for some reply. Finally Moriah murmured, "Thank you for—for confiding in me, Emily. I—I am very happy for you." She said no more, and Emily deemed it best to leave her alone with her thoughts.

When the door closed behind Emily, Moriah put a hand to her brow and choked back her tears. She had cried enough, she told herself. Besides, Emily's situation was quite different from her own. She rose and went to stare out the window that gave out onto the front of the cottage. Yes, Emily's situation was different, but Moriah knew very well that her friend had been speaking very practically to her. Emily's gentle words floated through her head. "One has to take risks in life . . . happiness is well worth fighting for . . . my fears may be groundless, after all." That last brought a chill to Moriah. What if her own fears were groundless? She thought of the letter that Justin had, after all, not written. And she thought of the earl calling him a man of "honourable, sound judgment." But then she recalled the earl's words that night in the garden. "The Abbey was just bait . . ." And Justin had denied that, their last night together, denied it when she would, indeed, have been prepared to put it all behind them! And then, unbidden there rose in her mind the strained and reserved face of Sarah Ashford. She'd been such a happy bride, and marriage had brought her only misery.

Moriah leaned her head against the window. No, the risks in her case were too great; she could not do it.

It was but a short time later that she heard the commotion below. She looked out the window and saw a gentleman dismounting from a chestnut stallion. Justin! She felt her heart beat rapidly at the sight of his powerful figure. He stood for a moment surveying the cottage and then raised his eyes to the upstairs windows. She knew a momentary urge to rush downstairs and into his arms — she missed him so much! But she checked herself, and despair engulfing her, she ducked out of sight. She did *not* wish to see him. Was that not why she had come here at first stop? And how could he have found her — and so fast? Surely the earl hadn't — No, for the earl had said she was wise to have gone away. But no matter. He was here, and what was she to do? She couldn't see him. Despite her resolve, she knew she would be clay in his hands.

And so she politely told Emily, when her friend came up not minutes later, to tell his lordship that she was indisposed.

Emily looked distressed and ventured that perhaps she *had* ought to see him. But Moriah was adamant, striving for a calm she did not feel and praying Justin would not storm the stairs of Emily's house. As a precaution Moriah kept her door ajar slightly, and as her room was near the landing, she could hear Emily's gentle voice making her excuses. Justin did not reply immediately, however, and she shuddered at what must be the stormy expression on his face.

In point of fact, Roane's face was bleak. He had raced in, felicitated Mrs. Shoup on her coming nuptials, and asked for Moriah in one breath. He was not surprised at her refusal, but having come this far,

410

he had not the faintest idea how to proceed.

"Mrs. Shoup—" he began.

"Emily," she interrupted.

"Very well, *Emily,*" he amended, smiling faintly, "as we are to be family. Then surely you must call me 'Justin.' " She nodded and his expression sobered. "I collect that she does not wish to see me. Indeed, I should be quite hen-witted should I not have figured that out. But I—well, I mean to say, I think it important that we talk." He looked up the stairs at the landing and thought he saw the quick movement of skirts. And then he noticed a faint shadow on the wall. Her shadow.

"I doubt it not, Justin, but I—Justin—that is, you wouldn't—ah—"

Roane tore his eyes from the landing and smiled at her. "No, Emily, I wouldn't," he reassured her, but his eyes ranged over the staircase again. Moriah was still there, unmoving, at the top landing. Dammit all, why didn't she come down? He could simply go after her, of course. There was no door betwixt them now. But suddenly he did not want to, or rather, knew that it would be the wrong thing to do. For the more he pursued her, the farther she would run. No, he needs must force her hand. It was the only way. And come to think on it, she did have a penchant for eavesdropping, after all.

"I shan't trouble you further, Emily," he said in a loud, clear voice. "But perhaps you will convey a message to Miss Landon. Tell her—well, the fact of the matter is, Emily, that I am getting married, and I thought she might want to know."

Emily's eyes widened in momentary alarm, then narrowed with suspicion. But Roane ignored her,

411

distracted by a loud gasp from above. He glimpsed the swaying of skirts and from the shadow on the wall it looked as if Moriah were swooning. His first thought was to dash up to her, but he checked himself. His pragmatic lady would never faint. And he would not go after her, not now. He had set the stage, as it were, and now *she* must act.

He stood stock-still, silencing Emily with a finger at his lips when she opened her mouth to speak. The tension was palpable as he waited, but there came neither sound nor movement from above. He cursed inwardly. Moriah was not ready yet. Perhaps she never would be. Well, he would do as Uncle George suggested and give her time. Now there was nothing else he *could* do.

Repressing a deep sigh, he turned to Emily. "Pray give my compliments to Miss Landon, Emily. Perhaps she will feel more the thing tomorrow and we—we may speak. At all events I—well, I—I bid you good day, Emily," he concluded softly.

"Good day, Justin. I—I am sorry," she whispered, and he bowed and took his leave.

Only when the door closed behind Justin did Moriah allow herself to grope her way to her room. Getting married! How could he? After everything that—No, she admonished herself. Why should he not? Moriah had spurned him time and time again. And a peer needs must wed and set up his nursery, after all. Yet she felt faint again at the thought of another woman sharing his bed, having his babies. She clutched at her stomach and edged her way into her room, sinking down on the bed. And who would he wed, so soon after he and Moriah had—had— Surely not Olivia Crowley, she thought in despair.

Olivia would make him miserable.

She bolted upright and grasped the bedpost. And what did she care how miserable he was? Was not misery what he had intended for Moriah? *Well,* she asked herself, wasn't it? Her hand began to tremble on the bedpost, for in truth, she did not know.

And what manner of man would declare his love for her one moment and propose to another the next? A man without scruples, without feeling, an inner voice shouted. A man who was hurt, a man who wanted to make you jealous, a quieter voice said. Go to him, see him one more time, the same voice told her. No—she could not face him now, when he was pledged to another. In despair she flung herself on the satin coverlet. She felt humiliated and confused, but the tears, which might have cleared her head, refused to come.

As she lay crumpled, dry-eyed, on the bed, she became aware that an overwhelming sadness, a sense of grief, had crept over her. And with it came understanding. She loved Justin—she could no longer deny it to herself. And whether or not he had meant all along to ruin her—well, it didn't signify. Not if he loved her now.

She remembered his tenderness and the way he held her, the way his deep blue eyes met hers with that devastating intensity. Oh, how could she ever have doubted his love? That inner voice came forward again, reminding her that he could destroy her in marriage. But the whole idea seemed absurd now, and even if 'twere possible—well, she could not know of a certain, unless she tried. What she *did* know was that without him, she would be desperately unhappy. She should have trusted him and trusted her own heart. And now it was too late. He was betrothed, and a gentleman could not rescind a promise of marriage. She knew well enough to what lengths a man would go in the name of honour, and she knew there was no hope for it. "One has to take risks in life," Emily had said, and Moriah had been unwilling to do so. And now she had lost all, irrevocably.

Chapter 35

Moriah could not sleep. The hot summer night air seemed to be choking her. She rose from the bed and went to the open window, but even that did not help. She had to get out of the house, out into the open. It was absurd, at this late hour, but she could not help herself. As if in a dream, she lit a candle and walked to the wardrobe. Her hand went automatically to her dark blue riding habit. Riding? What was she thinking? She had no idea. In truth, she wasn't thinking at all, and silently, she began to dress.

"George!" Emily whispered, suddenly jolted from sleep. "George!" she repeated, shaking him gently. "I hear noises."

"It's probably a cat," he mumbled from under the covers and threw an arm around her.

"No, George," she said urgently, sitting up and out of his reach. "I hear footsteps. Someone is on the staircase. Do you not hear it?"

George shrugged the blanket off his head and opened one large blue eye. Then he smiled. "Yes, now I do. Can't you guess, love? I'll warrant 'tis Moriah. She's restless, I don't doubt. She has much to think on."

"Yes, but where is she going?"

"Perhaps she's in need of some warm milk. Or a glass of brandy. It doesn't signify, Em. Leave the girl alone and come back to bed." He patted the pillow next to him but she ignored him, her ears attuned to the sounds from belowstairs.

"George! Did you hear that?"

"Hear what, Em?" he asked in a thick voice. "Come back here." He tugged at her arm but she squirmed away.

"The back door. I—I fear she's gone out!"

He did not reply for a moment and then, finally, he raised himself up on his elbow. "I believe you are in the right of it, Em. Is that not the stable door I hear creaking?"

"Oh my God, yes!" she exclaimed, pivoting her feet onto the floor. "George, we must stop her. She'll—"

"Emily! Emily, calm down," he said, reaching a hand to cover hers. "She is not some bird-witted, devil-may-care chit. There is only one place she would go now, and I, for one, would not be fool enough to stop her. Now come—"

"Oh, George! Do you—do you really think that is where she's go—"

"Yes, love, I do. Now come back—"

"B—but, George, it must be nigh on two o'clock in the morning! She—"

"Ah, then the night is young, my love," he murmured, grinning and inching close to her.

"George, you are quite scandalous! And that is much beside the point. We must not allow—"

"What we must not do is interfere, Emily," he interrupted firmly.

"But she is under my protection. I must have a care for—"

"No, Em. There is someone else to protect her now. She is in good hands. Now for Godsakes, come back to bed, woman!" he shouted and, grabbing her, put an end to all further conversation.

It was madness, sheer madness, to be galloping over the roads in the middle of the night. But she felt driven; she simply had to go there. She doubted that the hunting box would be locked, but it didn't signify. Even the woods outside the door held special memories. She was shaking as she held the reins and urged Ruby on, grateful for the moonlight that guided her. Never had she felt so desperate, so torn asunder. She had been afraid to pledge herself to Justin, afraid to live with him, and yet the thought of living without him was utterly devastating.

She did not bother stabling the mare, merely tied her to a tree and then walked unsteadily to the door of the hunting box. The handle turned and the heavy door swayed open. Darkness engulfed her as she closed the door behind her. Oh God, she thought, I must indeed be mad. Whatever am I *doing* here? Desperately, she groped her way along the dark corridor. Her head swam with images of Justin—Justin laughing, Justin angry, Justin holding her. She

417

could even smell the scent of him. She reached for the handle of the closed sitting room door, and then gasped aloud, frozen at the sound of footsteps.

The door swung open in the next moment, and she stumbled right into the wall of his chest. He caught her, then held her away from him, his eyes piercing hers in the faint candlelight from within the room. "Moriah!" he uttered softly, wonderingly.

She was shocked, mortified, yet felt a wave of heat at his touch. She stared up at him, dazed and speechless. He was in his shirtsleeves, his cravat loose and dishevelled, his dark hair tousled. Even so, she felt the power that emanated from him, that sense of energy she'd felt even at their very first meeting. She swallowed hard, then finally stammered, "What — what are you doing here?"

"What am I — for pitysakes, Moriah, 'tis *my* hunting box!" he exclaimed.

"Oh — ah — yes, of course. I —" she began, feeling very weak.

"I might ask *you* the same," he interrupted in a low voice.

"I? Oh, well, I — er — I — I could not sleep, you see, and —"

"Never mind. Come here," he commanded softly, and led her into the room, to one of the green and gold love seats. He pushed her gently down and then reached for the half-empty glass of brandy on the sofa table. "Drink this," he said, and she took the glass from him. *His* glass, she thought irrelevantly, and drank liberally.

Roane hovered over her as she took her first sip, then sat down on the opposite love seat. He leaned forward, his hand clasped between his knees, and watched her intently. She did not speak, nor did he press her. She drank again and, slowly, the color returned to her cheeks. He had never seen her look so frightened nor confused as she had moments ago. It had quite unnerved him. But now she took several deep breaths, her back straightened, and he could see her customary composure returning. He sat back and crossed his legs.

"Forgive me, my lord," she said at length. "I am intruding."

"Fustian! You know you are not," he countered, smiling faintly.

"I must felicitate you, my lord, on your . . . coming marriage," she said stiffly. Her face was calm but her eyes said otherwise.

"Thank you, Moriah. I—"

"This is rather—ah—sudden, is it not?" She clutched the brandy snifter so tightly that he feared it would snap. But he knew he must bide his time. Now that, by some miracle, he had her here, he did not want her storming out in but a moment.

"You might say that," he replied impassively.

"I see," she said. "It—ah—it is a warm night, is it not?"

Ah, the weather, he thought. Such a regrettably safe topic. But he was having none of it. "Very warm, my dear. Rather like another night, not too long ago, if I recall," he said pointedly.

His meaning did not escape her. Her cheeks flushed and she took a quick sip of the brandy, then set the glass down. "Perhaps I ought to be—"

"Are you not the least bit curious as to my nuptial plans, Moriah?" he asked, leaning forward again.

She clasped her hands tightly in her lap. "I should

419

not mean to pry into what is not my concern," she said repressively, with visible effort.

Roane blanched and checked the impulse to gather her in his arms. Instead he rose and went to sit next to her, careful not to touch her. She tensed but did not move, and he spoke calmly and deliberately. "On the contrary, my dear, I should think that it is very much your concern. After all, you and I—"

"My lord," she blurted, jumping up and moving toward the hearth, "I—er—do wish you happy, as I have said, but I really should not care to discuss it."

Never had he seen her strive so hard to maintain her composure. Her head was bent and her profile looked beautiful in the candlelight. He rose and strode to the hearth, taking her hands, forcing her to look at him. " 'Tis a pity, Moriah, that you wish not to discuss it for, in truth, I had rather not make wedding plans myself." She blinked in confusion and he lifted a gentle finger to graze her cheek. "Surely you know that it is *you*, and none other, that I would wed," he breathed.

Her violet eyes widened and he watched the anguish recede, to be replaced by a look of utter surprise.

"You mean you—" she began, and he nodded, allowing a slow grin to suffuse his face. "You're not going to marry someone—I mean—" She seemed incapable of completing the sentence and he shook his head, his eyes twinkling, his hands at his sides, waiting. "But I thought—"

"Yes, I know what you thought," he said tenderly.

"Oh, Justin," she cried and then, suddenly, she was in his arms.

"God, Moriah. I thought I had lost you," he

rasped, crushing her to him. And then he kissed her, his hands clutching her back and his mouth searching hers with all the desperation of the past days.

When finally he raised his head, he saw that her eyes were moist. "Oh, Justin, I've made the most dreadful accusations," she moaned.

"Hush, love," he whispered, stroking her brow.

"No, I must say it. I've been foolish and frightened, and I think . . . quite out of my head, ever since that horrid night at the ball. But I've been wrong, Justin, and I *do* trust you," she breathed.

"Thank you, Moriah," he said quietly, his thumbs caressing her cheeks as he gazed at her in wonder.

It seemed, however, that she wasn't finished, and he thought he knew what was coming. "And my behavior throughout has been far from exemplary. Why, when I think of the way I came to you, here, at first stop, so wantonly and—"

"Indeed," he mused, then silenced her with another kiss, this one soft and brief. "Hmmm. Painted Haymarket ware, I should say," he murmured, throatily.

At this her chin went up and her eyes flashed fire. "You needn't be quite so sanguine, Justin! *You* have not been a paragon of virtue, you know."

All trace of humor vanished from his face and he put her gently from him, his eyes piercing hers. "No, I haven't been," he said huskily. "And now if you have finished your spate of self-recrimination, shall I begin mine? Indeed, there is much I wish you to—to understand. But I had rather table it all for a long winter's evening before a roaring fire. Let us forgive each other and, above all, forgive ourselves. We have neither of us been saints, little one, but we are very

421

human, and I love you very much."

Her eyes welled up and tears coursed down her cheeks. He produced a handkerchief and softly dabbed them away. "I love you too, Justin," she whispered.

"Yes, I know, little one," he said tenderly.

She stiffened. "You know? But I have never—why, you—you puffed up—and then to hoax me like—"

"As to that," he interrupted imperturbably, putting a finger to her lips, "well, we shall have pound dealing henceforth, I promise." And then he added, his eyes dancing, "But tell me, Moriah, how *could* you have been such a hen-witted peagoose—*you,* my most practical, sensible lady—as to believe that I would—indeed, that I could possibly, after chasing you for days—contemplate marrying elsewhere?"

She turned away, putting the width of the hearth between them. "Perhaps I was not thinking quite clearly, but I had refused you so many times. And I know that a peer needs must marry and set up his nursery."

"You sound like my uncle!" he exclaimed, much amused and wishing they might cease talking and do something more . . . interesting. She turned to him and he caught his breath. The candlelight played on her golden skin and silhouetted her luscious figure. The familiar stirrings, which he had been so carefully suppressing, surged through him.

"You—you do *want* to, don't you?" she asked pointedly.

He darted toward her, hardly crediting what he'd just heard. He cupped her chin lightly in both hands. "Moriah! Perhaps you *are* hen-witted. After all this, you *still* question my wish to marry you?"

"No. No, not that. The—" she stammered and, to his amazement, began to blush, but she went resolutely on. "The nursery. I mean to say, you *do* want children, don't you?"

He dropped his hands and cocked his head. "Children? Well, I—I hadn't thought much about it But—but of course I want children, *your* children, whenever they come."

"Then you—you will not continue to—ah—" She blushed again and this time seemed unable to go on.

"To what, Moriah? I fear we are speaking at cross purposes."

Abruptly she strolled to the window, running her fingers along the heavy green curtains before turning to face him. " 'Tis of no moment, Justin. We—"

"On the contrary, love, I think it is of great moment, else you should not be so distressed. Now come, out with it. Did we not just agree to pound dealing?"

"I am not dissembling, Justin. 'Tis merely that a lady doesn't speak of—" At his raised eyebrow she stopped. "Oh, Justin. You have been . . . doing something to prevent—That is, when I first came to you, you said there were ways a man could—ah— prevent the—"

"Oh my God!" he exclaimed, striding to her as realization dawned. "You may also remember, my love, from that reprehensible interview, that we spoke of a—a woman doing the same. And that *you* were going to—ah—"

"*I?* How in the world would *I* know about such things?"

"I asked myself the same but—well, you seemed to know a great deal that you shouldn't have! And so I

423

assumed—" He stopped short, then laughed aloud, gathering her in his arms. "Oh, little one. We *have* been dealing at cross purposes. I do believe this means a special license for us. No long engagement nor elaborate wedding preparations for *you*, my love. Shall you—shall you mind terribly?" he asked gently.

"Oh no! In point of fact, I should not like a long engagement above half!" she assured him, then went quite red. "That is—I mean to say—" she stammered.

"My sentiments exactly," he ventured with a lecherous grin. He was beginning to feel very warm indeed and bent his head toward hers.

"That is not what I meant!" she retorted, backing away.

"No?" he asked dubiously, advancing on her.

She ignored the question and darted over to sit once more on the love seat. "Justin, how can we explain our haste?" she asked earnestly after a moment. Trust Moriah to wax practical. He schooled himself to patience. There was plenty of time later for—

"Very simple, my love," he replied, sauntering forward and easing himself down next to her. This time he draped a possessive arm about her shoulder. "You see, I am about to embark on a political mission in the north country for my esteemed Uncle George. I must depart next week, and I should like to have my wife accompany me."

Her lovely brow furrowed in thought. "Yes, I can see that that will serve. And, Justin, I am glad that you have decided to become involved in politics. The government needs men like you," she said, but her voice was troubled.

"You sound like Uncle George again, and you don't sound terribly pleased, love. Now, why is that?"

"Because I wish I could be of help to you!" she blurted. "And marriage to the daughter of a—a compulsive gambler can hardly be advantageous to your career, Justin. You ought to be—"

"Marrying the likes of Olivia Crowley?" he asked mischievously. "Tut, tut, my dear. I doubt that Olivia knows the difference between a weaving loom and a printing press, whereas *you*— And then there is the part about physical attraction," he continued, pulling her close within the curve of his arm and feeling his desire rise as her body pressed against him. "But I believe we've—er—discussed *that* quite thoroughly before. Besides, *you* are not without influential connections, love."

"I?" she asked, and he was pleased with the breathless note in her voice.

"Yes. I seem to remember someone very close to you, a most knowledgeable lady, who currently resides in Lancashire."

"Oh, Justin, *can* we visit Miss Billingsley?" she asked eagerly.

"I shouldn't dream of not doing so, little one," he replied softly, his mouth close to hers. "And now—"

"You know, Justin, Miss Billingsley—"

"Was most remiss in one area," he interrupted hoarsely.

"Whatever do you mean?"

"You talk too damned much!" he muttered, and then he kissed her, long and hard. A part of him knew he had to release her, but he couldn't. He had come so close to losing her; he needed to hold her now, needed her so badly.

He pressed her back against the pillows, his hands caressing her body with increasing urgency even as his mouth hungrily devoured hers. She clutched at him, warm and pliant, and her fervent response was nearly his undoing. But at last, his body aflame and his breathing ragged, he raised his head, and himself, from Moriah.

"I — I must take you back to Emily's," he rasped.

"Y — yes,"she whispered, struggling to sit up and straighten her hair. God, how he wanted her.

"It — it is not at all the thing for us to be here," he managed, extending his hand and pulling her up. Her hand burned in his.

"No. Of course not," she concurred, her eyes aglow with passion and love, as they met his with that special intensity that would always jolt him.

"There is . . . time enough next week," he said resolutely, trying to catch his breath, unwilling to let go her hand.

"Yes. I love you, Justin. I think I have done so for a very long time," she breathed in her husky voice.

"As I do you," he echoed softly. His eyes caressed her face, and then slowly, he led her from the sitting room.

"We really must go," he repeated, once they were in the vestibule.

"Yes, 'tis near dawn," she murmured.

" 'Tis only proper," he replied gravely, and then, quite suddenly, he grinned. "But then," he added devilishly, "we are neither of us saints, are we?"

"No, we are not," she answered readily, her wonderful violet eyes dancing.

At this he chuckled, a deep masculine chuckle of

426

delight. And then the Viscount Roane scooped Miss Moriah Landon up into his arms and marched her purposefully toward the stairs.

And Miss Moriah Landon snuggled closer and kissed him full on the mouth, thinking what a truly handsome mouth it was. "Pray do not—ah—over-exert yourself, my darling lord," she whispered as he reached the top landing.

To which sage advice the viscount gave a roar of joyous, triumphant laughter and dauntlessly bore his most pragmatic lady to the inviting bedchamber beyond.

Author's Note

In the post-Waterloo years England saw much labor unrest, both industrial and agricultural, especially in the north country. The many incidents of machine-breaking, bread-riots, and the like, as well as the radical reform rhetoric being espoused from soapboxes, engendered in the authorities fear of social chaos and organized revolution. It was this fear that led to the terrible Peterloo massacre of 1819, when militia charged on a peaceable assembly, killing some and wounding many people. Perhaps if there had been a real Viscount Roane and his Lady, such a disaster might have been averted.

ZEBRA ROMANCES FOR ALL SEASONS
From Bobbi Smith

ARIZONA TEMPTRESS   (1785, $3.95)

Rick Peralta found the freedom he craved only in his disguise as El Cazador. Then he saw the exquisitely alluring Jennie among his compadres and the hotblooded male swore she'd belong just to him.

CAPTIVE PRIDE   (2160, $3.95)

Committed to the Colonial cause, the gorgeous and independent Cecelia Demorest swore she'd divert Captain Noah Kincade's weapons to help out the American rebels. But the moment that the womanizing British privateer first touched her, her scheming thoughts gave way to burning need.

DESERT HEART   (2010, $3.95)

Rancher Rand McAllister was furious when he became the guardian of a scrawny girl from Arizona's mining country. But when he finds that the pig-tailed brat is really a voluptuous beauty, his resentment turns to intense interest; Laura Lee knew it would be the biggest mistake in her life to succumb to the cowboy—but she can't fight against giving him her wild DESERT HEART.

Available wherever paperbacks are sold, or order direct from the Publisher. Send cover price plus 50¢ per copy for mailing and handling to Zebra Books, Dept. 2169, 475 Park Avenue South, New York, N.Y. 10016. Residents of New York, New Jersey and Pennsylvania must include sales tax. DO NOT SEND CASH.

PASSIONATE NIGHTS FROM ZEBRA BOOKS

ANGEL'S CARESS (2675, $4.50)
by Deanna James
Ellie Crain was a young, inexperienced and beautiful Southern belle. Cash Gillard was the battle-weary Yankee corporal who turned her into a woman filled with hungry passion. He planned to love and leave her; she vowed to keep him forever with her *Angel's Caress*.

COMANCHE BRIDE (2549, $3.95)
by Emma Merritt
Beautiful Dr. Zoe Randolph headed to Mexico to halt a cholera epidemic. She never dreamed her caravan would be attacked by a band of savages. Later, she refused to believe that she could love and desire her captor, the handsome half-breed Matt Chandler. Captor and slave find unending love and tender passion in the rugged Comanche hills.

CAPTIVE ANGEL (2524, $4.50)
by Deanna James
When handsome Hunter Gillard left the routine existence of his South Carolina plantation for endless adventures on the high seas, beautiful and indulged Caroline Gillard learned to manage her home and business affairs in her husband's sudden absence. Caroline resolved not to crumble and vowed to make Hunter beg to be taken back. He was determined to make her once again his unquestioning and forgiving wife.

SWEET, WILD LOVE (2834, $3.95)
by Emma Merritt
Chicago lawyer Eleanor Hunt was determined to earn the respect of the Kansas cowboys who openly leered at her as she was working to try a cattle-rustling case. The worst offender was Bradley Smith — even though he worked for Eleanor's father! She was determined not to mistake passion for love; he was determined to break through her icy exterior and possess the passionate woman who lurked beneath her.

Available wherever paperbacks are sold, or order direct from the Publisher. Send cover price plus 50¢ per copy for mailing and handling to Zebra Books, Dept. 2169, 475 Park Avenue South, New York, N.Y. 10016. Residents of New York, New Jersey and Pennsylvania must include sales tax. DO NOT SEND CASH.

THE BEST IN HISTORICAL ROMANCES

TIME-KEPT PROMISES (2422, $3.95)
by Constance O'Day Flannery

Sean O'Mara froze when he saw his wife Christina standing before him. She had vanished and the news had been written about in all of the papers—he had even been charged with her murder! But now he had living proof of his innocence, and Sean was not about to let her get away. No matter that the woman was claiming to be someone named Kristine; she still caused his blood to boil.

PASSION'S PRISONER (2573, $3.95)
by Casey Stewart

When Cassandra Lansing put on men's clothing and entered the Rawlings saloon she didn't expect to lose anything—in fact she was sure that she would win back her prized horse Rapscallion that her grandfather lost in a card game. She almost got a smug satisfaction at the thought of fooling the gamblers into believing that she was a man. But once she caught a glimpse of the virile Josh Rawlings, Cassandra wanted to be the woman in his embrace!

ANGEL HEART (2426, $3.95)
by Victoria Thompson

Ever since Angelica's father died, Harlan Snyder had been angling to get his hands on her ranch, the Diamond R. And now, just when she had an important government contract to fulfill, she couldn't find a single cowhand to hire—all because of Snyder's threats. It was only a matter of time before the legendary gunfighter Kid Collins turned up on her doorstep, badly wounded. Angelica assessed his firmly muscled physique and stared into his startling blue eyes. Beneath all that blood and dirt he was the handsomest man she had ever seen, and the one person who could help beat Snyder at his own game.

THE BEST OF REGENCY ROMANCES

AN IMPROPER COMPANION (2691, $3.95)
by Karla Hocker
At the closing of Miss Venable's Seminary for Young Ladies school, mistress Kate Elliott welcomed the invitation to be Liza Ashcroft's chaperone for the Season at Bath. Little did she know that Miss Ashcroft's father, the handsome widower Damien Ashcroft would also enter her life. And not as a passive bystander or dutiful dad.

WAGER ON LOVE (2693, $2.95)
by Prudence Martin
Only a rogue like Nicholas Ruxart would choose a bride on the basis of a careless wager. And only a rakehell like Nicholas would then fall in love with his betrothed's grey-eyed sister! The cynical viscount had always thought one blushing miss would suit as well as another, but the unattainable Jane Sommers soon proved him wrong.

LOVE AND FOLLY (2715, $3.95)
by Sheila Simonson
To the dismay of her more sensible twin Margaret, Lady Jean proceeded to fall hopelessly in love with the silver-tongued, seditious poet, Owen Davies—and catapult her entire family into social ruin . . . Margaret was used to gentlemen falling in love with vivacious Jean rather than with her—even the handsome Johnny Dyott whom she secretly adored. And when Jean's foolishness led her into the arms of the notorious Owen Davies, Margaret knew she could count on Dyott to avert scandal. What she didn't know, however was that her sweet sensibility was exerting a charm all its own.